To Taki

Mike.

# YESTERDAY'S MAN

Also by M S Koll:

**The Chessman Enigma**
Diadem Books
ISBN-10:1478384476
ISBN-13: 978-1478384472

# YESTERDAY'S MAN

M S Koll

DIADEM BOOKS

All Rights Reserved. Copyright © 2014 M S Koll

No part of this book may be reproduced or transmitted in any form or by any means, graphic, electronic, or mechanical, including photocopying, recording, taping or by any information storage or retrieval system, without the permission in writing from the copyright holder.

The right of M S Koll to be identified as the author of this work has been asserted in accordance with the Copyright, Designs and Patents Act 1988 sections 77 and 78.

Published by Diadem Books

For information, please contact:
Diadem Books
16 Lethen View
Tullibody
ALLOA
FK10 2GE
Scotland UK
www.diadembooks.com


The views expressed in this work are solely those of the author and do not necessarily reflect the views of the publisher, and the publisher hereby disclaims any responsibility for them.


This book is a work of fiction. Names, characters and places are products of the author's imagination. Any resemblance to any person living or dead is entirely coincidental.

*For*

*My mother Anastasia who sadly passed away last year and will be greatly missed.*

# CHAPTER ONE

**IT WAS ONLY** five hundred yards from the cottage to the Village Local and David decided to walk. The rain had held off all day and though the skies were black and laden, he didn't think twice about using his car, after all he was going for a drink.

He'd reached about halfway when the heavens opened. It poured cats and dogs, giraffes and elephants, it was that heavy. David was a fit young man of just twenty-six so he made a dash for it. He still arrived at the door of the Dog and Affodil drenched.

As per usual the pub was quiet even though in most pubs it would be peak time, at half nine.

Barry the landlord handed David a beer towel for him to dry his hair and took his jacket to hang over the big open fire. His wife Louisa was sitting on a stool behind the bar reading a magazine.

Including David, the Affy, as the locals called it, had eleven customers, just enough to form a football team or more likely in these parts, a Choir.

He'd been in Llanbas nearly two months arriving in mid-January. On the whole, he'd been made welcome by the locals, both he and his brother Patrick, who was two years older and nine inches taller.

Patrick was at their newly purchased cottage, which he had managed to obtain on the back of a three-year lucrative contract with the massive Japanese Electronics Company Vitrax, which was only nine and a half miles away.

His hours were flexible; as long as he did the work he was fine. David preferred it that way; it enabled him to look after his older brother who was a bit slow and could only do manual jobs such as bricklaying, painting, carrying; he was good at carrying and strangely enough a great mechanic even though he had no formal training. Patrick was the strongest man he'd even seen.

Patrick didn't like socialising much—hardly drank and spent most of the night watching anything on TV. Sometimes after an emergency late at night, David would come home and find Patrick watching foreign films with subtitles which Patrick could hardly read or keep up with.

Both the brothers were born and bred in Taunton, Somerset, and when their parents died in a car crash they upped and moved to Bristol. Now they were living just eight miles from Cardiff. David was extremely ambitious and was continually saving his wages.

'So what will it be then Dai?' Barry had taken to calling him Dai. God knows why.

'A pint of best and whatever the old boy is drinking please,' said David.

Whilst waiting for his drinks, he took in the surroundings; the Affy had seen more affluent days in its two-hundred year old history.

There was only one room downstairs, apart from the kitchen and toilets. It was a good- sized room, could hold fifty comfortably. Wood panelling on all the walls, one large oak bar, two dozen assorted wooden chairs, eight pine tables and a few brass effects covered two of the walls. On one of the remaining walls, three pictures were hanging all depicting hunting scenes. There was solid wood flooring, stained and uneven through years of wear and tear and on the back wall stood a magnificent wrought iron fireplace surrounded by old-fashioned tiles and a marble mantelpiece. Above the fireplace, there was a painting; a large painting of a black dog romping through a field full of golden daffodils.

Hence the inn's name, Dog and Affodil, the Tudor name for Daffodil.

The pints were poured. David paid and carried them over to where the old man was seated.

The old man stopped scanning through his dog-eared scrapbook and looked up, recognised David and noticed the extra pint. He closed his scrapbook.

'How are you today Walter?' asked David.

'Same as yesterday, and the day before. I'm YESTERDAY'S MAN son,' said Walter.

David set a pint before Walter and then took a seat. He was by far the youngest in the place. Walter was probably the oldest, probably about seventy-five.

This was the fourth time since coming to the village that he had sat with the old man. He knew his name was Walter, that he lived alone in the village, had done so most of his life, had no children, no living relatives, kept himself to himself and carried that scrapbook everywhere he went, which included the toilet.

Walter intrigued David. For some reason he had empathy with him even though he knew very little about him. Walter rarely spoke—he would get on with his brother Patrick perfectly.

So, it came as a surprise when Walter asked him if he had bought his cottage or rented it.

'I bought it Walter,' said David.

'Through which Agents?' asked Walter.

'Morton and Sons,' replied David.

Walter hesitated, then vehemently spat out: 'Fucking Mortons, they're fucking bastards, don't trust them son!' And with that he rose, picked up his scrapbook and without another word, headed for the door and out into the pouring rain.

His beer was still only half-empty. David sat bemused and bewildered, wondering what the hell had got into the old boy. After a moment or two, conversation resumed in the pub and he couldn't feel their eyes on him anymore.

David finished his beer and sauntered up to the bar.

'Are you alright luv?' asked Louisa.

'I think so,' said David.

'Well, you look a little drained,' said Louisa. 'It's not like old Walter to have a go. Never says a word usually, keeps himself and his thoughts to himself.'

'Old Man,' said Barry, the Manager. 'He's not a day over sixty-five,' he added.

'He looks and acts it,' said Louisa, 'and anyway Barry, how do you know?'

'I just know. I think Terry once told me that he went to college with Walter,' said Barry.

'And Terry, how old do you think he is?' said Louisa.

'Told you, sixty-five,' said Barry.

'He's over seventy for Christ's sake Barry, you're nearly sixty,' said Louisa.

'I'm fifty-seven,' said Barry.

'Fifty-eight, going on fifty-nine, that's what you are,' said Louisa, now fed up with the conversation and going back to reading her magazine.

'I'm fifty-seven, Dai, don't you listen to her, and Walter is, say, sixty-five or six,' said Barry, pouring another pint for David 'on the house.'

'Thank you,' said David.

'Do you know what's in that scrapbook, Barry?' David asked. 'He keeps it really close.'

'No idea Dai, no-one here does either,' Barry replied. 'My guess is family photos.'

'He gave me the impression he had no family or relatives,' said David.

'Ah but he did once, about, oh, it must be twelve, fourteen years. First his wife dies, suicide, then within a few months his daughter is run over by a hit and run driver, she was only six or seven, then his wife's sister, who had moved in to look after the daughter. Yes, that's it, Iris, that's her name, dies of cancer and so within a year poor old bugger has no-one, except that old dog of his.'

'Christ, that's sad, awful, such bad luck,' said David.

'But that's not the end of it Dai,' said Barry.

'There's more?' said David.

'Yeah, his dog dropped dead two months after his sister-in-law died of cancer and he loved that bloody mongrel, used to bring it in here, it would lie down in front of the fire for hours,' said Barry.

'Unbelievable. If someone made that story into a film, people would say it was too far-fetched,' said David.

'But that's exactly what happened, isn't it Louisa?' said Barry.

David took a long drink of his beer and asked Barry how he kept the pub going with so few customers.

'It's a struggle,' said Barry. 'I've been here with my wife for sixteen years. The first half-dozen it was fine. We were of course younger. People came in for food, things were different; now it's all Gastro Pubs run by micro brewers—plastic food which comes readymade in a bag, tasteless lager. We're waiting for the market to rise and then sell.'

'To one of those micro brewer people?' asked David.

'No, they don't want out-of-the-way pubs like this. The Yuppies wouldn't come. No, I'm talking about the property market. We've a massive beer garden out back; big fore-front. The place is ripe for development into flats or even new houses,' said Barry.

'Will you be glad to go?' said David.

'Look around you Dai, what do you think?' said Barry.

When David finished his pint, he left. It was now just drizzling but it still didn't stop him taking a detour to go past Walter's cottage. Ten minutes later, he stopped outside a small dilapidated cottage. It stood out like a sore thumb.

It was in complete contrast to the house next door, a beautiful ranch-like spread with what looked like a swimming pool. It really was a lovely structure; no more than maybe ten years old.

The following morning, a Thursday, the local council's building surveyor also made a visit to Walter Cramp's cottage. He spent a total of five minutes there taking photos.

The next day as usual, David and Walter shared a few pints in the Affy, last night's walkout unmentioned. Walter was as usual morose and untalkative. He just nodded to everything David said.

Patrick was in the cottage finishing the last room that needed painting.

The letter came through the next day. It was from the local council on standard official stationery. In a nutshell, it required Mr

Cramp to mend the broken front wall and cut down the overhanging branches from the two trees as they were a danger to the public. They gave him a fortnight to arrange the same. Otherwise they would send in workmen and charge him accordingly.

Poor old Walter was very upset. He'd once owned a construction company, employing twelve men and could easily have done the work himself, but nowadays he just couldn't physically do any strenuous work on account of his health problems.

Walter realised he would have to bring in people who could do the work—not that he knew where to begin; it had been a long time since he was in the business.

David reached the pub just before nine and was surprised to find that a pint had been earmarked for him behind the bar, courtesy of Walter.

He could see Walter sitting in his usual position near the fire and that he had most of a pint still in front of him.

When he sat down, he greeted Walter, who he thought said 'Hello.'

After a few minutes of silence, Walter produced the council letter from his pocket and passed it to David, who read it and in all honesty, after seeing the cottage, wasn't surprised. He was nevertheless surprised it had taken the Council so long to act.

David handed the letter back to Walter who pocketed it, without saying a word.

'Do you need any help with this, financial or otherwise?' asked David.

'I have money David—that's your name, right?' said Walter.

'Yes, that's right,' said David.

'But I need someone to do the work and make sure that they do it right, so that I don't get any more letters,'

'Don't worry about a thing Walter, at eleven tomorrow morning someone will be there to do the job.'

'Are you sure?' said Walter.

'One hundred and ten percent. I'll finish my pint and go and arrange it,' said David.

The look of relief on Walter's face was a sight to behold and helping out would add some more money to his bank account.

When David got home, Patrick was watching a video, an old slasher flick; it was all blood, mutilations, gory. All the videos his brother had were the same.

'Patrick, I see you finished here.' David looked around. The job as always was perfect. He had to give Patrick his due.

'I've got another job for you across the village. Come on, I want you to see the job. We'll go in my car.' David had a four-year-old Honda, Patrick an eight-year-old small open truck. Both vehicles were in good mechanical condition. Patrick made sure of that.

Patrick pressed 'pause' on the video player and got up. He was used to taking orders from his brother. He could trust him.

At eleven the next morning David rang the doorbell to Walter's cottage.

On answering, Walter, who was still in his pyjamas, looked at the pair. David had obviously found a workman.

'Good morning Walter, this is my brother Patrick, he's going to do all the work for you. Now he's a good worker, Walter, doesn't waste time and doesn't say much, which should suit you down to the ground. He works in a local garage every weekday from 7 until 10 but can be here by 10.30.'

'Only one man?' said Walter.

'Just Patrick, he works faster than two,' said David.

'Money?' said Walter.

'You pay for the materials and six pounds an hour. Patrick will bill you on completion, when you've checked his hours and are satisfied with the work.'

'That seems fair, but only your brother,' said Walter.

'If you find him too slow Walter, just tell me and I'll make arrangements for someone else to do the work. Oh, and one last thing: Patrick doesn't stop, but drinks coffee every hour with milk and four sugars. Will that be okay with you? Would you like me to buy in coffee, sugar, etc.?'

'That will be okay. When does he intend starting?' asked Walter.

'In about an hour when we come back from the builder's place,' said David.

At half past twelve, Walter, still in his pyjamas, came with the coffee. He was absolutely amazed. The old wall had been demolished; no bricks in sight and two rows of the new wall had been laid. By two it was nearly two-foot high. By five o'clock the wall was up. The gate, rubbed down and painted, was ready to go on as soon as it dried.

Patrick was now pruning the trees, rose bushes and some other plants that were in the front garden.

Walter had never ever seen such a workman and he had been in the business for over thirty years. The job was perfection itself.

At six when Walter came out, now changed into some flannels and thick lumberjack style chequered shirt with another coffee, Patrick was sweeping up and they had the first exchange of words between the pair.

'Well done. Can you paint the windows and front door, Patrick?'

'Can,' said Patrick.

'The outside could do with a coat of paint. Can you do that, Patrick?'

'Can, easy, but I have no ladders,' said Patrick.

'Well it's dark now,' said Walter, 'best you do the other jobs tomorrow. I've got ladders in the back.'

Patrick nodded, finished his coffee, and got into his truck for home.

That night in the pub Walter had a lot to say to David.

Firstly, he wanted to pay Patrick ten pounds an hour because he was better than three men, not two. He was like a machine. Secondly, he wanted Patrick to do the entire house, inside and outside.

David agreed the money would come in handy. Unfortunately, he couldn't slow down his brother's work rate and eke out the job because his brother had only one pace—very fast.

'Young lad like you shouldn't be sitting here drinking pints with an old man. You should be out dancing, cinema. Tell me, have you met any girls yet?' Walter asked David.

'I've not the time,' said David. 'We need to work, me and my brother. Get ourselves set up, then we can enjoy ourselves.'

'Son, life goes too fast, enjoy yourself now, 'cause one day you'll wake up and be a "Yesterday's Man" like me,' said Walter, and that was the last thing he said for the next hour.

After three days, Patrick started to drink his coffee with Walter indoors. On the fourth, he started sharing lunch which the old man cooked. By the seventh day, they started having conversations of a sort.

Patrick started on the roof, then the attic, next the bedrooms and bathroom. It was beginning to look like a very nice cottage.

It took Patrick a total of fifteen days in total. He'd put in one hundred and fifty-two hours. With the cost of materials, it came to around two grand which Walter paid over in cash to Patrick, who without counting it paid it over to his brother.

A bond had been cemented between them. Patrick went nearly every day to see Walter and they talked for hours and hours.

The word had got around in the village and everyone and their dogs wanted Patrick to do some work for them. He was slow in the brain but fast with his hands. He was well liked in the small community.

On that Wednesday morning, Walter went for his biannual medical check-up. Patrick had driven him there in his truck and waited for him outside.

It was bad news. The Big 'C.' It had spread. Chemotherapy and radiotherapy might prolong his life six months or so, but it seemed to be too late. He had tops, a year.

When he stepped into the flatbed truck, Patrick sensed that something was wrong with his old friend. He didn't ask Walter because he was afraid of the answer.

Walter didn't volunteer any information. He didn't want his new friend to be sad.

When they reached Walter's cottage, Walter made coffee for both and then told Patrick to sit down. Patrick did, at the small mahogany dining table.

From somewhere Walter produced the scrapbook. It lay between the two of them.

'What's that then Walter?' asked Patrick.

'It's my life, Patrick.'

'I don't understand, Walter.'

'No, I guess you wouldn't,' said Walter.

'How old are you Walter?'

'I'll be seventy in August Patrick, but I very much doubt if I'll make it till then.'

'I don't understand, Walter.'

'I know son, you're a decent lad, a good heart and you're as strong as an ox. Tell me how old are you?' asked Walter.

'Two years older than David,' said Patrick.

'And David is how old Patrick?'

'He is twenty-six. Can we see what's inside the book now Walter, can we?'

Walter opened the book, cuttings from newspapers, photos, notes, letters and other types of correspondence. Patrick just looked through the pages, again and again. He asked no questions. He knew Walter would tell him when he was ready and he did.

That evening when he got home, he told David about the scrapbook. He told him all he could remember. He told him about the big house, about Walter's daughter, his wife, his dog and he told him about the group photo, ten people in all; all had rings around their heads.

'What do you mean, rings around their heads, Patrick?'

'Rings, round ones, David.'

'Of course they're round, show me.'

David grabbed an old newspaper, opened it until he came to a photo of some people and passed it to Patrick together with a biro.

Patrick drew rings around their heads.

'And the other photos, in the book, Patrick—did they have rings around them?'

Patrick shook his head.

'So Barry, you haven't seen Walter for three days now?' said David.

'No Dai, I wonder if he's taken ill?' said Barry.

'Strange, because Patrick says that he hasn't answered his door either and I've been working flat out day and night lately; a few problems at work,' said David.

'Your brother not much of a drinker, eh Dai?' said Barry.

'No, funny that, he just doesn't like to drink. Not that I'm the biggest boozer on the planet,' said David.

'People are drinking more at home now,' said Louisa butting in.

'I suppose they are. Much cheaper, but you won't get a good pint sitting at home or any decent conversation,' said Barry.

'You don't get any decent conversation here either,' said Louisa.

On the way back home, David took a gamble and passed by Walter's. He rang and rang. He was about to turn and carry on home when he heard the door being unlocked.

'Hello Walter, me and Patrick have been a bit worried about you. Are you feeling okay?' said David.

'Come in lad, it's cold outside. Do you want a cocoa or something?'

'No thank you Walter. I missed you down at the Affy; no one to talk to.'

'They're okay David, once you get used to them. I know they steered well clear of me. Think I'm some kind of nutter, but all in all they're a harmless bunch apart from Barry's wife—the woman's a right quean. Best you stay well clear of her,' said Walter.

'I understand you showed my brother your photo album. May I take a look?'

'Help yourself. It's on the table,' said Walter.

David looked through. He paused at the group photo newspaper cutting with the rings around their heads, seven men, three women. The caption underneath read: 'TONS MORE FROM MORTONS.'

David started at the beginning of the photos. A nice looking woman standing outside a cottage, surrounded by flowers, wild ones. Her age, maybe thirty. The same woman in different situations, always looking happy. Later photos of a baby, then a young girl playing and happy. Then the little girl with a dog; he couldn't tell the breed. Then pictures of the happy family, Walter, the woman, whom David assumed had been his late wife, the young girl, obviously his daughter and so on. The last but one was a picture of a large stone building, with two large double doors above the doorway. It read: 'W. R. CRAMP CONSTRUCTION LTD.'

In front of the double doors, Walter stood with about ten others all in overalls.

David felt he was prying. It didn't feel right looking at the skeleton of a man's life. He closed the book with trembling hands. He'd glanced at the cuttings. They were all to do with Mortons and another company who were solicitors. That was called Fenwick, Morton and Baines, a real mouthful.

Walter spoke as soon as he saw David close the scrapbook.

'Your brother Patrick has become my friend. He's a great lad but didn't really understand what he was looking at when I showed him my scrapbook, but you, David, are a different kettle of fish altogether. You're very bright, luckily for Patrick. You look after him. You know what that book represents, don't you?'

'The past. I think it's your late wife, daughter, dog, staff and…'

'The estate agents took everything I had, even my dignity and now I've run out of time. Year upon year I thought about it, made plans, all to no avail. I've run out of time,' said Walter.

'What do you mean you've run out of time Walter? Time to do what?' said David.

'To make the bastards suffer and pay for ruining a happy family.'

'We talking about Mortons?' said David.

'Of course we are but like I said, it's gone on too long and now it's too late.'

'Why do you keep saying it's too late Walter?'

'Because David, unlike you and your brother, I'm old and I've got a terminal disease. Four, six, eight months, only God knows.'

'Shit Walter, can't they do anything?'

'Prolong a stupid stubborn foolish and cowardly man's life a few months? No good to me.'

'You're none of those things, Walter. Like you said, you had a happy life, a nice wife, a beautiful daughter, a good company, one can't ask for much more.'

'Yes they can David, and do,' Walter said. 'I was just unfortunate. True, the day that I answered the knock on my door. I think about it every single day but every single day I sometimes get so confused with anger and stupid thoughts that I've learnt to keep myself to myself. Sometimes I've gone a week without talking to anyone, until first you, and more so your brother, made me realise that I was still alive and that won't be for long.'

'Do you want to talk about that day?' said David.

'What day, David?'

'The day this all started, or is it too painful too talk about it?'

The timing had been right, and it was.

'Fourteen years ago, November the fifth, bonfire day or night, anyway. It must have been a Saturday, about two. I never worked after one on Saturdays. The doorbell rang. I thought it was kiddies looking for a penny for the Guy thing, so I answered the door. I had a couple of quid in change for them.

'Anyway, it was a Mr Abraham Morton, local estate agent. When I say local, I mean Cardiff. Anyway, this man says they have buyers who would pay over the odds for my house and land. It's the house in my book with all the wild flowers.

'I tell him I'm not interested. He leaves a card and goes. To cut a long story short, my business needs expanding. We need a bigger workshop, modernise our tooling and take on a few more men to cover the amount of proposed work that was flooding in. So, I rang this Mr Morton. This by then was just before Christmas.

'We agreed a price for the house and the two acres of land. A very good price I might add. About 20 per cent over the market price. I had no worries about moving because I also owned this cottage which we were using as an office and storage. I got a few of the men to make it habitable and everything seemed to be going fine. At the time, they had recommended a firm of solicitors, Messrs Fenwick and Baines, and I dealt with the main man, a Mr Terry Fenwick. There was no Baines. It was just Fenwick and three girls.

'Two days before exchange, that would be the twenty-fourth of January, this Mr Fenwick, my so-called solicitor, together with Abrahim Morton and the buyer or a representative of the buyer, as the buyer was a limited company, came to the house.

'We had or they had planning problems. The Council had earmarked part of my land for compulsory purchase to build a new link road and some other things to do with mineral rights on the land.

'Now I was in a bad position. I had already borrowed money and purchased a suitable building. I had also ordered various heavy pieces of machinery on which I had already given a down-payment of twenty-five percent.

'Are you following all this David? They wanted to give me half of what we had agreed or they were going to pull out. I couldn't afford to lose a quarter of a million pounds plus, so I told them to get lost, the buyers that is, and asked Mortons to find me another buyer.

'If there were buyers, I never saw them.

'This went on for three months. I had signed a contract with Mortons; my business fell away. I was robbing Peter to pay Paul. I laid off staff and so on; a never-ending downward spiral.

'The bastards wanted me out. They put off buyers and didn't market the property at all. I had no chance. I started drinking heavily. For the first time in our marriage, we argued day and night. Money was tight. We were reduced to accepting hand-outs from friends and Mabel's sister Iris who sold up and came to stay with us as Mabel wasn't coping and was always seeing the doctor with some ailment or another.

'Then one day I came back from doing a small job in Penarth. It was about two o'clock and my Mabel had taken a cocktail of pills. I was too late to help and Iris was away.

'Three days after the funeral I sold out, losing an extra fifty thousand. I moved into this house. Then my little girl Susie got run over, on her way to school. I or Iris should have taken her, but Iris was ill and I too drunk. Again, it was my fault. What was left of my life disappeared the moment I heard about the accident.

'And here I am talking to someone I hardly know and expecting a stranger as such to care,' said Walter, by now exhausted from speaking. He hadn't said so much in nigh on fourteen years.

'The big house next door, who lives in that?' asked David.

'Louis Morton,' said Walter.

'He being who exactly in the family?' asked David.

'Father of Abraham, Lancelot and Deena.'

'Some strange names there. I mean who would call his son Lancelot?' said David.

'As you can see the Council had a change of mind; no problem with minerals, no new road. How convenient for the Mortons,' said Walter bitterly.

'Must be worth a bomb now,' said David.

'Million plus,' said Walter.

'Who exactly are the ringed people in this photo, Walter?'

'They're the people who should have less than me to live, but I will tell you anyway. You might need to know.

'This one is the head, that's Louis. Abraham's that one, then there's Lancelot and Deena, the daughter and youngest. That one is Israel Levy, he's the group's accountant and he's married to Tara... Fenwick Terry is that one. Eli Sampson is the General Manager. He's the one with a beard.

'That leaves us with Georgia who is Lancelot's wife and Gareth Jones. I'm not sure exactly what his role is.

'Lancelot is now of course a partner in the solicitors Fenwick, Morton and Baines. His wife Georgia owns a clothes shop, a boutique, I think the modern word is, in Cardiff, very expensive and high class.'

'I don't know what to say if truth be told. I'm not sure what you're asking of me,' said David, knowing full well what was being asked.

'Before you go any further, David, I'd like you to know I'm not a rich man. This house is worth say one fifty. I've twenty cash, a further thirty-five in the bank and fifty thousand in various shares,' said Walter dangling the juicy carrot in front of the ambitious David.

'Over a quarter of a million,' thought David, who didn't say anything. He was thinking, more like dreaming. It would take him and Patrick ten years to get that much if things went right for them.

He looked at Walter. He was a cunning old man. First, he befriends the 'vidiot' brother of his, then uses his ambitions, or greed as he probably sees it, on him to lure him. David liked the new word that he had invented 'VIDIOT'—an idiot who sits and watches videos all night.

'I have a proposal for you and your brother David, and for obvious reasons I need a fast answer,' said Walter.

# CHAPTER TWO

**THAT MORNING** it was so cold it began to snow. D.I. Karetzi wore the daffodil his mother had given him in his leather jacket's lapel; after all it was the first of March, St David's day.

Mike didn't feel like going into the office they called 4 'I's that day, neither did his car, a two-door Mercedes coupe.

As he drove slowly up Bute Street, wipers working overtime, he spotted the woman and child who were fighting against the elements heading in the same direction. Neither had a raincoat or umbrella, not that that would have helped much in the prevailing weather conditions, a mixture of high winds, sleet and snow flurries. The woman in one hand held a plastic bag and in the other a small child's hand. To Mike they looked as if they had just stepped out of a Dickens' novel, their clothes being rather shabby and old.

He came to a halt beside them and asked them where they were going.

The little boy, aged about six, maybe seven, told him they were on their way to school.

'Which school is that?' asked Mike.

Again, the little boy answered: 'St Leonards.'

'Where is it?' asked Mike, showing the woman his warrant card, so as not to scare her unduly.

This time the woman answered. She gave Mike the street.

'You can't walk there,' said Mike. 'It's at least fifteen, twenty minutes from here. Why didn't you wait for a bus?'

'We got no money, mister,' said the little boy.

Mike got out of the car. 'Please get in. I'm going that way. I'll drop you off.'

'We don't want any favours, thank you,' the woman said, on the point of tears.

'I'm not doing you any,' said Mike. 'Like I said, it's on my way, now please get in before you both get pneumonia.'

Mike pulled the front passenger seat forward and the boy climbed in. He then reset the seat and the woman got in. From the boot, Mike got out a large towel he had packed in his sports bag with his football gear.

'Dry your hair with this,' he said to the boy. The boy did so and then passed it to his mother.

'My name's Mike, what's yours?' he said to the boy.

'Daniel,' said the boy.

'And you?' Mike asked the mother.

'Angie,' she replied.

Mike drove steadily up and towards the school.

He stopped at a newsagent's and bought some chocolate bars, two sandwiches and various fruit juice drinks. On his return, he gave the bag to Angie.

'This is for Daniel's lunch break.'

'I can't accept that, thanks, but we will work it out,' Angie said. 'In a week's time I'll be able to claim and things will be better.'

'I'm sure they will,' Mike said. 'I'm not prying, Angie, and it's none of my business, but I'll feel a lot better if you tell me how you got into this position.'

'My husband Mark just got up one morning six weeks ago and left us, with no money, no food as such, nothing, and we haven't heard a word from him since.' She went on: 'The red tape—well, you must know, being a policeman and all, is mind-boggling. You can't get a straight answer from anyone. Hopefully now I've sorted some kind of benefits out.'

She then burst into tears and Mike felt so angry that people like her and the boy were in such a position.

'Don't cry again Mummy. It will be all right. Daddy will come home soon and we can all eat together like before.'

'When was the last time you both had a square meal?' said Mike.

'I had cornflakes last night. Mummy wasn't hungry,' said Daniel.

'Fuck,' said Mike under his breath.

Angie was still sobbing. Mike turned to the boy and asked him if he liked chocolate. He did.

'There's chocolate bars in the bag Daniel. Pick one and eat it before we get you to school.' He did.

It was now nine a.m., not that Mike had any pressing work. They in the office had done nothing but twiddle their thumbs for nearly two months. Not one case. It was very disquieting to say the least.

Back at 111 Nelson Street or 4 'I's as the residents preferred to call it, Amber Gilberts had cooked breakfast for DI Evans, and Charlie White.

Special Detective Inspector Mikhail Karetzi was usually late and only drank espresso for breakfast so the food available was just for the three of them. There was enough for six because Charlie eats normally. Evan liked double portions and triple portions sometimes weren't enough for Amber.

It was now a quarter past nine and they were in the middle of their breakfast when they heard the door downstairs opening. They assumed it was Mike as he had the alarm code and a key for the front door.

They were mistaken and surprised to see a six-foot tall, angular woman with cropped blondish hair, no make-up, age of about forty standing there at the living room door.

More surprising was that she was wearing a Chief Constable's uniform.

All three looked up but nobody stood up.

'I am your new Chief Constable, the name is Short.' She went on: 'I assume that I have the correct address and this is not a café, so please get off your backsides and report to me downstairs in the office." Then she added: 'NOW!'

'Yes Ma'am,' said Evan, being the first to stand.

'It's not Ma'am, Boss, Guv, Chief, it's Chief Constable Short, easy to remember and remember you will,' she said before turning and walking out to go downstairs.

'What happened to Clarke?' said Evan to Amber.

'Search me,' said Amber in reply.

'I think a few things are going to change,' said Charlie.

'And we aren't going to like them,' said Amber.

'And Mike's late,' said Charlie, whistling with nervousness.

They left their food and trooped off downstairs. The ashtrays had been binned as had a pack of cards. The wastepaper basket was now sitting on one of the desks. The Chief Constable was sitting behind one of the others.

They stood, all three of them like naughty schoolchildren called before the Headmistress.

Muriel eyed them carefully. She could see the Big, the Good and the Ugly. Only the Bad was missing. She'd read the reports: the Bad was only punctual in a blue moon.

She started with the Good, D.I. Evan Jones, a Chapel-going Christian, family man, good record. She looked at him directly. 'This is a non-smoking office, D.I. Jones.'

Evan nodded.

She then looked at the Big, and stated, 'We are not running a restaurant Ms Gilberts.'

She stood up to address Charlie, towering over him. Charlie felt intimidated. He didn't know why—after all he was a civilian.

Mr Charles White, aka Chalky. 'I have your record. How you got to working with us defies all logic. It seems that my hands are bound at the moment but I wouldn't consider your status here permanent.' That dealt with the Ugly.

'Now can someone here enlighten me as to when we can expect to see our colleague Special Detective Mikhail Karetzi, and whilst we're on the subject, can somebody explain to me what exactly Special Detectives do?'

No one could. Not that the Chief cared anyway, she was just marking time till the other one turned up.

'Do we have a screwdriver here?' said the Chief.

'We do have a set,' said Amber.

'Good, will one of you take down that ridiculous sign from above the front door? This is a Police Station.'

Charlie duly removed the 4 'I's sign that he had made as a Xmas present to the others.

After dropping off Daniel, Mike took Angie to the shops. They bought or rather Mike bought a coat for the mother, a raincoat for Daniel plus three shirts, a cap, two pairs of trousers and a pair of shoes. He used his own credit card, not the Corporate card. He then withdrew one hundred pounds and handed it to Angie.

It was one hell of a battle but Mike won out and she accepted on the condition that she would repay it one day.

It was now half ten and Mike decided to head for the office with Angie, so that they could phone the various departments to try to fast forward her benefits.

By this time, the new Chief Constable was seething but she was going to wait.

The others pretended to be busy filing, reading old reports, shuffling things from one desk to another. Deep inside the new Chief was laughing on one hand and raging with anger on the other hand.

It was difficult to believe that this banal ragbag bunch of people had achieved so much in so little time.

Getting the Chessman, Wales's biggest serial murderer was just one of their collars. She looked at them again. She still couldn't believe it.

Mike walked in. Young, badly dressed, woman with him, looked like she'd been crying. Her make-up was all over the place and as for her hair, it was a disaster, thought the new Chief.

'The bastard has brought in a hooker or maybe a girlfriend who looks like a downtown hooker, no class,' thought Chief Constable Muriel Short.

Evan made the introductions.

'And your friend, Special D.I. Karetzi?'

'Yes, this is Angie, I just picked her up this morning. I mean, she was caught in the snow storm and I gave her and her son a lift to school.'

'And why is she here?' asked the Chief.

'I was going to ask Amber to sort out some of her problems,' said Mike.

'I see you've also been on a shopping spree,' said the Chief.

'Yes, I bought Angie and her son some gear,' said Mike, getting a little pissed off with the inquisition.

'How did you pay, D.I. Karetzi?' asked the Chief.

'By credit card Chief, not that I see that it's any of your business.'

'It's not Chief, it's Chief Constable Short.'

Mike tried to suppress a smile but failed. This giraffe of a woman was called Short!

The Chief noticed but let it be. So this was Mr Bad. By the time she had finished with him he'd be Mr Nothing.

Mike took out a cigarette. Evan shook his head. Mike noticed that the ashtrays had gone. He returned the unlit cigarette to the packet.

'It doesn't take long, does it, D.I. Karetzi?'

'What's that then Chief... Chief Constable Short?'

'To understand the new rules,' said the Chief.

Mike didn't answer but walked to the desk and got a pen and paper.

'Write down all your particulars Angie, National Insurance number, date of birth, yours and Daniel's, address, husband's name, where you have applied to for benefits and when, and Amber will do the rest.

'Now we will call a taxi to get you home,' said Mike.

'Thank you. You are the most decent person I have ever met. Thanks for the clothes, the money, the lift. One day I will repay you. That I promise,' Angie said as she exited to wait for the taxi.

Oh my God, thought the Chief. He gave the tart money too and the Force was paying for this guy's sexual desires! Christ, he must be hard up—yet he's very good looking, fit, smart and he's stooping to women like that.'

Angie left and all eyes were on Mike.

'Do you have a watch, D.I. Karetzi?' said the Chief.

'Yes I do. You wish to know the time?' said Mike.

'I know the time and I also know you're two hours late,' said the Chief.

'If we had something to do I'd be here on time,' said Mike.

'I understand you carry a knife, D.I. Karetzi?' said the Chief.

'I do, about my person, I carry a folding knife,' said Mike.

'I would like you to hand it in. A policeman shouldn't be above the law.'

'I can't do that. It's my father's, or to be pedantic, was my father's. The only thing as such that I have of his,' said Mike.

'That's a direct order. It's not open to discussion D.I. Karetzi,' the Chief said.

'And I have given you a direct answer which also isn't open for discussion, Chief Constable Short.'

'Then in that case, I have no option but to suspend you, Detective Inspector Karetzi,' said the new Chief. 'I will not have insubordination in my force and I will not tolerate mavericks on my force, and one more thing before you leave, you cannot use police credit cards to buy streetwalkers clothes or pay for them for services rendered. You disgust me. I will look into this and I would prepare yourself for the consequences, D.I. Karetzi.'

'Chief, you have no idea what you are talking about, no one does,' said Mike, dropping his warrant and credit cards on the table. 'See you guys later,' said Mike as he left for his car.

'Not so fast, D.I. Karetzi,' said the Chief.

Mike turned. 'Yes,' he said.

'Mobile phone please,' said the Chief.

Mike plonked one of the two he still possessed onto the table and walked away. It wasn't quite the walk of shame but it was as near as one could get to it.

Once outside Mike lit up. Angie had already gone. He remembered the café on the other side of the street and headed for it. He was in a daze. This wasn't the way it was supposed to end.

'Now that your talisman has gone, let me explain why I'm here,' said the Chief. 'I know it's difficult to close this place down. There's no room for your type of policing in the modern force, but I am sure that after another few months of sitting on your arses doing nothing, you will make the appropriate decisions and retire or leave and find other suitable places to ply your trade. Do you understand me, Mr White?'

'I guess so,' said Charlie.

'Don't guess, Mr White, be certain you understand what I'm telling you.

'D.I. Evans, you have been on the force a long time. I'm sure we could arrange a full pension. Same applies to you, Ms Gilberts. Think about it, don't try to swim against the tide. You'll eventually drown.'

'What will happen here to this place?' said Amber.

Doesn't concern you,' said the Chief. 'Just think about what I've said. You have until the end of the month.'

One minute she was there, all six foot of her, the next gone, like a streak of lightening but with much more power and effect.

Mike ordered and sat alone. He was the only customer at that time. He pondered over his new unaccustomed position. He wondered if it was springtime in Archangel, his father's birthplace. He wondered about the strawberry blonde and he wondered how the café could make such a shit cup of coffee.

Whilst Mike was contemplating his future, Amber, Evan and Charlie were more than thinking about the present. Charlie had already written a letter of resignation which he had given to Evan, who put it in his desk drawer. Amber was too stunned to think, never mind finish her cold breakfast.

'How come we never got wind of Clarky's resignation?' said Evan.

'Who said he resigned?' said Amber.

For ten minutes they discussed the matter. Had the Chief resigned? If so, why? Had he been pushed aside again, and why?

When did it happen? Where did Short come from? Was she for real and so on, never coming to any conclusions.

The next call was from Mike. His first question to Amber was had she looked into the Angie problem?

'Yes and No Mike,' Amber replied.

David returned to his own cottage after he had finished with Walter. Patrick was engrossed in a gangster film—he seemed happy. The first thing he did was to look for his dictionary. He found it in the kitchen, together with the two Delia Smith cookbooks. It was only a small one but that's all he had so he turned to V and looked: no such word as Vidiot.

He wouldn't tell his brother about the financial arrangements he had made with Walter. After all he would always take care of him. He would concentrate Patrick's mind on the emotional side. It wouldn't be too hard to explain to Patrick why they needed to kill ten people that they had never met. Walter was Patrick's friend, his only friend. Someone Patrick looked up to, that was the key.

He opened the bag. A sawn-off shotgun with a dozen cartridges, unregistered; a rope with a noose, a sharpened kitchen knife with a seven-inch blade, which was at least twenty years old and therefore untraceable; a lethal cocktail of pills according to Walter and a bottle of GBL, an odourless and colourless paint stripper which again, according to Walter, would be lethal when mixed with a little alcohol.

Walter had indeed been a very busy man. He'd prepared carefully but events had overtaken him.

The last thing that David extracted from the bag was a Polaroid Instamatic camera. With ten films already inserted.

It didn't take much to convince Patrick. He would have gone out there and then and slaughtered the lot without any qualms—that was how eloquent David was and how stupid Patrick was to listen and believe David's sad story.

'It's not like Mike to hit on a bird like that Angie woman,' said Charlie.

'Don't be daft, Charlie, Mike wouldn't have looked at her twice. He took pity on her. Remember that day in the restaurant, Charlie, you Amber? Now don't tell me Mike's got ulterior motives,' said Evan.

'That's what I said, wasn't it?' said Charlie. 'Mike's always helping the less fortunate.'

'Then we have that old tramp,' Amber recalled. 'What's his name Evan?'

'Everard I think,' said Evan.

'And let's not forget him being afraid of heights and risking all trying to help the Chessman.'

'Let's help this Angie Dawson, shall we?' said Amber, picking up the phone.

Mike sat for over an hour in the café. He tested their tea. It was as bad as the coffee and their bacon butties—he left most of it. He paid up, got into his car and drove directly to the cemetery where he remained until he had nearly frozen to death.

He didn't want to be another cemetery customer. This time he drove to his mother's house in Penarth. She wasn't at home and he couldn't contact her as she refused to have a mobile phone.

Angie Dawson was another who didn't possess a mobile, but she did have a landline. Unfortunately, that had been cut off due to non-payment, so Amber had to write her a letter with the good news. Charlie volunteered to take it around by hand. Each put thirty pounds into the kitty for Charlie to buy some groceries and things for Mrs Angie Dawson.

Amber gave Charlie a list which included washing powder, washing up liquid, soap, squash, milk, eggs, bread, the list was endless.

Before making the purchases, Charlie took it upon himself to buy Angie a cheap umbrella. He then bought a second one for the little boy. Charlie paid from his own pocket. Mike's Good Samaritan approach was catching. In all, excluding the umbrella, the groceries came to just shy of a hundred. The extra nine pound odd again coming out of his own pocket.

At precisely five o'clock Charlie parked outside the home of Angela Dawson. He knocked and Angie opened the door. Fortunately, she recognised Charlie.

'Amber asked me to give you this,' Charlie said, handing over Amber's letter. 'From what I can gather, she's sorted everything out for you, pulled some strings here and there. She's good at that.'

'Please come in Mr, sorry I don't know your name,' Angie said.

'Charlie, just plain Charlie.'

There was poor, then dirt poor, and then this. The few pieces of brown furniture were falling apart, the carpet threadbare, the television old enough to be in a museum and it was cold, as cold as outside, if not colder.

Charlie noticed for the first time the little boy wearing his raincoat but still shivering uncontrollably.

'Hi there. I'm Charlie. What's your name?'

'Daniel, but you can also call me Danny.'

'Something wrong with the electric heaters Angie?' said Charlie.

'They're not working,' said Angie, 'only the small fan heater in Daniel's bedroom.'

'How come, they all broke down together?' asked Charlie.

'No, one by one, over the last year or so. They were very old. We got them second-hand about six years ago from one of those pawn-type exchange places,' said Angie.

'Oh, I forgot, I've got some groceries in the car, I'll bring them in,' said Charlie.

'Thank you Charlie but I cannot accept any more charity. I know you mean well but Mike—that's his name isn't it?—gave me one hundred pounds and I'll never ever be able to repay him, but I'll try, I swear I'll try.'

'I've been ordered to deliver these goods and deliver them I will. Come on Danny, you're a big boy, help me bring in the bags.'

'Okay Mr Charlie, I can carry a lot.'

'That's good because I'm not very strong,' said Charlie.

Together they brought in the bags. Angie was crying again. The little boy put his arms around her and tried to protect her. Charlie said 'Good night' and left. By then both were crying.

He got in the car and shed a few tears of his own. How could people live like that? One thing he had to admit, the place was very clean, but piss poor.

Amber and Evan sat talking. They were going to eat together. Amber had made a stew. Evan was in no rush. His wife Edna had gone to Edinburgh to visit their daughter Jasmine who had been promoted and moved to Scotland to carry on her new job.

Charlie phoned Evan and explained the situation. Evan told Amber and together they put the cooking on hold and headed for the nearest DIY superstore where they purchased a new twenty-eight inch TV and three portable convector heaters, which he dropped off outside the house before driving off.

They paid with Evans's corporate credit card. He'd thrown caution to the wind—his days were numbered anyway.

Charlie knocked on the door and this time Danny answered.

'Hello Mr Charlie,' he said.

'Hi there, big boy. We've got some more carrying to do,' said Charlie.

'Where's your mum Danny?'

'Upstairs Mr Charlie, she's in the bathroom.'

'Well, let's hurry up and get these boxes in Danny.'

'What's in them, Mr Charlie?'

'Let's open them and see,' said Charlie. 'Let's give Mummy a surprise, shall we?'

'Yes please. Mummy's stopped crying now, Mr Charlie.'

'That's good, Danny. Very good.'

'Is that a television Mr Charlie?'

'Yes Danny.'

'Is it new?'

'Yes Danny.'

'Can we put it on now Mr Charlie?'
'Once we've tuned it in, you can.'
'What do you mean, tuned it in?'
'You'll see Danny. It won't take long.'
And it didn't. Ten minutes and it was on.

By the time Angela had come downstairs, two of the heaters were on full blast, the third unpackaged and ready to move to another room, the T.V. tuned in and playing.

'Don't say anything please, Angie, and please don't cry. I must go now,' and Charlie left.

By the time he got into his car Angie was blubbing her eyes out. All this from one meeting with a stranger, a policeman at that.

'Why are you crying Mummy? Mr Charlie and Mr Mike are very nice men. Don't you like them?'

'Of course I like them, Daniel. They are very, very nice men.'

The room was warming up. Angie crossed to where her son sat and cuddled him. They would make it thanks to that lovely policeman whom she thought was trying to pick her up. How wrong could one be!

The first meeting that they had was at Walter's home. It was a Saturday night.

'Please listen carefully David, as you know we can't go into this all gung-ho. Every erosion of these bloodsucking leeches must be to a plan. Alibis must be in place. One must beware of CCTV cameras. They're everywhere. Disguises to a certain extent if unavoidable, but planning is of the upmost importance.

'One last thing; don't use your own voice on the telephone and never use your own telephone or mobile if it has any connection to our business. I've been thinking about this for years and I have formulated a plan for the first victims.'

When Walter had finished, David asked a few questions, received satisfactory answers, made the necessary adjustments and reconciled himself to doing the job the way Walter had mapped it out.

Monday couldn't come quick enough for Walter or Patrick. David though was beginning to have some doubts but a quarter of a million was a lot of money. He and his brother would be set up for life and the doubts faded into insignificance.

'So Charlie, what are we going to do?' Evan asked. 'See the month out, then give in our resignations like Amber advises? That way we go into a new financial year or give them in now and let Short walk all over us.'

'Walk all over us!' said an angry Amber. 'The woman's already done that and we can't do anything about it, except sit it out. No resignations, nothing! We just sit here.'

'That's okay for you Amber, but I joined up all those years ago to police, to stop crime, to catch criminals, not to sit here playing cards.'

'Anyway, it's your deal Amber, and remember you owe me twenty match sticks from the last game,' said Evan.

'Do you think we did the right thing changing the front door lock?' asked Amber.

'Course we did,' said Charlie. 'Stops undesirables trying to break in and steal all the computer gear.'

'So did the old lock,' said Evan.

'Yeah, but by undesirables I mean Chief Constable Short,' said Charlie.

'And when she finds out that the locks have been changed, what's our excuse?' said Evan.

'That some nasty tried to break in and ruined the lock,' said Charlie.

'Now look Evan,' Amber said, 'I need to cook and eat; you need to smoke your pipe and eat, Charlie needs to doze off occasionally and eat. All these things, including our present activity, are outlawed by the new Sheriff in town.'

'What are you making for lunch anyway Amber?' Evan said, lighting up his pipe.

'Wait and see Evan, it's only half nine.'

Mike was bored. He didn't know what to do. You could only do the gym for a couple of hours. You could only run for an hour tops. It filled in the day but the evenings, he worried about the evenings. Sit at home and watch television—not his style; go out partying, more like it, but the drinking would be too much; women, no, not the ones he knew anyway. He sighed, sat down with his coffee in his favoured leather tub chair and promptly fell asleep.

It was ten to five when David made the call from a Cardiff phone box.

The receptionist answered and David asked for the Managing Director. It was personal and he could not tell her the nature of his business. The receptionist passed on the message to Mr Morton and asked him if he wished to take the call.

Abraham Morton was intrigued and took the call.

'Abrahim Morton here, with whom am I speaking?' he said in his best upper class voice.

'You can call me Mr Smith for now, which of course is not my real name. At this moment in time I cannot reveal my name. All will become apparent to you very shortly if you can bear with me for a few minutes,' said David.

'Okay, go ahead Mr Smith, tell me why I'm talking to you,' said Mr Morton.

'You're talking to me because I am in a position, or to be precise, my clients are in a position to purchase three, one million pound plus homes within a half hour's drive from Cardiff. Does that help you, Mr Morton, to prolong our discussion?'

'It sure does Mr Smith, please go on.'

'I am what you call an Agent, a Sports Agent and within the next month I will have three sportsmen, all foreigners here wanting immediate access to properties.'

'I'm following you Mr Smith.'

'It's very important that nobody but nobody knows that I am in Cardiff, otherwise I risk losing my deal as others may step in, hence the subterfuge.'

'I see,' said Morton. 'There is no problem with the houses; we have quite a few on our books that would be suitable. How would you like to proceed?'

'Well, you have the brochures ready, we will pay top dollar, no bartering and I will be at your office at eight tonight. That is if you can make it then of course. Unfortunately, I have a little piece of business I need to complete first.'

'That I can do. Any other requirements, Mr Smith?' said Morton.

'Yes, I would like to see a solicitor. Preferably someone who you work with closely, so that I can get a precise timescale on everything and a copy of his standard contract. Can that be done?'

'Give me a minute Mr Smith, whilst I make contact with someone we work very closely with.'

A minute passed.

'A Mr Terry Fenwick will be here at eight as arranged,' David said and added: 'One last thing: I know I sound paranoid but please be alone with Mr Fenwick, nobody else, no CCTV cameras, you understand. I've very big money riding on this lot. I can't afford any mistakes. In two weeks' time it will all be done and dusted.'

'You can rely on me,' said Morton.

'Will see you at eight then,' said David, closing the phone.

He was six pounds lighter. That's how much he had pumped into the phone box. 'Bloody crooks,' he muttered to himself as he walked back to his car.

As Abrahim Morton drove his eighty-grand Mercedes back home to his flat, he calculated that between the two firms, they would rake in about a hundred thousand pounds—not bad for taking one extra lousy phone call.

Of course he could have asked Lancelot to attend the meeting but he didn't want to frighten off Mr Smith, who seemed cagey enough as it was. He couldn't say, 'and this is the solicitor, good man, he's my brother, by the way.'

He, Abrahim, had no interest in sport of any kind but he'd read somewhere that these agents were making millions. He wondered how much Smith was making out of his deal.

Nevertheless, a hundred grand was not to be sneezed at and he was happy. Since the divorce, five years ago, he lived alone, never spoke to his ex and fortunately they never had any children so he devoted his time to the Company. It had expanded enormously. They now owned seventeen sites, over a hundred properties which they rented out and had their fingers in many pies.

Abrahim's father was still Chairman but apart from board meetings never interfered in and of the day-to-day business which Abrahim loved.

Louis, his father, could be found either on the local golf course, where he played a round or two whenever the weather permitted or in his indoor swimming pool which was on the side of the house.

Terry and Abrahim sat together around the small boardroom table. They had already started celebrating. Both were drinking Scottish Malt Whisky, neat.

CCTV cameras were off as per Mr Smith's request and both were smoking cigars, Davidoff Havanas. A third glass lay on the table as did the box of cigars together with a cutter.

Patrick parked the car half a mile from the office of Morton's Estate Agents and they walked the rest of the way. It had stopped raining a few hours previously but it was extremely cold. Both were wearing leather gloves to protect their hands and to avoid leaving any fingerprints.

Patrick was to take out the younger man Morton, David the other one on a given signal from David who was carrying a leather briefcase which contained the knife. In his coat pocket he had a bottle of whisky in which he'd already mixed the GBL.

Morton buzzed them in. It was now exactly eight p.m. At least they were punctual. But there were two; he only expected one, a Mr Smith.

'Best get another glass Terry, there's two of the buggers,' Abrahim said.

'Welcome to Morton's. I'm Abrahim and this is Mr Terry Fenwick, the solicitor,' Abrahim said holding out his hand.

'I'm David Smith and this is my colleague who, how can I say, watches my back.'

'I see,' said Morton shaking David's hand and ignoring Patrick.

'Can I take your coats?' asked Morton.

David took off his coat and handed it to Abrahim who hung it up. Patrick didn't move.

'Right then, follow me please David. We're in the boardroom. Please sit down.'

David sat then indicated to Patrick to sit.

'Please help yourselves to the cigars and whisky, or if you prefer something else, I am sure I can facilitate you,' said Abrahim.

'Thank you. I like whisky and actually I have brought with me my favourite brand which we can all drink to celebrate on conclusion of our business; till then I will take a glass of this, which is a fine brand, but nowhere as good as the Tullibardine.'

David poured himself a large one. 'Before we progress Abrahim, the CCTV cameras?'

'Switched off,' said Abrahim.

'Thank you. As explained, my position is delicate.'

'I have six houses here that meet your criteria,' said Abrahim wondering why on earth this Smith chap would keep his leather gloves on.

David read and re-read. No one spoke. A good five minutes passed before David asked Abrahim if he had a road map.

Abrahim did and brought it to the table.

'Could you please show me where these two places are on the map?' Abrahim did.

It took another five minutes before David separated three of the six and placed them in front of Abrahim. 'These are the ones I want,' David said.

Abrahim noticed that they were all in villages west of Cardiff and very near to each other. The total price 3.2 million.

'We will pay the full price, but the sellers will leave all the furniture such as curtains, carpets, light fittings, beds, cupboards, white goods in kitchen, oven and whatever. My people must be able to move into a furnished house.'

'I don't foresee any problems there,' said Abraham.

I bet you don't, thought David. All your Christmases have come at once.

'You will act on our behalf?' asked David of Terry.

'Would be pleased to,' said Terry.

'Timescale?' asked David.

'Can do in three weeks,' said Terry. 'Would you like to know our rates?' said Abraham.

'Whatever they are, it's fine. Those amounts of money are inconsequential,' said David.

'Have we concluded our business for the time being?' said Terry.

'We have. I will take this contract and the three brochures and will be back in three days. Would you like a deposit when I return?' said David.

'Ten percent will be sufficient,' said Abraham.

'And you will have a word with the owners and get them prepared,' said David.

'Will do, like I said I don't see any problems, do you Terry?' said Abraham.

'None at all,' answered Terry.

'Then in that case, we will celebrate with a proper drink,' said David who now rose and went into the other room where he retrieved his bottle of laced whisky from his coat.

On returning, he was careful not to show them the top, holding it in such a way that they could not see that the seal was broken.

He made a big thing of opening it. Both Abraham and Terry had drained their glasses in anticipation of a higher quality Malt. Again David had left most of their whisky in his glass.

He poured each of them a good measure then raised his glass as a toast.

'To the future collaboration.'

Both Terry and Abrahim took a sip, then two. It was an acquired taste but for a hundred grand they would acquire it.

'So do you like it? Would you like me to bring you a case when I return?'

Before they could answer, David raised his glass again. 'Here's to my two new Welsh friends.'

Both drank again.

David wasn't sure how long the stuff took to work and what were the symptoms. If it took much longer, he would have to give Patrick the signal and he really wanted to avoid that.

On the third drink, they began sweating and realising something was amiss. Thirty seconds later and they were writhing on the floor.

Having ascertained that both were dead, David took out the camera and took two photos. Their work was done.

He put his whisky bottle into his briefcase, together with the camera. He found a toilet and hand basin and washed out his glass, which he dried and replaced with the other glasses in the kitchen. He then took out the remainder of the GBL and poured it into the half-empty bottle of the Morton's whisky. He then washed and cleaned their glasses before pouring in some of the poisoned whisky.

He put on his coat, and together with Patrick, lifted the deceased into their chairs. He let the two cigars burn themselves out in the ashtray.

On the way out, they switched of the lights and walked back to the car.

David now drove the car to Dinas Powys where they parked and waited.

They waited for over two hours, but eventually got their reward. A half-cut Gareth Jones came out of the pub and started walking unsteadily towards his home.

David stopped the car next to the slow moving Jones and asked him for directions to Wenvoe. In the meantime, whilst Jones was rearranging the details in his mind, Patrick stepped up behind him and broke his neck.

Patrick then picked him up like a rag doll and carried him to the nearest lamp post where he dumped him. David took another photo and they left. This time they went directly home.

Before leaving David emptied Jones's pockets of money and credit cards. He also took his watch and ring, all this to make it look like a mugging gone wrong.

A friend of Gareth Jones found his body half an hour later. He was also on his way back from the pub.

At first, the police on the scene thought that the victim had suffered a heart attack, but soon realised he had a broken neck.

The SOCO team were called in and photos were taken from every conceivable angle.

The bodies of Morton and Fenwick were found at ten past seven by the cleaner, Mrs Alibi. She nearly passed out when she realised that the two were not sitting drinking whisky and discussing business. They were sitting motionless and dead.

She went into the small kitchenette and stood over the sink. Her head bowed, she thought she was going to be sick. After a while, she felt better but her mouth was dry. She opened the kitchen cupboard and took out a glass. It hadn't been cleaned properly so she rinsed it out a few times before filling it with cold water and washing down two Aspirin tablets. She could now face the police whom she telephoned from her own mobile. She was careful not to touch anything.

Chief Inspector Roger Appleby was first on the scene. They took a statement from Mrs Alibi. At first, it was suspected that the two gentlemen had formed some kind of suicide pact but there was no note. It was suspected that they had been poisoned. They dusted for fingerprints and waited for the rest of the staff to come in to take theirs.

The *Chronicle* and *Echo* had a field day as did next morning's *Western Mail* and various other national papers. As yet, the police had not connected both sets of murders.

The hullabaloo had quietened down significantly by Thursday. The police now suspected a connection. Every contract concluded or not over the past two years that included either Morton's or Fenwick's was being scrutinised.

Over forty people were helping police with their enquiries.

As the Chief Inspector told the reporters, they had not ruled out the possibility that it was just a coincidence that the three men were well known to each other and that Jones was a victim of a mugging that had gone wrong.

Deep down he knew he was talking rubbish but he liked to keep an open mind.

Walter spent all day looking at the three photos. From his scrapbook he had extracted the group photo.

There were now red crosses on three of the ringed faces. He'd already passed over twenty thousand pounds cash for David and was in the process of transferring his shares.

David realised that all calls to both the estate agents and the solicitors were being monitored by the police. For two days he'd followed Sampson around various villages' and towns' letting properties. Apart from when he was driving Sampson was never alone. Again, Sampson's house was like a fortress. A police car passed every ten minutes or so and in the house there were six children, a wife and a live-in nanny. Outside work this man didn't have a life. He never went anywhere, no pubs, no restaurants, no cinema, no football game; once at home, forget it.

If there was any way, it would have to do with the car; an accident, something, but what? Murder was a tough business to be in, David decided. He switched to Levy, the Group's Accountant. Now Israel did all his work for the Mortons from one of the estate agency's back rooms but he also ran a private practice mainly from home. He too was married. Could he, David, go for a consultation as a client? He very much doubted it. He didn't have the correct credentials. All involved with Morton and Fenwick's were being very careful, so for the time being Israel Levy was also a no-go.

Lancelot and his wife Georgia; two young children. He had to mark them down as possibilities, but they lived in one of those very posh apartments down on the Bay, difficult to get in and out.

Now that left Deena, married and divorced twice. She dealt with mortgages for their customers at Morton's. Again, she had her own separate room in Morton's Head Office in Cardiff. So far, he had not been able to find out where she lived. Did she live alone? Was it accessible? Did she have a boyfriend or girlfriend? What were her hobbies? He would hardly go online and find out.

The following day, Friday, David, having no work on, waited for Deena Morton to leave. She drove a BMW, red sports car and drove it fast.

Again, she lived in an apartment overlooking the mouth of the River Severn in Penarth.

'Shit,' said David. 'Not another bloody apartment.' He parked up near Deena's car. She was going to go back out, otherwise she would have garaged it.

He took a stroll, listened to some music on his car radio, had a coffee from his flask, another stroll, another coffee and eventually she reappeared, all dressed up like a tart.

As she came out, she spoke to a character in a long brown camel coat. They seemed on friendly terms. That was the fourth of fifth time that David had clocked him. 'Plain clothes cop,' David reckoned. This looked like another write-off.

They were still talking when a taxi pulled up. The man with the brown coat opened the door of the cab for her and said something which David couldn't quite catch. He followed the cab back into Cardiff where it dropped her off outside a casino.

She was obviously well known in there because a doorman rushed out and opened the door of the taxi and held open the glass door of the Casino for her to enter.

David drove off. He wasn't a member. Wouldn't become a member unless he could get hold of some new ID.

When he returned, Patrick and Walter were watching "Dracula's Monster" or something like that on TV. It was crap and in black and white but both seemed to be enjoying it.

Walter looked at David who shook his head. Then Walter carried on watching the film.

Saturday morning and both David and Patrick were in Penarth. The man in the brown coat was again there walking up and down the promenade. Deena surfaced at eleven, waved to brown coat, got into her car and headed off. David followed.

The bloody bitch was going clothes shopping. Patrick was getting edgy. He hated shopping and David found it difficult to keep his brother's mind on the job.

By three Deena had had enough and ate at a small Bistro from where she made at least half a dozen calls. When she had finished the lazy sod hailed a taxi to take her and her shopping the half a mile to where she had parked.

'What do we do now David?' asked Patrick.

'We head for Penarth and wait,' said David.

'Wait for what?' said Patrick.

'I don't know,' said David.

'Okay bro,' said Patrick satisfied for the time being.

Her usual space was occupied when Deena arrived home so, she with brown coat's help, unloaded her shopping and drove the hundred or so yards to an undercroft parking space. David followed and handed the knife to Patrick. It was his turn. He'd only done one.

It was dimly lit in the undercroft. Patrick looked around, saw nobody and advanced on his prey, hiding as best he could behind other cars as he reached Deena who, at the last moment cried out, but not before Patrick had plunged the kitchen knife through her heart. He wiped the knife clean on Deena's trousers, just as David had told him, before running back to the car.

David drove slowly away from the undercroft in the opposite direction to the apartments. He turned and used the minor roads to get them out of Penarth.

When they got back home, he changed to his proper number plates and drove off to Comeston Lakes where he dumped the knife and Jones's watch and rings all in different places.

After five minutes of waiting, brown coat tried to raise Deena on her mobile. When he didn't get an answer he ran to the undercroft where he found her. He called it in…

'I'm sorry Walter but no photo, too dangerous.' Walter was unhappy but hoped that one of the local rags might oblige with one.

The *Wales on Sunday*'s headline on the front page in big block letters simply said 'MORE MURDERS AT MORTON'S.'

Those headlines sold an estimated forty thousand more copies than average. On Monday, only half of Morton's staff turned up for work. The others either phoned in sick or didn't even bother to make excuses; they were scared.

On Monday morning, Miss Jennifer Nightingale flew to Paraguay. She was going on a special fact-finding tour of the native Indians of that country and would be unable to communicate with family and friends for most of the three-week expedition.

Unknown to her this would have a devastating effect on her boyfriend and fiancé, Desmond Harris who, after seeing her off at Heathrow Airport in London, decided it wasn't worth going into work. Although his title was Sales Manager, in realty he was no more than a glorified key holder for the properties Morton's' had on their books, either for sale or rent.

'So Charlie, what would you like to do today, play cards, or play cards? It's your choice,' said Evan.

'Very droll,' said Evan. 'I would like for Mike to be here and for us to have a case to crack,' said Charlie.

'What's happening with this Morton's business Amber?' Evan asked.

'A little bird tells me that they have two main suspects and to expect developments in the next 48 hours,' said Amber.

'Obviously someone working at Morton's or the other guys, Fenwick's,' said Charlie.

'Makes sense,' said Evan, 'but to my mind there's got to be at least two involved. It will be interesting to see what their motive is.'

'This guy in the *Chronicle*, Alex Symonds, isn't he the one that came down here early December and wrote us up a good piece?' said Amber.

'Yes, Alex Symonds is a reporter you could trust. I like the man; has some dignity, for a reporter that is and he likes a drink,' said Evan.

'Can we share the matches out again?' said Charlie. 'I keep losing and running out!'

Charlie took a dozen or so matches from Evan's pile and thy carried on playing cards.

On Tuesday morning when Desmond Harris turned up for work, one of the few who did, he was confronted by a D.I. Foster and a Detective Sergeant Mills who requested that he went with them down to Cardiff Central for another interview.

They made him a coffee and the three sat around the table.

Chief Inspector Appleby began the interview by asking Harris to confirm what he had told them about his movements on the night of the murders in their first interview.

Harris sighed. 'Look, it's all written down in my statement.'

'Please tell us again,' said D.I. Foster.

'Okay, I finished work at about half-past five, then picked up my girlfriend from where she works and we went to her parents' house.'

'What did you do there, Mr Harris?'

'Well, we had a meal and just talked, watched something on tele but mainly we talked.'

'And you say you left about eleven?'

'That's right, about eleven maybe a little before, say ten to, quarter to.'

'Your girlfriend is the only one who can vouch for you as the parents were out until eleven thirty.'

'We've spoken to them. You seemed to have missed out that particular fact from your statement, Mr Harris.'

'What fact?' said Harris.

'That the parents weren't there,' said D.I. Foster.

'I don't see what the problem is,' said Harris.

'The problem, Mr Harris, is that Mr and Mrs Nightingale weren't there,' said Foster.

'Let's move on,' said Appleby. 'Where were you Saturday evening, Mr Harris?'

'I was with my girlfriend from about one in the afternoon, till Sunday night.'

'What did you do?' asked D.I. Foster.

'What do you mean, what did we do?'

'Exactly what I said—did you go out and eat, did you go to the cinema, a bowling alley, a pop concert, bingo?'

'That's enough Peter, let Mr Harris answer in his own time.'

'Well, Saturday we went for a walk, bought some wine and some readymade meals and went back to mine. Sunday we got up late, read the papers, ate lunch, ham and pineapple pizzas, then went to her parents' house where I helped her to pack and get organised for her trip. I left about nine for my place and returned the next morning at eight to drive her down to London.'

'Did you see the parents, Mr Harris?' asked the Chief Inspector.

'Yes I did, in the morning,' replied Harris.

'And your girlfriend, where can we contact her?' asked D.I. Foster.

'My fiancé cannot be contacted for three weeks. She's in Peru, the Andes or somewhere.'

'How convenient,' said Foster.

'Are you trying to say something? Am I missing something? I don't like the way…'

'I think you need a lawyer, Mr Harris.'

'Why would I need a lawyer?' said Harris.

'Because we're going to charge you,' said the Chief Inspector.

'Can I phone my father to arrange a lawyer?' said Harris.

'Yes,' said the Chief Inspector.

'We got him boss. He looks the sneaky type,' said D.I. Foster, who then proceeded to tell the whole precinct. A cheer went up. Drinks that night would be on Foster and for once in his life he didn't mind. The Super was informed and he passed on the good news to the Chief Constable.

Two hours later, poor Desmond Harris had been cautioned and arrested and was now in custody. Both the *Cardiff Chronicle* and the *South Wales Echo* picked up the story quickly and their front page headlines respectively read 'MAN ARRESTED OVER MORTON'S MURDERS and MORTON'S SUSPECT HELD.'

All the radio and television stations broke the news to their respective audiences. Everyone was on such a high that they forgot the little matter of motive.

Walter and David laughed. Patrick couldn't understand why but joined in anyway.

Mike spent the day catching up on all the Poirots he'd taped; he loved the simplicity of the plots, the era, everything, especially Souchet who he thought was perfect from his voice to his mannerisms.

The day passed quickly. A few glasses of Pinot Grigio, a few non-filter cigarettes and film after film with no advertisements to hold up the stories; he fast forwarded when the commercial breaks were on.

By eleven Mike was exhausted. Doing nothing all day did that to people who were used to doing things. He switched on the television and immediately turned to Ceefax. He wanted to read the football latest. Whilst flicking up and down the pages, the news bulletin on BBC1 was saying that the Morton's murderer had been apprehended and charged. Must have been one of the staff, thought Mike and switched off.

For the first time in years, Mike overslept and was woken by his cleaner.

'For the love of God, Detective K, you still sleeping and the madman is killing people everywhere. What is wrong with you? Go to work, catch this man. It's your job. I will tell your mother, you should be ashamed of yourself.'

'Mrs Alibi, take it easy. It's not my case and anyway they've caught the man who was responsible.'

'Fooee, I never heard so much stupidity and I never thought I'd see Alice's boy sleeping when there was work to do.'

Mike got up. He was only wearing his boxers. 'Mrs Alibi, the man has been caught. It's all over. No need for anyone to worry.'

'I said Fooee. They got that stupid boy Desmond. Do you think they would invite him for a drink?' Mrs Alibi said.

'Please Mrs Alibi, you're not making any sense. Who is Desmond? Who hasn't offered him a drink? And they call me crazy.'

'Okay if I make you a large espresso will you listen to me or are you too smart to listen to Mrs Alibi, your mother's friend for twenty-five years.'

'Anything you say Mrs Alibi. Can I get dressed now?' Mike said, heading for the en suite.

In the lounge, coffee and cigarette in hand, Mike asked his cleaner, or more likely his mother's spy, to take a seat which she reluctantly did. He now realised why he never brought any women back on a Tuesday night because it was Wednesday the following day morning and Mrs Alibi would appear. Usually he was up by eight, ready by half eight.

'May I talk to you now?' said Mrs Alibi.
'It hasn't stopped you thus far Mrs Alibi.'
'And don't be cheeky to an old lady.'
'Go ahead Miss Marple,' said Mike.
'I do the contract cleaning for Head Office, and I found the bodies of Mr Morton and the other person.

'I arrive at six-thirty and find that the lights are out but the door is not locked or the alarm for which I have the code. I suspected that somebody has already come in early. This happens maybe once a month when they have a lot of work on.

'I clean the immediate area first, as is my normal practice, then I do the eight individual offices, finishing with the boardroom, kitchen and toilets. I assume that whoever came in early is in the boardroom working but when I open the door the lights need switching on, so obviously I switch them on and see the two sitting around the table. I say 'sorry' and am about to leave when I realise something is wrong. I look closer and see that they are dead.

'I feel sick so I rush to the kitchen to throw up in the sink but for some reason I can't. In my pocket here, like this...' She showed Mike her pocket. 'I carry aspirin tablets, I take two out and open the cupboard for a glass. I get one which is dirty and a little damp. I rinse it out and take the tablets after filling it with water.

'I call the police and wait for them to come. They ask me some questions and I leave in a hurry. I've never seen dead bodies before, do you understand?'

'Mrs Alibi, I'm not sure what you're trying to tell me. I don't see anything untoward or unusual. The killer, after finishing his job, switched off all the lights and walked out.'

'Detective K, you're not listening or maybe you're just not a good detective. Listen, the glass, someone probably, the killer, had used that particular glass. It was still damp. He attempted to clean it but didn't do a good job and please remember, did I tell you there was a third empty glass, unused on the boardroom table, together with an Atlas and house brochures?'

'Well maybe this Desmond chap had a drink with them. He's some kind of Manager isn't he?'

'Don't make me laugh. In that place even the tea lady would be a manager. They give these people titles but not money. Do you see?'

'Do you know this Desmond, Mrs Alibi?'

'Yes, once or twice a week he is in first sorting out keys and putting them on various people's desks. He's a nice young lad, twenty-four I think he told me once. Wouldn't and couldn't hurt a fly.

'Not to Mr Abrahim; he's a nobody. Invite him in for a drink; I don't think so, and how did he poison them, tell me that Detective?'

'What makes you think they were poisoned, Mrs Alibi?'

'No blood anywhere. Both men were wearing white shirts, easy to notice blood.'

'Look Mrs Alibi, it's not my case but for us to charge this Desmond bloke, it means he doesn't have an alibi, unlike you, Mrs Alibi,' Mike said stressing her surname.

'That is very clever Detective K but I'm telling you it is not Desmond Harris, so get down there and find out who it is.'

'It's not that simple, but I hear you. You have a point or two and I'll get someone to look into it,' said Mike wishing she would just get on with the cleaning.

'The road atlas, what about that, why would they need an atlas, you tell me Detective K?'

'They're estate agents, Mrs Alibi. They were probably looking up some place.'

'Fooee, what kind of estate agent doesn't know his own area inside out and remember Desmond would also know.

'Now Detective K, get your act together and go and kick some ass.'

Good idea, thought Mike, I must get out of here till she's gone.

Whilst showering Mike wondered if she'd said ass or arse. Quite the detective was Mrs Alibi.

Mike left his apartment and started walking to clear his head. Never mind Mrs Alibi, it was he who needed the aspirins.

Half an hour later he'd got himself to town, bought a newspaper and was sitting in one of those new coffee houses drinking his second espresso of the day.

Four glasses, one clean, two still with drink in them and one washed out and put back into the cupboard. An atlas, open at which page, brochures, fingerprints, Desmond, keys, door unlocked, alarm off, CCTV cameras must also have been off, why? His mind was racing. They, assuming it was the same person or persons, they go to Dinas Powys and take out another employee. How tall is Desmond? Is he a big lad or what?

No alibis by the sounds of it. Is he stupid, did he just go home and no one knew he was there, no one to vouch for him, for all three incidents, where or what is his motive? Was there anything missing from the offices? Why try to make the Jones' killing look like a robbery, why, was all this just one big coincidence?

'Fuck it,' he felt a headache coming on again. He asked the waitress if she had any aspirins. They did and he took them.

How the hell did someone get poison into their drinks? Nothing made any sense.

Mike rang Amber. 'Hi, Mike, we're missing you, come down.'

'Hi beautiful. The boys there?' said Mike.

'Yes, we're all here, playing cards as usual,' she said.

'Listen Amber, I've heard nothing from Short. I think I'm on my way out but I need for you to get me everything you can on this Morton business,' said Mike.

'I'll try Mike, but it's getting difficult to even phone and say hello these days. It's as if Central especially are keeping it tight; not letting anyone into their party.'

Mike heard Charlie. They were on loudspeaker. Charlie was singing: 'It's my party and I'll do what I want to, do what I want to.'

'Okay,' said Amber, 'that's enough Charlie.'

'Did you know Amber, Charlie was the lead singer in a group before he tried his hand at something else,' Mike said.

'Sure,' said Amber, 'and I was a limbo dancer a few years ago.'

'Leslie Gore 63,' said Charlie.

'I'm serious Amber,' said Mike.

'What about, Charlie or the information on this Morton thing?'

'Both Amber, both; what's important right now is that they've got the wrong man which means everyone will become complacent and pay for it with their life or lives.'

'Why do you think that?' shouted Evan.

'My cleaner told me,' said Mike.

'Have you been drinking Mike?' said Amber.

'No, I'll explain when you all come down to mine tonight, say eight. I'll order some food from Angelo's and…'

'Mike we've got to go. It's her majesty, Chief Constable Short. She's trying to get in and we've changed the lock and code. See you at eight.'

Evan let the Chief Constable in. She was fuming but waited until she got into the office.

No hellos or good mornings from Short.

'Who changed the lock and why?' she said.

'I did,' said Evan and Charlie in unison.

'Both of you?' said the Chief Constable.

'Yes,' said Evan, 'someone Superglued the lock after attempting and failing to get in.'

'Why would someone want to get into a police station?' said Short.

'Because we have a hundred grand's worth of equipment I suppose,' said Evan, pointing to the computers and such on the back wall.

'Well I will need a new key and the new code if that's not too much trouble, and I would like them before I leave.'

Charlie took off a key from his bunch of keys and then took a piece of paper, wrote down the code and handed both to Short.

She didn't say 'thank you.'

'So what have you decided?' said Short.

No one answered.

'Look,' she said, using a much softer tone, 'I know it's difficult but we don't need this place anymore. Two of you are ready for full retirement and you, Mr White, have only been with us a few months. We will give you all a month's wages and, well, that's it.'

Still no answer

'As you might have heard, we have up and coming officers who are our future. New ideas, new strengths; they bring different things to the table. Take, for instance, the Morton's case—solved, no problem. We've got university boys clambering to join us. The Force needs different disciplines in this day and age.'

'And what if you have the wrong man?' said Amber.

'We haven't,' said Short. 'Anyway, think about what I have just said. We can sort it out to everyone's satisfaction.'

'What if this Harris bloke didn't do anything? What if he's a victim of circumstances? What if everyone lets their guard down because they think they've got the killer and the real killer kills some more?'

'A lot of "what ifs" Detective Jones. We've got the right man, believe me.'

That evening at the Queens, a police pub as such, they were celebrating. Chief Inspector Appleby, D.I. Foster and another dozen or so were drinking the bar dry.

D.I. Foster forgot it was his wife's birthday and that he'd promised to take her out; he was celebrating.

In another part of town, there were more celebrations but of a quieter kind.

Chief Constable Short, Chief Superintendent Freddie Fowler and top Crown Prosecuting Services Office Alan Wilson were having a meal. The Champagne was flowing freely.

Walter and David had made an appearance at the Affy. Patrick was at home watching TV and in Mike's apartment on The Bay, four people were enjoying pizzas from Angelo's.

'Well did you get any info Amber?'

'Not much. This Harris boy has only his girlfriend/fiancé as an alibi for all four murders but she's away in Peru or somewhere and can't be contacted for four weeks. At Harris's flat they found leather gloves which had been cleaned with some kind of bleach and were discoloured and he only had two kitchen knives, one for cutting bread and a small one for peeling vegetables. That's it Mike. Oh, and he, of course, has access to all the keys, codes and personnel files.'

'And his motive?' said Mike.

'No motive as yet but he was treated like a tea boy and they think he just snapped and went on a killing spree.'

Mike told them what he had learnt from his cleaner Mrs Alibi.

No one was impressed.

'My money is still on Harris, Mike. Sorry, but all this nonsense about glasses, atlases doesn't make sense,' said Charlie.

'I have to agree with Charlie,' said Evan.

'Okay,' said Mike. 'One last thing, Amber, do we have details of this Harris; I mean height, weight etc.?'

'We do Mike. I've got it here. Age 25, height 5'7", weight 10st 8lbs, no distinguishing marks, brown hair cut shortish.'

'That's fine Amber,' said Mike, getting up and coming back with two large thick books.

Mike picked up a copy of *The Echo*, read, put it down, then picked up another, read it, and taking a pen, circled a few words on page three.

Everyone looked on. 'Tell me Charlie, how tall are you?' asked Mike.

'Five eight, eight and a half,' said Charlie.

'Try again Charlie, Evan's 5'8" and you're a bit shorter,' said Mike.

'Okay I'm say, five seven and a half and weighed 11st 2lbs, this morning,' Charlie said.

'Good, I'm just a tad over six foot. If I step on these books I become 6'2", the same height as Gareth Jones.' Mike pointed to the ringed sentence in the paper. 'Now Charlie, come from behind me and try to break my neck.'

Charlie did. He tried but couldn't get enough leverage because of Mike's stooping and because of the height difference.

'Why did you stoop?' said Amber.

'Because that's the way drunks walk. Their eyes are fixed to the floor,' said Evan. 'And Gareth Jones was 14st plus. Not an easy bloke to bring down,' said Mike. 'Even drunk, he has height and weight advantage.'

'I reckon we ought to get your cleaner to work with us,' said Amber.

Everyone laughed.

'So what do we do now?' said Amber.

'You can ring up this Chief Inspector Appleby's boss and mention what we have just talked about,' said Mike.

'Can't do it Mike,' said Evan.

'Why on earth not? Until you resign you're still a police officer Evan.'

'It's not that. It's Appleby's boss,' said Evan.

'What about him?' said Mike.

'It's Fowler,' said Evan.

'Oh Christ, no, don't tell me it's the guy who threatened us because he was under the assumption we stole his car,' said Mike.

'We did in effect steal his car and that guy has got a long memory,' said Evan.

'We'll send a fax or something to Appleby. At least then we have a record,' said Mike.

By ten they had all had enough and went home, leaving Mike alone once more.

He listened to some of his father's old fifties and sixties American albums for an hour or so and then went to bed.

At eight the following morning Amber sent a fax to Chief Inspector Appleby. By nine the Chief Constable was on the phone to Amber giving her hell. By half nine Charlie had walked into town from the office and found himself a telephone box.

It took him a while to locate Alex Symonds but eventually he did and had the *Chronicle*'s Chief Reporter on the line.

'So who am I talking to?' asked Symonds.

'Somebody who has a story for you.'

'Does this somebody have a name?' said Symonds.

'No, this is your classic anonymous phone tipster,' said Charlie.

'Fine, tell me what you have,' said Symonds.

Charlie did.

'Christ,' said Alex Symonds on finishing his conversation with Charlie.

'Linda!' he shouted from his desk, 'get me everything we have on that Chessman business, and I mean everything.'

With every file in front of him, computer working overtime, Alex was now ready to follow up and ascertain the few things he needed. First, he called Mrs Gilberts and asked to speak to D.I. Karetzi.

He wasn't in the office and she would not confirm that he had been suspended. Yes, she did remember Alex but could not comment on Mike's position. A second call to his man in Cardiff Central confirmed that there were rumours but no-one was quite sure. A third call to Mr Brian at Tangent didn't help. The man obviously didn't know or didn't care.

Six calls later and Alex was ninety-nine percent sure but he still felt uncomfortable. That one percent was the difference between a massive front-page spread and a one paragraph throw away article hidden somewhere on page seven. Alex got in his car and drove down to 111 Nelson Street.

He pressed the buzzer.

'Answer that will you please Evan,' Amber said, her mouth full of doughnut.

'Yes,' Evan said.

'It's Alex Symonds from the *Chronicle*,' Alex said. 'I rang earlier.'

'It's Symonds again from the *Chronicle*,' Evan called out to Amber.

'We've no comment to make,' said Amber. 'He's wasting his time.'

'Let me speak to him,' said Charlie.

Evan handed Charlie the intercom connection.

'Is that Alex Symonds?'

'It is,' said Symonds.

'We would like you to understand that we have no comment to make on Detective Inspector Karetzi. Will you please now go away and let us get on with our work.'

'Fine, then in that case, I see no reason to trouble you any further,' said Symonds walking away happy in the knowledge that he was now a hundred percent certain.

The second guy who answered the buzzer was the guy with whom he had spoken in the morning, the anonymous tipster. He'd detected that bit of a cockney accent. It was unmistakable and the guy wanted him to know that it was him.

'Well, he seemed to accept that quite easily,' said Evan.

'Strange that, you can't usually get these people off a potential story for love nor money,' said Amber, biting into another jam doughnut.

Mike was having lunch in a small pub in Cowbridge with Tanya, the airhostess. Their on-off relationship was waning. Both felt it had run its course. In truth, Tanya had found somebody more committed and Mike was still searching for a strawberry blonde he had once met fleetingly.

'You look very sad today Mike, but you must have realised we couldn't go on like we have been doing in the last three or four months. We can still be friends, can't we?'

'Of course we can,' said Mike. 'Where can I drop you off?'

'At the airport if it's okay with you.'

At the airport they kissed and parted. Both knew they couldn't be just friends and both were happy with that.

The next morning's headlines 'COP HERO SUSPENDED' did not sell any extra copies. People were more interested in murders, not police heroes who, after all, were paid by the taxpayer to do their job.

Mike showered, shaved and made himself a coffee for breakfast. He was about to light up his first cigarette of the day when he got the call from Evan. It was about the newspaper article.

'Thanks Evan, but I've got to go get to my mother before someone tells her.'

Mike drove like a madman, normal for him, to his mother's house in Penarth. The door was ajar and he could hear the sound of a woman's voice coming from the lounge.

He walked straight in. His mother Alice, Mrs Alibi and two others of that age were looking at the *Chronicle*'s headlines.

His mother, on seeing her only child, started crying. Mike moved swiftly to throw a protective arm around her.

'Look Mam, this is not what it seems. I've just been rested whilst they work out what my new unit does.'

'And the others, are they suspended too?' said Alice.

'Look here son,' said one of the old ladies, 'everything I read here is more than good. They're singing your praises from the rooftops. This reporter Alex Symonds is one hundred and ten percent for you, so who have you rubbed up the wrong way?'

'The new Chief Constable, Muriel Short,' said Mike, embarrassed by the attention he was receiving.

'Is she a gay or does she carry a white stick?' said the other old lady that Mike didn't know.

'Diana, for goodness sake,' said Mrs Alibi.

'Well she must be either blind, a raving lesbian or very stupid to sack the best man in the Force,' said Diana.

'Ladies please, I've only been suspended, no more than that,' said Mike, knowing different.

'I'm your mother's oldest friend,' said one. 'My name is Andrea. I knew your father because I also worked down on the docks. Your father was a good man, as you are. We understand you cannot tell us everything and we don't wish to pry, do we ladies, but we can all read. Is it something to do with the Morton fiasco, because Beatrice has told us all about how they are holding the wrong man and we all agree with you on that score, isn't that so?' she said turning to the others who all nodded.

'I cannot really talk about it,' said Mike. 'You understand.'

'But we can Mikhaili,' said his mother.

'You must prove them wrong and you will get your job back,' said Diana.

This is ridiculous, thought Mike, his temper edging up. He was about to put them in their places when his mother started blubbing like a baby. This time Andrea put her arm around her.

Mike pulled up a chair. In for a penny, in for a pound, he thought.

'Why don't we all have a nice cup of tea or something and discuss the Harris case.'

His mother and Mrs Alibi made the tea. Mike couldn't bring himself round to calling her Beatrice, and Diana produced some cake.

Andrea poured the tea and cut the cake into six pieces. Everyone helped themselves to milk, sugar and a piece of cake except for Mike who didn't take milk and didn't fancy the cake.

When they all settled down, Mike spoke. 'I'll be the... let's say, for want of a better word, the prosecutor asking the questions. You in turn can act as Counsel for the Defence. My first question to you is, where is Harris's alibi?'

The women talked. Mrs Alibi answered. 'His girlfriend or, as we understand it, his fiancé.'

'Where can I find this fiancé? I understand that she is in Peru or Paraguay and cannot be contacted.'

'Our answer to that is, when was this trip arranged? I bet it was a long time ago.'

'Right,' said Mike, a good point.

'How come nobody else that is involved during those days saw him? He didn't go to the cinema, bowling, restaurant, pub, unusual to say the least,' said Mike.

'Do you go to the cinema, restaurant, pubs, Detective Mike?' said Mrs Alibi.

'I do,' said Mike.

'Do you keep all the receipts, tickets, bills from these places in case you might need them for an alibi sometime?'

'No I don't, but Harris is making out that he was either in his flat or his fiancé's flat all the time. I repeat "all the time".'

'So he had better things to do! After all, they wanted to be alone because they wouldn't be seeing each other for a month.'

'True,' said Mike.

'Did they eat during this period?' said Andrea.

'They must have,' said Alice. 'You can't live on love alone.'

'But they didn't order any takeaways,' said Mike.

'So they had food in the fridge, freezer, cupboard. Did anyone check the bins to see if what he said they ate, they actually did eat? Everything these days is packaged.'

'I can't answer that,' said Mike.

'Would you have checked if it was your case, Mikhail?'

'Yes Ma'am, I would have.'

With his next question, Mike was in for more than the pound.

'He only had two kitchen knives and Deena Morton was stabbed with what we think was or is a kitchen knife.'

Nearly all four laughed. 'No one has a full set. Do you? Think about it,' said Diana.

'Detective Mike doesn't,' said Mrs Alibi.

'We also found bleached leather gloves in his apartment.'

'What an idiot,' said Andrea, 'and that's why he didn't have a drink. He goes to all the trouble to get rid of a kitchen knife but doesn't bother with the gloves.'

'Don't forget the poison Andrea, the watch, credit cards, rings; he's one smart cookie is our Harris. He dumps all the incriminating stuff apart from the leather gloves.'

'It's all consequential,' said Diana. 'I've watched more than my fair share of police programmes and hairs, foreign fibres, something to match up Desmond with the killings; I'll answer for you in a word—None.'

'Unless of course they're railroading the poor bastard and taking short cuts to achieve a result,' said Alice, his mother.

'And what's his motive? I know the lad. He's not ambitious, otherwise he wouldn't be there. He's not jealous of anyone. He has a company car, a nice girlfriend, his own little flat and lots of time ahead of him,' said Mrs Alibi.

'Okay, okay ladies, we all agree it's not Harris, but he's the only one in the frame,' said Mike.

'Well we have talked about this and know two things: it wasn't Desmond and it must have been two others known to either Mr Morton or Mr Fenwick. I would say two strangers to the area because they had brochures of houses and a road map on the table and also Desmond isn't strong enough or cunning enough to poison Mr Morton and Mr Fenwick. And one last point, surely Desmond would have put the alarm back on. He knows the code,' said Mrs Alibi.

'That would have gone against him, Mrs Alibi, if he had locked the door and activated the alarm system. It would have been obvious that the killer worked in the estate agents office,' said Mike.

Mrs Alibi nodded. 'That's right, never thought of that.'

'So you think there were two: one drank, the other didn't. Is that correct?'

'That's the way we see it,' said Mrs Alibi.

'He then cleans one glass, not properly and replaces it to make us think there was only one perpetrator,' said Mike.

The ladies nodded in unison.

'Wouldn't it have been easier to replace the clean glass—no washing it, no drying; that's what I cannot understand. It doesn't make sense.'

'Another thing that I can't get my head around is the lack of fingerprints anywhere.'

'They were wearing gloves,' said Diana.

'Yes, I agree, but if you were having a meeting with two people wouldn't you find it a little disconcerting? It's a little weird wouldn't you think?' said Mike.

'Possibly one was a bodyguard or chauffer. He wouldn't take his gloves off,' said Andrea, 'and that's why he didn't want a drink.'

'Mikhail, I would say that somebody phoned and made an arrangement to meet with Mr Morton for some big business, as they were obviously expecting them. Surely the phone records have been checked,' said Alice.

'They must have. I'm sure they did,' said Mike.

'And the cameras, why were they off?' said Diana.

'Well, my colleagues would say that Harris switched them off,' said Mike.

'Possible,' said Andrea. 'He would know where they were situated and could avoid them, until he got to the box.'

'Lots of imponderables,' said Mike.

'So what next?' said Mrs Alibi.

'I'm going to go home, call some colleagues again, go through what we've talked about and put it to the unit dealing with the case.'

# CHAPTER THREE

**JUST OVER** four miles away Walter and David were also planning their next move.

'Look David, the stupid police—and take my word for it, they really are stupid! Have you read today's *Mail, Echo* or *Chronicle*?'

'Yes I have. I assume you're referring to the front page, Walter.'

'What normal company or institution in the world would suspend their best man! It's illogical. It doesn't say why. He probably wasn't PC enough or maybe he didn't salute a superior or whatever they do.'

'So what are you saying, Walter?'

'I'm saying that even these idiots will come to the conclusion eventually that the man they're holding isn't the murderer. They are slow but now is the time to strike again.'

'You mean today?' said David.

'No, I mean in two, three days' time. They won't be expecting it but it needs a few days.'

'Sampson will be the easiest,' said David.

Brian knocked on the Director's door. He'd been summoned to the big man's office. He felt a little uneasy as he always did when it was a one to one with the Director.

'Come in Brian, come in. Coffee, tea, cold drink?'

'I'm fine,' said Brian.

'Well, sit down, sit down and have a look at this,' he said pointing to the *Western Mail*. 'Go on, read it, have a good laugh. That long streak of piss who calls herself a Chief Constable has just opened Pandora's Box and all hell is heading her way,' said the Director, who was happily chuckling away.

'She's just gone and suspended that Kanasta Detective. I wish I was a fly on the wall down there,' said the Director.

'We have a man down there, don't we Brian?'

'No Mr Director, we pulled all the Cardiff boys out when we sold up to Lord Henry Pritchard.'

'We had no choice, Brian. Too many important people got on our backs. I still don't know how those boyos manoeuvred that one.'

'Those boyos, Mr Director, gave us the bloody run around from day one when you think about it.'

'Do you think this Kanasta would work for us, Brian?'

'I doubt if D.I. Karetzi would,' said Brian. 'He seems to have his own agenda.'

'Pity,' said the Director. 'But I'm looking forward to what happens next down there in Wales. I've a feeling it might be quite interesting and I don't think I'll add my four penn'cth into the mix.' With that he picked up the phone and asked his secretary to get him the assembly leader first, then Lord Henry Pritchard, then the Home Secretary in that order.

'Why did Clarke go?' said the Director.

'He was caught having an affair with Emma Andrews from the Assembly by a private detective working for her husband. He was going for a divorce and citing the Chief Constable whose wife was also aiming for a divorce and still is I think.'

'So he resigned?' said the Director.

'Pushed out on a full pension due to illness is the official line Sir,' said Brian.

'And where did they find long tall Muriel?'

'As you know, Sir, she was the Kent Deputy Chief—remember? You met her at Dowell's party up here in London last year.'

'Of course I remember her. How could I forget someone as obnoxious as Short? She needs cutting down to size and I think she's just run across the person who will oblige her.'

'Is she a lesbian, Brian?'

'She's not married, Sir.'

'Fine, looks like my first call's coming through. Thank you Brian, keep me advised of any developments.'

'Will do, Mr Director,' said Brian.

What a ridiculous question, Brian thought to himself. Is Short a lesbian? How the hell was he supposed to know? He was married with two kids.

This was the time for one of his smelly cigars and Alex Symonds was about to proceed downstairs and out into the car park for a smoke when Linda rushed in, a pile of typed sheets in her hand.

'I think you should read these, Alex.'

Alex took the sheets. A woman given clothes and money by D.I. Karetzi, name and address supplied. Another man helped out after a crash, name and address supplied. A policeman in Llandudno, another in Swansea, one more in Cardiff, all praising D.I. Karetzi and showing their support.

'About thirty so far have either phoned, texted or emailed, it's incredible. I don't think we've ever had such a response. These people have gone out of their way to contact us and were still getting more.'

'What shall we do with them?' said Linda.

I'll go and have a word with Joe, see if he'll let us use them as another front page.'

Joe Pinder, Editor, read some, looked up at Alex and told him to stick it under a 'Your Comments' section.

'But Joe, this is big,' said Alex.

'The story's finished Alex. We milk it with a few more public comments and that's it. He's not Superman saving the world is he? And Alex, the cop ones without names and addresses, roll them up in another part, say two hundred words or so, you know, "Cop respected by his peers shit".'

Alex walked out. It was time for a cheroot.

'Who exactly is this bastard, Muriel,' asked her lover Brenda.

'Which bastard Brenny?' replied Muriel.

'The one in the news, all over the front page, the one with the Russian name,' said Brenda.

'Ah, that bastard. He's just a nobody who got lucky with some high profile case, a real male chauvinist, unruly, unmanageable and unwanted in my force.'

'He's making a lot of waves, Muriel.'

'Enough to get him drowned, Brenny. Anyway, let's not talk about lowlifes like him. Do you fancy a drink and an early night?' said Muriel.

'I want us to go out as a couple. Go and eat somewhere, act like normal couples do,' said Brenda.

'Look Brenny, you're still young—plenty of time for that; right now it's best we keep a low profile and slowly I can introduce you to people as my partner. The time's not right now.'

'When will it be the right time, Muriel?'

'When I tell you, Brenda.'

Muriel got her own way as she inevitably did with most things. They stayed in and after a few drinks, Brenda had forgotten their conversation. Muriel was happy and remained so until the following morning when the 'Cack hit the proverbial fan.'

The Director of Tangent, an arm of MI5—or was it the other way around?—rang as did the Home Secretary, some newspapers, some idiot from the Welsh Assembly and Lord Henry Pritchard.

She didn't give a rat's arse what the people thought. She would do the job her way, as Sinatra used to sing, but the call from Lord Pritchard disturbed her.

She went to the files and took out the contract agreement for 111 Nelson Street. Twice she read through the whole contract and at least half a dozen times Clause 19 and 19a. It was a little ambiguous. It seemed that a unit of four police people had to work in the building for a period of ten years, otherwise the Landlord, Lord Pritchard's company had the right to review the agreement or contract and cancel such contract with just a week's notice.

Technically, of course, she had only suspended D.I. Karetzi but worryingly all resignations or movement of the units had to be passed by Lord Pritchard as did all replacements and or recruits.

However, if the Chief Constable recommended that one or all of the unit had been found guilty of misdemeanours then under the terms of the contract, if such misdemeanours could be proved, then the Chief Constable could take the appropriate action.

What a labyrinth of legal jargon saying nothing, yet everything. Who could decipher this crap either way? She needed more than an insubordination charge and her opportunity came with the announcement that D.I. Karetzi was on the Radio Wales phone-in, talking about the Morton's Murders.

'So what exactly is he saying?' asked the Chief Constable.

'Well, he's finished now,' said Sergeant Dicks.

'So what the hell did he say, Dicks?'

'He said that the man that has been arrested for the Morton's Murders is the wrong man. He said it about five times. The show's presenter couldn't seem to get much sense out of him,' said Dicks.

'That doesn't surprise me. Ring D.I. Jones in Nelson Street. Tell him I want him and his partner at Cardiff Central within the hour.'

Dicks contacted Evan who contacted Mike. Mike refused to go but Evan explained that as a colleague and friend it would be wise to play the game.

Mike and Evan sat alone in the main interview room. A policewoman had brought them some coffee. Mike's throat was dry—what he needed was a stiff drink, not warm coloured water.

Evan couldn't stop fidgeting. For the umpteenth time he counted the chairs in the room, still six. He played with his pipe; he was dying to light up.

'I'm sorry to have kept you waiting, Detectives,' said the Chief Constable, a stupid smile on her face. 'I think you know Detective Superintendent Fowler, and this is Chief Inspector Appleby, D.I. Foster and P.C. Williams.' The latter had a pen and notebook in his hand, but no chair to sit on. There were no seats for DI's Karetzi and Jones either.

The Chief Constable started the ball rolling. 'I have heard a tape of your phone-in with Radio Wales today. Would you like me to replay it for you D.I. Karetzi?'

'No point. I know what I...' said Mike.

'That's good, because you made some very controversial statements,' said Fowler. 'Actually, the same statement five times.'

'I'm not sure,' said Mike. 'What did I say five times?'

'That you believe we have the wrong man in custody,' said Fowler.

'Yes, that's what I said. It is of course just my personal opinion,' said Mike.

'And mine,' added Evan.

'How did you come to this ridiculous conclusion, Detective?' asked Appleby.

'I just looked at the facts. They don't add up. I looked some more and still they didn't add up,' said Mike.

'Did you collaborate with your colleagues Mrs Gilberts, Mr White and D.I. Evans?' said Fowler.

Mike hesitated. 'We did discuss the matter.'

'Did I or did I not suspend you, D.I. Karetzi?'

'You did,' said Mike.

'Can I say something here?' said Evan.

'If it's relevant,' said Fowler.

'We discussed the case outside office hours in Mike's, that is D.I. Karetzi's home, together with many other subjects,' said Evan.

'And who exactly was there?' said Fowler.

'All of us,' said Evan.

'Why were you there?' said Fowler.

'I invited them for a cup of tea and a piece of cake,' said Mike.

Mike turned to P.C. Williams. 'Are you getting all this down Constable? Please note my name is spent with a "z" not an "s".'

'So what other things did you talk about?' said D.I. Foster.

'Nothing important as such,' said Evan.

'We will decide if it's important or not,' said Fowler.

'I don't think so,' said Mike.

'What's that meant to mean D.I. Karetzi?' Chief Constable Short said.

'What people discuss in the privacy of their own homes is not your concern, Chief Constable Short.'

This is some cool cookie, she thought, best they got down to the nitty-gritty.

'Look, D.I. Karetzi, let's talk shop, take a step back and think about why in your opinion Harris is innocent of the charges that he is being held for,' the Chief Constable said.

'I can't do that,' said Mike.

'Why not?' said Fowler.

'Because there's a wall behind me,' said Mike.

'Cut the smart talk Karetzi, just tell us why Harris is innocent,' said the Chief.

Mike told them.

They all began sniggering.

'So let me get this right Mr Hero Detective. You together with your mother, cleaner and two old friends of your mother's worked it out. Are you fucking serious?' said Chief Inspector Appleby.

'Let me put you and your pensioners in the picture,' said Fowler. 'We did check the bins, and yes, two pizza boxes were in it. They could have been there six days, so what? The knife is missing, but the leather gloves have been bleached. According to Harris, he made a mistake and bleached them when they became discoloured with paint, pure rubbish of course. We did check the phone records. First thing we did. We are after all proper detectives here.'

'The phone records, that's the key,' said Mike.

'Look, there was a phone call to Mr Morton via the receptionist at 16:55 hours from a phone box in Central Cardiff. We've got about thirty odd sets of fingerprints. We believe that Harris made that call pretending to be looking to buy some expensive properties. That was the hook for our Mr Morton,' said Appleby.

'Have you tried to get in touch with his fiancé?' said Evan.

'We have. No luck as yet but they will have their story and alibi set out. It won't do us much good getting hold of her. To be completely honest, we think they did it together,' said Fowler.

'And this Harris, all five and a half foot of him brought down Gareth Jones, did he?' said Mike.

'Don't be sarcastic Detective. It's obvious the guy was pissed, probably fell over, tripped, bent down to pick something up, who knows; we got Harris,' said Appleby.

'But Morton knows Harris, you're talking rubbish,' said Mike, his temper rising. 'You've got fuck all.'

'You're bloody jealous, that's what it's all about isn't it? Suspended cop, not a hero anymore, so he shoots his big mouth off to all his so-called fans. This is the real world, D.I. Karetzi. Remember Constable to spell his name with a "z" not an "s",' said Fowler.

'I have some good news for you two,' said Short. 'I'm lifting your suspension as of now, D.I. Karetzi, and I have a case for your team. It's all in this envelope.' Short pushed over an A4 size manila envelope. 'Here is your credit card, mobile phone and of course your warrant card.'

'This *misper* case, recent is it?' asked Evan.

'Very recent, just one year, maybe thirteen months or so,' the Chief said, smirking; the others were laughing.

'Thirteen months,' said Evan.

'Lucky for some,' said Appleby.

'Is there a problem?' said Short.

'You know we haven't a chance, not one in a million—thirteen months, my God, when was the last sighting?' said Evan.

'Thirteen months ago,' said Short. 'Surely South Wales's finest superheroes can hunt down one *misper*,' said Fowler.

'Yeah,' said Mike, 'no probs. We will get in our new BMW and drive around till we find him.'

'Don't think I've forgotten that you stole my car,' said Fowler, livid with rage.

'No I won't. I'll replay the tape, that always reminds me of our meeting,' said Mike.

'You're just scum,' said Fowler, getting up.

'And you're just the stagnant, stinking piece of pond life we sit on,' said Mike, also standing confrontationally.

Within ten seconds, everyone was on their feet. Fowler and Foster inched forward as did Mike.

He looked Fowler in the eyes. Fowler backed off, but Foster moved closer. Without moving or looking at him Mike said, 'Don't even think about it.'

Evan said, 'I'd listen if I was you, Detective Foster.'

'He's no problem to me,' said Foster.

'You're the problem, you yourself, now back off,' said Mike.

'Back off Foster,' said Chief Constable Short. 'Now.'

It still took Foster a full five seconds to respond. He didn't want to lose face.

One by one, they exited the interview room. The Chief Constable, followed by Fowler, Appleby, Evan and Foster, who slammed the door shut behind Evan, then turned and threw a punch at Mike catching him on the shoulder.

Mike staggered but was saved from falling by the wall. He saw the next punch coming and avoided it. Foster on the other hand didn't avoid the hammer blow Mike threw smashing his nose and completely taking him off his feet. Constable Williams seemed in a trance and was just beginning to react. He dropped his notepad and pen and was about to intervene when he realised that it was all over.

Mike turned to him and said, 'He's slipped and caught his nose on the table, got it, otherwise he will be in big trouble. He threw the first two punches.'

'Yes, I saw it all,' said the Constable.

Evan had come back in, saw Foster on the floor with a broken nose. He was followed shortly by Appleby who surveyed the scene before asking, 'What the hell happened here?'

Foster by now had come to his senses and mumbled, 'I slipped Rog, hit my head on the table, broke my nose.'

Mike and Evan left. Appleby turned to Foster and said, 'He told you not to think about it, you stupid bloody idiot. Go and see a doctor.'

Outside both Mike and Evan lit up. Fowler was talking to the Chief Constable, and P.C. John Williams was telling everyone who would listen how the Russian with a 'z' in his name took out Foster with one punch. Foster would never live it down and he'd never forget it either. All he had to do was look in the mirror.

Mike told Evan what happened and they then headed back to the office in Nelson Street.

'Good to see you back,' said Amber.

'Yeah Mike, the team's together again,' said Charlie.

'So what happened at Central? Who was there? What did they say? Come on tell us all,' urged Amber.

Evan did, just leaving out the little fracas at the end.

'Something wrong with your hand, Mike?' said Charlie, noticing the swelling around the knuckles.

'His fist accidentally ran into D. I. Foster's nose,' said Evan.

'Only after he had two pot-shots at me,' said Mike

'You need some cream on that,' said Amber.

'Are you always thinking about food, Amber?' said Charlie, laughing at his own pathetic joke.

'I meant medicinal cream Charlie,' said Amber.

'I know,' said Charlie.

'Look, we have been given a case—missing teenager,' said Evan.

'How long?' said Amber.

'How long, Ace 74,' said Charlie.

'Thirteen months,' said Mike ignoring Charlie.

'They're taking the Mick,' said Charlie.

'No Charlie, in this case, they're taking the Mike. The Chief Constable wants us out so gives us a thirteen month old Misper.'

'Is that the file?' said Amber.

Evan passed it over and Amber read out loud. 'Jason Conley, age 16, address blah, blah, blah, last seen walking home from school.

Parents, grandparents, friends, locals, shopkeepers all interviewed. No note, letter, telephone or text call, mobile dead blah, blah, blah.'

'Is that it?' said Mike.

'One sheet of paper,' said Amber, 'and this photo.'

'Nice looking boy,' said Amber.

'Yeah, blonde hair, blue eyes, good physique,' Evan observed. 'Did he have many friends? Was he good at sports? Academically was he bright?'

'Not the brightest, reasonable at sport, not good, few friends,' said Amber reading on.

'Girlfriend?' said Mike.

'No mention of one,' said Amber.

'Parents together, other siblings—the address is a good one,' said Evan.

'One sister older by two years, parents well off, father a local butcher,' said Amber.

'Where do we start?' said Amber.

'With the sister and non-existent girlfriend,' said Mike.

'So you're saying there should be a girlfriend,' said Evan.

'That's what I'm saying. Look at the picture, he's one handsome boy, Charlie.'

'True,' said Amber. 'Does seem strange he didn't have a girl.'

'Maybe he had gay feelings,' said Charlie.

'Surely then he would hide them from the others and the best way of doing that is by being seen with girls,' said Mike.

'Let's go through the motions then,' said Charlie. 'No way we can get a result and everyone knows it.'

'It's not even a matter of let's prove them all wrong. Every card in the pack is stacked against us,' said Mike.

'I'm so bored,' complained Amber. 'All I do is cook and eat, so I'm going to do something and you lot will help. This is a missing kid, he deserves our best shot.'

'Amber, the boy is 17 now,' Evan said. 'He probably doesn't want to be found.'

'He's missing, might be dead. If we don't owe the boy anything, fine, but surely his parents should know what happened to their only son, wouldn't you Evan? Would your father and mother, Mike? Of course they would. Let's do something, please boys. We must. It's our job, like it or not.' Amber was on the point of breaking down.

Charlie, Evan and Amber looked at Mike.

'Why are you all looking at me?' said Mike.

'Because, Mike, this is an unusual situation and we need your unusual methods to have a chance, even it's one in a million,' said Evan.

'But Evan, I've no idea where to begin. Thirteen plus, no sightings, no contact, what does that suggest to you?'

'It suggests that he is dead,' said Charlie.

'I've heard of cold cases but this one's in the deep freezer,' said Mike.

'So it's preserved, we've got a chance,' said Charlie.

'Yeah, a fat one,' said Evan.

I'm going to start and see if we have any *mispers* in the last two, three years that are unaccounted for,' said Amber.

'I'm going to have a cigarette,' said Mike, looking around for the ashtrays.

'They're upstairs in the dining room, lounge place, said Evan. 'That's where we can smoke or, of course, outside.'

'That's not on, Evan—why can't we smoke here, and where's the 4 'I's 'I's sign gone from outside?'

'This is an office Mike, a public place of work and Short told us to dump the sign,' said Evan.

'Right then, Charlie, could you go and purchase two signs for me, one saying lounge, the other office, and before you go please put up our 4 'I's 'I's sign where it was before,' Mike said.

'Are you sure Mike? You're asking for a whole heap of trouble,' said Evan.

'Elvis did that one in '75, said Charlie.

'Which one?' asked Evan.

'Trouble,' said Charlie.

'Put the sign up, Charlie,' Amber said, without turning from one of the computers where she was working. 'Otherwise you will have trouble.'

On Charlie's return, Mike, who by now had found the ashtrays, lit up only his third of the day. He liked to smoke about half a dozen daily, but lately this had crept up to ten or so.

'So, listen up everybody,' Mike said. 'I am designating this room as a lounge, and the new office will be the old lounge upstairs. So Evan, if you need to smoke your pipe and you happen to be upstairs, I'm afraid you will have to come down here to smoke, is that understood?'

'You've got to be joking,' said Evan.

'No, Mr McEnroe, I'm dead serious! Nowhere does it state which room is to be utilised for any specific purpose, isn't that so Amber? You have a copy of the contract between Lord Pritchard, the Landlord and the South Wales Police Force.'

'Mike is correct,' said Amber, again totally concentrating on her computer screen.

'How did you know that?' said Charlie.

'I didn't until Amber told us,' said Mike.

'Do you know it's six?' said Evan.

'What you doing tonight Evan?' Mike asked.

'Nothing, Edna's still in Scotland visiting Jasmine,' said Evan.

'And you, Charlie?'

'Not much, Maggie's on nights, why Mike?'

'No reason, just asking,' said Mike, wondering why he'd asked.

'If you're all angling for something to eat, said Amber, 'let me tell you this: someone needs to go out and do some serious shopping.'

'I suppose that's my job,' said Charlie.

'You're sure the clairvoyant Charlie,' said Mike.

'And soon I can foresee four new tyres for my car paid by my employers for wear and tear,' said Charlie getting up and crossing over to Amber.

'Eight pork chops, big ones, two pounds of Maris Piper potatoes and two large trifles please Charlie.'

'Take my card, it's on the desk,' said Amber.

'And four bottles of Pinot Grigio Charlie, the most expensive you can find,' said Mike.

'18!' shouted Amber, within a fifteen, twenty mile radius of Cardiff.

'What period are we talking about?' said Evan.

'Three years,' said Amber.

'That's one every two months,' said Mike.

'Hang on boss, I'm just printing out the stuff, give me a mo.'

They waited.

'Right,' said Amber, 'these are only the ones aged eighteen or under, seven girls, eleven boys, ages range from 13 to 17. Three of these were found within days, by either us or parents. Three committed suicide, two reported dead, and seven have been in contact or sighted since.'

'Three left, is that including ours?' said Mike.

'Yes, the other two are Lizzie Brown, two years ago from Bridgend, age fourteen and Joanna Morgan from Llandaff, age sixteen, two months before Jason,' Amber stated.

'Since our boy, have there been any *mispers*?' said Evan.

'Two, one had run away, found three weeks later begging in London, and one caught shoplifting twice in two days in Bristol.'

By now Charlie was back with the food. Amber got up excitedly. She was ready to start cooking and Charlie took her place around the desk.

'Charlie, please go up and get Amber back down. We need a photo of this Joanna Morgan girl,' said Evan.

'I can't Evan, sorry, not when she's cooking. She'll kill me. Why don't you go, Evan?'

'You're more sort of her, you know…'

'Age, is that what you're trying to say Charlie, and no, I don't want to feel her wrath; cooking and eating are sacrosanct to Amber.'

'Don't look at me,' said Mike.

'Alright, let's do without the photo,' said Evan. 'Two missing persons, roughly the same age, living only a couple of miles apart, disappear within 43 days of each other…'

'Okay, said Charlie, 'boy and girl fall in love, they keep this love a secret, girl runs away, finds somewhere to live or work or both, contacts the boy and he also vanishes.'

'Fair to simple, full of holes, all they had to do was wait six, seven, eight months, declare their love and no one could have done anything about it. I mean the girl is now eighteen, nearly nineteen, the boy not far off eighteen, and how come no one knew about them—difficult to hide,' said Mike.

'But it's all possible, Mike,' said Charlie.

'Yes, and maybe that's what's happened. I've heard stranger things.'

'Maybe he got her in the club and forced their hand; maybe they wanted the baby, maybe she aborted the child,' said Evan.

'We need her file. I'm sure they would have seen a connection,' said Mike.

'Who?' said Charlie.

'Our boys,' said Evan. 'They would have been very thorough, I can assure you. *Mispers* aren't taken lightly. In the back of your mind, you fear the worst, abduction for purposes of prostitution, white slavery, porn and snuff movies, they all go on Charlie, much more common than you think,' said Evan.

'So what do we need to do?' said Charlie.

'Interview both sets of parents and maybe grandparents, siblings, teachers, sports, hobby angles, best friends of each. We must find a connection a thread that ties them together. We need all the interview statements for both, Joanna's files, everything, and we need a big blackboard,' said Mike.

'The last one, the blackboard, big bugger. We got one—I'd say it was two meters by one and a half,' said Charlie.

'We don't do meters or kilos here,' said Evan. 'We're old school, feet and inches, stone and pounds.'

'Fine,' said Charlie. 'Whatever the size, it's under the bed in the spare room.'

'What the hell were you doing looking under beds, Charlie, or shouldn't I ask?' said Mike.

'Let's get it down then Charlie, we can put the thing up tonight,' said Evan.

'You've got me mixed up with Arnold Swartzanigger. The thing weighs a ton. You do tons?' said Charlie.

'Tons we do Charlie, but if you ever meet Arnold, I would suggest you don't use his surname, your pronunciation sucks.'

'So can we see Jason's room, Mr Conley?'

'After fourteen months and you come around and ask to see my son's room! You people are bloody useless. You've already made Eva cry. Fourteen months and you've got not one inch further in your investigations. I doubt if you ever actually made any. You lot got a nerve.'

'Mr Conley, we know this is very painful but we have a dedicated unit looking into this case with fresh eyes,' said Evan.

'Come on then, we've left it as it was just in case,' said Mr Conley.

The room was big and surprisingly very tidy. Everything was neat and orderly. On one wall there was a Cardiff City team picture.

'Anything missing, Mr Conley?' asked Evan.

'Only his money box. That one was emptied of cash, otherwise nothing.'

'Do you know how much money was in there?' asked Evan.

'At least two hundred. He was a saver, my son. Never spent a penny unless he really needed to.'

'Did he like sport, Mr Conley,' asked Mike.

'Followed City, first took him to Ninian Park when he was seven,' said Mr Conley proudly.

'Why did he stop supporting them then?' asked Mike.

'How did you know that?' said Mr Conley.

'Picture up there is over three years old,' said Mike.

75

'Just stopped going. Didn't seem interested anymore. Jimmy used to call for him to go and Jason would feign illness or something. Jimmy just got the message and stopped calling.'

'When did this start Mr Conley?' said Mike.

'About four, maybe five months before he disappeared,' Conley said, tears now beginning to roll down his cheeks.

'I think we've seen all we wanted to Mike,' said Evan.

'Yes,' said Mike. 'Just one thing: your daughter, when can we talk to her?'

'Why do you need to talk to Julia?'

'Just some more background stuff,' said Mike.

'Well, you might just catch her. She lives just down the road, No. 40.'

'Thank you Mr Conley, and your wife Mrs Conley too. Please tell her that we are sorry if we caused her any distress,' said Mike.

'I've been expecting you Detectives,' Julia said. 'Will you be long because I need to get to the shops and buy my husband's birthday card and present.'

'Not too long,' said Evan. 'Is this your daughter Mrs, Julia, I'm sorry, I don't know your name?'

'It's Mrs Labins now and yes, Karen is my daughter.'

'She's beautiful, Mrs Labins,' said Mike.

'Thank you,' said Julia.

'Can we ask you a few questions about Jason?' said Evan.

'Yes, as long as you're quick.'

They asked, Julia answered.

Next, it was the turn of the grandparents, four of them, then Jimmy and Cliff, two good friends of Jason's. It was a teacher's turn next. Luckily, he was at home; another one was watching City play, but already they had a rounded picture of Jason.

'So Evan, what do we have?' said Mike. 'Let's compare notes.'

'As I see Jason is thus,' said Evan. 'Good looking boy, average at sports, academically, few friends, decent parents, no drink, drugs, problems, saved his pocket money, worked where he could, when he could part time, good school attendance records and as for girlfriends, I doubt if he ever even kissed one. I don't see the connection with Joanna. How did they meet, when? Sorry Mike but I can't put the two together, even though we haven't spoken to anyone from Joanna's side.'

'Nor can I Ev, but that is the only thing we've got to work on,' said Mike.

'Back to the office then. Maybe Amber or Charlie have something we can use,' Evan said.

Neither Amber nor Charlie could help. Between them they had made calls to Joanna's parents and one set of grandparents. The other set, from the father's side, lived in Inverness and had done so for over fifteen years.

'So are you telling us that Joanna was just an ordinary, nice looking girl, lots of friends, academically very bright. Parents say she was Oxbridge potential. In other words Joanna had a very bright future. Is that it?' said Evan.

'Boyfriends?' said Mike.

'No steady, lots of friends but no steady,' said Amber.

'We will have to check with the teachers and some of the friends. I just can't buy into this Miss Goody Two Shoes,' said Mike.

'Hobbies, everyone has hobbies,' said Evan.

'Normal young girl, things like music, clothes, rugby,' said Charlie.

'Stop there Charlie, did you say rugby?' said Mike.

'I did. One of the cheerleaders for some amateur league team, the Valley Pirates play out of Pontypool or Pontypridd, anyway Ponty something,' said Charlie.

'Never heard of them,' said Mike.

'Nor have I,' said Evan, although I must admit league is making inroads in South Wales. I mean Celtic Crusaders is in the Super League playing against teams such as Wigan, Leeds, St Helens and the rest, big time in that world,' said Evan.

'So how did she end up doing that? Her school—would it be involved in any way?' said Mike.

'Doubt it. The team aren't local. She only did it for two years. Stopped about three months before she disappeared,' said Amber.

'But we have our first connection. Jason supported Cardiff City but lost interest just months before he disappeared,' said Mike.

'Cannot see the connection, Mike. City generally play on a Saturday. The Pirates play on a Sunday,' said Amber. 'We thought of that. Anyway I've got the names and addresses of six of the cheerleaders; two are from her school, the others from various schools in the Pontypool area.'

'Are you playing tomorrow Mike?' said Evan.

'No Evan, I'm banned for two games; tomorrow's the second one,' said Mike.

'Why don't we go and see them play then Mike?'

'Who, Evan?'

'The Pirates of course,' said Evan.

'I'll find out where they're playing and at what time,' said Amber.

'Anything else?' said Charlie. 'I've got to go.'

'Nothing,' said Amber, 'and thanks for all the help today.'

'It's my job,' said Charlie. That is my day job, he thought to himself as he left the premises and headed directly for the Cutty Sark where he hoped he could get the details for his other job. The one he did at night.

'So Slim, what do you have for me?' said Charlie.

'Big one Chalky. Politician, second job banker.'

'So he deserves to be done,' said Slim, who was short of money.

'What do you mean, Slim?'

'Politician, banker, robbing us in every single which way.'

'Tory is he?' said Charlie.

'Don't know, can't tell the difference,' said Slim.

'How much, Slim?'

'Usual, one third,' said Slim.

'Quarter,' said Charlie.

'Quarter then,' said Slim.

'We have plans, Slim?'

'All in here; position of safe, CCTVs, Alarms, the lot, Chalky.'

'Any family or servants?' asked Charlie.

'No family or servants. Politician and wife in London all day tomorrow, leaving early morning, attending some banquet. Will stay in second home overnight. Wife will return alone,' said Slim.

'How much we talking about, Slim?'

'Min 40, 50K but don't touch anything else Chalky, money's dirty, won't be reported to the police.'

'Dirty, Slim?'

'Yeah, bribe money for services rendered. Twice a year he travels to Switzerland and deposits what he's collected during the period,' said Slim.

'See you anon then Slim,' said Charlie. 'Think I'll take a drive, see what I'm up against.'

# CHAPTER FOUR

**DAVID** looked at himself in the mirror. With his dyed hair, false moustache and stern looking glasses he looked twenty years older. He practised his new signature. Brevington-Hill sounded posh enough and Jonathan was a good strong name to use as his Christian name. He had two pieces of luggage, a small leather holdall and a large briefcase which could take the sawn-off shotgun and camera. He was a little worried about the cartridges for the gun but Walter had assured him they were fine. The problem for David was that everything only had a certain shelf life, but Walter wanted it done efficiently and quickly so he wouldn't have risked dud ammunition.

He'd already picked the house to view. It was less than half a mile away from Mr Eli Sampson's. It was partially secluded, detached with grounds of about a half-acre. It was on for 495, they had come down from five and a half. Now he had two problems left. Would the estate agents work on a Sunday and if they did, how could he guarantee that Sampson would be the one showing the house. The second problem he'd covered as best he could by choosing an expensive house near to where Sampson lived. Would the commissions, nearly ten grand, swing it for Sampson to work on a Sunday?

One other point in his favour—the owners were currently away on holiday.

Patrick dropped David off near Cardiff Central. David was wearing the only suit he owned, a navy blue one. He only had three ties, one was a khaki coloured one and this is the one he opted for, to go with his white shirt.

David noted the arrival time of the next London train. He bought a coffee and sat down and waited. He was wearing black gloves. It was cold both inside the station and outside.

He finished the coffee, leaving it where he sat. There were no bins anywhere in sight. He did though remove the cap and place it in a napkin before pocketing it.

The London train arrived only a few minutes late and disgorged its human cargo who all rushed like maniacs to the gates.

David joined them and then joined the queues for a taxi. He was about eighth in line.

'The Adam Hotel, please,' David told the taxi driver.

On arrival, he paid the taxi driver off and headed straight for the reception area.

'Good afternoon. I'm Brevington-Hill and I have reserved a room until Tuesday.'

'I'm afraid we don't have your reservation Sir. I'm sorry but I can't find anything.'

'What bloody idiots. Sorry, not you Janice, my bloody office. They just can't seem to get their act together. Do you have any rooms?'

'We do Sir.'

'Well thank God for that,' said David. 'Can I pay in cash, now, in advance?'

'No problem Sir. That will be two hundred and eighty pounds including breakfast.'

David paid up, had his bags taken up to the room. That cost another fiver.

At a quarter to five he made the call. No, they didn't do Sunday showings.

Pity, because he was leaving Monday early morning for London.

However, she would check to see if anyone was available. David gave his name, room number and telephone number of the Adam's Hotel.

It took only ten minutes for her to ring David back. 'Would two p.m. be in order?' she asked.

'It would,' said David, thanked her and closed the phone. From his mobile he called his brother, gave him exact instructions. He was to be in the alleyway at precisely twelve thirty. He hoped his brother

Patrick understood his instructions. It was difficult for him to grasp certain things. Those that didn't concern cars or physical work.

At fifteen minutes past twelve, David changed shirts. He now had on a blue button down shirt. The white shirt and khaki tie he put in the small leather holdall. He shaved with an electric shaver and put that back in his bag. All he now had out were a toothbrush, toothpaste and a bottle of aftershave. He zipped the bag shut and opened the window of his first floor hotel room. He leant out. It was still raining. It was twenty-five to by the time Patrick arrived. He was five minutes late. He couldn't find the small alleyway that ran next to the east side of the hotel.

David saw him and whistled. Patrick looked around. David whistled again; this time his brother saw him and moved to a position of where he was directly underneath the window. Patrick waved, David waved back and then held the leather case out of the window before dropping it into Patrick's outstretched hands, without a word passing between them. Patrick walked off; bag in hand and David shut the window. He was uncomfortable wearing gloves, but necessary.

It was five to three and the second half was about to start. The Pirates were up by seven points and looking good for a win. From the secretary cum manager cum player when required Evan had got every team-sheet for the last five years, the time of the Pirates inception. Mike had collared the cheerleaders—only two knew Joanna.

That morning they had interviewed the parents and three friends including a girl called Patsy who was Joanna's best friend.

The teachers they would do the next day. They had a book full of notes but nothing that helped.

Charlie in his second job had easily gained entrance to the MPs and Banker's home, located the safe and was now attempting to open it. It was five past three.

'And this is the kitchen Mr Brevington-Hill. A lovely size, nearly thirty-eight square metres with a southerly aspect, all your usual mod-cons plus some extras but the *piece de resistance* I have yet to show you. It's down this way, the cellar. Please follow me.'

David did and he was very impressed. A full sized snooker table, a well-stocked bar, leather sofas and armchairs, a few coffee tables, and still the room looked empty.

The carpet was at least an inch thick, a little worn but still worth a pile. David smiled to himself, then turned and spoke.

'This carpet must be worth a pile Mr Sampson.'

Sampson smiled a false smile. It was one of the things he did well. He wished he could get on with his spiel and go back home and enjoy another bottle or two with his wife and play with his four sons and two daughters, the oldest being only twelve. He usually only did rental properties but with all the problems recently he was helping out with sales. It was only a few minutes from home. He couldn't refuse old man Morton, he owed him. Little did he realise that he would pay with his life.

'The previous owners had some kind of music studio down here. It's completely soundproof. Mr Ellis of course changed it into this,' he said waving his hands around the room.

'Is that a toilet?' said David.

'Yes it is,' said Sampson.

'May I use it before we go up?' said David.

'Of course, please go ahead,' said Sampson.

Leaving the briefcase David entered the toilet. In his pocket he had some cotton wool which he stuffed into both his ears. He counted to fifteen slowly and then flushed the toilet.

'Is there anything you wish to see again, Mr Brevington-Hill?' said Sampson, slyly glancing at his watch. It was twenty past three.

'No, I've seen enough, but I would like to show you something of interest Mr Sampson.'

Both were standing at opposite ends of the snooker table, David where the reds were and Sampson in the baulk area, where the yellow, brown and green balls were all in a line.

First David placed his briefcase on the table, then he opened it and in what seemed like one movement, lifted the sawn-off shotgun and fired both barrels.

The first caught Sampson in the neck, the second three inches below the first.

Sampson slumped, his head flopping onto the table and catching the green ball which spun into the left centre pocket.

To David, who had never fired a gun of any type in his life, the noise was deafening even with the cotton wool stuffed in his ears.

'Three points Mr Sampson, well done, but I think your break is over.'

Putting the shotgun in his briefcase, he proceeded to walk to the door when he remembered the camera. He retraced his steps and took one photo. He noticed that the table's green baize was slowly turning scarlet. He left the spent cartridges. Five down, four to go.

When he reached the ground floor, he called Patrick and told him to expect him in about five minutes. It actually took him seven to reach the preordained meeting place.

Within forty minutes, Walter had the photo in his hand. It was now a quarter past four. Mike and Evan were having a drink with the Valley Pirates players who were celebrating a fine victory. Mike bought the first two rounds, Evan the next one. Both Mike and Evan only had a half each and at five called it a day and left. Mike drove back to 4 'I's.

Sharon Sampson started panicking at around half past four. By five she had contacted everyone she knew. Eli was nowhere to be found and was not answering his phone.

Eventually the lady who had arranged the showing contacted Sharon Sampson and Sharon called in the police. They found the body at six. It made the nine o'clock news and ruined the Chief Constable's sex life, amongst other things. She then proceeded to ruin Chief Superintendent Fowler's evening, who gave Chief

Inspector Appleby a mouthful before he got blotto on a mixture of vodka, whisky and beer.

It took Charlie nearly four hours to get into the safe. He could have broken into the Bank of England in less time.

There were thirty-one thousand only in the safe and that really pissed him off. The MP's passport and various small gold nuggets were also in the safe. He decided he wouldn't touch them as he had promised Slim. They could be kosher and bring a load of unnecessary heat to bear down on him.

Charlie, his blood boiling with frustration, grabbed the passport and ripped out the first three pages which he put in his pocket.

He replaced the remainder of the passport in the safe and left. When Charlie got home he burnt the three passport pages, took Slim's quarter out of the 31K and hid the remainder under the floorboards.

Mike was at Angelo's, eating alone when he got the call from Amber. There had been another Morton's victim, an Eli Sampson. She'd just seen it on the news. She had also spoken to Evan.

Mike carried on eating his calamari. It wasn't their case. Five people murdered from the same company in less than two weeks.

At half nine he received another call. This time it was his mother. She and Mrs Alibi had just had a cup of tea together and were wondering what Mike and the others in the force were doing about getting the right man.

'Look Mam, it's not my case. I've told you before. I've told the necessary people that it wasn't Harris but I can't do any more and for the record I wouldn't be doing any more than what's being done.'

'You do something Mikhail,' Alice said. 'We give you all the clues and what do you do? You sit in Angelo's eating.'

'I've got to eat and it's no good ringing me. I cannot do anything. I've my own cases to chase. I've got missing lads to find, so can I finish my meal and get some sleep? I've been working all day,'

Mike said, his veal getting cold and the other diners getting a little tired of his voice, especially as he was now beginning to raise it.

Eventually his mother let him go and he could return to his meal. It was cold and he'd lost his appetite.

Angelo was now at his table. 'Don't worry Mike, I'll get you some fresh food, otherwise your Mother will be complaining that you don't eat enough or properly.'

'I'm fine Angelo, just bring me a large brandy,' said Mike.

'You sure?' said Angelo.

'Yes, Angelo, I need a good drink followed by a good sleep, followed by some breaks in this case we're working.'

Mike had his drink, drinks; his sleep intermittent and dream-laden. The strawberry blonde, his lost love featured in most, but no breaks regarding the missing duo.

All Monday they talked over their notes, Charlie writing everything up on the blackboard.

At ten Evan phoned one of the teachers who taught and knew Joanna well. He listened and when finished turned to Charlie and said, 'Top class student, very clever, no problem. She would have easily, in his opinion, got the grades for Oxbridge.'

Charlie marked it up.

'What the fuck are we missing here, Evan? Two *mispers* both without reason disappear without trace. Are they dead, living in the same country where nobody knows who they are or doesn't care or has under guard or drugged or working illegally or a mixture of these things?' said Mike.

'Look Mike, I don't think they were abducted. Can we agree at least on that?' said Evan.

'We can,' said Charlie.

'Amber?' said Evan.

'I agree,' said Amber who was now into her eighth chocolate biscuit.

'You Mike?' said Evan.

'Agreed Evan, so they left home for a reason and they don't leave together as we know and they don't know each other.'

'As we think we know,' said Charlie.

Just as Amber was about to demolish the last remaining chocolate biscuit, the buzzer sounded. Amber answered. It was the Chief Constable together with two high ranking Scotland Yard Detectives, both Chief Inspectors, one called Michael Lincoln, the other Anthony Ford.

Amber quickly ate her biscuit and went to the door to greet the trio personally.

Evan dispatched Charlie upstairs to fetch a few more chairs.

At first glance, it seemed that Scotland Yard had sent Little and Large. Ford was thin and little with floppy hair, glasses and brown moustache. Lincoln was tall, about six one and fat. No moustache, no glasses.

Both used the same tailor. They were both grey and old fashioned, the only difference being that Lincoln's had used twice as much material as had Fords.

'Scotland Yard have kindly sent two of their best men to help us with the Morton inquiries and they wish to have a general word with yourselves,' the Chief Constable said.

'Is this formal or informal?' said Evan.

'Whatever you wish it to be,' said Ford raising himself on his toes.

He still didn't look any taller.

'Would you like to talk here or in our office?' said Mike, lighting up.

Ford looked around but didn't say anything. It was obvious what he was thinking.

'This will do fine,' said Lincoln, but the Chief Constable Short could not contain herself.

'This is the office and I have stated quite clearly that this is a no-smoking area.'

Mike, who was standing, as were the others, crossed the room, opened the door and pointed out the 'lounge' sign.

'But this is the office D.I. Karetzi,' said the Chief Constable.
Lincoln smiled.
'Not any more,' said Mike. 'We've had a little change around. Nothing in the lease prohibits us as to what use each room has.'
'You can't do it. This is obviously the office. It has the computers, screens, desks, phones.'
'I don't wish to contradict you Chief Constable Short but we can do it, we have the landlord's permission. Amber can show you proof if you wish.'
Lincoln smiled again.
'I see you people are working on something,' said Ford, pointing at the blackboard.
'Yes, it's a missing person mystery,' said Charlie.
'We've only been on it a few days,' said Evan.
'How long has this person, or is it two, been missing?' asked Ford.
'Over a year,' said Evan.
'Christ,' said Lincoln, looking at Ford, 'and what have you got to work on?'
'Nothing,' said Amber. 'Absolutely nothing.'
'Aren't you the unit that collared the Chessman and another bunch of cases including a sixteen-year-old bank job?' said Lincoln.
No one answered.
'And you're working a thirteen-month missing person case?' said Lincoln.
'Let's all sit down,' said an embarrassed Chief Constable, 'and talk about this Morton business.'
'To be honest with you,' said Mike, 'we're lucky we were given this. For three months we've been sitting here playing cards and drinking coffee.'
'That's enough, D.I. Karetzi, they haven't come to hear about your working conditions,' said the Chief Constable.
They all sat down. Amber offered them coffee and biscuits. All except the Chief Constable accepted. The Chief Constable noticed

that they had a fridge, a freezer and toaster in the room which grated on her; everything about this group did.

'It comes as no surprise to you that this guy Harris is innocent?' said Lincoln.

'None at all,' said Evan.

'So what take do you have on this?' said Ford.

Mike told them.

'Motive—there we have a slight problem because there doesn't seem to be one,' said Lincoln.

'There is,' said Mike.

'Would you like to speculate, D.I. Karetzi?' said Ford. 'Would any of you?'

'Revenge,' said Charlie out of the blue.

'For what? They couldn't have all done something to someone,' said Lincoln.

'As a firm they could,' said Amber.

'Fine, let's run with that. They sold someone's house under its market value. They overcharged somebody too much commission—no, I don't see it,' said Ford.

'Over the last five years they have sold some 1800 properties,' said Lincoln, just beating Amber to the last biscuit.

'It's a massive job,' said Ford.

'This latest murder, no clues,' said Mike.

'It was simple,' said Lincoln. 'Man rang from a hotel here in Cardiff, made an arrangement to have a viewing. A Jonathan Brevington-Hill, aged about forty, difficult to say, as he was obviously in disguise, no fingerprints in house or hotel. Two shotgun cartridges were left at the scene of the crime; nothing else. Detached house, a little off the beaten track, soundproof room, paid in cash for two nights, picked up by taxi from Cardiff Railway Station, picked up at Hotel by taxi but not from the house. That's it.'

'Any comments?' said Ford.

'I have a few observations,' said Evan.

'Shoot,' said Lincoln.

'I would say that our man is younger. It's very easy to make yourself look older but very difficult to make yourself look younger. He's local, he knows where this Sampson lived and expected him to do the viewing as he lived near the house in question. He has an accomplice, someone drove him out of the area, a man in a suit with two cases would stick out like a sore thumb in those rural areas, and lastly he will kill again. It looks to me that he's trying to ruin Morton's.'

'One briefcase only, that's all he had according to the taxi driver who took him to the viewing. He's adamant about that,' said Lincoln.

'And the other item of luggage,' Evan said. 'This holdall was not in the hotel room.'

'And can we assume he was wearing gloves in the taxi?' said Amber.

'Correct on both,' said Ford.

'Was he caught on any CCTV cameras at any station?' said Charlie.

'Still looking into it,' said Ford.

'We're looking for two people, one average height, maybe a little shorter, age probably thirtyish and a taller guy six foot plus, one who is fit and strong. The taller one probably doesn't drink, or if he does, very infrequently and little. The brains of the two is the smaller one, the one that shot Sampson and poisoned the other two. Now I am a betting man and my money is on a pair of hitmen who are being paid by someone else,' Mike said lighting up. Lincoln did too and a few seconds later Evan fired up his pipe.

'You are crazy. How did you get from one man in a disguise to two hitmen, D.I. Karetzi?

'A lot of people do call me that and maybe I am,' Mike agreed. 'I like to get results in any which way that I can, Chief Constable Short, but I have one more question: was there more than one type of whisky at the first incident?'

Ford looked at Lincoln. The Chief Constable looked at them both. Lincoln nodded very slightly but before Ford answered, Mike butted in.

'There were two different types but you only found one bottle, isn't that so?'

'That's right, we only realised this—that is the connection—two days ago. How the hell did you know?' Lincoln said.

'Elementary, Mr President. The killer, killers, brought with them their own, already tampered whisky because it would be impossible to have done anything in the victim's presence.'

'Well deduced Detective, excellent, but what's this President business about?' said Lincoln.

'Ford, Lincoln, Kennedy, Reagan, all American Presidents,' smiled Mike. 'My mind wanders along strange paths sometimes.'

'Incredible,' said Lincoln. 'What do you say, Chief Constable Short?'

'I like to have all my facts on hand, not conjectures,' said the Chief Constable.

'Like Milo de Venus,' said Mike.

Everyone, with the exception of the Chief Constable, smiled or laughed.

'Shocking Blue did Venus 1970 I think,' said Charlie.

'Is that one of your jokes Mr White?'

'No Chief Constable Short, it's another one of his observations,' said Mike.

'Have we finished here?' said Evan. 'We still have a case to follow up on.'

'I think we're just about done,' said Ford.

'Check the railway,' said Mike. 'It's important to find out where he came from because it sure wasn't London.'

'Thanks,' said Lincoln, standing, 'and good luck with your missing persons case. Thirteen months,' he said, shaking his head in disgust.

Outside Lincoln had to ask the Chief Constable: 'Why aren't these people working on the Morton Murders?'

The Chief Constable didn't answer.

'Did you see how many biscuits that Lincoln ate?' said Amber.
No-one answered.
'Seven! My, can that man eat,' said Amber.
'He sure can,' said Charlie, thinking that Lincoln would have to up his rate at least four times to get anywhere near Amber.
'Well, I feel better,' said Evan, handing Mike a pencil, which Mike absentmindedly took.
Five seconds later, his knife was out and he was whittling down the pencil to a one inch stub.
'She tried to belittle us, Mike,' said Evan.
'Who did Evan?'
'Short,' said Evan.
'I think she was the one who came out bad,' said Mike.
There is something not kosher with that woman,' said Charlie.
'What do you mean Charlie,' Mike asked.
'Charlie's trying to say that Short is a raving lesbian,' said Amber.
'No I don't think it's that,' said Charlie.
'So is she, or isn't she?' said Evan.
'Guaranteed,' said Amber.'
'No big deal,' said Evan.
'To whom?' said Mike.
'To anyone,' replied Evan.
'Do you remember Charlie, our late, great Chief Constable Clarke?' said Mike.
'Oh no, don't tell me we want more photos please Mike, not that again,' said Charlie.
'Let's think about it. What do we lose? Those in favour don't raise your hands,' said Mike. 'Good,' he said, after a pause, 'that's carried unanimously.'
'But I didn't raise my hand,' said Evan.
'Nor did I,' said Charlie.
Amber started laughing.

'What's so funny?' asked Evan.

'You lot,' Mike said.

'Don't, repeat don't raise your hands if you want to go ahead with the photo shoot,' said Amber.

'That's tomorrow's job, Charlie,' said Mike.

'Where am I supposed to start? She knows who I am. She's seen me Mike. It's crazy,' said Charlie.

'Amber, can we get an address for Short?'

'Yes Mike.'

'Then no problem Charlie. Work it out.'

'I'm not happy with this at all,' said Charlie.

'Don't worry Charlie, I'm not either,' said Mike.

'Let's do some work,' said Amber.

'We have come to a dead end. There is nothing we can follow up on. For whatever reason two people just disappeared and do not want to be found and we don't have any leads, do we?' said Mike.

'There is something I've been thinking about,' said Evan. 'I've been racking my brain to understand why would six young girls volunteer and train to become cheerleaders to a group of amateur rugby league players playing in front of fifty people and a dog or two? The weather is foul; there are no facilities as such. They don't get paid. It's hardly Old Trafford or the Millennium Stadium, is it?'

'Because they are interested in the players, not the conditions. The sport itself. They are infatuated with the players,' said Amber.

'Something along those lines,' said Mike.

'Didn't you get every team sheet for the past five years from the coach or manager bloke?' asked Mike.

'I did. They're here on my desk,' said Evan.

'How long was Joanna a cheerleader?' said Amber. 'And when did she start?'

Evan read out the dates.

'Let's take six months of the season before she started until, say, three months after she disappeared,' said Mike.

'Thirty-four players,' said Evan.'

'That's a big turnover,' said Mike. 'Only thirteen are on the field and five on the bench. That's a total of eighteen,' said Mike.

'We can eliminate whoever of those thirty-four who has played this season. How many is that, Evan?' said Amber.

'Hang on, I'm not a computer,' said Evan. 'Fourteen,' he said, 'including those who have been on the bench.'

'That leaves a nice round twenty. What happened to them? Did they go abroad, get injured and leave the game, play for some other team?' said Mike.

'I have the coach's telephone number. He owns a garage by day,' said Evan.

Evan hunted down the number and rang. He was on the phone for thirty minutes plus.

Mike, Charlie and Amber waited patiently. Eventually Evan put down the phone and his pen.

'Okay, that man is like a walking encyclopaedia,' Evan said. 'One died, another struck lucky and joined Hull K.R., three injured and out of the game, one joined the army, four play for other teams in the league, two are playing Union, one moved to New Zealand--new job, and the rest he has no idea about. They just drifted out of the game.'

'That leaves seven,' said Amber.

'Does the coach have their contact numbers, addresses? At one stage, he would have rung them at various times to arrange training and things,' said Mike.

Evan phoned again. This time he came back with four mobiles and two landlines.

'That's only six,' said Amber.

He remembered that Dai Morgan retired to run a pub, the Red Cat in Caerphilly.

'Right then, you take these two, Charlie. I'll take these two and you, Amber, the other two. I'll use my mobile and you can use the two landlines. I think Evan has done his fair share of phoning.'

'Any of you got a Gary Powers?' shouted Charlie.

'Yes Charlie,' said Amber.

'Cross him off, don't bother ringing. I'll explain in a mo,' Charlie said.

'I'm done,' said Mike.
'And me,' said Charlie.
'What about you, Amber?'
'Nearly there. Just waiting for this Tony Brown to come to the phone,' Amber replied.
'Let's start with you then Charlie,' said Mike.
'I rang this David Priest, married, four kids, oldest nine, retired at same time as Gary Powers, opened up a sport's shop here in Cardiff. Powers is Gay. Peter Price's phone, dead,' said Charlie.
'Yes Amber, anything?'
'Well I didn't bother with Gary Powers but Brown left because he was on drugs, did six months for possession and other related crimes,' said Amber. 'As far as he can remember, they had groupies everywhere and made good use of them but the cheerleaders they kept well away from, as they were all underage. The girls wanted to but the players kept their distance, as far as he knew.'
'That's roughly what Priest said. None of the players would touch them even though the girls threw themselves at them,' said Charlie.
'And you Mike, anything?' said Amber.
'I lucked out, numbers not in use,' said Mike.
'So we have three guys left but I think we're barking up the wrong tree,' said Amber.
'I'm not sure of that,' said Mike.
'The players wouldn't touch them with a bargepole. They all say that,' said Charlie.
'But if they did, they would keep it quiet from their teammates Charlie, wouldn't they?' said Mike.
'I guess so. It makes sense,' said Charlie.
'It makes a lot of sense,' said Evan.

'That leaves us with Peter Price, George Montgomery and Phil Leinster,' said Amber. 'But it could be any one of the twenty. For that matter it could be somebody still playing.'

'We could be completely on the wrong track,' said Charlie.

'I would say that's more probable than possible,' said Mike.

'What's probable, Mike?' said Amber.

'That we are on the wrong track,' said Mike.

'Do you think this Joanna girl is or was a "dell",' Charlie asked to no one in particular, not that anyone could have answered him.

'Sorry Charlie, did you say "dell", like Del boy?'

'Yes Evan.'

'Is that Cockney slang for what exactly?'

'A "dell" is a virgin,' said Charlie.

'That doesn't rhyme with dell, Charlie,' said Amber.

'I know. I never said it did,' said Charlie.

'Anyway, what difference would it make if she was a virgin?' said Mike.

'No difference, just thought I'd ask.'

'For Christ's sake,' said Mike. 'Let's get on with it. We have three names. Let's hunt them down.'

'Firstly I think we should have something to eat,' said Amber. 'Egg and Bacon do?'

'That's nice,' said Evan.

'Just a bacon sandwich for me Amber,' said Mike.

'And you Charlie?'

'I'll have an Adam and Eve on a raft, that's two fried eggs on toast to you Amber.'

'Charlie how many times have we discussed this slang talk business? Can you give it a break,' said Mike.

'Sorry,' said Charlie.

'Tell me Charlie, what would you call scrambled eggs?' said Amber.

'Wrecked eggs on a raft—and if I just wanted two friend eggs, I'd say eggs with their eyes wide open. Got it Amber?'

Amber got it.

She'd learnt something new, completely useless, but new.

After eating, they started ringing each and every one of the remaining thirty. They asked one question only: did they know the whereabouts of Price, Montgomery or Leinster? After near on two hours they had knowledge of both Montgomery and Leinster. Both lived in the area and for different reasons both could be eliminated from their inquiries.

'Trust us to end up with Price,' said Evan.

'What's wrong with Price?' said Charlie.

'It's one of this region's most common names. I mean how many Montgomery's do you know, one I bet, the golfer but spelt differently, and as for Leinster, it's a region in Eire with a great rugby team and we end up looking for a Price,' said Evan.

'You got me there Evan. I don't follow any sport so I've not heard of either of the two guys you're on about.'

'One's a region, like a county in Eire, Charlie,' said Evan.

'But,' said Amber, 'how many Peter Donald Price's are there? That cuts it down.'

'I've heard of McDonald's,' said Charlie.

'Very clever,' said Evan.

'Don't worry boys, I'll deal with it. Shouldn't take me too long,' Amber said.

'How you going to go about it?' said Evan.

'Ask Charlie,' said Amber.

'Something quite legal, eh?' said Mike.

Amber shrugged her massive shoulders and smiled. Charlie looked on innocently.

'Why don't you lot look into our other case? The one we were assigned and let me get on with my work,' said Amber.

'Okay,' said Evan. 'Where are we going to start—with Jason?'

'Well, from what we can gather, there is the possibility he's gay or has gay tendencies. Handsome lad, no girlfriends,' said Mike.

'No connection with Joanna,' said Evan.

Charlie wrote 'Gay Scene' on the blackboard and underlined it twice. Then wrote the word 'KEY' in block letters next to it.

Evan stood up, walked to the blackboard and wrote the word 'Diary' with a question mark next to Joanna's name.

'Yes, I've been wondering about that,' said Mike. 'It seems strange that she didn't leave a diary. Maybe it was incriminating in some way and she took it with her.'

'Did she run away by herself or with someone and if so, why?' said Charlie.

'They were in love, she was pregnant, any number of reasons,' said Evan.

'What people will do in the name of love,' said Amber, looking up from one of the computers.

The buzzer went again. It was Little and Large, better known as Chief Detective Inspectors Ford and Lincoln.

Charlie let them in.

'Thought we could talk a little easier without your Chief around,' said Ford.

'I see you've made some progress on your *mispers*,' said Lincoln, pointing to the blackboard.

'Possibly,' said Evan.

'That's fast work,' said Ford.

'It all depends,' said Mike. 'Can we interest you guys in a cup of coffee?'

Both declined.

'Do you know anything about food, Chief Inspector?' Charlie asked.

'If eating a lot is knowing a lot then I'm an expert,' Lincoln replied, patting his huge stomach.

'In that connection would you have any idea what Adam and Eve on a raft would be?' said Charlie.

Lincoln looked puzzled; he rubbed his chin then said, 'Eggs on toast.'

'Brilliant Chief Inspector, well done,' said Charlie.

'How did you guess that?' said Mike. 'It must have been a guess surely?'

'Half and half. I can see from the plates on that desk that you've just eaten. I can see the remains of eggs on three and on one of the three, breadcrumbs, that I assumed to be toast, whereas the others don't have breadcrumbs. I guessed that the toast must be the raft, but I must admit I've never heard that saying before,' said Lincoln.

'Could you lot stop talking about food, you're making me hungry,' said Amber, 'and by the way, Cardiff, Monmouthshire, Vale, Rhondda, Bridgend, Newport, Caerphilly, Merthyr, I've gone through the lot and we have two P.D. Price's, one's sixty-eight and the other's the right age but blind.'

'Shit,' said Mike.

'Can you check the rest of the country? One thing that also might help us—did he speak Welsh?' said Mike.

'Why?' asked Charlie.

'He was born somewhere near Brecon where I think a few, quite a few speak Welsh,' Mike said. 'If that is the case, he could have headed for the areas where Welsh is spoken by more people. He would blend in easier. Does that make sense to you all?'

No one spoke.

Mike decided that silence was a spurious critic and decided to carry on with his theory.

'Look, this Price was only twenty-eight when he stopped playing; according to everyone he was good, played full back, scored tries, was man of the match on many occasions, had a nice job as a P.E. teacher, swimming instructor and games master in a small public school just outside Newport, yet gave it all up, no notice, nothing—and disappeared from the face of the earth. What we need is a list of all public schools and other independents. We need to contact all the top teams in Super League and the semi-professional ones up North.'

'If he's a Welsh speaker then North Wales especially, North West and West Wales would give him a living in a number of different ways,' said Evan.

Ford and Lincoln looked on. It was now gone seven and no-one seemed in a rush to get home.

'Sorry about this,' said Mike.

'No problem,' said Lincoln, but Ford kept glancing at his watch.

'Now how can we help?' said Evan.

'Two different types of whisky,' said Ford. 'A Glenlivit bottle, still on the desk and what we now know to be a Tullibardine, which I had never heard of and we cannot find anyone around here who stocks it. Boys at Central had it analysed in Scotland. No sign of the bottle or container that it was brought in.'

'Mike, can you help with this?' said Evan.

'Yeah, was distilled in Perthshire, not a great malt, a bit sweet and creamy for my taste. I'm not sure they still produce it. Whoever bought it must have bought it in Scotland a while ago,' said Mike.

Ford and Lincoln looked at Mike, unbelievingly. Evan noticed their puzzlement and said, 'Mike's a whisky connoisseur.'

'Anything else to go on?' said Evan.

'He had a coffee in the station before going to the Adams Hotel in a taxi, but no coffee top from the container, a very careful man,' said Ford.

'Hotel room; anything there?' said Mike.

'Nothing. Anyway, they had already cleaned and re-let the room when we went down. Very efficient staff here in Cardiff,' said Lincoln sarcastically.

'No witnesses anywhere for any of the incidents,' said Ford. 'Five murders, no witnesses.'

'And still we haven't got a motive. We're checking every sale for the last five years, re-interviewing the staff, those who are brave enough to come to work. Business is drying up. Morton's are tottering on the brink of disaster. This has brought them to their knees,' said Ford.

'Well, they had better start praying,' said Mike.

'What do you mean Detective?'

'If they're on their knees they may as well pray,' said Mike.

'That's not funny Mike,' said Evan.

'Evan, while all this has been going on, what have we been contributing? Nothing. We're looking for Romeo and Juliet and the Chief Constable is laughing at us,' said Mike.

'You're paranoid Mike,' said Evan.

'Three months, how many cases did we get, Evan?'

'None, and now we have five murders in our field of experience and what do we get? A fucking *misper* and no disrespect to you people, but why bring in Scotland Yard?' said Mike.

'Beats us. We've been wondering that since we came down yesterday,' said Lincoln.

'I would have thought the locals could handle it better than us outsiders and just going off on a tangent for a second, can anyone tell us what happened to D.I. Foster's nose. I understand he slipped and you were the only person present when he did, D.I. Karetzi,' said Ford.

'Question; if it's money, where is it coming from and why is he or she paying for it?' said Mike.

'Answer; to obtain more money than he's paying out, much more money or just for revenge,' said Evan.

'Question; after Morton's, who are the biggest estate agents and would they stoop to literally killing off the competition?'

'Answer; no way. These are victims of a personal grudge,' said Lincoln.

'Question; how long does one keep a personal grudge?'

'Answer; sometimes forever,' said Amber.

'Question; who's next on the list?'

'Answer; everyone of any power at Morton's,' said Lincoln.

'Question; why not get the top man first?'

'Answer; they want him to suffer and logically if that is the case, he will be last,' said Ford.

'Question; should we then just concentrate on his past, not the firm's.'

'Answer; no, maybe a few of them are involved,' said Ford.

'Question; what will they do if Morton's folds. Will they still pursue the staff?'

'Answer; without a doubt Mike. This is personal, of that I'm sure,' said Evan.

'Last question; do we agree that there are at least two working together, which is unusual in this type of crime. Are they ex-forces of some type? Are they maybe related? Are they being paid to do a job, or are they doing this for their own personal reasons?'

'Answer,' said Lincoln. 'I think they are good amateurs on a personal mission. Look at their equipment, a kitchen knife, an old shotgun, poison. I mean, poisoning in this day and age and they are youngish, not old, and I think they are local, they know the area.'

'I agree,' said Mike. 'They are bound to slip up somewhere. Firstly they need transport, they need time, money because they need time, maybe that's why they're in a hurry. They haven't the money, or the time.'

'I like it,' said Lincoln. 'We've taken up enough of your time. Thanks, and if you don't mind, we will call on you during the next three or four days.' Lincoln rose from his chair and shook hands with everyone.

Ford did the same, not because he wanted to but because his partner had set a precedence.

It was ten past nine, everyone wanted to go somewhere, Mike and Evan home, Charlie to the Cutty Sark and Amber to the kitchen upstairs where she had some lamb kebabs ready for grilling.

The Right Honourable Alistair Macintosh arrived home in Cardiff at five to ten. His first act was to have a stiff drink before opening the safe and depositing another ten thousand pounds.

The money had gone, but the jewellery had been left untouched and surprisingly so had his passport. Weird, leaving the safe open. He wandered around the room. Everything was in its rightful place. A quick walk around the rest of the house confirmed that nothing had been taken. Two silver Mont Blanc pens worth hundreds each were on the desk.

Okay, so thirty-one thousand pounds was missing and he couldn't contact the police, but he could replenish that within three or four months. He was about to close the safe when he noticed that his passport seemed a little shapeless. He picked it up and immediately knew that someone had tampered with it and on closer examination, found that three pages were missing, torn out.

He put it into his pocket and closed the safe just a few seconds before his wife Myra came into the room carrying a couple of bags of shopping.

'I've lost my passport. Don't know where or when. I'll have to report it and get another issued,' he said.

Myra said she would have a good look around. It had to be somewhere. Alastair let her get on with it whilst he lit up the fire in the lounge.

Bit by bit he fed the fire with the remains of his passport.

It was Wednesday morning. Mike was first in to 4 'I's. Amber was eating breakfast, a four egged herb omelette and what seemed like half a loaf. He poured himself a coffee, no milk, no sugar.

'You're early today Mike,' Amber said.

'I am, had to avoid the cleaner. It's her day to clean and tell me what a lousy Detective I am,' said Mike.

'Don't be stupid and get yourself something to eat. You'll wither away playing all this sport and your various other activities.'

'I've not been fortunate lately with other activities,' said Mike, as he watched Amber devour the food at a rate of knots.

'Any luck with Price?' said Mike.

'Yes and no. Yes, we found another in Bangor; and no, it turned out to be a woman.'

'I have a list though of P. Price's and D. Price's. Only seventy-two,' said Amber.

'Only!' said Mike.

'That's about it Mike, a lot of cold calling for you and the other two men in my life.'

Ten minutes later and all three men were on the phone. Amber had now turned her attentions to a cream cake, her excuse being that it would go 'off' unless she ate it. It had been in the fridge all of twelve hours. It obviously had put up one hell of a fight, but its three friends hadn't made it past midnight the previous night.

At eleven, they stopped, thirty-three down, and everyone feeling a little dispirited.

After his tea and biscuits and on his third call, Charlie struck gold or possible gold.

'May I speak to a Mr Peter Price, please?' Charlie asked.

'Speaking,' said Mr Price.

'This is the Four I's Heir Inheritance Agency and we are trying to track down a Peter Price who has been left a legacy in a relative's Will.'

'It cannot be me, although any help would be most welcome,' laughed Mr Price.

'Why cannot it be you?' said Charlie.

'Because all my folks are alive and well.'

'The gentleman in question died in South Africa, where he has lived alone for the best part of sixty years,' said Charlie.

'I don't know anyone in South Africa and I'm certain I don't have any relatives out there,' said Price.

'Well Sir, to eliminate you, would you kindly answer a few questions. You can be very surprised in this business.'

'Sure,' said Price. 'I'm off work today. I've got the flu.'

'Sorry to hear that, Mr Price. I've just three simple questions—age, where born and if you have a middle name?'

'I'm thirty next month, born in the village of Pencelli, near Brecon and I do have the middle name of Donald after my grandfather.'

'I'm very sorry Mr Price for raising your hopes, you're not the man we're seeking. I hope you get over the flu quickly. Once again, sorry for disturbing you.'

'I knew it couldn't be me,' said Price, closing the line on Charlie.

'I've found him,' said Charlie, standing up and waiting for a response.

'Well done, Charlie!' said Mike, Evan and Amber all at once.

'Let's have his number Charlie,' said Amber.

Charlie read it out. Amber started matching it up to an address.

'Got it, 76A Twyforth Avenue, Llay.'

'Lay, as in what chickens do?' said Charlie.

'No Llay as in small place, spelt with two LL's, a couple of miles North of Wrexham,' replied Amber.

'How many miles to this place Amber?'

'I'd say about 200, of which three quarters are on the A40, M50 and M5,' said Amber.

'Beamer outside Evan?' said Mike.

'Yes Mike, she's tanked up, tyres and oil okay and ready to go.'

'Be about four hours up, four down and maybe two in Llay. Should be home by midnight all going well,' said Evan.

'I'm going,' said Charlie.

'You've got Short. You've got her address. Take a flask of coffee and some sandwiches Charlie and don't forget your camera.'

'If she was a brama it would be a pleasure, but…'

'Charlie,' said Mike.

'Sorry Mike, I forgot.'

Mike and Evan left, Mike driving.

'What's a brama Charlie?' said Amber.

'A good looking broad,' said Charlie.

'Do you make these up, Charlie?'

' 'Course I don't. They're all pukka words, mainly from the twenties and thirties,' said Charlie.

Siren on, headlights flashing, blue lights and Mike at the wheel, got through the roadworks on the M4 in quick time and they hit the M5 in less than an hour. Another one and a half hours of motorway driving and they were approaching Nantwich on the A500.

At three, they stopped in Holt and refuelled and used the men's room in a small café where they had a coffee.

All was well until the puncture on the A483. Mike fought to control the car, which fortunately was only travelling at forty as they had just come off a roundabout and hadn't as yet built up speed.

The car careered first to the right then to the left where it bounced off one tree and hit another full on coming to a shuddering halt. The car's airbags inflated and did their job.

Evan was bleeding from his forehead and in a state of shock, the passenger side having taken most of the impact.

Mike was slumped over the wheel; his right arm felt numb and was dangling on his side. His left hand still gripped the steering wheel tightly.

Evan spoke first. He asked Mike if he was okay. Mike said that he thought he was.

'And you, Evan? Where's that blood coming from?' That was the first time Evan realised he was injured.

'Switch off the engine Mike,' said a dazed Evan.

'Can't, got no feeling in my right hand.'

'Well, it's not broken,' said Evan. 'You would know if it was.'

Evan opened his door, got out and with the back of his jacket sleeve attempted to wipe the blood from around his right eye.

Three times he used the same action until he could see clearer. He went around the bonnet of the car, opened Mike's door and unfastened his seat belt before helping him out. He then switched off the engine.

'What exactly happened, Mike?'

'A puncture, driver's front,' said Mike, pointing with his left hand to the deflated tyre. 'We've got a towel in the boot and we've got some water in the glove compartment—or we did have last time I looked.'

The water was indeed still there and, together with the towel, Evan managed to stem the blood coming from his forehead.

Feeling was coming back into Mike's arm and hand slowly but surely.

They had removed the blue lights when they had stopped to refuel. Luckily, the car was off the road and had left no debris on the road. Apart from the puncture, the front passenger door was heavily dented as was the wing. The grill and headlights were a write-off and the radiator a goner.

The car wouldn't be going anywhere under its own steam for quite a while.

As the police car approached, Mike had full feeling in his arm and was now smoking one of his non-filter cigarettes. It was only his second of the day. He knew he had to give them up.

Evan was on the phone to Amber. She said it was best to use a local garage for the repairs and not to have it brought back down to Cardiff. She would arrange everything from the office.

'Who was driving?' asked the younger of the two traffic police.

'I was,' said Mike.

'Lose control, did we Sir?' asked the same officer.

'Yes, actually I did. Luckily no other vehicle was involved,' said Mike.

'Have you been drinking?' asked the young one.

'No,' said Mike.

'Driving a tad too fast, I would say,' said the other policeman.

'We are Policemen,' said Evan, handing them his warrant card. Mike did the same.

'I'm afraid I'm going to have to ask you to take a breathalyser test Sir,' said the younger one.

'Why?' said Mike. 'It's obvious I haven't been drinking.'

'Not to me Sir. I see skid marks and I see a wrecked car. It's my duty to test you.'

'It's your duty to help and use a little common-sense,' said Mike. 'Your first priority is to see to the wellbeing of the passengers, either or both could have internal injuries and you've not once asked us if we are okay.'

'Ambulance is on its way,' said the older.

'Now can we get on with the test, please Sir, or would you like us to take you in?' said the older.

Mike took the apparatus and blew into it. It was clear.

'That just leaves the dangerous driving Sir—you yourself admitted as much.'

'I did not,' said Mike.

'You said that you lost control of the car,' said the older one.

'Of course I lost control after the bloody puncture, you moron,' said Mike.

'Did you call me a moron?' said the younger policeman.
'Yes,' said Mike. 'You're a stupid idiot with the mental age of an eight-year-old.'
'You will regret that statement,' said the older of the two.
'I don't do remorse and I've just about had enough of your crap,' said Mike.

The ambulance arrived just in time. They patched Evan up and thought it best if both went with them to the local hospital for a check-up.

Both declined. They had work to do. Within seconds of the ambulance leaving, a Simm's tow truck arrived to pick up the car and take it and its passengers into Wrexham.

'You cannot take the car. The driver was advised not to until it has been inspected by our people in situ and probably down in the pound,' the older one said.

'And you two will accompany us to the station where you can have a little talk with our Super,' said the other who was now brandishing a pair of handcuffs.

'This is not going to end up nicely for you two,' said Evan.

'Especially if you even try to lay a finger on either of us,' said Mike.

'You,' said the younger, looking at the Simm's driver. 'Hang around, we will need a witness if these two try to resist us when we make an arrest.'

'I'm off,' said the driver. 'I've not part of this.'

'Stay,' said Evan.

Mike phoned Amber, asked a question, received an answer and turned to the policemen.

'Now please listen carefully boyos,' he said. 'You've wasted enough time: get back in your car and go and help some little old lady cross the road.'

'Right, let's have 'em Ted,' said the older who stepped forward straight into Mike's knee in his private parts. The younger one reacted so slowly that he was on the floor, Mike's foot on his neck, a kick from Evan in his private parts that hurt more than a kick from

Mike would have. Evan was wearing heavy brown brogues, Mike light moccasins.

Mike used the older one's handcuffs to cuff them together. He indicated to the tow truck driver to get the car ready for towing. Evan phoned Amber, a Chief Inspector and Sergeant were on their way. Within minutes, they pulled up behind the other police car, four in total.

It was obvious who the Chief was. He introduced himself as Chief Inspector Merson and shook hands with both Mike and Evan.

The two policemen were still sitting on the floor handcuffed to each other. Merson looked at them in disgust.

'Can he go now?' said Evan, pointing at the truck.

The Chief had a quick look around and nodded. 'Please don't do any work on the car until my boys have a look at her,' he told the Simm's man.

The driver nodded. He wanted away but did have some story to tell the boys down at the pub that night.

'I understand you boys are on a case up here?' said the Chief.

'We are Sir. A *mispers* case, over a year old. Not sure if it's the right bloke but still got to find out.'

'You guys were involved with the Chessman case, weren't you?' said the Chief.

'That's us,' said Evan.

'Fantastic job; old friend of mine Ray Davies from Llandudno. Said you were the best he'd ever come across and Ray knows his stuff.'

'Top man Ray is,' said Mike. 'Have a lot of time for him. It was a pleasure working with him. He helped us a lot. If you speak to him soon please give him our regards.

'Will do. Now can I do anything for you?'

'We need a car and driver for a few hours,' said Evan.

'Where you going right now?' said the Chief.

'Llay,' said Evan.

'Right, my sergeant and I will drop you off in Llay, then he can drive me back to the station and come back when you give him a call. Here's the number. It's Jones, Clive Jones.'

'Thanks Chief, very kind of you,' said Mike.

'No problem,' said the Chief who then turned to the two still handcuffed and still sitting policemen and said, 'I'll deal with you two bloody plonkers later.'

'If you could drop us off at the top of this Twyford Avenue and pick us up at say seven, we would be extremely obliged,' said Evan.

Mike looked at his watch, an Omega and a present from the Jones's family. It was five past six.

Mike and Evan said their goodbyes and thanks to the Chief and then waited for them to drive off. They did not want anyone to know the exact address; after all, they could be completely wrong; coincidences in police work were common.

A few minutes' walk and they were outside a large Victorian-style end of terrace house. It was divided into two flats, ground floor, one flat, the other on the first floor. Evan rang the bell that had a small plaque with an 'A' written next to it. The door opened automatically and they were now confronted by another two doors. They waited and a young man came to the door. He looked like the Price they were looking for.

'May we come in?' Mike asked, showing the man his warrant card.

'What do you want?' said the man.

'A word with you Sir,' said Evan.

'Am I in some kind of trouble?' said the man.

'May we come in please Sir and we will explain?' said Evan.

'Who's that Pete?' asked a young girl's voice from somewhere inside the apartment.

'It's the police, Jo,' said the man.

'What do they want? Have you gone and annoyed the upstairs people again?'

'I don't think so love,' Peter said making room for the detectives to enter.

'We were just about to eat,' said Joanna, coming into the lounge where the three men stood looking at each other.

Her hair was shorter and darker and she'd filled out a little, in a good way, but there was no mistaking Joanna Morgan. She was still a stunner.

'So are you going to tell us why exactly you are here?' said Peter.

'We've come up from Cardiff,' said Mike.

'Good for you,' said Peter, getting butterflies in his stomach.

'Are you Peter Donald Price?' said Evan.

'You the guys who phoned me this afternoon pretending that I might be in line for some money?' said Peter.

'That's right,' said Evan.

'And you are Joanna Morgan?' said Mike looking into Joanna's large emerald green eyes. 'Your parents are worried sick,' said Evan.

'So why are you here to take her back? She's eighteen and doesn't have to go anywhere she doesn't want to.'

'That's correct, and we haven't come to try and get you to go back home, although I'm sure both sets of parents would love to see their grandson,' Mike added.

As if on cue, a baby started crying in one of the rooms off the lounge.

Joanna got up and after a few minutes brought in a lovely, happy faced, smiling bundle of joy. 'This is Mark Anthony,' said a crying Joanna.

Peter got up and comforted her.

'You're a very nice family,' said Evan. 'You should share your happiness with those who love you.'

'We *are* happy,' said Peter, 'but it's been tough. It's all my fault. I succumbed to, to…'

'We all make mistakes Peter, we all make mistakes, but don't compound them,' said Mike.

'We were in love,' Joanna said. 'We only slept together the once. I was only sixteen and I wanted Peter to be the first and only one. I became pregnant and we took the decision to move away. I could not bring shame upon my family. I miss them like crazy and I know Pete misses his mum and dad.'

'We don't have any friends up here. Pete's trying to hold down three part-time jobs to keep food on the table. We can't afford to go out. We're trapped in this small flat. It's hell but our love keeps us together and we will fight on for the baby's sake,' said Joanna, kissing her little boy.

'It's not so bad for me,' Peter put in. 'I meet people during the day. I'm a relief teacher, a part-time barman and help out at a local gym. I go everywhere by bike, can't afford a car and Jo, only time she goes out is to the market to buy groceries. We only have the phone because of my work. I need to be in contact with the various educational establishments in the area.' He continued: 'As you can see all our furniture is second hand. It's been tough but hell for Jo.' He paused before going on: 'I'm ashamed. I had a good job, lots of friends, decent parents and Jo could have walked into Oxford or Cambridge University. One moment of madness, just that one moment...' He sighed, cuddling Joanna with an intensity only a person deeply in love could muster.

Mike looked around the room. He felt sad. Why did they have to find them? All they had done was open old wounds for them.

'We couldn't even afford to get married,' said Peter. 'Sounds daft but we had more than enough on our plates to worry about and as the time has slowly passed, we have more pressing worries like making it to next week.'

'I have an idea,' said Evan. 'Please give me a moment to explain it to you. You might turn it down, that's up to you. Like I said, it's only a suggestion.'

Evan carried on. 'Give me a family photo. I'll have copies made and enlarged. I will approach your parents, both sets, tell them that you are well and happy, give them a photograph and see what their reactions are. Under no circumstances will I tell them where you live or any contact number.'

Mike butted in. 'Take it from me, you will make them the happiest people in the world. It will open up the way for both of you to return to your roots with baby Mark. Think about it, at least four doting parents, friends, decent job, financial stability and a chance to have the wedding you desire. It's only right. You've both got grandparents. What are they, seventy, eighty? Don't they deserve to see their great grandson who will be brought up in a loving atmosphere?'

There was hesitation. Joanna shook her head. The baby was content for the time being. He was lucky he couldn't know what kind of hell his loving parents were going through.

'Think of Mark Anthony. He deserves the best he can get in life. Give him the chance. Like I said, it might not pan out the way I think it will, but doesn't the little boy deserve everything you can get for him?'

Joanna, still crying, passed the baby to her partner Peter, then got up and headed into the small kitchen. She returned within a minute holding a picture of the three of them. It was a six by four, a nice picture. It had been taken at Christmas.

Evan took it and thanked them. It was over and it was ten past seven.

'I'll ring you tomorrow,' Evan said. 'Don't worry, as from this moment your luck and life will change for the better.'

As they went out Mike turned. 'Just one last thing, do either of you know a Jason Conley?'

Neither did. Mike didn't expect them to give him any other answer.

'One thing Mike,' Evan said, as they walked back up the road.

'Small photo on the mantel shelf, Evan?'

'How did you know I was going to ask you that?' said Evan.

'I'm psychic,' said Mike.

'Good, can you tell me what time we will get home tonight if at all,' said Evan laughingly.

True to his word, Sergeant Jones was waiting at the top of the road.

'Sorry we're a little late Sergeant.'

'Not a problem. Everything go as planned?' he said.

'Yes, we've had a good hour and now we need to get to Cardiff, so could you get us to Wrexham station?' said Evan.

'Best you go direct to Shrewsbury. You would have to change at Shrewsbury anyway. That okay with you?'

'That's fine. How far is that, Sarge?'

'About thirty, forty minutes or so.'

Jones the driver made it with twenty minutes to wait for the last Cardiff train.

They said goodbye to Jones the Sarge, had a smoke outside the station, bought a few cans of beer and boarded the train when it came in from Crewe. It was due to arrive at Cardiff at 23:04 hours.

Mike phoned Amber and told her that the Joanna Morgan investigation was now closed. They had tracked her and Price down.

Amber wanted to know every detail. Mike told her. He didn't mention the run-in with the local Wrexham boyos.

Ten minutes into the journey and Evan took off his right shoe, looked at it carefully and put it back on.

'That was a good kick, Evan. Edna home yet?'

'Coming Friday night with Jazzy. Why do you ask?' said Evan.

'It's your white shirt, Evan.'

'What about it?'

'It's now changed colour to red, or one of the collars has.'

'I know Mike, I'll wash out the shirt but my forehead, five stitches. How am I going to explain it away to Edna?'

'Tell her you cut yourself shaving Ev.'

'Ha ha, very funny Mike, and I use an electric shaver which I've had for many a year.'

'You'll think of something Ev.'

'If you tell her the truth Evan, she won't let me drive you anywhere again and it will take you double the time to get anywhere.'

'At least I'll get from A to B in one piece,' said Evan, looking at his shoe again.

Charlie had been waiting nearly two and a half hours outside the Adams family house or that's what he'd named it. It was monstrously hideous. Chief Constable Muriel Short lived inside. It suits her down to a 'T', thought Charlie.

Flat dark shoes, blue pinstriped trouser suite, long brown wig over her cropped blonde hair and her falsies, some bright pink lipstick and a pink blouse, Muriel Short was ready, but as usual Brenda wasn't.

'For Christ's sake Brenda, get a move on. You wanted to go out and you take nearly two hours to get ready. Where do you think we're going, to the Palace?' Muriel shouted.

'Starlight's better,' Brenda shouted back.

It was worth the wait. Brenny looked like a porcelain doll, just five foot four but all woman and only twenty-eight. Muriel felt good. She'd had six months of heaven and expected a lot more. It had cost her new clothes from Brenda, dentists for Brenda, car, manicures, cosmetics, weekends away, but by God, it was worth it.

She called for a taxi. It would meet them a hundred or so yards up the road, one of the reasons she wore flats, the other reason was her height; even with Bren wearing high heels, she was still a good five inches taller.

They walked out hand in hand. Charlie was alert. For a moment, he didn't do anything. These were the wrong people.

He got out of his car and followed the couple with his eyes. A taxi stopped and picked them up. What he guessed rightly to be prearranged.

The lights were still on in the house. Charlie was getting a little fed up.

It was eleven when Charlie broke. He called Mike. No one else was coming out, of that he was sure. Short was still inside, probably watching television or something.

'Yes Charlie, where are you?' said Mike.

'Outside the Chief's house, I've been here nearly six hours,' he lied.

'And no-one's come out or gone in during all that time?' said Mike.

'Chief went in at about seven and two women came out about half nine,' said Charlie.

'But not the Chief?' said Mike. 'They drove off'?

'No, they walked hand in hand to the top of the road and took a passing taxi.'

'That was lucky,' said Mike.

'I think they had prearranged to meet up with the cab at that point,' said Charlie.

'Why didn't they want the cab to come to the door?' said Mike.

'Beats me,' said Charlie.

'There are two cars still in the driveway Mike, a silver Audi and a Smart car.'

'Very odd,' said Mike.

'We've arrived,' said Evan.

'Hang on Charlie, be with you in a minute. Now tell me what did these two look like?'

'Well one was tall, dark hair, wearing trousers, the other was shorter, mini skirt, high heels, dark hair, page boy style and yes, both wore bright red lipstick.'

'Could the taller one have been Short?' said Mike.

'Not unless she sprouted some big bazookas,' said Charlie.

'Okay Charlie, go and activate the Audi's alarm and wait to see who comes out,' Mike said.

Charlie did and then ran back to his hiding place. The alarm went on and on. Eventually somebody contacted the police who came and disarmed it.

By now, Mike and Evan were in the office.

'Starlight Club,' said Amber according to Vice. 'It's the best in the city, food, show, the works.'

'Head for the Starlight Club Charlie. I've a feeling the tall one's inside. We need pictures.'

'I'm not going in there Mike,' said Charlie.

'Why on earth not?' said Mike.

Charlie could hear Evan laughing.

'I'm not dressed properly,' said Charlie who was wearing jeans and a black shirt with a zip-up nylon jacket.

'Get in there Charlie. No-one's going to bite you,' said Mike.

'I'm not going in, do you understand me. I'll wait outside.'

'Come and pick me up Charlie. We will go in together. Will that make you any happier?' said Mike.

'Not particularly,' said Charlie, checking himself out in the mirror.

'Twenty pounds,' said Mike.

'That's right Sir, ten pounds each.'

Mike handed over the money and they walked in. They headed for the bar where Mike ordered two bottles of lager.

There were about six hundred inside; some were eating, some drinking, some talking and the rest dancing to a Kylie Minogue song played by a chap with pink hair and a pink suit.

Couples were kissing everywhere, men with men, women with women. Everyone was dressed up smart. The place was clean and everyone was having a good time, everyone except Mike and Charlie.

Cameras were clicking everywhere. Charlie's was at the ready. Somebody accidently touched Mike on the arse. Mike didn't do anything because he didn't want to draw attention, then someone tried to hold his hand. Mike pulled it away and moved to the other side of Charlie.

'That's them,' Charlie said. 'Over there dancing under the pink flashing light. See them?'

'I do Charlie. You're right, the tall one's got a fine pair on her. I'm not sure if it's our Chief, the long hair, lipstick, not her bag, but I can't be certain.

'Look, they're kissing,' said Charlie.

'Get some shots in, Charlie!' Charlie did. He took a dozen in all.

On the way out somebody grabbed a piece of Charlie's arse—another accident?

They got out and breathed the fresh air.

'Not my scene,' said Mike.

'Nor mine,' said Charlie.

They dropped off the camera at the office and Charlie drove both his colleagues home. It was the end of a very long day.

Thursday morning Mike turned up at twenty past nine. Charlie and Evan had already been there half an hour and were ninety-five percent sure it was the Chief Constable in the photos. Amber was a hundred percent sure. Mike came in at ninety.

'Okay, forget Short,' Mike said, getting up and walking towards the blackboard where in red chalk he wrote in big fat block letters just the two words 'STARLIGHT CLUB.'

'Why you ask me have I put that up on the board? It's for Short. I want to see her reaction when she next pays us a visit.'

He then passed Evan the photos of the Price's. 'You've got some people to see with the good news.'

'I'll walk down the road with Charlie. See if we can borrow another car from the pool. Keep us going until ours if fixed,' said Mike.

Sandy and Curly were having a cuppa when Mike and Charlie walked in. In his hurry to get up Sandy spilt his all over his newspaper. Curly spilt his all over his overalls.

'Morning,' Mike said.

'Good Morning,' said Sandy.

'Two things only Sandy, one I need a car for a week or two whilst the Beamer gets sorted in Wrexham; we had an unfortunate accident.'

'Detective, the car has to come back here for any work or repairs. We never use outside people on our own cars, that's the rule.'

'Sandy this is an exception to the rule. It's in Simm's garage, Wrexham. I don't intend discussing it. You sort it out with them. Tell them about the rule, tell them anything you like, we just need a car,' said Mike.

'We have a problem there Detective,' said Sandy.

'Of course we do Sandy, every fucking time I come in here we have a problem to sort out and I have a rule which states that any problem can be sorted out without resorting to violence,' Mike said.

'There are no cars available for around two weeks, when we are expecting seven new cars; well, when I say *new*, I mean new to us. They're a year old,' said Sandy.

'What type?' said Mike, taking out his knife and opening up the blade.

'New models of the type you have but have been already designated to members of the Force,' said Sandy.

'Do these designees use them to travel throughout the length and breadth of Wales?' said Mike.

'I've no idea Detective,' said Sandy.

'Can you tell me the names then Sandy?'

'I'm afraid I can't Detective. Believe me I would give you any car if it was up to me but it's not,' said Sandy.

'Look Sandy, I understand your reluctance but can you at least assure me that all those designated are of higher ranking than myself—it will make me feel better,' Mike said.

Sandy paused and then said to Curly, 'Tell them Curly.'

Curly opened one of the steel filing desk drawers and took out a red folder. 'Four Superintendents, two Chief Superintendents and one other.'

'One other, what's that meant to mean Curly?' asked Mike.

'Civilian,' said Curly.

By now Charlie had seen enough. He excused himself and wandered around the garage. Sandy kept a wary eye on him.

'This civilian, does he have a name?' said Mike, now cleaning his fingernails with the knife, not that they were dirty but it gave him something to do.

'No names, Detective,' said Curly.

Mike took two quick strides and backed Curly into a corner. He was still holding the knife. Curly panicked and blurted out that the civilian was the Chief Constable's private secretary.

'Thank you,' said Mike.

Curly had a hand around a large screwdriver, which was lying on the desk.

'You don't want to be screwing around with me Curly,' Mike said, smiling.

Curly let go of the screwdriver.

'We will bid you good day then, gentlemen. Please keep us advised about the progress of our car,' Mike said.

By now, Charlie was back and they left together.

'I think we handled that very well,' said Curly.

'Aye, we were just great. I suggest you go and use the toilet Curly,' Sandy said, before sitting down and finishing off what remained of his cold tea.

'Do I have another job on for tonight Mike?' Charlie said.

'You do Charlie.'

'Let me guess,' said Charlie. 'A filing cabinet in a garage, a red folder, seven names?'

'Spot on but we also need the mileages of all these people for the past year. Will you have any trouble getting in Charlie?'

'I think I have the alarm code. I'm not sure but the number 3649 is written next to the light switch near the front door where the alarm box is mounted and, as for the front door, easy,' said Charlie.

'Do you know Mike, I've done more breaking and entering for the police since I came to work for you, than I have for the previous five years.'

'Today just goes to show you,' said Mike. 'You can't trust anyone these days.'

By two, Evan had returned.

'Do you know it's days like this that make me glad that I chose policing as a career. I can honestly say it was one of the most satisfying days of my life,' Evan said.

Evan went on to tell them how happy both sets of parents were. How, without exception, they broke down and cried with relief that their children were alive and well and how proud they were to have a grandchild.

'I've got two envelopes here, one with a cash cheque of three thousand pounds from Price's father, so that they can buy a car, his words, and one containing twelve hundred pounds cash from Joanna's parents for them to buy baby clothes and stuff for Mark. Joanna's parents are both on a week's break from work. They are going to do up the big spare bedroom for the couple so they have somewhere to live and a box room for the baby. I left with the father Jacob, who was on his way to buy paint and wallpaper.'

'Can you arrange for the money side of things, Amber, whilst I phone them with the good news?'

Evan did. Joanna answered the phone. Peter was at work.

'I'm going out for half an hour,' Mike said.

Mike was true to his word. He was back in thirty minutes, holding a massive boxed teddy bear. A card was attached to one of the bear's ears. It read 'To Mark Anthony' and signed 4 'I's.

'I got this one, Teddy Bear, Elvis 1958,' said Evan.

'Nearly,' said Charlie. 'Year was 57.'

'That's a nice gesture, a big teddy bear,' said Amber. She didn't bother asking how Mike had paid for it. She knew it would have gone down on the Corporation's Credit Card.

'I'll get it sent by DHL or equivalent,' said Amber, 'and I'll enclose the cheque and cash,' she added.

'I wish all missing persons' cases were so simple. What about Jason? We've not one lead on that one?' said Evan.

'We were going to look into the gay scene,' said Amber.

'I think we can give that a miss,' said Charlie.

'I think it's the Starlight for you, Charlie,' smiled Evan. 'Mike tells me it's all happening there.'

'I will tell you something Evan,' Charlie said, 'it's the cleanest club I've been in, the food looked bloody good, once in it wasn't unduly expensive, the customers were all smartly dressed, the staff polite and efficient. I couldn't fault it in any way except when someone tried to touch me up.'

'Charlie's right, Evan, most of us have a misconception of those types of clubs. You can add to Charlie's point another one; they play recognisable music with tunes to them, not this bloody head-banging shit.'

'Look, we can't just sit here twiddling our thumbs, there must be something we can be doing which will help our cause. Let's all go back to the point where he was last seen, shall we?' said Evan.

'What for?' said Mike.

'I don't know, Mike, give me another idea,' Evan said. 'We've exhausted everyone we can interview. They don't seem to know anything. Do we interview them again?'

'No Evan, you're right, let's go and have a look,' Mike said. 'It's only a few miles down the road.'

'Can I make a suggestion?' asked Charlie.

'Sure Charlie, go ahead,' said Evan.

'Why don't we do a question and answer thingy. I like them, something might crop up,' Charlie said.

'Best you do the questions Mike,' said Amber who had now completed the packing and addressing of the teddy bear.

'Question: Did he know where he was going to go after leaving school? That is, had he arranged something with somebody?'

'Answer: Stargazers sang Somebody in 55.'

'This isn't the time for that, Charlie,' said Evan. 'Give proper answers like this; he took no clothes, that we know of, other than those he was wearing for school, but he did take the money he had saved.'

'Did he have a gym bag or large satchel?' Mike said.

'I'll check on that,' said Evan.

'You don't need to,' said Amber, 'he disappeared on the Friday. He played football that afternoon. It's all here in the interview with Mr Pope, teacher who actually ran the game.'

'Question.'

'Look, I've got to say it, every time Mike says Question I think Moody Blues 1970,' said Charlie.

'And I Charlie will get the Moody Blues if you interrupt us one more time, so I say again; Question: Assuming it was premeditated and he had spare gear in his bag, then it's logical to say he was met by someone.'

'Answer: Agreed, because he left a good fifteen minutes after school finished. Most kids can't get out fast enough,' said Amber.

'Question: Why did he stop supporting or following Cardiff City?'

'Answer: Because he had something better or more important to do,' said Charlie.

'Question: What could be more important than following City?'

'Answer: Most things Mike,' said Evan.

'Question: Name one?'

'Answer: He watched sport on TV. He went out with his friends. He had a girlfriend. He wanted to be left alone. Hobby of some kind, lots of things, Mike.'

'Question: Assuming he was in collaboration with somebody, I ask you what could be the connection with such a person. Obviously an older person, who drove. I'm lost at this point.'

'Answer: I don't have one,' said Evan.

'Nor do I,' said Charlie.

'It's the key question Mike—who picked him up, where did they go and why?'

'Question: His parents are decent folk. They didn't argue or row with their son, no animosity. He blanked his friends, his teachers can't help. He was just your average lad, so what was he running away from?'

'Answer: Or whom,' said Amber.

'Question: Did he have a mobile phone?'

'Answer: He did, but the last known call was to his mother to say he would be in late that day as he was going to the cinema with some friends,' said Amber.

'Question: What time, what type of phone and when did the parents start worrying? By that I mean when did they call in the locals?'

'Answer: 16:15 hours, pay as you go and a few minutes before midnight,' said Amber.

'Question: It goes without saying that the parents tried to contact him on his mobile?'

'Answer: They did. They phoned all his known friends. The father drove around the area. They contacted the local hospitals, even the taxi companies,' said Amber.

'Question: Has anything turned up like his school blazer, his mobile, watch, anything at all?'

'Answer: Nothing Mike,' said Amber.

'Question: Did we search the area near the school thoroughly?'

'Answer: Yes, the school grounds, the school itself. They talked to the bus drivers on his route, some shop owners. We couldn't have done much more. They even had two dogs down at the school,' said Amber.

'Question: Has that sudden urge to remain at home on Saturdays connected in any way to his disappearance?'

'Answer: How do we know he stayed at home? He could have gone and played football or whatever with his friends, or he could have just hung out at whatever happened to be the new "in" place where the boys meet girls, smoke, have a beer, talk.'

'Okay Evan, we get the point, but he blanked his friends so if he did go out he went alone, secretive like. He didn't want anyone to see him,' said Mike.

'Question and Answer,' said Charlie. 'Let's go re-interview the parents. Were they with him on Saturdays, either one of them? That will settle it.'

'Six o'clock, we'll go, both should be home from work,' said Evan.

'Another point,' said Amber. 'On the night of his disappearance, where were both the parents? Jason phoned at 16:15 at the house. Were they both at work? Someone answered the phone.'

'It could have been the sister, what's her name Evan?'

'Julia I think,' said Evan rifling through his notes.

'Was she living at home then?' said Mike.

'What about Saturday afternoons? Maybe she could tell us what he did all day,' said Evan.

'I think we need all the phone records during that period,' said Mike.

'We've got them Mike, nothing unusual. Everybody and their uncle has been through them including me,' said Amber.

That killed the conversation. It was a good five minutes before anyone said anything and that was Charlie who wanted to know if there were any biscuits.

There were. Amber hadn't eaten them all.

'You seem a mite perturbed Mike,' Evan said.

'I'm not sure that's the correct word to us. I am, let's call it, more disturbed than confused Evan.'

'Something isn't right in this Jason case,' said Mike with a touch of melancholy.

'You're thinking what I'm sure we're all thinking. The parents are involved somehow or other,' Evan said.

'I am, Evan,' Mike agreed. 'I'm not looking forward to re-interviewing them. I'm afraid of what we might find out.'

'Do you want me to go with Evan?' asked Charlie.

'You can come, Charlie,' Mike affirmed. 'I want you to have a good look around the house, on the outside and the street as a whole.'

'And I'm looking for anything in particular, Mike?'

'No Charlie, just note everything, take photos too—and we will go in your car, Charlie.'

The Chief Constable had travelled to London for a conference. She drove using her silver Audi which was much more comfortable that the Smart car which generally she only used for around the city.

For the life of her, she couldn't understand how the car alarm was set off. There were no high winds, no trees nearby, no sign of any damage by a bird or other animal. It would remain a mystery to her but if it happened again, then that would require some CCTV cameras to be erected for the outside, front and back.

Her biggest worry was the Morton affair. For now she'd covered her arse by bringing in the two Scotland Yard men but if they failed and that's the way it was looking, and God forbid there was another murder, there would be an outcry. At least she had the others in Nelson Street tied up with a missing person's case.

Of course, because she had left early she did not know that a *mispers* case had been solved; the fax was on her desk awaiting her return.

'We should leave now,' said Evan. It's nearly six.'

'We're sorry to bother you again Mrs Conley but we've just a few last questions. If it's inconvenient we can return later on.'

'No, please come in. Jim's watching the news. I'll tell him. Would you like a tea or coffee?'

'That's kind of you but no thank you. We won't take up too much of your evening,' Evan said.

Jim Conley entered the room. He was smoking a pipe.

'Dutch, is it?' said Evan.

'Yes, do you smoke a pipe?'

'I do,' said Evan.

'Would you like to try some?'

'No thank you Mr Conley.'

'It's Jim, and my dear wife is Emily.'

'We would like to know what Jason did on Saturday afternoons after he stopped going to the matches with his friend.'

'Well, I don't rightly know,' said Jim. 'I work for a local butcher and on Saturdays we close at noon and then go for a pint in the Black Horse, which is about thirty meters from the shop, with my two colleagues and come back home. I then get washed and changed and me and Emily would invariably go shopping and have a coffee in town. We would return say five thirty, latest six and settle down for an evening of television.'

'And Jason?' said Evan.

'Well, he was either in his room listening to God knows what or watching TV,' said Jim.

'Anyone else in the house with him?' asked Mike.

'Julia was home sometimes but she mostly liked to go out with her friends on a Saturday,' Emily said.

'And on the Friday of Jason's disappearance, were you all at home?'

'Yes we were,' said Jim.

'Are you a hundred percent sure about that?' asked Mike.

'Of course I am. How could I ever forget that night? I dream it every day. I always will. I don't sleep, I can't, it's hell. He left no letter, just the one phone call to say that he would be going to the cinema with friends. I took the call.'

'We go out for dinner or to the pub on either a Wednesday or Thursday, never on a Friday,' said Emily.

'Have we been of help?' asked Emily hopefully.

'Every bit of information is of help,' said Mike.

'Have you made any progress of any sort?' asked Jim. 'Is there a glimmer of hope? We need to hear something, Detectives, just that our prayers are not going unheeded.'

'It's a puzzle, Mr Conley. We have a few of the pieces and slowly we hope to get enough to form a picture. One thing I do guarantee you, we are doing our upmost to solve your son's disappearance.'

'Thank you,' said Emily. 'May God be with you.'

'May I ask if you are practising Christians?' said Evan.

'We are Roman Catholics and attend our church every Sunday without fail,' said Emily. 'And our children, they too attended regularly with us. Lately our Julia has lapsed a little,' said Jim.

'Actually we would like another word with Julia,' said Evan.

'Then you're in luck. She'll be dropping off little Karen any moment now. We're babysitting,' said Emily.

'She's a beauty that one,' said Mike. 'How old is the little girl?'

'About 10 months, is that right Jim?'

'Yes, that's right love,' said Jim, who had moved towards the front door to let his daughter and granddaughter through.

'Hello again. There, Mrs Labins, can you spare us a few minutes of your time?' Mike asked.

127

'My husband is outside waiting in the car,' Julia said.

'Just two minutes, no longer I promise you.'

'Dad, will you tell Dominic I'll be a few moments? Tell him I need to use the toilet.'

Jim exited the house without speaking.

'Now what do you want this time Detectives?' said Julia, stubbing out her cigarette in the big ashtray that was lying in the middle of the kitchen table.

When they had finished, they thanked Julia who went out in a hurry, only turning at the door to say, 'See you later Mum.'

Mike took out a twenty-pound note from his pocket and when Jim was distracted and Emily at the door seeing off her daughter, Mike flicked Julia's spent cigarette onto the note before folding it three times into a secure paper parcel before putting it into his pocket.

'Have you got a handkerchief?' Mike asked Evan, who produced one and handed it to Mike.

'Is it possible to have one last look at Jason's room?' said Mike. 'We could have missed something.'

'You know the way,' said Jim. 'Help yourselves.'

'What are we doing here, Mike? Why the cigarette butt?' said Evan.

'DNA. I need the baby's and Jason's. Those yellow memo note things stuck up there will do,' said Mike, taking all six. 'Now Evan, you explain to Jim in the kitchen that we need to borrow these to have a record of Jason's handwriting. Tell him we will photocopy them and return these originals tomorrow afternoon. It's important you keep Jim in the kitchen whilst I try and get a sample from the baby in the lounge.'

'Oh Mike, I don't like this one bit, this is serious stuff! Where you going with all this anyway?'

'Evan, I don't have a clue where this is going, or if it's going anywhere. Please hold your nerve here, Evan. It could be important. We must take some risks. No-one else is doing anything, are they Evan?'

Downstairs Evan asked Jim if he could come into the kitchen in order to show him what they had taken from Jason's room.

Mike wandered over to the carrycot that Karen was in.

'She's got beautiful skin, must run in the family,' Mike said.

'Yes Karen's lucky, she's got lovely blonde hair, blue eyes and lovely skin,' said a proud grandmother.

Mike bent over and with Evan's handkerchief wiped the dribble from around the baby's mouth. He also picked up some loose blonde hairs.

'I'm sorry Mrs Conley, I didn't realise that we have been here nearly an hour. I'll go get my partner and leave you in peace.'

'It isn't a problem Detective, like I said we will cooperate and help in any way we can,' Emily said.

'Thank you Emily, you've been very understanding. Evan, are you finished?' Mike shouted.

'I am. Jim doesn't mind us taking the notes. He doesn't want them back,' Evan said to Mike as they left the house.

'You're sweating, Evan,' Charlie said as they both clambered into the car.

'What we're doing in there Mike, lifting DNA samples from mothers, babies, missing boys, what were you thinking? We can't use it as evidence. If it proves anything, we never had permission to take the samples. Forget losing our jobs, we can get sued to high heaven and I don't know what else,' said Evan, now sweating even more as he thought about the consequences of their action.

'We going for the garage, Mike?' asked Charlie.

'Yes, in for a penny, in for a pound,' said Mike.

'What's this about a garage?' Evan asked.

'Sandy's garage. We're going to break in and copy some documents, that's all.'

'That's all! I see us being inside before the nights out and they will throw away the keys when they find the DNA samples.' Evan wiped his head with one of Charlie's back seat cushions.

'We can drop you off Evan at the office. Give the samples to Amber and if things don't go our way you can bring us a file hidden in a cake.'

'Mike, you've got to get serious. This isn't a joke. We can't go breaking into police compounds and garages. It's madness,' said Evan.

'It's crazy I know, Evan, but if we succeed it will be like scoring the winning goal in the FA Cup Final,' said Mike.

Charlie stopped the car and turned in Evan's direction. 'Evan we all owe this man. If I don't do it he's crazy enough to try it himself because he thinks it's important, so what am I supposed to do, let Mike ruin himself? At least I know what I'm doing when it comes to this type of work.'

'Drive on Charlie,' said Evan.

Charlie stopped the car thirty yards away from the garage. In the shadow of a large adjoining building, he left the car idling over.

'Now I'm going to use the code we have. If the alarm goes, drive off and don't worry about me, I'll be okay,' Charlie said.

Mike got into the driving seat, Evan in the front passenger seat. All they could see of Charlie was the powerful small torch he was holding.

'He's in,' said Mike.

'How do you know?' said Evan who was in a better position.

'No light,' said Mike.

'What's he after exactly?'

'Mileage charts for last year and the designated names of those receiving the new cars, Evan.'

'He's been in there nearly six minutes,' said Evan.

'Here he comes now,' said Mike.

Charlie opened the back car door, got in and said, 'Piece of cake, no file required.'

Evan laughed out of sheer nervousness.

After arriving back at their office and handing Amber the three DNA samples, they sat around the table and waited for some small lamb chops and corn on the cob.

They ate with their fingers. They had a lager each and didn't talk throughout the meal.

'Charlie, what did you see?' asked Mike.

'Houses, gardens, fronts and a lot of people who looked out from behind their curtains.'

'Nothing strange or unusual?' said Mike.

'Zilch. There's a lane running at the back but every house has a six foot brick wall,' said Charlie.

'What do you now think of the parents Jim and Emily?' said Evan.

'They know nothing. They really are hurting,' said Mike.

'I concur with that, but the daughter is a different kettle of fish. She didn't exactly lie but didn't tell us the whole truth,' said Evan.

'The body language said it all,' said Mike. 'Couldn't look at either of us in the eye, head down, full arm cross gesture, fidgeting with that ashtray. She's something to hide.'

'There is something going on with the father too,' Mike said. 'She didn't even bother to wish him a goodnight or thanks, and it was noticeable that Jim didn't want to tell her husband that lie about her using the toilet.'

'And why didn't she want her husband to know that she was talking to us, and why has she stopped going to church?' said Evan.

'Well, she was of no help with Jason. We still don't know what he did on Saturday afternoons,' said Mike.

'I don't think I've ever seen a bonnier little baby. She's like a living doll, blonde hair, blue eyes, creamy skin. She'll break some hearts one day and yes, Charlie, I know Living Doll by Cliff in 1960 or so,' said Evan.

'Was that her husband outside waiting in the car?' asked Charlie.

'Yes, that's Dominic,' said Evan.

'Strange that then,' said Charlie.

'Well, you said his daughter has blonde hair, white creamy skin, blue eyes, is that correct?'

'It is Charlie,' said Evan.

'The guy in the car, the husband Dominic, I would say he's a Greek or Arab, a Med Arab, very dark hair, colour of Mike's, brown skin, wide nose; isn't it unusual that the daughter hasn't taken one of his features?' said Charlie.

'Unusual but not impossible,' said Amber, 'and of course the other possibility is that this Dominic is not the father.'

'If I remember correctly, baby Karen is now ten months old so she was born in May, the year before last, some month's after Jason disappeared,' said Evan.

'And it was around about then, when she started missing out on church,' said Mike.

'But what does all this mean? Jason phoned at quarter past four from school, walked out and disappeared, pre-planned from what we have gathered so far,' said Charlie.

'Why did he leave? Who helped him, and what did they do next?' said Evan.

'Answer the first and we will be able to fathom out the next two. That should be enough to bring closure.'

# CHAPTER FIVE

**MIKE** tried to turn back when he had reached Andreas but unfortunately for him, Andreas had clocked him and came rushing out. Andreas was a good barber, one of the best if not the best, but alone with him, as the only customer, no way.

'Ah Mikhail, you come for haircut, yes?'

'No Andreas, I've come to ask you out for a date.'

'This some kinda Russian joke Mikhail?'

'No Andreas, it's just a Welsh bloke being sarcastic; of course I've come for a haircut.'

'You like Greek coffee?'

'No, I'm fine, thanks,' said Mike.

'I make anyway, so I get you one, best coffee in the world, makes your brain good,' said Andreas wandering off.

'Makes your brain dead,' thought Mike, bloody disgusting stuff and he liked his coffee, black. Mike prayed for some more customers. Maybe the rain was putting them off.

'Okay you sit, Mike, no hurry,' said Andreas, handing Mike his large cup of what looked like crude oil. It was then that Mike noticed that Andreas had flipped the 'Open' sign to 'Shut.'

'You can smoke now Mikhail.'

'Thanks Andreas,' Mike said, settling down for another one of Andreas's pearls of wisdom.

'You know when I was young I joined a ship for one year. Went to America, South America and back to home. I learn many things Mike.'

'I'm sure you did Andreas. Now I suppose you would like to impart some of that knowledge on to me.'

'I am long time in this country Mikhail and, like you, I'm still a foreigner.'

'Andreas, I've told you before, I was born here. I don't know anywhere else, and I love it; the rain, the sport, the green lush lands, everything.'

'But you don't know. Have you seen my country? Best food, best Ouzo, cold beers, sun, blue seas, beautiful women; you would like it.'

'I'm sure I would Andreas. Now what about this haircut?'

'I tell you Mikhail, on ship they tell me, if you want to know about food ask a Frenchman. If you want to know about warm beer, ask an Englishman. But if you want to know about women, ask a Greek.'

'Well, I'd like to find one, Andreas.'

'You okay Mikhail. You find plenty but not for you the babies, eh? Now this type of woman you find in Greece. Many, many of them everywhere. I will tell you the story of when I was in Salonika. I meet this one…'

By now, Mike had closed his eyes and more importantly his ears. He really didn't want to hear about Andreas's sexual conquests. All he needed was a good haircut.

'Where the hell is Mike?' said Amber. Charlie looked at his watch. It was nearly ten. Mike was always late but only by ten or fifteen minutes. He picked up his mobile and was about to phone when Mike walked in.

'You've had a haircut Mike,' said Evan.

'Good morning Evan. You're on the ball today.'

'It's called observation,' said Evan.

'Now everyone knows what I've been doing this morning. Can I ask what you've all been doing?' said Mike.

'Apart from tea-drinking and cake-eating, we have sifted through various bits of information that we have accumulated, namely Karen is Julia's daughter. No luck on Jason because Mike, he didn't lick the damn notepad things. They're self-adhesive like modern stamps,' said Amber.

'Anyway, can you tell me why we need Jason's DNA?' asked Charlie.

'To eliminate him from being Karen's father,' said Mike, 'that's why.'

'Shit, that's disgusting. How can you think along those lines?' said Charlie.

'For his disappearance Charlie,' said Evan.

'I see,' said Charlie, 'but incest?'

'Look Charlie, you said yourself Dominic, Julia's husband doesn't look anything like the baby,' said Mike.

'Yes, but you took the samples before I told you that,' said Charlie.

'It's my mind Charlie, it works in mysterious ways sometimes,' said Mike.

'Right, what are we going to do about it?' said Charlie.

'Get Dominic's,' said Amber.

'How, without alerting him or the parents?' said Charlie.

'I don't know yet. I've got a bloody headache. I've been listening to Andreas the Greek for nearly an hour. Lesser mortals wouldn't make it out of the barber's, especially if they've been unfortunate enough to be offered a coffee,' said Mike.

'Turkish,' said Amber.

'Yes, Turkish-style, but Greek.'

'But we have news on the car business,' said Amber.

'Last year's average mileage was 8,000 miles; apart from two, one was nearly three times that and the other didn't have a car!' said Charlie.

'Would that be the civilian?' said Mike.

'Yep, a Miss Brenda Aston, age twenty eight and private secretary to the Chief Constable.'

'Mike, it's the one in the picture. She has her own address, a small flat in Whitchurch and drives a Fiat,' said Evan.

'Pure nepotism,' said Amber.

'Well, she can forget the car,' said Mike.

'You haven't asked who did the 23,600 miles, Mike,' said Amber.

'No, it's unimportant,' said Mike.

'Unimportant but interesting,' said Amber. 'It's Foul-mouth Fowler.'

'Um, that's interesting,' said Mike. 'I wonder why he's burning rubber at that rate.'

'I've made tea,' said Amber. 'Anyone interested? We could also have a sandwich; keep us going till lunch.'

Only Amber and Evan had tea and sandwiches. Mike had coffee and Charlie just a Coke.

'Question,' said Evan. 'Is it possible that Jason is the father?'

'Answer: yes, he had the time; every Saturday afternoon, and we do not have Julia's movements for the same periods,' said Amber.

'Question: if that is the case, it would have killed their parents, so Julia would have helped him go away somewhere,' said Evan.

'Answer: that's a possibility but what role does Dominic play in all this?' said Mike.

'Question: if it's Jason's, does Dominic know?' said Evan.

'Answer: 'I doubt it,' said Charlie.

'Look,' said Amber, 'it's Friday; he works just two hundred yards away in the Tate's Insurance Building. I bet he will go for a midday drink with his mates—there's a pub next door.'

'Difficult,' said Charlie, 'we got to find another way.'

'I agree,' said Evan.

'Look, let's go anyway. We've nothing better on, have we?' said Mike.

They sat in the pub for nearly two hours. Dominic didn't appear.

'You know his car Charlie,' said Mike.

'Yes, it's a green Mondeo,' said Charlie.

'Let's see if it's parked around here,' said Mike. Ten minutes it took them; it was easy. Green Mondeos aren't thick on the ground.

'Damn,' said Mike, looking through the window. 'No half bottle of water or soft drink, ashtray is shut, so we don't know it he's a smoker. Too much of a risk breaking into it.'

'Let's get back Mike, this is pointless,' said Evan.

As they walked back, Amber called Evan on his mobile. Little and Large were coming in at four for another chat.

'So no luck with Labin?' said Amber.

'Not yet,' said Mike, 'just a matter of time.'

'So do you know what Lincoln and Ford want?' said Evan.

'No,' said Amber, 'no idea.'

They didn't have to wait long. Lincoln and Ford were early. Both were wearing big smiles.

'Guess you have good news?' said Mike.

'You guess right, Detective,' said Ford, making himself at home and sitting down. Lincoln still stood; at near on twenty stone it might have done him good to take the weight off his legs but the chair wouldn't have been as happy. Before anyone managed to speak, the phone rang. It was Mr and Mrs Morgan. Their daughter had just contacted them. They were moving down within the week. Amber passed on the good news.

'Don't tell me you've closed a mispers case, the thirteen-month-old one,' said Lincoln.

'Yep, that was the happy parents,' said Charlie proudly.

'I would have bet a thousand to one against that result,' said Ford.

'So you've heard our good news, now what's yours?' said Mike.

'We have a suspect, a John Anderson, age thirty-seven, divorced, no kids. Last address Dinas Powys. Last seen five days ago,' said Ford.

'Why this guy?' said Charlie.

'Run-in with the estate agency two years ago; joint deal on some property, said the agency cheated him,' Ford said. 'He lost over a hundred and fifty grand as did the Morton family and Fenwick the solicitors. Anyway, he threatened that he would kill them all, not once but on many occasions during a period of about three months after the collapse of the deal. He was initially not a suspect as he had moved to Australia. A little checking and we found him to have returned to the UK five month ago. Further checks and we located his whereabouts; a small flat in Dinas Powys. We raided the place this morning; no one has seen him for five, six days.'

'Before you ask,' Lincoln put in, 'he's six foot tall, strong, he's a builder and no, we didn't find any incriminating evidence in the flat apart from a pair of rubber gloves and a book on guns. Oh, and he only had one kitchen knife, small blade.'

'So why are you telling us Sir?' said Evan.

'We need someone else's ideas on this man,' said Lincoln. 'We can't really work with Appleby and Foster. They are still convinced it's Harris, even though his girlfriend has been contacted and collaborated with everything he said. He has of course been released but I'm sure Appleby and Foster are keeping him under surveillance. To be honest, they don't want us there and we've been ordered to stay until this Anderson has been apprehended.'

'He fits the bill, does Anderson. What would you say Mike?' said Evan.

'I agree Evan, but why disappear now, why not before? If it's him surely he's not finished?' said Mike.

'That has bothered us. How did he know we were on to him?' said Ford.

'Maybe he has an accomplice still working at Morton's or even the police station,' said Charlie.

'Aye, another point,' said Lincoln. 'We know he must have an accomplice, but we don't have a lead on anyone else. This man seems to have no friends.'

'Coffee anyone?' said Amber. 'I've some really lovely chocolate biscuits; they're new to the market.'

'Love some,' said Lincoln. Lincoln now sat down. He was nearer the biscuits that way. 'So Detectives,' he asked, 'can you shed any light on this? Where would he run to, will he try another hit? Is he staying with his accomplice? Anything will be of help here.' Lincoln spoke between mouthfuls of biscuits. It was one race he was destined to lose. Amber beat him hands down in the fast eating game.

'Did he take his car?' said Charlie.

'No,' said Ford.

'Suitcases?' asked Charlie.

From his case Ford produced a dozen or so photos and laid them on a desk. They were photos of every part of Anderson's flat, including two open wardrobes.

'No suitcases, left in a hurry,' Lincoln said. 'Milk was six days old, bread was going off, cups unwashed.'

'I don't think he's your man,' said Mike.

'What?' said Ford.

'I said I don't think Anderson's your man,' Mike repeated.

'I heard what you said the first time Detective. Can we know why you have come to this conclusion?' asked Ford.

'It's just my opinion from what I hear and see,' said Mike.

'Let's have your opinion then please,' said Lincoln.

'Okay, Anderson has been back in the country five months, working and living in Dinas Powys. He then reads about the murders. He's got to assume that he's suspect No 1—after all, he did threaten to kill them all. He has a problem, maybe because he's a loner and doesn't know anyone in the area. He hasn't a decent alibi—he was probably at home alone watching TV. Then he reads about Harris and thinks thank God they've got the murderer. Then it's obvious it can't be Harris; it could be his accomplice but now he's back as suspect No 1 either as the main man or as the accomplice. Again for whatever reason he doesn't have a reliable alibi. He thinks about it and decides it's only a matter of time before the Police get to him so he does a runner. He doesn't take his car because everyone can trace it. And then we have these pictures: look at the mess? The man's dirty and untidy; the killer is meticulously clean and careful and very tidy.'

Lincoln put his head in his hands. This is not what he wanted to hear. Ford just said, 'That's crazy.'

'Is it?' said Evan. 'Sounds right to me.'

'And me,' said Amber.

'I don't think he went far,' said Charlie.

'Why?' said Ford.

'Because he knows or thinks that you will cover all the train stations, buses. He's lugging around a heavy suitcase,' said Charlie.

'Why would it be heavy?' asked Lincoln.

'It's full of tinned food, a knife or two, water, a few warm clothes. I would search any disused barns, outbuildings, unused property in the area but it won't solve anything. He didn't do any of the killings—he's just another Harris with a different name,' said Charlie.

'Okay, but I'm still not entirely convinced,' said Ford.

'And you, Chief Inspector Lincoln?' asked Evan.

'You've blown some holes in our theory,' said Lincoln.

'Let's find Anderson and then we will know. Until such time I suggest no one says anything to the Press,' said Ford, still nursing the possibility of it being Anderson who committed the murders.

Lincoln and Ford bade the unit their goodbyes and exited, the smiles wiped off their faces and replaced with frowns.

'I'm telling you Mike, those boyos from London need to get some brains,' said Evan.

'They're okay Ev, what would we do? They've got no proper leads. They don't know the area, the people; Appleby and Foster are probably not helping them much, if at all. At least they are trying,' said Mike.

'I'm off,' said Charlie.

'Something important going on tonight Charlie?' asked Amber.

'Could be, I have an idea,' said Charlie picking up an envelope and carefully sliding it into his pocket.

Amber looked at Evan, then at Mike; both men shrugged their shoulders. Neither had a clue where Charlie was off to.

'I think I'll go now,' said Evan. 'Need to tidy up the flat before Edna and Jasmine get home tonight.' Evan retrieved his umbrella and left.

'That leaves just us two, Mike. Want to dance?'

'I'm not in the mood for dancing,' Mike sang.

'Okay,' said Amber. 'You hungry?'

'No thanks,' said Mike.

'Going out tonight, Mike?'

'I am Amber, on a blind date. My friend Toby and his wife have arranged it for half seven. Fiona's been trying for years to arrange it with one of her friends. I couldn't fob her off any more. She was beginning to suspect I was gay.'

'I think everyone can vouch that you're not,' said Amber.

'Too bloody late, Amber, and to top it all we're going to some kind of Portuguese place.'

'Don't worry Mike, you'll get on fine with the lady.'

'I'm not worried about The Lady, I'm worried about my stomach.'

Amber laughed. She loved this crazy man.

It was half five when Charlie returned. He just stood in the middle of the room grinning.

'What you got Charlie?' Mike said.

'Mike, I don't have a title or a badge. I share a desk but I am street smart.'

'That you are. You have your own desk but you're of no fucking use in the Starlight Club Charlie.'

'Nor are you Mike. I saw the guy with the black moustache touch you somewhere intimate. I was expecting at least third world war to start up right there. I still can't understand how you held your cool.'

'I'm a professional detective, Charlie, just like you're a professional street smarty. Now you going to tell us why you're smiling or do we have to guess?'

Charlie felt in his pocket and extracted the envelope he had taken before leaving. He opened it and emptied the contents onto the desk nearest to him. A two-inch long cigarette butt.

'Labin's,' Charlie said.

'How did you get that?' asked Amber.

'I reasoned like this: if I was a smoker and worked on the fifth floor of a large building, what would be the first thing I would do on finishing work and getting out onto the street?'

'Have a fag,' said Mike.

'I waited. Saw him light up, followed him and picked up this dog end when he discarded it,' said Charlie.

'You're not only streetwise but a bloody brilliant detective, Mr White,' said Amber.

'Hear, hear,' added Mike.

Mike took a taxi at seven, found the restaurant, the Caldo Verde and still had nearly a quarter of an hour to wander around the adjoining streets whilst he had a cigarette. By the time he'd walked around the block the others had arrived, but Mike could only see his friend Toby sitting at a table. Thank Christ for that. Maybe his date couldn't make it, thought Mike. Now he wouldn't be lumbered with some bloody plain cold fish who'd only be interested in his brain.

'Hi Toby,' Mike said.

'Hi stranger,' Toby replied.

'You playing tomorrow Mike? Big game. We've got to win to stay up,' said Toby.

'Yeah, I'll be there. Down at Malins Village, isn't it? Noon kick-off,' said Mike.

'We've still got a few years left in us Mike. We've been friends for over twenty years and defensive partners for eight. I miss you when you're banned, which is happening with increasing regularity lately, Mike.'

'Don't worry Toby. Where is Fiona and …?'

'Dorothea, Mike,' said Toby.

'Dorothy,' said Mike.

'No Mike Doro-*thea*, means 'Gift of God.'

'I'm not particularly religious, Toby.'

'Here they come, Mike.'

Mike automatically ran his fingers through his curly jet-black hair. It didn't make much difference. Both men stood. By the time the girls had crossed the room Mike had appraised his blind date and he thanked God he wasn't blind—she was beautiful. Short dark hair, hourglass figure, five-seven, eight in her stockinged feet. He hoped he was right about that part—he liked stockings—big brown eyes, long slender fingers. No rings, bangles or bracelet. Square cut nails painted pink to match her lipstick. Skirt blue down to the knees. Low-cut white blouse hiding what looked like good-sized firm breasts. High heels. He'd just got down to the three-inch cream belt, which was tied at an angle around her slim waist when Fiona spoke.

'When you've finished ogling my friend Mike, can I formally introduce you to each other?'

Fiona did and they all sat down. It was now Dorothea's turn to do a little ogling, whilst Toby ordered some champagne. Six plus, coal black eyes, good teeth. Lovely hair most women would be proud of and that teardrop scar under the left eye. Fiona was right; this man looked like a film star. Pity he was a cop.

'Shall I order for everyone? Starters and the wine? I eat here with clients quite a lot.'

They all agreed and Toby ordered. The food came. A few plates of petiscos, the Portuguese equivalent to the Spanish tapas or Greek Meze, and as a special favour to a good customer, a couple of plates of salgados or spicy pastries which are usually eaten only as snacks throughout the day.

'So what are we about to eat here Toby?' asked his wife Fiona. A worried look had crossed her face.

'Right, this is *salade de poluo*, tender pieces of octopus in vinaigrette. This *flgada oder iscas*, which as you can see is thin slices of fried liver on bread.'

'Don't worry about the names Toby, just tell us what the ingredients are,' said Mike

'Okay, this is a salad of dried cod in oil and vinegar, this another salad of white beans, onions, eggs, parsley in oil and vinegar. This is diced pig's ears and that one is squid fried in their ink. This is *moelas*, just, well, spiced chicken stomachs.'

'And those, that look like cakes, what are they?' asked Dorothea.

'They are the *salgados*, that's bread filled with paprika sausage; the small croquettes are dumplings made with dried cod, potatoes and herbs. The deep fried triangles are filled with ground meat and seasoned with curry, piri-piri and mint and called *chamucas* and the half-moon shaped deep fried choux pastries are filled with crabmeat. I've ordered some Vinho Verde.'

The wine was excellent as were most of the starters; a few such as the spiced chicken stomachs might have tasted good but no one was willing to try them except Toby who had eaten them before.

For their main course, the ladies both ordered grilled Turbot with a green salad. The men plumped for *bife á calé*, steak flash fried and covered with a sauce made up of potato flour, milk, mustard, butter and lemon juice, which came with homemade French fries. Mike was impressed as he was with the red Reserva wine, which came from the Douro region in the north of the country around Vila Real.

By now Mike had learnt that Dorothea was well off; a widow of six years with one grown-up daughter of eighteen who was attending Cambridge University, lived in Llandaff and wrote for various magazines, mainly the fashion pages.

In the seventy minutes they had been in the restaurant, Dorothea had learnt that Mike's real name was Mikhail, that his father was Russian, that Mike was a Special Detective Inspector in Cardiff, that he had never married, was unattached, had a great smile and was Toby's defensive partner in some kind of football team. After her fish course, Dorothea excused herself as did Fiona. They were both smokers and wanted to go outside and have a smoke. At least it wasn't raining and the Caldo Verde had three small tables covered by an awning with the name emblazoned in green across it.

Each of the three tables had three chairs and an ashtray. Everything was aluminium and light for ease of carrying back inside when service was finished for the day. The girls sat down, both smoked Consulate Menthols. Fiona spoke first.

'Well Dor, what do you think of Mike?'

'I like him. He's rugged, handsome and looks a little dangerous. I've never ever come across anyone with coal-black sparkling eyes before. Does he wear contacts Fiona?'

'I don't think so, I mean who in their right mind would pick black ones? I very much doubt if they even make them in black.'

'And that scar; at first I thought it was actually a real teardrop.'

'Yes, Dore, I've always wondered how he got that.'

'Strange a good looker like him isn't married or in a stable relationship of some sort,' said Dorothea.

'I think he plays the field, that's what I can gather from Toby,' said Fiona.

'Do you know what's weird, Fiona? It's like I know him, that we've met before, but surely I would have remembered.'

'He's been in the papers a lot, Dore, not his picture but a description of sorts. He's quite a celebrity—caught a whole bunch of miscreants, including some serial killer that terrorised the country for a period of about six months.'

'I remember now; it was someone called the Chesspiece, no, Chessman, and again just recently people were writing in wanting him to be on the Morton thing.'

'Yes, he'd been suspended for some reason,' said Fiona.

Just then Mike came out. 'Mind if I join you girls? I'm dying for a smoke.' The girls had finished but sat there and waited for Mike to light up. Dorothea noticed the non-filter cigarettes and the gold and silver Dunhill lighter that matched his Omega watch. Mike took three long drags and flicked the remainder of the cigarette into the gutter.

They all got up and re-entered the restaurant. Mike held the door open for them.

'I took the liberty of ordering the sweet. The Portuguese are not too hot on sweets, so I've ordered *Tigeladas*, they're light, fluffy, thick pancake-type puddings. Does anyone want cream with them?' Toby asked.

Nobody did but everyone wanted coffee. The pancakes came— they were delicious.

'Now would anyone like a Port or a nice Madeira? They have exceptional ones here,' said Toby. The consensus was for the Madeira and Toby, after consultation with the owner, ordered a rare fifteen-year-old Sercial, a subtle dry Madeira. That too went down well. It was now half past nine and Toby asked Mike and Dorothea if they would like to come around to the house for a nightcap; after all, they could all fit into a taxi.

After a small discussion, it was agreed that Mike would drop off Dorothea in one taxi and carry on home and Toby and Fiona would take a separate taxi. Toby called for the bill. Mike insisted on paying but Toby would have none of it and won out in the end. He promised Mike that he could pay next time.

The taxis arrived within seconds of each other and they all said their goodnights before getting into their taxis. Dorothea gave the driver the address and they departed. It had just started raining. Mike was now in a position to look over Dorothea's legs. He liked what he could see. She was wearing either tights or stockings. It was hard not to stare but he got away with a quick peep or two.

Dorothea had noticed Mike's roving eye. She wanted to smile. She was proud of her long shapely legs and was pleased when people noticed them. She was extra pleased that Mike seemed to approve. Mike turned and faced Dorothea. He wanted to plant a long deep kiss on her pink mouth but asked instead if he could come in and use the toilet facilities. She had no problem with that.

'Would you like a drink Mike?' she asked, adding, 'I have some interesting whiskies at home.'

'My favourite tipple,' said Mike. Things were really beginning to look up and he was ready—he always was.

The taxi driver smiled. He loved it when the bloke was going to score; it usually meant a much bigger tip. He was right—Mike tipped over the odds. Dorothea's house was actually a maisonette comprising the first floor and attic of a large Georgian house. It had its own entrance. The rooms were expensively but tastefully decorated. Dorothea took Mike's jacket and hung it up.

'The bathroom's through there,' she said pointing. Mike had forgotten that he needed to use the toilet facilities. He went in , washed and dried his hands, flushed the toilet and then stood in front of the mirror, before deciding it was too late to have a face lift and that the face he could see before him had got him this far and hopefully would get him a lot further.

Dorothea was sitting on a fabriced chair, her legs curled underneath her. 'The drinks are on the glass table, help yourself. Mine's a scotch with a dash of Whisky Mac, no ice, but if you need some there's lots in the freezer.' Mike chose the Grouse, a good blended whisky. He poured two and added a splash of Mac, swirled the liquid in the glass and set one down in front of her. He noticed the ashtrays; she followed his eyes and nodded. 'Go ahead and smoke Mike, you know I do.'

Mike bent down and lit her menthol for her, then he tapped out a cigarette of his own and lit up before sitting on the large sofa opposite her. He noticed the size; it was bigger than a single bed. He raised his glass and said, 'Here's to whoever had the foresight to arrange blind dates.'

She replied, 'Then here's to Fiona.'

'Fiona,' Mike said, taking a sip.

Israel Levy was good with numbers. He also was good at poker. Money was his goal, his everything. 'Normal' souls would be in mourning for his late colleagues, but for him money was the important thing.

There was still four of them playing; the other two had already lost too much and left. Israel had about eight thousand pounds worth of chips and was about to go all in with a low straight flush. Chang, the owner of three Chinese restaurants, followed; he had an ace high flush, same suit as Israel Levy. Both had hearts. Big Mal, local nightclub owner, had a full house, aces over fours. He was also feeling confident. Before the all-ins, the pot had eight thousand pounds and now it was going to total twenty-six. Smithy the fourth player had already folded and he had less than five hundred pounds in front of him.

Big Mal flipped over his two cards. 'Shit,' said Chang, chucking in his flush. Israel milked the moment for as long as he could before turning over first the two, then the three of hearts. He scooped the money and started putting it into piles of a thousand, twenty-eight piles in total plus a few odd chips.

'You lucky bastard,' said big Mal.

'I am, aren't I?' replied Israel.

Two more hands and Israel had the whole thirty thou that had been brought in by the players for the session. It was still early, just gone ten p.m. Chang and Big Mal left for the casino where they could get credit and play and Smith poured himself a drink; it was his house so he didn't have to move. Israel cashed in the chips, collected his coat and left. He'd only drunk soda water as was his practice when he played cards so he was sober and in a position to drive back home to Tara and have a proper drink.

His Alfa Romeo was parked nearby and as he walked towards it, he counted himself a very fortunate man. That was about to change. The pistol pointing at him was a replica but it looked real enough to Israel.

'One word motherfucker and it will be your last,' said David, enjoying scaring the shit out of Levy. 'Get into your car,' said David, 'and drive.' Levy did.

'Look, I'm wearing a Rolex and I've just won ten grand in a poker game, it's yours,' said Israel, 'Just let me go.'

'Shut up and drive,' said David, looking at the side mirror to make sure Patrick was following.

'So,' said Foster, 'why were you in hiding, like a criminal, tell me, arsehole?'

Appleby looked on. It wasn't going to be easy breaking this Anderson down, but he was going to give it his best before Ford and Lincoln turned up and got all the credit.

After stringing him up and taking the photo, David counted the money—thirty thousand pounds—the lying bastard. He said he'd only won ten. The Rolex would be worth two, three grand but David left it.

Before leaving the scene, David phoned Walter, who told them he had to go out and would see them at midnight. Walter took the bus, the last one out into Cardiff and after finding himself a phone box he dialled Cardiff Central Police Station. He left a message for the Chief Constable.

He gave the duty seargent the exact position of where to find Levy's body and said that there would be two more the following day unless Detectives Karetzi and Jones were assigned immediately to the case.

He caught the last train home. On the way back he calculated the odds: he needed high profile detectives to follow the case. He would leak them enough information to catch David and Patrick; he needed the world to know why Morton's and Co were being eliminated.

He would have his day. What could they do to him: imprison him, hospitalise him, what? He had four, five months left; he wanted his fifteen minutes of fame. People needed to know: he would avenge his wife and daughter.

Evan was still hugging and kissing his wife and daughter when he got the call.

'Problem dad?' asked Jasmine.

'Big one—looks like we've just been assigned to help in the Morton's case; there's been another victim. I've got to go. Sorry Edna, food's in the oven. I've done a chicken.'

'You go Evan, we're okay,' said Edna.

Mike had progressed. Dorothea was now on the couch with him. He'd done a little preliminary investigating and confirmed that she *was* wearing stockings. The call from Evan curtailed any other ideas that he had. He gave Evan the address. Dorothea was as pissed off as Mike; they exchanged telephone numbers and Mike promised he'd be in touch soonest.

Mike and Evan were the last on the scene. The circus was in full swing. Short was there acting as ringmaster. Appleby and Foster the clowns were there; Little and Large, a SOCO team, six uniforms, a photographer, the local press, a doctor and the fire authority had a presence. Levy's body was still swinging from the rope. It was a grotesque sight—everyone was just standing there and watching.

'Who is he?' asked Evan.

'Israel Levy, accountant for Morton's and Fenwick's,' said the Chief Constable.

'What are we doing here?' asked Mike. Short told them all about the call.

'That's strange,' said Evan.

'Bloody strange,' said Mike.

Mike spotted Alex Symonds, chief *Chronicle* reporter and someone he could trust. He walked over but before he even managed to say hello, the Chief Constable had bounded over and in a loud booming voice advised Mike not to fraternise with the Press. A few of the onlookers felt embarrassed. Foster, the one with the broken nose, smirked.

'Hi Alex, nice to see you again,' Mike said.

'Same here. You on the case Mike?' the reporter asked.

'I'm not sure,' said Mike.

The Chief Constable knew that she had to keep calm and keep things under control, so she just ignored Mike's conversation with the Press.

'Excuse me,' said Chief Inspector Lincoln, 'but there seems to be a lot of chiefs here—who is going to run this show?'

'I am the most senior officer, local officer I mean, apart from the Chief Constable,' said Appleby.

'D.I.s Karetzi and Jones have still got their missing persons case to follow up on,' said Foster laughingly.

'How's your nose Foster? Want me to re-straighten it?' said Mike.

Foster scowled and turned away.

'Forget the missing persons case for now,' said the Chief Constable. 'Chief Inspector Appleby will be in charge, under the watchful eye of Chief Superintendent Fowler, who will of course be reporting to me. You two will help chief Inspector Appleby with his inquiries. Is that clear to everyone?'

'And what about us?' asked Ford.

'I think you should make your reports and leave us to get on with it,' said Appleby.

'I will have to ring London,' said Lincoln.

'You can ring anyone you like, but your presence is not required here anymore,' said Appleby.

'Is that correct, Chief Constable Short?' asked Lincoln.

'It is,' said the Chief Constable. 'Good night and thank you for your help,' she added before turning and heading for the car.

'You heard her,' said Foster, 'now get back to wherever you came from.'

'Let's get on with it then. Cut the man down, cordon off the area, get the car down to Forensics, tyre marks, the usual and let's have a search: fifty, sixty meters all around the area. Oh and D.I. Karctzi, get rid of your mates,' said Appleby.

'Which mates?'

'The fucking Press,' said Appleby.

'Yes Sir,' said Mike, trudging off to where the pressmen were huddled together.

'So Mike, looks like you're one of the monkeys.'

'Monkeys, Alex?'

'Seems that Chief Appleby Einstein is the organ grinder. Isn't that so?' said Alex.

'Guess that's the way it's panning out, Alex.'

'The guy's an idiot, Mike. They've still got that Anderson down at Central. Maybe they think he broke out, strung up Levy over there and then came back and waited for them to continue the interview,' said Alex.

'You need to go now Alex, before I get into trouble,' said Mike.

'I'll be in touch Mike. Come on lads, they don't want us here,' said Alex.

Appleby clicked his fingers. 'Over here everyone, not the Press, just the detectives. Has anyone advised his family?' Appleby said. 'Best you do that D.I. Jones and tell me, do you really need an umbrella? It's hardly raining.'

'Hardly is enough for me,' said Evan dryly.

'Does anyone have his movements up to the time of his death?' said Appleby.

'Maybe Jones can throw some light on it when he speaks to the family,' said Foster.

'It's D.I. Jones, D.I. Foster,' said Evan.

'Come on, chop-chop, let's get on with it,' said Appleby.

Evan found out that Israel Levy had been playing poker, which he did every fortnight on a Friday. He found out where and with whom. Evan then passed on the message to Appleby, who sent Foster and a uniform to Paul Smith's house where it was ascertained that Levy left the house just after ten with thirty thousand pounds in his hand.

Chief Superintendent Fowler, Chief Inspector Appleby, D.I.s Foster, Karetzi and Jones all sat in one of the interview rooms. Ford and Lincoln were outside typing out their reports.

'So he left at five past ten, ten, fifteen minutes tops to get to his last resting place, say ten twenty. The message was received at ten forty-five. Everyone okay with that?' said Fowler.

'Maybe he knew his assailant or assailants,' said Foster.

'Two fresh sets of tyre marks, one of course the Alfa, the other the killer's,' said Appleby.

'So, this is the way I see it,' said Fowler. 'One's in the Alfa with Levy, the other following him. Obviously, Levy was driving the Alfa; we will see what the Alfa throws up—we might get lucky!'

'My money's on one of the card players. They knew that Levy had 30 grand cash on him and just waited and followed him,' said Foster.

'Why the hanging?' said Evan.

'Is there a message there?' said Appleby.

'It's like a game of Cluedo. We've got deaths by poison, by strangling, by stabbing and now hanging,' said Appleby.

'It's nearly one a.m.,' Appleby continued. 'I want a house-to-house around this Smith's house and a proper daylight search of the crime scene. D.I. Foster can do the crime scene search. D.I. Jones the door-to-door and D.I. Karetzi the background search on Levy's involvement with Morton's. I'll have a dozen uniforms on standby for you, Foster, and you, Jones, you start at seven sharp, here in this station and let's talk to the poker players.'

Alex Symonds received the call at one a.m. It had been a long day but he took it. That was one of the problems of being in the newspaper business, you never knew when the next break would come—you had to follow every lead.

'Symonds here,' Alex could hear the box being fed—someone had put a load of money into this call. Alex again said, 'Symonds on the line.' At last a very faint voice asked him if he was the newspaper guy. Alex replied that he was. Was he party to the scene in the woods last night? He confirmed that he was.

'Who's calling?' said Alex.

'Yesterday's Man,' said Walter. 'Listen young man, listen carefully,' said Walter. Alex did.

'Chief Constable Short, this is Alex Symonds from *The Chronicle*. I was one of the reporters in the woods last night. I have to advise that I'm recording this message.'

'It sounds important,' said Short.

'Well, it's seven minutes past two in the morning, Chief Constable, and I need to change the paper's headlines now.'

Three minutes later and Alex had closed the phone. He was now rearranging the wording of the headlines. The Editor had to be informed but lives were at stake and he couldn't foresee any problems.

Once back in the car David had to ask Walter what he was playing at.

'Look David, we need maximum headlines and these two, Karetzi and Jones will get them. They're local heroes, the public love them,' said Walter.

'Why do we need this publicity? We're opening ourselves up for a fall and that's not in our agreement Walter,' said David.

153

'David, you've seen my Will, you stand to be a rich man. Three, four months, that's all I got, let me at least have my fun. I've waited a long time. The photos help but I need everyone to know. I want to see it in black and white,' said Walter. 'Now can I take off these bloody gloves?' said Walter.

'Yes Walter, you can.'

# CHAPTER SIX

**THE CHIEF** called a meeting.

'I received a phone call yesterday, a very disturbing one. This is today's paper, my hand has been forced, there is no choice. I can only tell you that the case will be handled solely by D.I.s Karetzi and Jones. I don't expect anybody in this room to like it but believe me I have no choice. So now please call in Karetzi and Jones and we will see how they wish to proceed. You are still answerable to me,' said the Chief Constable. 'Is that clear?'

Mike and Evan entered.

'Of course it is, but I cannot understand why he wants them on the case,' said Fowler.

'I don't know either. How would you suggest we start the ball rolling?' said the Chief.

'Firstly, we release Anderson,' Mike said. 'Let's not waste any more time on him. Then, as the Chief Inspector Appleby said, let's do the house-to-house. D.I. Foster can be in charge of that, a search of the crime scene, anyone can do that whoever's available on duty, and if we can bag up everything you have on the Morton's case and have it sent around to Nelson Street a.s.a.p. we will begin sifting through the evidence.'

'Don't forget the poker players,' said Evan.

'And your missing persons case,' said Appleby.

'Oh that,' said Mike. 'We should have that wrapped up by Monday.'

'Are you telling me that you've found him?' said an incredulous Chief Constable.

'Won't be long now,' said Mike, warming to his story.

'I can't believe it,' said Fowler, 'it's not possible.

'Everything's possible,' said Evan

'Can we get on with it then?' said Mike.

'I will see you later,' said the Chief Constable.

Mike nodded and left together with Evan.

They drove back in their separate cars. Mike in his Merc, Evan in his Rover. It was eight o'clock when they sat down for a coffee and smoke. Mike's first of the day. He would give up soon.

'So now we are on the Morton's case,' said Amber, 'thank God because I've a bit of surprising news. Dominic Labin is the baby's father.'

'Shit,' said Mike.

'Where the hell does that leave us?' said Evan. 'And we told Short that we've solved the case as such.'

'Has anyone called Charlie in?' said Mike.

'Yes,' said Amber, 'he's on his way.'

'First things first,' said Mike.

'What's that then?' said Evan.

'Find out what exactly Alex Symonds was told, word for word. He might have taped it. Where did the call originate, age of caller, and any other thing of use,' said Mike.

'You've missed the main point Mike,' said Amber.

'Have I?' said Mike.

'Yes Mike, why does this person insist on you and Evan leading the case? Does he want to make you look like fools, does he know either or both of you, have you wronged him in some way?' said Amber.

'How about, does he expect more publicity?' said Evan. 'We've been in the papers for one reason or another lately. We're very high profile.'

'If we're doing *how abouts*,' said Mike, 'how about it being the Chessman's ghost or his long-lost brother trying to exact revenge of a kind on us?'

'That's weird,' said Charlie, who had just walked in ahead of the Chief Constable.

Mike and Evan stood up; both were smoking. She indicated with a flapping of her right hand in an up and down motion for them to sit. Both did, still smoking.

'Is this still part of the house, Mrs Gilberts?'

'Yes Chief Constable Short,' Amber replied.

'And the stupid sign outside?'

'Part of the house, makes it more homely,' said Amber.

'And this?' she said pointing to the blackboard.

Amber shrugged. 'It's a blackboard, Chief Constable Short, and I'm not offended in any way.'

'I know what a blackboard is, Mrs Gilberts. I'm talking about what's written on it. Specifically these two words here…' She pointed to the words *Starlight Club*.

'Oh that, part of our inquiries into the mispers case, it's a gay establishment. Mr White and I have visited at least a dozen times. Charlie, that is Mr White, takes his camera and we take loads of pictures.'

'I think they are doing drugs through the club in a big way,' said Mike.

The Chief's heart accelerated. She felt nauseous and dizzy. She turned away from the group, her face had turned colour; somehow she kept control.

'Are you all right Chief Constable Short? Would you like a glass of water?' said Evan.

It took a while for the Chief to speak. First she had to get her composure back.

'Yes, I'm fine thank you. At Central you were saying that you're near closure on the mispers case. By the way, congratulations on the other one, that was a turn-up for the books.'

'I bet it was,' said Mike.

'Detective Inspector Karetzi, I've suspended you once, don't push your luck I won't hesitate to do so again.'

'I have no quarrel with you Chief Constable, no axe to grind, but you really must get off my back. For three months you leave us doing nothing. You try to force my colleagues to resign, when things don't go the way you want. You give us an unsolvable missing person's case, which we will have closed within a week, not the seventy weeks the others had, just a week and now you threaten me with suspension. What the fuck is your problem, Chief? You want my resignation, I'll give it to you before you leave. However, I would think carefully about making your wishes come true. Things don't turn out the way you expect. Whilst I'm on the subject, we need one of the new cars—police before civilians I say.'

'You are rambling on. You're digging a grave for yourself, Detective. You're acting like a school kid having a tantrum.'

The bell rang. 'It's Symonds,' said Evan.

'Well, let him in,' said Amber.

Mike stood face-to-face with the Chief Constable. 'Decision time, Chief, suspension, resignation, both or harmony, which I translate as letting us get on with the job, where we have priority as Specials to use whatever means we can get.'

Alex Symonds heard it all. Mike, having said it all, lit up another cigarette and blew the smoke towards the ceiling. He watched as it drifted and dispersed. The Chief Constable sat down. Amber poured her a cup of coffee and added milk. Amber decided that anyone that skinny didn't use sugar, so offered none.

'Right Alex, I'm off in half an hour to play football,' said Mike. 'I want to know word for word your conversation with our informant.'

'Look, I'll recall it best I can,' said Alex.

'No you won't,' said Mike, 'you let us listen to the tape.'

'The tape Mike? I've no idea.'

'Give us a break Alex, don't waste time. I know you've got a tape, you record everything.'

'It's private. I can tell you what's on it but otherwise I'm breaking confidence.'

'Alex, since the Chessman business, we've built up a rapport. We're friends working on the same side. Do you really want to withhold evidence and ruin any titbits that we could throw your way in the future?' said Mike.

Alex delved into his pocket and threw a tape onto the table.

'Thank you,' said Evan.

Amber played it back and forth half a dozen times before handing it back to Alex.

'Your comments first Alex. You must have thought about it,' said Amber.

'I have. The call originated from a Cardiff phone box. The caller didn't try too hard to disguise his voice. I would say he is over sixty-five years of age and his description of the crime scene was second-hand. He didn't give me the precise location, therefore I must deduce that he is not our killer, just someone who has a peripheral role. I don't think he is the mastermind—he seems a little soft in the head if you know what I mean.'

'So he rang for a reason,' said Charlie. 'Firstly, he had to get your attention Alex. This he did by giving you the location but his main purpose was to get Mike and Evan on the case, hence the threats of more dead bodies.'

'He's after publicity. Why ring me? The person to ring is the Chief Constable. My problem is why he wants publicity—he or they have made no demands and we have six bodies,' said Alex.

'This part, where you ask him who's calling and he answers *Yesterday's Man,* what's that all about, Alex?'

'For the last two hours I've been through back issues of the paper, nothing on *Yesterday's Man*,' said Alex.

'Is that some kind of clue?' said the Chief.

'God knows; okay, let's say he's old, say seventy. He's had his better days, maybe something there,' said Evan.

'There was this bloke Andrews, Chris Andrews, he had a big record but in the early sixties, 63 or 4 I think, that was called *Yesterday's Man* or was it *Yesterday Man*?' said Charlie.

'Interesting Charlie, but I don't think that will help much,' said Evan.

'I guess not,' said Charlie, 'thought it worth a mention.'

'He's brought Morton's to breaking point,' said Alex. 'They've closed the main office in Cardiff. The other two are struggling. Staff have been sacked. As for Fenwick's they're on the ropes, just two left of the family. Louis the father and Lancelot the son.'

'You say he, but it's they, two maybe three of them. What do they want? Not money,' said Mike.

'Could it be father and sons or two brothers and one son, or three brothers?' said Charlie.

'There could be a woman involved,' said the Chief.

'Maybe,' said Amber.

'Possible,' said Evan.

'Look,' said Mike. 'I've got to run. Game kicks off in twenty minutes.'

The Chief Constable walked to the door with Mike. 'If you're ever rude or sarcastic with me again Detective, I'll have your badge and the only game of football you'll be playing in will be in the prison yard against other low-lifes.'

'Chief, I understand where you're coming from, please don't forget the car. Miss Aston won't mind, of that I'm sure,' and with that he walked out. Again, Alex Symonds caught the conversation.

On returning to his office, Alex called Brian in London. He told him everything. Brian told him that the voice profiling of the tape had tendered a certain amount of information. One: the age of the caller was between sixty and seventy. Two: the caller was not highly educated. Three: he probably had worked with his hands, not behind a desk. Four: the accent was of a man probably not born in Wales, but of having lived there for a long time, most of his life. Five: The accent was a Cardiff area accent. Six: Alex's cheque was in the post.

'So Brian, what news from our man in Cardiff?' said the Director. Brian told him: 'I told you that the new Chief Constable would come unstuck with that Ruski boyo. I'll bet you anything he's onto her sexual tendencies and has already got photos. It's only a matter of time; she's going to run into a big storm with those boys. I still wish they worked for us.'

'Anything you want me to do about the Morton business, Mr Director?' said Brian.

'Not of any interest to us, Brian, but I wouldn't worry—Karetzi and Jones will get them.'
'Can I send them the voice profile Sir?'
'Yes, why not. It's an interesting puzzle, keep me up to date on it, Brian.'
'Goodnight Mr Director.'
'Goodnight Brian.'

With results elsewhere going the Casuals' way, the draw was enough to keep them up. The team celebrated in the local Bear Inn from four until they were thrown out at nearly eleven o'clock by which time only five of the twenty-three players and management were still standing upright. Of these five Toby and Mike were still coherent enough to have a meaningful conversation. They talked football, football and Dorothea. Fiona picked them up and got them home.

Sunday morning and Mike just couldn't move. Apart from his head, which was spinning like a top, his body ached; his muscles were hurting and his hands still trembling. Three double espressos didn't help, nor did the large malt. There was no way he could retrieve his car and drive to Penarth to take his mother Alice to the cemetery. He couldn't even muster up enough energy or for that matter enthusiasm to go and buy his half a dozen Sunday papers.

He wanted a bacon sandwich but didn't feel like making it, so he settled for a piece of toast, which somehow he managed to burn. He opened the doors of the balcony. The cold wind and rain hit him hard, so he moved back to his chair and just sat there, day dreaming. He thought of Dorothea, he thought of the strawberry blonde, he thought of his late father, of his fight with the Chessman. He thought a lot and was nearly asleep when the phone rang.

It was his mother Alice. He told her he wasn't well and couldn't come. His mother said she'd come down after the cemetery and make him something to eat. He managed to fob her off; he really wasn't up to making the bed and Hoovering before she came.

Toby rang next to see if he was still alive; Toby sounded worse than him.

Four hours and two cold showers later, Mike was ready to face the world but first he needed something to eat. Sunday was a bastard of a day for finding something to eat at lunchtime. Everything was geared for families. The carvery was king on Sunday, even in most pubs. Nevertheless, he needed something more substantial than burnt toast so he made the effort and ventured out.

It was days like these that he wished he had a more stable relationship. He walked briskly and as if on automatic pilot arrived outside the office. He let himself in; he could smell food; he couldn't quite distinguish what it was.

'You okay Mike? You look like you've been in through the wringer, you're soaking. I suppose you overdid the partying last night?' said Amber, taking Mike's jacket and handing him a tea towel.

'You don't miss a trick, Amber. I've always said you're a better detective than me.'

'Well it doesn't take a Holmes to see that you've walked here in the rain and that you didn't drive because you're still probably drunk and I bet you haven't eaten, just black coffee.'

'Spot on Amber. Can you now tell me what the score was? I've forgotten.'

'Well you certainly scored a few against Short, Mike.'

'I did, but I have a feeling that a few might have been home goals, Amber. We will see in the near future no doubt.'

'What do you mean, home goals, Mike?'

'When you score against your own team.'

'I don't think so, Mike. Now do you fancy a little duck?'

'You did say duck, didn't you, Amber? My hearing's not too good this morning.'

Amber laughed. 'Here, drink this, rum is good for you.'

'Thanks Amber, but I'm not sure anything liquid is good for me today.'

'Drink it Mike, we will eat soon and then I'll get you a taxi to get you home. You need to relax.'

By the time Mike got back home he was feeling much better. He had his papers; he could now take it easy. After about forty minutes Symonds was on the phone. Morton's Estate Agents' offices in Dinas Powys was ablaze. Fire fighters were on the scene trying to get the fire under control. As far as he knew nobody was in the building, all staff had been accounted for.

Amber rang within a minute of Mike replacing the receiver. She'd rung Evan who was on his way to the fire, as was Charlie. Mike called a cab and arrived a few minutes after Evan and Charlie. D.I. Foster, together with two uniforms, were keeping back the onlookers. The fire was now under control. The Chief Fireman was leaning on the fire engine, walkie-talkie in hand. For some reason, it seemed the right time for Mike to light up his first cigarette of that day. A passing fireman gave him a dirty look. Mike gave him an even dirtier one.

Charlie saw Mike and came over to him. 'Hi Mike,' he said.

'Hi Charlie, been here long?' Mike asked.

'Long enough to know that the fire started in two places simultaneously,' said Charlie.

'Arson,' said Mike. 'Have you got a camera with you Charlie?'

'No Mike, but Alex's boys have. He's over there. See him?' said Charlie.

'Right, I see him, let's have a word with him Charlie.'

'Hi Alex, thanks for ringing. I see you've got a photographer down here,' said Mike.

'Yes, Jimbo's a top man,' said Alex.

'Can you call him over, Alex? I need a word with both of you.'

'Sure Mike,' said Alex, whistling to get Jimbo's attention.

'Now, if you can help me out here, whatever the cost, we will reimburse you. I need photos of all the crowd, lots of them; and I need photos of every vehicle within two hundred yards of here.'

'Impossible mate,' said Jimbo.

'Do you have another camera matey?' said Mike. 'Yes? Well, give it to Charlie, that's this bloke, that way we will halve the time. Charlie can do the cars, you the crowd.'

'No way my friend,' said Jimbo.

'Friend I am at this moment Jimbo, and it's best I remain one,' said Mike.

'Beach Boys '68, Arrival a few years later, both sang Friends,' said Charlie.

'Do it Jim,' said Alex.

'But Alex,' said Jim, wondering what the guy with the white hair was talking about.

'Just do it now before they disperse,' said Alex, who had just realised that the white haired guy was the one on the phone. It was the cockney accent that gave him away.

'On your head be it Alex,' said sulky Jimbo.

'Thanks Alex, we will bear all the costs,' said Mike.

Mike and Alex moved to where the Chief Honcho was speaking with Evan and Foster.

'I understand it's Arson,' said Mike.

'Who are you?' said the fireman chief.

Mike showed him his warrant card.

'Another one,' said the fireman.

'Yep,' said Mike, 'another one. Now will you confirm it's arson?'

'Not until we have done our investigations,' said the fireman. 'It would be amiss of me to speculate.'

'When will you be able to confirm that it was Arson?' said Mike.

'We will be in a position to identify the cause within two or three days after the building is secured and safe for us to begin our investigation,' said the fireman.

'Can you tell me when you expect to start this investigation?' said Mike.

'Tomorrow around noon,' said the fireman. 'Look, D.I. Karetzi, that's the correct pronunciation isn't it?'

'Yes,' said Mike.

'It's not a big deal. No one was injured, no stock involved. Could be just an accident. An electrical malfunction or one of the computers or electrical system. I'm not ruling out anything.'

'But I am,' said Mike, 'everything except arson; a fire doesn't start in two different places at the same time, does it?'

'Who told you that?' said the fireman.

Mike didn't answer but just walked away to find Charlie. Evan was hot on his heels. They found Charlie. He had finished.

'How many, Charlie?' said Mike.

'Eighty-nine,' Charlie replied.

'Get Alex and Jimbo, if he's finished, and get back to 4'I's. Evan and I will meet you there. If you have any problem, tell Jimbo that we will have some money for him.'

'Okay Mike, see you anon.'

'Evan, can you give me a lift to my car if it's still there and I'll follow you to the office?'

Evan drove to where Mike had left the car, which fortunately still had four wheels—it wasn't the best of areas—and then took off for the office.

Mike beat him with a minute to spare. Evan wasn't surprised. Mike was a very dangerous driver in his view.

'So we are all gathered together on a Sunday night to discuss today's events,' said Alex sarcastically.

'I'm here to collect some cash,' said Jimbo, 'and then I'm gone like dust.'

'Have we got any petty cash Amber, for Mr Dust here?'

Amber opened a desk drawer and produced forty pounds.

'Is that it?' said Jim.

Amber took out another twenty. Jimbo didn't move. Another twenty and he was gone. Amber started processing the photos, nearly two hundred in all.

'Did I tell you that I have had some more thoughts on our mysterious caller?' said Alex.

'No, you didn't,' said Evan.

'Well, apart from being old, say seventy, he's got a mild Cardiff accent. I would say he's not originally from these parts. I would also hazard a guess that he is not or was not a white collar worker, he probably was or is a tradesman of some sort.'

'That's very observant of you,' said Evan.

'It's my job,' said Alex, 'to be observant.'

Mike looked at Alex in a way that made Alex feel uncomfortable but didn't comment. Alex was relieved. Mike was very astute normally. Today though he seemed to be labouring a little. Mike wasn't up to speed. He needed to relax. Alex was up to something but Mike didn't have the time or inclination to delve any further.

'That reminds me,' Evan said. 'Did D.I. Foster bring us all the documentation and files on the Morton cases?'

'He did. We found nothing out of the usual,' said Amber.

'I've got to get home,' said Mike. 'I'm no use to anyone here. I just can't concentrate.'

'It's Sunday. Edna and Jasmine have been home nearly a day and I've hardly seen them,' said Evan. 'Tomorrow's another day.'

Alex was first to leave, followed by Mike and Evan. Charlie stayed another five minutes and had a cup of tea with Amber before packing up and leaving. Amber was left to her own devices. Food had literally taken a back burner but Amber would make up for it later.

'Why couldn't we watch the fire, David?'

'Because Patrick, never mind, we couldn't. You can see it on TV later.'

'Have you changed the tyres yet?' asked David.

'Just the front ones, like you said,' said Patrick.

'That will do. Where are the old ones Patrick?'

'In our garage, David.'

'Good,' said David, 'I'm going for a walk. I need to do some thinking.'

David had walked near-on one and a half miles before he stopped. He had made a decision. There would be only one more death, enough was enough. Walter had to go—he wouldn't share this with his brother Patrick. He would have to do it alone but first he needed to check out Walter's house, make sure the Will was in order and that there was no incriminating evidence tying Walter, Patrick or himself to the murders.

'What part of *no car* can't you understand Brenda?'
'What part of *no car, no us* can't you understand Muriel?'
'You're acting like a baby, Bren.'
'And you're acting like my mother, Muriel.'
'Don't you understand that they probably have pictures of us in the club! They could ruin my career and then where would we be? Can you tell me that, Brenda? Of course you can't, all you can think of is the car. For Christ's sake, think like a grown-up. I warned you about going out so much. I've hardly been in the job a minute and all you care about is a fucking car.'
'Muriel, it's not the car and you know it. It's you, pushing people, using your rank. You pushed that bloody detective too far. You were warned he was smart and dangerous. The last Chief told you, that guy from MI5, that Lord Henry; you tried to crush him to prove to yourself that you could break him. Muriel, the guy's a fucking hero. He doesn't care a shit. He's breaking you and you're giving in like a little pathetic puppy.'
'Are you saying that you fancy him, Brenda?'
'I don't know him, Muriel. All I know is that he will win, because you're not strong enough to deal with him. You promised me the car, so go get him. It's the car or us. What's it to be?'
'I'll get you a car, Brenda.'
'I want the BMW, the red one, the one you agreed that I should have.'
'I said I would deal with it, Brenda, I will get him in tomorrow, first thing. Him and his partner, who seems more logical.'

Mike poured himself a Macallans and no water—you drink a good malt neat. He sat and picked up a newspaper. His mobile rang.

It was Evan. After finishing, he got up and wrote a letter. He dated it and included the time of 0800 hours for the following morning. He found an envelope and put it in. He didn't bother to address it.

The Chief Constable had her offices in a separate building to the station. Mike and Evan arrived five minutes early. Evan made sure of that. They waited in the first office, which doubled up as a waiting room. A sergeant, two uniforms and a civilian were seated at desks. Two were working computers, the Sarge and the civilian going through paperwork. The phone rang and the civilian answered it. He then got up and asked Mike and Evan to follow.

They passed through another office with another two civilians and then into another room where the Chief's private secretary took over and asked them to wait whilst she ascertained that the Chief was free. Obviously she was. Evan went in first, Mike followed. Prior to entering, he turned to the PA and said, 'Thank you Brenda.'

The Chief didn't bother to stand—that was a bad sign. She didn't bother to wish a 'Good morning' either, another bad sign. Evan said 'Good morning' but Mike didn't.

They stood until the Chief said that they could sit. Two chairs were provided on their side of a massive oak desk.

'This is off the record for now,' she said. Mike pulled out the letter he had written the previous evening and placed it in front of him. The Chief eyed the envelope with suspicion but didn't comment on it.

The Chief swivelled her chair to a position where she could see more of Evan than of Mike. She crossed her legs and folded her arms. Mike turned his chair so that he could see her full in the face.

'Do you know why you are here, Detectives?'

'No,' said Mike, 'mislaid my crystal ball.'

'You're here because I've had numerous complaints about your general behaviour.'

'Who has been complaining?' said Evan.

'Too many to ignore,' said the Chief.

'Have these people filled in complaint forms, Chief Constable?' said Evan.

'Not yet,' said the Chief.

'Well, that will give us a couple of months breathing time,' said Mike.

'Give it a break Detective. This is serious and you're not talking to one of your low-life friends.'

'That's true Chief, I can't classify you as a friend.'

'You just won't give yourself a break, will you Detective?'

Mike didn't answer.

'Can you tell us what you want, Chief Constable Short?' said Evan.

'I want you to stop behaving like comic book detectives. And start doing your job by the book.'

'We have achieved results,' said Evan

'You've been lucky and had a lot of top class help and backing, but you've ruffled too many feathers and that is going to stop. As from this moment, you will go through me. If you want to interview someone, you first inform me. If you want to go somewhere, through me. If you want to go to the toilet, through me. If you want to buy a pencil, you do it through me. Are you getting the picture of how we will be working together in the future? If I say "sit", you sit. If I say "stand", you stand. You take your orders directly from me and don't question them. Is that plain enough English for you?'

'Excuse me, Chief Constable Short, but apart from Brenda listening at the door, is this still an off-the-record conversation?'

The Chief glanced at the door. This wasn't getting any easier.

'What happens if we make a mistake or can't follow your particular directives?' said Evan.

'Then I will be forced to disband your unit and your careers will come to an abrupt end,' said the Chief, swinging her chair back to its original position and unfolding her arms.

'Have either of you anything to say?' said the Chief.

'I do,' said Evan. 'I think you are treating some good people like dirt under your feet, and I for one cannot work under these ridiculous rules.'

'You will get used to doing things my way, the correct way, D.I. Jones.'

'Are you telling us we cannot have the new car?' said Mike.

'You're not even getting the old one back, never mind a replacement. And I want the corporate credit cards back, and that includes Mrs Gilbert's. No more perks for you two, and of course don't forget the mobile phones.' The Chief leant back on her chair. She felt good. She would crush the little bastards. She was all-powerful and the two in front of her knew it.

'The Accounts Department will of course go through your expenses with a fine toothcomb. I'm positive they will find a lot of discrepancies. One more thing: get rid of our ex-jailbird Mr White and find someone more suitable for the post. I suggest we give him two weeks' severance pay. He can leave on your return.'

Short couldn't help herself. She wanted to hurt them, especially Karetzi, the male chauvinist pig. 'You see Detectives, I hold all the aces.'

Evan squirmed. She did indeed seem to have covered everything. He would write up his resignation on their return to 4,I's but he was worried about Mike, who was very quiet. Maybe he was lost for words; too stunned to speak.

It looked as if the interview or whatever it was had come to an end. Evan started to rise until a restraining hand pulled him back down into his chair.

'I think we are finished,' said the Chief, noticing that Mike had pulled Evan back into a sitting position.

'You are,' said Mike.

'Are you addressing me, D.I. Karetzi?'

'I am, and I said you are.'

'You are Detective?'

'Yes you are finished—your career will disappear just like one of my cigarettes.'

'I know they call you crazy Detective, but you're talking in riddles.'

'You and your PA. It's a perfect description for Brenda, Personal Assistant. Might be lovers. We as men of the world find it quite acceptable but would the readers of various newspapers be so open-minded? Would they like to see pictures of their Chief Constable canoodling in a drug-infested gay club? Would they wish to read that the so-called assistant is driving around in a car provided by the public? Would they understand that their Chief Constable is twice the assistant's age and pushed through the necessary paperwork for this car, whilst the detectives in charge of the area's biggest case were turned down and resigned because their hands were tied every which way during which time our killer wipes out a whole family one by one? Will the readers understand why the Chief Constable who is provided with a car and driver needs another two cars?

'Will all this manage to make today's *Chronicle* and *Echo* and tomorrow's *Sun* and *Mirror*?

'Now Chief, you might say to me, proof and I would say I wouldn't be mouthing off in the Chief's office if I didn't have the documentation and the tape that's running in my pocket. No Chief, that's my resignation.' Mike pushed over the letter. 'The date's today's date. The time 08.00. Evan will testify that I gave it to you on entry. Everything I have said is as a civilian to a police person, to use the correct terminology. Go ahead, read it. Your four aces aren't good enough where the jokers are wild.'

'You bastard, you fucking bastard!' the Chief said, a few tears breaking through her hard made up face.

'I am, Chief, I'm a crazy bastard.' Mike got up and walked to the door. He opened it and looked at Brenda. 'Miss Aston, would you please take this down: *I will not be getting a new car.* Write it twice, no, three times. I want you to understand it. I've explained the car position to Miss Aston. I think she's taking it rather well under the circumstances, Chief.'

The Chief Constable ripped up the envelope containing Mike's resignation into four pieces. Mike leant over, scooped them up and put them in his pocket. The Chief looked at him. Mike shrugged. 'Second nature to me Chief, I see evidence and I take it. You never know when you have to prove something. It's what we detectives do.'

Evan had now come to life again. 'Where do we stand, Chief?' He too had dropped the 'Constable Short.' 'Is it back to work for us or is it Symonds's place of work; there is a lot going on.

The Chief had recovered; she didn't make Chief without a problem or two. 'Tea or coffee, detective?'

'Coffee would be nice Chief Constable.' Evan had now added the 'Constable.' The 'Short' he wasn't ready for yet.

The coffee came. The Chief's change of attitude didn't extend to ashtrays and Mike wasn't going to push his luck.

'This is going to be difficult, detectives. I've been hasty and a little stupid. You two are my best detectives. I've read your files; they are very impressive. You do get results, maybe by cutting corners or by luck. Possibly, because of your unorthodox methods, but you both have a problem with authority. Do we agree on that?'

'If authority and red tape gets in the way or holds up our investigation, then yes, I would agree we have a problem,' said Evan.

'But on the other hand, we can get on with authority if they are being reasonable and try to understand what we're about,' said Mike.

'Will we have any future problems? I mean, are we going to have any more of these set-to's, gentlemen?' said the Chief Constable.

'No Chief. May I make a small suggestion?'

'Go ahead, Evan.'

'Why not give our old car to your PA? It's only a year older than the ones coming up in a week or two. It's a good car, low mileage, nice colour. Mechanically perfect. Just the radiator and a wing and a bumper to fix. It should be nearly ready by now.'

'That's a good idea, Evan, and of course you will have the new one.'

'That's the idea, Chief, we need a car badly. You need not lose face, Miss Aston wants a good car, everybody is happy.'

'That's a good solution Evan, thank you,' said the Chief.

'Also Chief, with regards to our credit cards, I mean the corporate cards, of course the department can only accept bona fide payments whatever's connected to the job. That's what we want reimbursed. No more, no less; no personal stuff,' said Evan.

'That won't be a problem,' said the Chief.

'As for the mobiles,' said Mike, 'I think we were on our fifth or sixth each, Chief. We were being bugged by MI5 or MI6 or the Tangent people, possibly all three so we only use Pay as You Go and change them continuously.'

'How did you know you were being bugged?' said the Chief.

'We have our own ways,' said Mike. 'That's why we have some strange expenses that you might have to turn a blind eye to, Chief.'

'Mr White?' said the Chief.

'Chief, he's okay. He does things we can't do or be seen to be doing. He's indispensable, as is Amber. Her grocery bills are high. You're going to have to turn another blind eye to them but you must consider that sometimes we're doing sixty, seventy hours in the office a week and don't have time to go out and eat or smoke.'

'Okay Mike, I hear you, but I'm beginning to get a little worried.'

'Why?' said Mike.

'Because I'm getting to like you two.' Everyone laughed.

'Evan,' said Mike, pointing to Evan's briefcase.

Evan opened up his case and took out a large manila envelope and passed it to the Chief.

'Photos and negatives from the Starlight Club,' said Mike.

'Thank you,' said the Chief.

'We don't have a problem with authority, we have a problem with red tape when coupled with misused authority,' said Evan.

'We must be allowed to be Detectives and use our initiatives to solve cases without all the hassle we seem to be getting from our own,' said Mike.

'Do you mean people like me?' said the Chief.

'No, Mike didn't mean you, as such Chief,' said Evan.

'Yes I did,' said Mike.

'Okay, let's start again,' said the Chief.

'Of course Chief. Amber makes up the reports every Friday and posts them to your office on a Saturday. She doesn't trust faxes or emails. You will know what's going on. Whilst we're on the subject, can we talk about the mispers case?' said Evan.

'Fine, I'm all ears,' said the Chief.

Jason Conley went missing about fifteen months ago. His older sister Julie married a month later a Dominic Labin. They have a daughter Karen who is about ten months old,' said Evan.

'Who is the father?' asked the Chief.

'Dominic is,' said Mike.

'I'm not following you,' said the Chief. 'Are you sure about this Dominic being the father?'

'Positive,' said Mike.

'How, without DNA samples?' said the Chief.

'We took samples from all four, all four, well three anyway. Dominic, Julie and Karen.'

'Covertly, Evan?'

'Yes Chief, without their knowledge and therein lies our problem, Chief.'

'And the problem is?' said the Chief.

'Well,' Evan said, 'it's our contention that prior to Jason's disappearance, he was regularly, over a period of three, four months, sleeping with his sister. Every Saturday afternoon, we think. She fell pregnant but was also sleeping on and off with her boyfriend Dominic. For one reason or another, she thought it was her brother's and to avoid bringing shame on her family, she helped Jason disappear and then quickly married Dominic.

'Now when the baby is born it looks just like the mother, nothing at all like this Dominic who's got Mediterranean blood running through his veins. So, now that confirms Julie's fears that the father is her brother. We know different of course but can't tell her. We think she knows where her brother is and that they are in constant communication. That's about it.'

'You can't get her phone or mobile records, you can't interfere with her mail and we don't have the manpower to follow her. Is that a summary of the situation?' said the Chief.

'It's easier than that,' said Mike. 'She wouldn't use her land phone, her husband would check the bills. The same with the mail, too risky. Her husband could easily pick up the mail. That leaves her mobile, which we could arrange to get hold of but it might not show anything. It's hard to get info from one of them unless it's a dial-a-friend type of entry or she might even use a phone box. It's a nightmare.'

'My advice to you is drop the case,' said the Chief. 'This Morton's thing is big. I've entrusted the whole thing over to Nelson, so deal with it in any way you feel like. I don't care one way or the other. My career is in your hands.'

'We will do our best, as always,' Mike said. 'It's important that we remain Special Detectives, it gives us more clout and lets us into more places. We need some kind of message to all our stations, stating that this case holds prevalence until further notice.'

'Count it as done. Go get them boys; you're my dogs of war,' said the Chief, 'and thanks for these,' she said holding up the manila envelope.

On the way out, they found Brenda crying softly into a small handkerchief.

'I think the Chief requires your presence, Miss Aston. Everything is sorted out, no need for tears,' said Mike.

It was raining. Evan unfurled his umbrella. It was only twenty yards to Mike's car.

'Where you going Mike? This isn't the way to 4,I's,' said Evan.

'We're going to pay Julie one last visit,' said Mike.

'And what are we going to say, Mike?'

'I've no idea Ev, not one.'


'Not you two again. What is it this time, collecting for the Policeman's Ball?'

'No Mrs Labin, we need a word. It's about your brother. Do you wish to talk here or down at the station?' said Evan

'Come in, don't make too much noise,' Julia said. 'The baby's just gone off to sleep. Please sit down and tell me what you want.'

'We have reason to believe that you know the whereabouts of your brother Jason and we also believe that you are in regular contact with him,' said Mike.

Evan followed this up without delay: 'Now before you answer us we would like you to know the following fact: Dominic your husband is Karen's biological father, one hundred per cent, not ninety-nine per cent but one hundred per cent. We cannot tell you how we came to have this information. Suffice it to know that we have proof and that it would be very simple for you to check this out for yourself.'

'Of course he's the father!' said Julia. 'Why would I want to check it out and under what law can you obtain information on me and my family?' She added: 'I will sue you for everything.'

'I see,' said Mike, opening up his phone and calling Amber. Charlie answered.

'Charlie, Mike here. I want a search warrant for the Labin residence, the Conley residence, any outbuildings, and when you get that, get two sniffer dogs with handlers and four uniforms, pronto.'

Mike got up, as did Evan. 'I'm sorry to have bothered you. I suggest that you take the baby out for a stroll when the team gets here. It might be a bit traumatic for her and you.'

'Please Detectives, don't go! I can see the DNA thing myself. I mean, will I understand it?'

'Yes you can, but you would see it as evidence in court if you try to sue,' said Evan.

'Can you stop this search warrant thing?'

'We could, but it will have to be done sometime,' said Mike.

'Please stop it and let me see the DNA results. Then I might be able to help you.'

Mike dialled again and again Charlie answered it.

'Forget the warrant and dogs. Get the DNA results from Amber for the Labins and bring them to their address. Thanks Charlie,' Mike said.

Within twenty minutes, Charlie was knocking on the door. Julia looked and looked. Her hands were trembling when she put them down. She breathed a massive sigh of relief before she started sobbing. Charlie retrieved the results. Mike offered her a cigarette. She took it even though it was non-filter. He lit it for her and she inhaled deeply.

'Before you say anything Julia, let me make our position clear,' Mike said. 'We are only interested in solving your brother Jason's disappearance. We only wish to find out that no harm has come to him and that he's okay. Whether or not he wishes to speak to his family is his business; he can do as he pleases, it's nothing to do with us. Do you understand, Julia, we are only involved up to the time that we know he's okay. We are not in any way interested in where or what he is doing. We must by law tell your parents that he is alive but we cannot give them any further information.'

'And we are in no way interested to know why he ran away,' Evan added. 'Do you follow what we are saying, Julia?'

'My husband doesn't know I'm in contact with him. Nobody does. I'll get him on his phone. I usually can around this time of day. Jason, is that you? Good, are you well? Good. I'm going to ring you in about two minutes, okay? I've someone at the door—bye for now. Look, I'm going outside in the back to call him. I need to tell him some private things before you speak to him.'

'That's fine Julia. Call us when you've finished,' said Evan.

'What's she going to say to him?' said Charlie.

'She's going to tell him that the baby is not his and that he should make the necessary arrangements to get in contact with the parents.'

A few minutes passed. Julia came in, phone in hand and gave it to Evan.

'Hello, I'm D.I. Evan Jones of the South Wales Police Force Missing Persons Unit. I'd like to ask you some questions to ascertain that I am speaking to the correct person. Full name, address before you left, date of birth, parents' names, schools attended, date that you last attended school, favourite football club.'

As Jason answered, Evan repeated the answers out aloud. Mike checked them with Amber on his phone.

'Thank you Jason. That's it for us—we are now closing the file. Good luck to you. I'll pass you on to your sister now.'

After Julia had finished, she thanked them and led them to the front door where she said goodbye. She was crying when they left. Mike was driving so Evan called the Chief and left a message: 'Jason Conley located alive and well. Case closed.'

'I think we called it right,' said Mike.

'We did. For all that time they thought that Jason was the father, like we did at one stage. Anyway, another case solved and we're down to doing something about this Yesterday's Man,' said Evan.

'Where the hell do we start?' said Evan.

'At the fire,' said Mike, turning around the car and heading for the burnt-out shell of the former Morton's Estate Agents.

A Derrick Soames was the fire investigating officer. He was all dressed up in protective clothing and refused entry to Mike and Evan.

'Could you at least let us see the photos that have been taken?' said Evan. He could, later on that day.

'Was it deliberate?' asked Evan.

'Yes, it's arson all right. The seat of the fire, that is the origin, was at two separate points: near the front door and through a window at the rear. I would say they used an accelerant, probably petrol, what I would classify as a Class B fire but then we have all these common materials in an office—wooden desks, paper etc., which of course is classified as a Class A.'

'Are you positive about the petrol—it couldn't be something else?'

'No, from pictures, when it was burning we had yellow flames creating black smoke, indicating that an accelerant such as petrol, acetone—that is, a liquid solvent used in the manufacture of paint, or paraffin.'

'I see,' said Evan. 'What about the paper and desks?'

'Yellowish red flames, greyish brown smoke,' replied Mr Soames.

'These fires common? I mean, what type of person starts these fires?' said Mike.

'More common than you think here in the UK," said Soames. "We have over 300 incidents daily. It's considered a white collar crime. Arsonists set fire for financial gain, usually to collect on insurance or to destroy company records or documentation.'

'And in this case, Mr Soames, an estate agency in the middle of a town—where is the financial gain there?' said Mike.

'Strange that. I'm based locally; the Morton murders have been headline news. Are you by any chance the Detectives dealing with the case?' Mike and Evan both nodded. 'Right, well, this wasn't done for financial gain by either Morton's or a competitor; after all, Morton's is finished as such. I would say off the record of course, that this is the work of somebody who has a completely different agenda.'

'What do you mean Mr Soames?' asked Mike.

'In my opinion, whoever the perpetrators are, they want to completely break and humiliate Morton's for some perverse reason and they want the whole world to see them fall from their lofty position,' Soames said.

'Do these arsonists like to hang around and watch their handiwork, Mr Soames?'

'In general yes, but in this case I would say no. They will get their pleasure and kicks not from the fire but what damage the fire will do to the Morton's empire,' said Soames.

'Revenge. Could that be the motive?' asked Evan.

'Probably,' said Soames. 'The clues are hidden somewhere in the distant past.'

'Yesterday's Man,' mumbled Mike.

'What's that?' asked Soames.

'Nothing,' said Mike.

'Thanks for your insight,' said Evan. 'Please don't forget the photos, here's the address.' He handed Soames a card.

'That was interesting,' said Evan.

'Very. I think we need to have a look around the head office and then sometime soon have a word with Mr Louis Morton and Mr Lancelot Morton,' said Mike.

'Wouldn't it be funny if the Queen knighted the son? Sir Lancelot has a nice ring. Don't you think, Mike?'

'Aye it does,' said Mike. 'Somehow though I don't think it's going to happen.'

They arrived and parked outside the main Morton's Estate Agency. They waited five minutes before Charlie arrived with one of the staff who had keys. All four entered and started to have a look around. Tim the staff member followed them around until Evan told him to go and sit in the reception area, which he was reluctant to do until Evan took out his handcuffs. Then Tim scurried to the reception area and sat down.

'What we should do,' said Charlie, 'is go through every desk one at a time and see what we come up with.'

Two of the desks were locked. Charlie unlocked them. No newspaper clippings, diaries, cryptic notes. Nothing that threw any light on the murders. They did the same with the kitchen cupboards, again nothing. They got out into the small yard, just a plastic table with four chairs and a few potted plants.

Evan called Mike and Charlie over. He was in Levy's office. He pointed to a photograph that had been framed and hung on the wall. Charlie took it down. 'I think most of the victims are on this. This is Levy, this is Deena Morton, Gareth Jones, if I'm not mistaken,' said Evan. 'I assume this one, the oldest is Louis Morton.'

'Charlie, could you bring in Tim?' said Mike. 'Who are these people?' he asked. Tim told them.

'Get the photo out Charlie, I want to see who took it and the date,' said Evan.

Charlie did. No name, no date, just a number.

'Any idea when this was taken Evan?' asked Tim who shook his head but said, 'It's pretty old, I mean none of them look like that.'

'Have you got Lancelot Morton's number, Tim?' asked Mike.

'It's in the book,' said Tim.

'Well, go and get the book please Tim.'

It took quite a few rings to get Lancelot to the phone. He was most helpful. The photo was about fifteen years old, taken by the *Western Mail* as part of an advertising campaign when Morton's and Fenwick's did their first major joint venture. Mike asked a few more questions and made arrangements for them to meet the next day at nine.

'One more call to Alex,' said Mike.

'Do we need this photo?' Charlie asked.

'No Charlie, put it back in the frame and hang it up,' said Evan. 'Mike's asking Alex for a copy of the newspaper cutting; he will know someone on the *Western Mail*.'

'I can't understand why you dragged us to this crumbling terraced house in the middle of nowhere,' Lancelot said.

'Yes, what's the idea?' said Louis Morton, Lancelot's father.

'It's safe and it's the only place one can have a smoke on duty,' said Mike.

'Are you mental, Detective?'

'He's crazy Mr Morton but these are our best people, take my word for it.'

'My Christ,' said Louis, 'half my family and friends have been slaughtered and who do we get on the case? A bunch of bloody comedians.'

'Mr Morton, please forget your prejudices and concentrate on the matter in hand.'

'Which is what exactly?' said Lancelot, brushing his blond fringe away from his eyes only for it to bounce back into the same position again.

'I can see that you don't have one positive clue between the lot of you. Please tell me that I'm wrong,' said Louis.

No one spoke.

'I thought as much. Six murders and you haven't a clue!' Louis said. 'You're a sorry lot and now you want to waste our time answering inane questions.'

'With all due respect, Mr Morton, this unit has only been on the case a few days,' said the Chief Constable.

'And what about the cowboys who worked? *Worked* being the operative word, before this lot. What did they come up with? Nothing of course,' said Lancelot, brushing his fringe back for the tenth time.

'And whilst we're at it, what kind of bloody police station is this, and what kind of dress is this? Where's their uniforms. Only this one is wearing a suit and you,' he said looking at Mike, 'got a hot date, have you? We're out of here, come on Lancelot, let them play at being policemen, we've got better things to do like arrangements for more funerals.' Louis Morton stood up. Lancelot followed suit.

'I think they are leaving you till last. Mr Louis. Lancelot is next or maybe it could be Georgia, but either way they are leaving you Mr Louis till last; you're the key to this whole mess,' said Mike.

'Now you might not be too worried for yourself, Mr Louis, but Lancelot and Georgia, well, they have children, your grandchildren, so please sit down and try to act like responsible adults,' said Amber. The Morton's sat back down. The Chief was impressed.

Mike lit up. Evan packed his small clay pipe while Lancelot looked on in disgust. Evan passed the photo of the group across to Mr Louis who glanced at it and looked at Evan.

'That's old,' said Louis.

'I know,' said Evan.

'Good,' said Lancelot, 'now that that's all sorted, out can we go?'

'We have come to the conclusion that our killers are after revenge for some wrongdoing by your good selves, or what they perceive as wrongdoing,' said Mike. 'They, and I say *they* because we believe that there are at least two, want Payback. They want to see you suffer, hence the ridiculous methods of killing. They want the utmost publicity in which they can revel as they watch you disintegrate.'

'We think this goes back a long way, possibly fifteen or twenty years,' said 'Evan. So if we can cast our minds back that far, what would we have?'

'Twenty years ago I was still at Uni,' said Lancelot, 'then law school.'

'I said before that you, Mr Louis, are the key to this. It is something that you and Fenwick were both involved in, possibly also your eldest son Abrahim.'

'Nonsense, Detective, we've done thousands of deals over the years. In any market there are dissatisfied customers but dissatisfied to such an extent that they would wipe out a whole family, well, I don't see it,' said Louis. 'We keep a file, files on any disputes or correspondence with customers who have a complaint, however minor. I assume that you have been through these files, Detectives.'

'Not yet,' said Amber. 'We haven't had the time, what with the fire and the closing of another case that we had been following.'

'So you have all the facts and files that you need, yet you call us in and ask my father, who is in a state of shock, to recall events from twenty years ago. You lot really take the biscuit,' Lancelot said angrily, flicking back his hair for the umpteenth time.

'I have the name and address of a good barber, Mr Lancelot, would you like me to give you the details?' Mike said.

Lancelot stared at Mike with disdain, then shook his head from side to side.

'Do you have any financial problems, Mr Louis?' said Evan.

'No we don't. The Estate Agency only accounts for one tenth of our finances,' said Louis.

'Why is it important? Or are you thinking that we burnt down our own agency for the insurance money?' said Lancelot.

'It is important, we know the building was leased not freehold and you didn't have 'loss of earnings' cover, Lancelot. The importance of my question concerns the perpetrators who didn't know,' said Evan.

'You've lost me,' said Louis.

'Me too,' said the Chief Constable. Charlie would have agreed with the Chief and Louis but was too embarrassed to let the others know.

'Look, our perps are blinded by rage, revenge, call it what you like,' said Evan. 'They are under the assumption that they are breaking the Morton's financially, yet in reality they are hardly denting the company. They are people not in the business, not in any business I would say. It gives a profile on them: not too smart blue collar workers or at best menial white collar types.'

'And it also proves that they are not known to you as friends, competitors or move around in the same circles,' said Mike.

'That's a start,' said Louis, 'but hardly enough to get us a collar, be it a blue or white one.'

'Nice one Louis,' said Charlie, forgetting whom he was addressing.

'I mean that's clever, Mr Morton,' said Charlie who had now changed colour from white to Charlie Red. It was the first time in a month that Lancelot had seen a smile on his father's face.

'One more thing,' said Mike, 'we think that one of them is old and probably planning everything and the other or others are much younger and actually carrying out the deeds. We don't think the older guy is participating in any way. That's the part that's bugging us: what the hell is his role and why is he helping us?'

'Helping?' said Lancelot.

'Well, someone phoned us to tell us where to find Mr Levy. He called himself Yesterday's Man. We have deduced that his age is between 60 and 70. Not especially well educated, not born and bred in the area. Not much really,' said Mike.

'So do we think he's the loaf of bread?' said Charlie. Everyone turned and looked at Charlie questioningly.

'Don't take any notice of him,' said Amber. 'He sometimes speaks cockney cant or the language of the underworld as spoken by cockneys and I think loaf of bread translates to the head, the boss, the man. Have I got it right Charlie?' said Amber.

'Dead on,' replied Charlie.

'So do you, Detective Karetzi, think that the older one is the boss?' said the Chief.

'Difficult one Chief. I don't know. These people have a very peculiar relationship,' said Mike.

'They could be related; father and son or sons, grandfather and grandsons; cousins, brothers, there's lots of possible permutations,' said Evan

'What are your plans Mr Morton?' asked the Chief.

'We have a funeral to attend to tomorrow and in a week's time we as a family are leaving for a six-week break in Sicily. Everyone is going: Maria, Abraham's wife, the kids, all of us. Private plane all arranged; we cannot go on living like cooped up animals,' said Louis.

'Up until then we will maintain the round the clock security,' said the Chief.

'Will you want to see us again before we leave?' said Lancelot.

'I don't think that will be necessary,' said Mike, 'but we need to keep in contact, something might crop up.'

'That's fine, we will leave some numbers with the Chief Constable,' said Louis.

After they had gone the Chief sat and had a coffee with them. She wanted to congratulate them on the Conley case.

'We really need to make some inroads into this Morton business. Do you want more manpower, help from Scotland Yard? What can I do?' said the Chief.

'I wish there was something,' said Evan, 'this is proving harder to deal with than the Chessman case. At least we had something to work on. Here it's all guesswork, complete guesswork,' said Evan.

'Educated guesswork, Evan,' said Amber.

'Yes, but are we still in primary school, Amber?' said Mike.

'Don't be so despondent Mike,' said Charlie.

'Maybe we should have a question and answer session,' said Evan.

'I'm not up for it,' said Mike.

'Is that some sort of game?' asked the Chief.

'Well, it's kind of,' said Charlie.
'How's it played then?' asked the Chief.
'Well someone, usually Mike, asks the questions and the rest answer those questions.'
'Come on Mike, let's play,' said the Chief.
'Okay,' said Mike. 'But be warned, it usually is just a waste of time.'
'No it isn't,' said Evan, 'something always comes out of it.'

Question: 'What's the motive?' said Mike.
Answer: 'Revenge,' said Evan
Question: 'What type of revenge?'
Answer: 'For financial loss,' said Evan
Question: 'What type of financial loss?'
Answer: 'Something involving property,' said Amber
Question: 'When did this happen?'
Answer: 'Fifteen, twenty years ago,' said Amber
Question: 'Why wait for your revenge all this time?'
Answer: 'Because our man wasn't in a position to exact revenge until now,' said Charlie.
Question: 'Why not?
Answer: 'Because he wasn't physically or financially capable,' said the Chief.
Question: 'How is he now in such a position?'
Answer: 'Because he has come into some money, either won some or been left some,' said Charlie.
Question: 'He is still using help: how did recruit this help?'
Answer: 'If he came into money, he's paying someone to help,' said Evan.
Question: 'They are not professionals. I know they've made no mistakes but these are amateurs, not professionals.'
Answer: 'They could be relatives,' said Charlie.
Question: 'Why do they want the publicity?'
Answer: 'Only the instigator, that is the one who wants the revenge, wants the satisfaction of the publicity. The others are

doing this for other reasons and I would say they don't like the publicity,' said the Chief.

Question: 'Are they leaving Louis until last?'

Answer: 'Yes, because he is the head of the family, of the group. Maybe the person who actually started this whole ball rolling,' said Evan.

Question: 'Do we let it be known the Morton's are going away on holiday?'

Answer: 'I think it best not to. We can lay a trap that way,' said the Chief.

Question: 'Why did Yesterday's Man help us, and will he again?'

Answer: 'Maybe he wants us to get him so that he can tell the world why he did what he did. Maybe it means that much to him he wants everyone to know his story,' said Charlie.

Question: 'If you were the top jewel thief in the world Charlie, would you want everyone to know it was you?'

Answer: 'You mean like a Raffles? Then, yes, I would like everyone to know how clever and good I was, but I still wouldn't want to get caught.'

Question: 'Can we draw him out through the newspapers, print something that upsets him enough to make him make a false move?'

Answer: 'There could be a way, through the papers; we will need a bit of co-operation though,' said the Chief.

Mike: 'End of question time ladies and gentlemen.

'I enjoyed that,' said the Chief, 'beats doing paperwork all day long and very useful too.

'You were saying something about having an idea for the newspapers, Chief,' said Evan.

'It's only a rough idea at the moment. We think our Yesterday's Man craves the publicity, so we take this away from him, pretend that we have shifted our enquiries to a pair of known London gangsters who were seen at the scene of two of the murders. They were owed money by the Morton's for various property deals in London and came to collect, couldn't and decided to exact their own form of justice as a lesson to Mr Louis Morton who they want to force into paying up. Probably with huge amounts of interest. These two criminals have melted into the underworld but the net is closing in on them and their London bosses. It's only a matter of time,' said the Chief.

'Do we tell Alex the truth or not?' said Evan.

'The truth,' said Mike. 'He wouldn't believe the other crap anyway; he's a shrewd operator is Alex.'

'Let's call him in, let him make up his own exclusive,' said the Chief.

'He always does, Chief, he's a fucking reporter, but a good one,' said Mike. 'Sorry about the French, I get carried away sometimes Chief,' added Mike.

'Yes, I've noticed,' replied the Chief.

'I don't like it Mike, not one bit, it's a pack of lies,' said Alex.

'Come on Alex, lies and reporters go hand-in-hand. What's different about this?' said Mike.

'I'll tell you what's different: when we write a piece there is an element of truth amongst the untruths. This piece is total garbage. If my readers ever get wind of this I'm finished. I'll have no credibility. You're asking a hell of a lot of me,' said Alex.

'Put the violin away Alex, and get out the drums and lead us into battle. Remember, when we get these bastards you've got another bloody exclusive. You will be Sir Alex of the *Chronicle*,' said Mike.

'Very funny Mike. May I suggest a more probable scenario?' said Alex.

'What's that?' said Evan.

'That my editor takes my drumsticks and beats the living crap out of me before showing me the door to the dole queue.'

'Amber, bring our man a glass of rum, maybe it will give him some backbone,' said Mike.

'No Amber, bring a new brain, the one I've got is still functioning,' said Alex.

'You're still upset Bren, how many times do I have to explain to you, they had me tied over a barrel and were about to roll me over a cliff,' said Muriel.

'But they gave us the photos and negatives, so now they have nothing,' said Brenda.

'Keep on dreaming, nothing is that simple with the people in Nelson Street—I've seen first-hand how they operate. They're good, always one step ahead,' said Muriel.

'Okay, okay, I'll take the older car, but next year I'm going to be first on the list, Muriel.'

'I think we can arrange that, Bren.' And with that the Chief Constable had finished with the subject for the time being.

# CHAPTER SEVEN

**WALTER** read and re-read the front page. Were these people that stupid? Gangsters from London! And he thought that these new people who had taken over the case were meant to be the cream.

He took a sheet of paper; he drew a square house, four windows, a door and a chimney with smoke coming out of it. On the side, he drew three matchstick men, one big one and two smaller ones. Then with a red biro he drew an X through the house.

In one of the drawers beneath the television he had self-sealing envelopes and stamps. He wiped the sheet of paper with a cloth. He wasn't sure about fingerprints on paper and using the address that he had from a previous cutting he wrote 111 Nelson St, Cardiff with the post code underneath. After putting on the stamp, he wiped down both sides of the envelope and put it into his overcoat pocket.

He rang Patrick. Fortunately, he wasn't working that day but David was. Patrick came around in the flat bed and they drove the few miles to Penarth where they had a coffee and where he posted the letter.

Before they left Penarth, he rang Alex Symonds and told him that he was crazy and barking up the wrong tree. He also told him that he had sent a letter to the detectives working out of Nelson St. Alex rang Amber and told her what he had heard from Yesterday's Man. He would be around in the morning to see the letter and offer any help that he could.

Mike was back to sharpening pencils with his knife. Evan and Charlie were playing cards. Mike called Dorothea on her mobile. He got no reply and he didn't leave a message; he didn't like talking when no one was listening. He tried again half an hour later and got the same result. He didn't feel like dining alone, so he searched through his papers for some inspiration.

There was Doctor Barbara, beautiful but a non-drinker and vegetarian. He mentally crossed her off the list. Then there was Tanya the air hostess; the problem there was that they had split up. Vicky the barmaid had slapped him hard when he had tried to get to first base. He could still feel the stinging on both cheeks. Tina, too loud, never got a word in edgeways with her. Then there were some whose telephone numbers he'd kept. There were obviously good reasons why he kept them but he couldn't remember the 'why.' But there was one he really wanted. Mike had no name, no number, no idea who she was. He called her the Strawberry Blonde. He closed his eyes and daydreamed of her. It wasn't as good as having her with him but it sure beat having nothing to daydream about and a few minutes later he left for home, he'd had enough and he'd run out of pencils.

After a while, sitting watching daytime rubbish TV, he got up, went into the kitchen, opened the fridge and stared. A few ripe tomatoes, some black olives, a chunk of parmesan cheese, some eggs, bacon, three bottles of diet coke, butter and marmalade. He closed the fridge. Nothing in there that he fancied, so he looked into the larder. A few tins of Heinz tomato soup, a tin of corned beef, some tinned tomatoes, plum not chopped, some pinto and some borlotti beans, chilli peppers, Tabasco, Worcestershire sauce, hot West Indian pepper sauce, olive oil, vinegar, black and white pepper, salt and garlic.

He closed the larder, poured himself a Macallan and lit up a cigarette. He leant on one of the kitchen units and blew smoke rings out of the window, which he always kept open. He was after all on the third floor, even Charlie would have a hard time getting up to the window and he was one of the best, if not the best.

He worried about Charlie; he'd heard about a few break-ins since Charlie had come and worked at Nelson St.; one at a jewellers in Newport had Charlie written all over it. He was certain that Evan also had his reservations but they both owed Charlie and if you didn't know, then you couldn't do anything.

Without thinking, he started humming an old Louvin Brothers classic. After a while he remembered the first couple of lines and broke into song: 'When I'm dreaming, I dream, I dream of you.' And again he thought of the Strawberry Blonde. Nearly six months and just one quick sighting, seconds only from across the street before he lost her.

Mike finished his whisky and headed back to the kitchen. He was hungry. He re-opened the fridge door and made a decision. He would have spaghetti *alla puttanesca* or in plain Anglo Saxon English, a whore's spaghetti. According to Andreas, the Greek barber, it was just a cheap quick meal that prostitutes could make between customers to keep them going. Andreas was a mine of useless information, though this one did have a ring of truth about it.

Mike opened a tin of anchovies to which he was partial and chopped them into one-inch pieces. He then chopped some garlic and diced an onion and sautéed the lot in olive oil. He slowly added some chopped chilli peppers, black olives and diced tomatoes. He would have also thrown in some capers but didn't have any. Black pepper and salt were also added and he left the mixture simmering for fifteen minutes to reduce to the consistency he liked.

Mike poured it over the spaghetti, which he had cooked *al dente* and with that he grated a lot of parmesan over the food and ate. After finishing, he remembered the parsley, which he usually put on top. It didn't matter, he had none anyway.

'Of course I want dessert, Jazzy. Have I ever not wanted apple pie and custard?' Edna laughed and patted Evan on the stomach. 'You should think of going on a diet Evan.'

'I'll start tomorrow,' said Evan.

'Good,' said Jasmine, not realising that tomorrow never comes.'

Charlie didn't like the film. He hated weepies but he'd promised Maggie. The damn thing was surely coming to an end. He popped some more popcorn in his mouth and closed his eyes. Hardened criminals should be forced to watch endless films like this in prison, he thought, that would stop them re-offending.

At the Daffy in Llanbas Village, Walter, David and Patrick sat together. The old man was getting sicker by the day. It was obvious to everyone. It was quite busy, mainly because Barry and Louisa, mine hosts, had reduced prices by forty pence and because it wasn't raining, all the customers were local. David excused himself, told Walter and Patrick that he had forgotten his mobile phone at home and needed it because he was expecting a call from his superiors at work, which might be urgent.

He drove directly to Walter's house, opened the front door with the key that he had had copied and searched for the Will. He was getting extremely worried about the old man. Patrick had told him about the phone call. It's as if he wanted them to get caught. He was losing his marbles. Maybe he'd already lost them; either way the old man was a liability and had to go, but first he had to check the Will.

David looked around. He found the Will, it hadn't been altered. Everything was still going to him and his brother. He replaced it where he had found it and left, going onto his own house and picking up the pills that Walter had originally given him.

He returned to the Daffy. Walter was on his second pint. Patrick still on his first half. David said he needed to have a word with Barry and Louisa; he'd only be a minute. Patrick carried on talking about cars. Walter wasn't that interested but listened. He really liked the boy, who although backward, had a good heart.

'Let me get you both a drink,' said David. 'I'd like a word in confidence, if I may'
'Sure,' said Louisa.
Barry poured a pint for himself and a large G&T for his wife.
'Haven't seen much of you Dai boy,' said Barry.
'That's what I want to talk to you about. It's Walter, he can't get out much now. He's terminally ill and we seem to be his only friends so we kind of look after him,' said David.

'What's he got?' asked Barry.

'It's the Big C: maybe two, three months at most, terminal, but what's worrying me is that he refuses any medical help and these past few days he's been talking about how he can't take the pain any longer.'

'The poor old bugger,' said Barry.

'That's not all,' said David. 'He's talking about taking his own life.'

'That's awful,' said Louisa. 'I'm sure he really doesn't mean it.'

'No, I guess he doesn't but it's sad to hear him saying things like that. I really like Walter and he really gets on with my brother Patrick. Look at them. Anyway please don't say anything to anyone. You know how proud Walter is.'

'You can rely on us,' said Louisa. Mum's the word.'

'Thanks,' said David, walking away and back to his table. Within an hour everyone in the village would know. Louisa had the biggest mouth this side of the Severn and that suited David's plans to a 'T.'

They waited for Walter to finish his drink then left, Patrick driving. They dropped off Walter and then went to their own house where a war film had just begun on TV.

David let Patrick get into the film then told him that he was going for a walk. But he took the car and drove near to Walter's where he parked in a secluded place, before walking on to Walter's with the half bottle of whisky that he had taken from the house.

He knocked on the door. Walter still in his pub clothes answered the door and let him in.

'I thought we'd go over my plans for Lancelot and his wife, Walter. Would you like a wee dram of Scotch? I've brought some; it's getting colder by the minute outside.' Walter declined. He didn't like spirits so David got a glass and poured himself one.

'So what have you got planned David? It's not going to be easy getting near them. I suppose the remainder have round-the-clock security,' said Walter.

David was beginning to think he couldn't go through with it. His plan had seemed feasible. A cushion over the mouth and nose, starving the old man of air, but Walter would put up a fight and he didn't have Patrick to hold him down. Pills in the whisky, but Walter wasn't drinking. It had to look like a heart attack or suicide.

Walter was obviously in pain and was waiting on David. 'Let me just think it through in my mind Walter, I need to get it clear before I tell you my plan,' David said.

'While you're thinking, I'm going to make myself a cup of cocoa,' said Walter, rising unsteadily to his feet and turning slowly in the direction of the kitchen.

David, sensing an opportunity, stood and with all his might shoved Walter towards the floor. Walter stumbled, tried to reach out for some support but failed and went crashing head-first into the fire grate splitting open his head from the centre of his skull to just above his right eye.

David wasn't certain, but after a few moments he realised that Walter hadn't moved and was dead. The perfect accident as far as David was concerned.

David drank his whisky and then went into the kitchen and washed out the glass. Walter had eight other similar glasses and using a kitchen towel David selected another and placed it first in Walter's right hand, then on his lips. He now placed the glass on the table and poured in some whisky and a dozen or so of Walter's pills. He wiped the pill bottle clean and took it over to Walter, placing that in his hand and returning it to the table. He did the same with the bottle of whisky, after first pouring some down Walter's throat. He then searched first the kitchen, then Walter's bedroom. There was nothing to tie Walter to Morton's or indeed himself and his brother Patrick.

In the lounge, he found some cheap rings and a silver cigarette case and a good gold watch, which he left as he did the money, about fourteen hundred pounds. He left the Will and some old photographs, from what looked like his schooldays, but took the scrapbook, which also held some loose photos, taken by David and Patrick, of their victims. He looked around some more and then switched on the TV.

He found a piece of plain paper and a biro, which he put near the glass of whisky. On the way out he left all the lights on. David was only carrying the scrapbook and his empty whisky glass and all Walter's tea bags. He drove home. Patrick was still watching the war film.

In the morning, David was up before Patrick. He dropped the glass outside and picked up the pieces, which he put straight into the bin. He then ripped out all of the newspaper cuttings and letters from the scrapbook and burnt them in the sink.

Patrick started work in the garage at seven and would usually pop in to see Walter if he had time because it was on his way. They would usually have a chat and a cup of tea. Walter wasn't big on breakfasts but did love his tea in the morning.

'Patrick, can you go in a little earlier and drop off these teabags to Walter? He said he'd run out last night and I forgot—he's probably gagging for a cup. Walter's usually up by six.'

Fortunately, both David and Walter used the same brand, so all David was doing was returning what he had taken the night before.

'And you can tell him I'll probably see him this afternoon. I've got a small job on this morning and Patrick, please keep your mobile phone on, you know how to use it. Just keep it on; sometimes I need to get in touch with you.'

For a full five minutes Patrick rang the doorbell. No answer, so Patrick rang his brother.

'Patrick for crying out aloud, ring him on his phone,' said David. 'You don't have his number? Okay, I'll get him, just wait there,' said David.

David rang; the last thing he wanted to hear was Walter's voice; that would be his worst nightmare.

He was relieved that he didn't get Walter on the phone. It confirmed that he was dead or at least in a coma. He needed to get there quickly, so he jumped into his car and drove the half mile or so to Walter's house. Patrick was sitting on the step.

'I couldn't get an answer either Patrick.' His brother hated being called Pat. He said it was a girl's name.

'Let's go around the back and see if we can find him. Maybe he's outside,' said Patrick.

'Climb over the wall and open the gate will you Patrick.'

Patrick did as his brother requested. They tried the kitchen door; it was locked. The curtains hadn't been drawn and it was difficult to see through the patterned lace net curtains, but if one looked carefully they could just about make out certain contents of the room. They could see a table, bits of chairs that the light was on and one of Walter's feet. David let Patrick see it first.

'I think Walter's had an accident Patrick, I'm going to phone the Police.'

It took nearly twenty minutes for someone to arrive. He asked a few questions before they showed the policeman Walter's protruding foot. The constable rapped hard on the window five, six times before deciding that they needed to get in.

'Does anyone have a key?' he asked.

'Would we be outside in the cold if we did?' said David incredulously at the constable's stupidity. David made a mental note to dump the key that he had in his pocket, the key to Walter's front door.

'We should get a locksmith down,' said the constable.

'Forget the locksmith,' said Patrick. 'He could be badly hurt, we need to get in now.'

'You're right, there's a small glass window in the kitchen,' said David. 'I can get in through that, I'm small enough.'

The constable broke the window and they cleared all the jagged edges from around the frame. David climbed in and into the kitchen sink which was directly beneath the window. He then opened the back door for the constable and his brother.

All three went into the lounge/dining room where they found Walter, dead from a cracked skull.

'Poor bastard,' said the constable. 'Looks like he had one too many and slipped hitting his head on this fire grate.'

'He was my good friend,' said Patrick, tears running down his face.

'I'll get a doctor down. You try to console your brother, he's taken it very badly,' said the constable.

'They were very good friends, despite the large age difference,' said David, feeling bad seeing his brother in such a state and knowing he was the cause of it.

Walter's local doctor arrived a half hour later. He pronounced Walter officially dead. Cause: accidental, no more, no less. It was obvious even to a small child.

Patrick was in no fit state to work that day so David dropped him off back home before returning to Walter's. On the way back he wiped the key clean and threw it into some heavy grass on some wasteland that he passed.

Amber wore rubber gloves to open the letter. All four of them looked at the drawing of the house with the three matchstick figures.

'This is meant to be a clue,' said Amber.

'Maybe we could pass it off as a Lowry and make a fortune,' said Charlie.

'I see three people; one big and two small,' said Mike.

'You saying that an adult and two kids are doing in the Mortons?' said Evan.

'No, I guess not,' said Mike.

How about a strong man and two normal people?' said Charlie.

With a pencil pointed at the larger of the figures, Amber said, 'That my dear detectives is Yesterday's Man, he's the oldest.'

Someone was at the door. It was Alex. 'Sorry I'm late,' he said. 'I see you've started without me. Any ideas on what it means?'

Amber told Alex what they thought.

'And the house, why the X through it?' said Alex.

'I would say that these three figures don't like estate agents,' said Charlie.

'So why pick on Morton's? There are hundreds of them out there,' said Evan.

'And why include the solicitor, the accountant? I would say this is a personal vendetta against this particular group,' said Mike.

'It's something involving one house, not more, otherwise he would have drawn more houses,' said Alex.

'A house sale or purchase that went wrong, hence the X through it,' said Amber.

'I like it. I like it a lot,' said Mike.

'Don't like it too much Mike, we've checked every sale, every conveyance, every complaint for the last twenty-three years,' said Amber.

'I've got the top twenty problematic cases on the file and believe me it was difficult to come up with more than a handful. I'll print out some copies. You will see what I mean, I've got them in order of severity,' said Amber.

'Go ahead,' said Alex, 'I can stay for an hour or so; business is quiet on the newspaper front.'

Amber printed out copies, passed each of the men one.

'Have you made No 14 on our list up Amber?' said Evan.

'No Evan, on the day of exchange Mr and or Mrs Brown, the vendors, removed the toilet from the bathroom and took it with them. Mr Brown was by the by a qualified plumber. They said it was worth over a thousand pounds and that Mr Brown would replace it the next morning. The matter was resolved amicably. Cardiff Central spoke to Mr Drayton, the buyer, who still resides in the house.'

'Have all these twenty been checked out then Amber?' said Alex.

'All apart from No 2 and No 5 on the list,' said Amber. 'The ones with an asterisk next to them.'

'Why not these two? Well, No 2 emigrated to Australia seven years ago and Cardiff Central couldn't trace them,' said Amber.

'And No 5, Mr and Mrs Everton,' said Mike, 'divorced.'

'Mr Everton now lives in Southampton and refuses to speak to us and Mrs Everton; now Mrs Parks, lives in Dunfermline and can't talk to us. She's very ill and was recently admitted into hospital,' said Amber.

'They couldn't have got further away from each other, could they?' said Charlie.

'How long's the guy been living in Southampton?' said Mike.

'Six years. Well, can we at least find out if he's been in Southampton over the last three, four weeks. Is he in work?'

'We have no idea,' said Amber, 'but I will ask the local boys to check it out for us.'

'I expect him to be clean,' said Charlie.

'I agree,' said Evan.

'So we have nothing as usual,' said Evan.

'Only this,' said Mike, picking up the letter with a tissue.

'What about the staff at Morton's and Fenwick's? Maybe we should speak to them again,' said Evan.

'You mean ex-staff. I don't see Morton's re-opening in the near future!' said Mike.

'They will just change the name after selling it from one Ltd company to another,' said Alex.

'True,' said Amber.

'They can run with the losses. It's not that big a financial problem to them,' said Alex.

'It's not about money, is it?' said Charlie.

'You talking about the murders?' said Evan.

'Yes, it's about revenge, isn't it?' said Charlie.

'It is, Charlie, but three like-minded people get together hell bent on revenge out of thousands of sales done through the years,' said Mike.

'Well, I'll leave you people to fathom it out and provide me with my next exclusive,' said Alex.

'Anyone ring on our new car or even the old one?' asked Mike.

'Nothing,' said Amber.

'We're not progressing on anything much,' said Evan.

'Let's have a coffee,' said Charlie.

'And a few biscuits,' said Amber.

The few biscuits included sandwiches and cakes. 'Maybe we should pay Sandy a visit, it's long overdue. Let's find out what the hell is going on with our car.'

Sandy and Curly were both working on cars, one underneath a Merc and the other under a BMW. Mike moved to the Merc and Evan with Charlie to the BMW. The music was so loud you wouldn't have heard a bomb being detonated in there.

Mike kicked one of the protruding feet. There was a twitch and movement hell bent on coming out from underneath the car, so Mike put a foot on his knee and put downward pressure on it until he could hear the screeches above the music. Curly who was by now out from under the BMW was told to kill the music by Evan. He hesitated, so Charlie went across the garage, picked up the radio and dropped it. It still spewed out music but Curly rushed across and closed it down—it was his radio.

'Hello Sandy,' Mike said, easing off slightly on the knee, 'come to find out what happened to our car!'

'It's good news, Detective. Good news all round. Your car's in the paint shop. It will be ready tomorrow, but if you wait another three days, you can have one of the new ones,' said Sandy.

'I'll have the old car for two days then; make sure it's delivered to Nelson Street at ten, tomorrow morning, and tell Brenda she can have it when you deliver the new one.'

'Have a nice day Sandy, you too Curly. Ten sharp Sandy, I really don't want to come down at five past ten tomorrow morning, have too much work on,' Mike said taking his foot off Sandy's knee and letting him move from underneath the car.

They walked back slowly, Charlie sharing Evan's umbrella, Mike just getting soaked.

'Mike, why don't you just get an umbrella?' said Evan.

'If Charlie got one, then I wouldn't have a problem Evan,' said Mike.

'How did they know about the Chief Constable's Private Secretary, Brenda Aston, being in line for their car?' said Curly.

'Ring up the paint shop Curly. Tell them that the BMW had better be ready to move at nine a.m. tomorrow morning,' said Sandy.

'You're not actually going to deliver the car to them, are you Sandy?'

'Of course I'm not, you are.'
'Shit, I'll go and chase up the paint boys,' said Curly.

On reaching outside the office, it got into Mike's mind that he'd promised to go and see his mother Alice.

'Evan, could you do me a favour and take me to Penarth? I'd drive myself, but then if you're with me I won't have to stay too long talking to my mother's cronies. I'm just not in the mood for small talk today,' said Mike.

'Sure Mike, my car's just down there,' said Evan.

Mike knocked and then entered. The door was always unlocked. He'd warned his mother a hundred times but she still thought she was living in the '50s.

'Mikhaili, my son, how did you get here?' said Alice, Mike's mother.

'My partner Evan Jones drove me down. Why do you ask?'

'I thought maybe you swam here Mikhail, you're wet through.'

'Look Mam, I come to visit you and you give me earache about my hair being a little wet. Let me introduce my partner Evan Jones. Evan, this is my mother. Mrs Alibi you know and Mrs Diana…,' said Mike.

'Just Diana will do. Are you married Evan?' said Diana.

'I am,' said Evan.

'That's nice, I keep telling my son he needs to find a good woman and have some stability in his life,' said Alice.

'You forgot the grandchildren, Mam.'

'Yes, and that. It's very important. Do you have any children Detective Jones?' said Alice.

'One daughter, Mrs Karetzi, and its Evan.'

'Can I take your umbrella? You see Mikhail, sensible people like your partner Evan get married, have babies and use an umbrella,' said Alice.

'Sit down, have some tea, some cake. Homemade, Diana brought it round,' said Alice.

'Thank you,' said Evan, eyeing the cake.

'Not you Mikhail. Take off your jacket and put it in the airing cupboard, then go into the bathroom and use a towel to dry your hair.'

'Yes Mam,' said Mike.

Mike was still in the bathroom when Mrs Alibi asked Evan if they had closed in on a suspect for the Morton's murders.

'I can't really talk about it,' said Evan.

'That's cop talk for they haven't made any inroads,' said Diana.

Evan's face reddened.

'And as for that rubbish printed in the *Chronicle*, who comes up with these stupid ideas? Some form of entrapment, was it?' said Mrs Alibi.

Evan said nothing. He wished Mike would hurry up.

'Not even a baby would believe that business about gangsters, London boys at that. As if we didn't have our own home-grown Taffia bad boys here in Wales,' said Alice.

Evan put some more cake into his mouth and chewed slowly. That way he didn't or couldn't speak.

Mike walked back in, hair now dry but now more unruly. He sat down and poured himself a cup of lukewarm tea. It just gave him something to do; the room was very quiet.

'Your partner, Detective Mike is not giving much away,' said Mrs Alibi.

'Giving much away about what, Mrs Alibi?' asked Mike.

'I said *not* giving much away about the progress or lack of it on the Morton mysteries,' said Mrs Alibi.

'It's because Evan does not realise he's in the presence of three Miss Marples,' said Mike.

'Well?' said Alice, looking at her son.

'The ladies know that the article in the *Chronicle* was at best a waste of space,' said Evan.

'I'll tell you what we will do, we'll play a game. I'm going to give you a drawing and a name and you can tell us what it means,' said Mike.

'I love games,' said Diana.

Mike drew the house, the three figures and then wrote Yesterday's Man underneath and left it on the table before saying, 'Come on Evan, let me show you the garden and we can have a smoke whilst the Marples decode our puzzle.'

Once outside, but under the cover of a small canopy, Evan wanted to know why he called one woman by her Christian name and the other by her surname.

'Simple Evan, she's also my cleaner.'

'I see,' said Evan, not any the wiser.

The detectives were outside for about five minutes before going back in.

Mrs Alibi had been elected as spokeswoman. 'Are you ready Detectives?' said Mrs Alibi.

'We are,' said Mike.

'This is the older person, the Yesterday's Man,' Mrs Alibi said pointing at the larger figure. 'These two are younger, could be accomplices, probably his sons. The cross through the house represents a deal, a property deal gone wrong in which they feel the other party, namely Morton's were to blame.'

'We also think that whatever happened it was a long time ago, hence the name "Yesterday's man" and that this person is now seeking revenge,' said Alice.

'So why has he waited so long to exact his revenge?' said Evan, now getting into the swing of things.

'Maybe the two smaller figures are his sons and he was waiting for them to grow up,' said Alice.

'Makes sense,' said Evan.

'So have we passed?' said Mrs Alibi.

'Not quite, we have checked every property deal involving the Morton's group and have come up with nothing untoward,' said Mike.

The room went deathly still.

'I'm assuming that you've checked their private house purchases and sales, commercial and land dealings.'

'Not really, we've skirted around them,' said Mike.

Skirted, I guess that must be more police speak for, sorry we didn't think of checking any of that,' said Mrs Alibi.

'We bow to the experts,' said Mike.

'Ladies, you are magnificent,' said Evan.

'We need to get back to our office. We have a lot of work to do,' said Mike.

'Nice meeting you all. Thank you for the tea and the cake, that was really nice,' said Evan.

On the way back, Evan ribbed Mike about getting all his work done by his mother and friends of hers. Mike's answer was to agree with Evan. After all there was an element of truth in it, even though he knew Evan was only joking.

'I don't see how we completely dismissed the Mortons' personal property dealings or their commercial enterprises,' said Evan. 'Next time we have a problem we should go direct to your mother's Mike, it might save us a lot of time,' said Evan.

Amber was alone, Charlie had gone home. Mike told her to look into the things that had been discussed with his mother and friends. Amber said no problem and carried on eating.

Jasmine had gone to see her old friends in the department store. She'd missed them. Promotion was fine but Edinburgh was a lonely place for someone new to the city. Just as any new unfamiliar place would be.

Mike got into his car. It had gone five. He drove slowly up to the city centre. Traffic was extremely heavy. It was still raining and Mike had his lights on. For the fourth time that day he tried Dorothea. This time he struck lucky: she answered the phone and seemed very happy to hear from him. Mike was at the very point of making arrangements to meet when he saw the bus. It was travelling in the opposite direction to him. He couldn't mistake the hair, even with the condensation on the windows of the bus. The hair was strawberry blonde. Mike's first reaction was to end his call by pressing the key, which switched off his phone. His second reaction was to make a U-turn and follow the bus, but a barrier prevented him doing so.

Mike turned left at the first available place, then right and right again. One more right and he was on the same path as the bus. Unfortunately he didn't know which bus. There were at least half a dozen ahead of him and those were the ones he could see. For fifteen minutes he followed them, passing them one at a time as they stopped to drop off and pick up passengers. Twice he nearly had an accident but he persevered until he realised how futile it was.

He stopped the car on a side street, put on his hazard lights and got out. He felt like screaming in frustration but settled on lighting up a cigarette and inhaling deeply. Was he cursed, would he ever find this elusive butterfly that flitted in and out of his life and dreams? Mike remained there in the same position for a while. It was still raining, not heavily but enough to have anyone on the streets either scurrying for cover or using their umbrellas. A passer-by advised him that it was raining. Mike told him to go forth and multiply, then carried on smoking. The passer-by gave him the pointed forefinger sign when he was about thirty yards away. Mike laughed; he was depressed but still laughed.

He remembered Dorothea but his mood wasn't convivial enough to warrant ringing her back. He got in his car and drove straight back to Penarth. His mother was alone; her friends had left. She was watching the news on TV. She was surprised to see him and she immediately began to worry. Her son was worried about something. She helped him off with his jacket and put it in the airing cupboard again. She fetched a towel and handed it to Mike who was sitting in an armchair staring at the TV but not taking anything in.

She let him have his space. He would tell her his troubles when he was ready, of that she was sure. At this very moment her one and only child Mikhail looked very unhappy and deep in thought. His father Demetri was the same; like father, like son.

Alice made Mike a large black coffee the way he liked it and put an ashtray on the small table next to his chair. The coffee was cold before Mike spoke. 'Mam, I know what to say but I don't know how to say it.'

'You just take your time Mikhaili, there's no rush,' Alice said. It was strange she thought. Her son always called her 'Mam,' not 'Mum' like other children called their mothers. Maybe it was his father's Russian blood, maybe in Russia children called their mothers 'Mam.' Mikhail was close to his father; it was a pity they didn't have another child, a brother or sister for Mikhail, but the good Lord never blessed them with another. God knows they tried. Mikhail was a good son, a good man with a big heart, but as a mother she knew that since his father had gone, her son was a little lost. He played too hard, worked to excess. His good friends had moved on or away. Others like Toby had married with children; at least he seemed at ease with his new partner Evan, who seemed a very decent type but was much older than her son and married with a child.

Mike interrupted his mother's thoughts. 'Mam, I have met a girl, a beautiful girl, well woman, really, three years or so younger than me I think. I know it's the right one and I've been around. Do you understand what I am saying, Mam? I love this woman. She occupies a lot of my time to the detriment of my work. Today I saw her. She was on a bus. I know I must move on but can't. I have other girlfriends, they're only a phone call away but I'm not motivated enough. One, two dates, then finish. Most times they finish with me. Somehow I force them into it. I'm drinking too much, other times I'm not eating properly. When I'm busy I'm not too bad but I'm beginning to make elementary mistakes as you and your friends pointed out today. For some reason the others in the team look up to me. I've led them into many a problem that we could have avoided. It all boils down to my mind being on this woman instead of the job.

'Today I could easily have broken a mechanic's knee. He'd done nothing wrong. I just wanted my own way and he couldn't facilitate me. That wasn't the only time I've been over-zealous and still my colleagues rely on me. It's too much, they have too much faith in me and follow blindly, but it's the only way we can get results. They've become my friends. Evan, I didn't think I would last a day with him, yet I'd call him a friend. Chalky, a petty crook, well a bit more than petty, has already saved my life twice. I'll always owe him and yes, we are friends, good friends. Then we have Amber, a twenty-stone black woman of sixty. She's always there for us. She's the glue that keeps the unit from falling apart. Do you understand, Mam? Do you understand what I'm trying to tell you?

'It's difficult to explain. I've become lethargic in my thinking, in my movements. I don't really know what I want. I'm glad the season's over. I can't get motivated for the training. I just want to play and go home or party, another thing which I find I can't handle anymore.

'I was better when we were after the Chessman. He was always one step ahead but was continually making inroads and closing the net. Then after we got him they leave us doing nothing for three months and then give us a fifteen-month missing person's case. I mean a "mispers" case, ridiculous.'

Mike suddenly and without warning stopped talking. Alice went and sat on the arm rest and put her arm around her son. She was crying. Mike wanted to but didn't want to show any further weakness in front of his mother.

It took a while but when Alice stopped crying she took a seat opposite her son. She wished Demetri was there, but he wasn't. It was up to her. She was his only living relative. She was his mother.

Mike took a gulp of the cold coffee. He then lit up. He'd said a lot, probably too much. He didn't want to burden his mother with his troubles. He'd only meant to tell her about the strawberry blonde.

'Now Mikhail, do you want another coffee? That one's cold.'

'It's fine Mam, just fine. I'm sorry; I think I've upset you. That's not why I came around.'

'What's this girl's name Mikhail?'

'I don't know Mam. When I met her, the only time face to face, I didn't ask her what her name was. I gave her some flowers I'd bought for Evan's wife Edna. I knew she liked me. She drove off. I saw her today on a bus but couldn't get to her. She's absolutely beautiful, strawberry blonde hair, lovely calm face. I know she's the one for me, if only I can find her. But I've no clues, no car make, name of the area where she lives or works, nothing.'

'It was the same for me, Mikhail, when I first set eyes on your father. Love at first sight. Who would have thought it would work out okay. A little Welsh girl with a Russian ship's engineer with no papers living in a hard communist country. Yet here we are. You dream son, dream as much as you like. It's good to have hope but don't make these dreams your master. Live, enjoy life. Other opportunities will present themselves. You'd be surprised. As for your work, give your best, son. If others are relying on you, they are for a reason. They trust you, things will work out.'

'You've been reading too much Rudyard Kipling, Mam. I think that part about dreams was from a poem of his called "If".'

'Then Kipling was a very clever man,' said Alice, 'he wrote sense.'

'He was also a top class baker Mam,' said Mike, breaking into a smile.

'Now him, I know about,' said Alice.

'You make everything sound so simple Mam.'

'It's because everything *is* simple Mikhail. You've got to see things in such a way that you're only left with simple.'

'Do you want me to fix you up with some eggs and bacon? And maybe it's best you sleep in the spare room tonight.'

Mike didn't need much persuading; he was hungry and tired.

'Don't forget the toast Mam,' said Mike.

'I remember, thick hard toast, left out of the toaster for five minutes. Then lashings of butter and marmalade as a base for the two eggs. Black pepper and salt, crispy bacon and a few tinned plum tomatoes.'

'How do you remember all my little idiosyncrasies?' Mike smiled.

'How could I forget them?' said Alice.

Whilst his mother was in the kitchen cooking, Mike gave Dorothea a call from his mother's landline. Again she answered in seconds. 'Hi Dorothea, it's Mike. I don't know what happened with my phone, it just went dead. I'm actually phoning from my mother's landline. I'm in Penarth; I came to see my mother.' They spoke for a while before Mike said, 'I'll pick you up at eight tomorrow then. I know a little Italian restaurant, which you will love. Wear the same clothes so that I'll recognise you. Yes, I know I'm picking you up at your house. I thought maybe we could carry on from when I was rudely interrupted and had to leave. Just when we were getting to know each other.

'Okay Dorothea, see you tomorrow. Good night.'

Alice heard every word that Mike said. She smiled. What a lovely name, Dorothea. She hoped that this girl lived up to her name, a gift from God, just what her baby needed right now.

Mike was nearly asleep when he spotted the books. He got out of bed and scanned the titles. One was a book of poems by Rudyard Kipling. He glanced at the index, found the page that he wanted and left it open on the bookshelf. He smiled, got back into bed and slept well. That night he didn't dream.

The house was cleared. The will was found, together with a total of £3,400. Two thousand was in an envelope marked 'funeral expenses.' All Walter's effects went to various charities. The only stipulation being that the various charities had to pick them up within a week of notification. All documents were to be burnt and he requested to be interred next to his wife and daughter in the local cemetery.

Patrick searched high and low for the scrapbook that David his brother had already burnt. David had been thinking; now with Walter gone, there was no need for any more risks but unfortunately, there needed to be one more. The Police wouldn't give up especially if the killing stopped suddenly. There had to be one more; a soft touch, that should keep the idiots looking in the wrong direction.

Five still worked in the last Barry branch on High Street. He didn't know any more than that, but as from tomorrow there would only be four. After all, they didn't have that much work on.

That evening, he went down to Barry and parked well away from the High Street. It was four o'clock and David was surprised how busy the place was. It had a village atmosphere, bars, cafes, butchers, bakers, quite a few decent clothes shops, hairdressers, a few newsagents, a grocer's. Their biggest problem seemed to be parking. There were shops long before cars. He counted four other estate agents in the street.

At five, two women came out and started walking together. That left three, of which one he could see through the shop window working at a desk. After a few minutes a man came out, waited a few moments and was picked up by a woman in a small blue Mercedes. Probably his wife, because he gave her a peck on the cheek. A girlfriend would have got more than just a peck on the cheek. Two minutes later another man left, leaving just the one still inside.

Five past six and the lights went off in Morton's. A few minutes later a young man of twenty or so came out and double locked the door. He turned left and headed at a brisk pace up the street towards the main town. David had a hard time keeping up with him. This chap was in one hell of a rush.

After fifteen minutes of brisk walking, he stopped outside a small terraced house. David stopped too. He was a hundred yards behind and was glad of the rest. He was breathing heavily. After a while, he started up again just in time to see the man draw the front curtains.

David counted the houses in the street from the corner to the young man's. His was the eighth; they all looked the same. He found the alleyway and counted the eight houses down; with the aid of a few bricks he found nearby, he could see over the wall and into the small paved yard and kitchen. There were no lights on anywhere in the house and apart from the front room, no curtains were drawn. This guy was obviously saving on electricity.

Around the front, it was as before. No lights on upstairs. David waited around a further ten minutes until he was sure that the young man lived alone, then at a reasonable pace headed back to his car. He drove round the streets until he was comfortable with his exact whereabouts before stopping outside Domino's Pizza in Holton road, Barry's main street where he ordered a ham and pineapple pizza. It was now just gone nine p'm. David ate the pizza about five hundred yards from the estate agency's young employee's house. On finishing, he carried the empty box to No 16 and rang on the bell. In his right-hand jacket pocket, he carried the homemade cosh, a sock containing a large round pebble. The door was opened. It was the young man.

'John Thompson?' said David.

'No,' said the young man.

'This is No 16 isn't it?' said David.

'Yes, but there is no John Thompson living here,' said the young man.

'It's a pizza delivery from Domino's, already paid for, Mr Thompson,' said David.

'Look, I'm not Thompson and I haven't ordered a pizza, okay?'

'I have an address Sir, just a second if you wouldn't mind,' David said placing the pizza on the floor and reaching into his pocket for the homemade cosh. It took one heavy blow to the poor unsuspecting young chap who collapsed onto the floor. Fortunately, for David, he had fallen backwards and David seized the opportunity to kick the pizza into the hall and close the door behind him.

The young man was rising to his feet in a daze. Two more heavy blows to the head and he was gone. David dragged him into the front room where he knew the curtains were drawn and he couldn't be seen. He sat the young man on the sofa. The TV was on; it was 'The Bill.' David sat on a chair, watched for twenty minutes. It was quite interesting. The ending though was pure fiction. They caught the man who had bludgeoned his boss to death. He'd left a few clues.

On his way out, he smoothed the carpet where he had dragged the young man, picked up the pizza box in which he placed the bloodied sock and pebble and walked out into the street. It took him fifteen minutes to get back home. Patrick was watching TV. He didn't mention anything to his brother.

It was now half nine, so he asked his brother if he wanted a drink. Patrick didn't so David walked to the 'Affy' and had a couple of pints.

Before going to pick up Dorothea, Mike tidied up his apartment. The sheets on his bed had only been on for a couple of days of which one he had slept at his mother's. He stocked up on drinks, nuts, especially cashew nuts, his favourite, raisins and things like that. He'd also bought milk and all the necessary items for a good breakfast, hopefully for two.

They hit Angelo's at half eight and left three hours later. Mike only had a total of three glasses of wine. Mike wanted to have all his wits about him until later. Dorothea had drunk another three. Apart from a matching blouse and skirt she was wearing what she wore at the Portuguese restaurant. Mike looked forward to a very eventful night of fun and excitement. As a couple, they were getting on great. There were no moments of silence. Everything was as Mike could have wished.

It was Jack Garner's girlfriend who found him. After finishing work in a local pub, Helen, the girlfriend immediately called the police.

Mike opened a bottle of champagne and poured it into two long fluted glasses. This time they sat next to each other. Mike didn't want to rush things. He had all night but did want to test the water a little so he kissed Dorothea long and hard on the mouth. There was no resistance. She wanted it as badly as Mike.

They took a sip of champagne. Now there was no conversation—it was time for action, not words. This time Dorothea instigated a long passionate kiss and that tasted much better than the champagne. Mike slowly and deliberately unbuttoned the four little ivory buttons of her blouse. She was wearing a low cut red bra, which Mike eyed with awe. He helped her out of the blouse, which he casually dropped onto floor. He now took some time to undo a few buttons of his shirt and slip it over his head. The zip on the back of Dorothea's skirt posed no problems and Mike started to unbuckle his belt when the damn door buzzer was activated. Mike froze. He glanced at his watch. It was near on midnight.

It was Charlie who had been dispatched by Amber to collect Mike whom she had assumed had drunk too much and take him to Barry.

'Yes Charlie, what are you doing here? You have a problem, something happened?'

Charlie told him and Mike said he would be down in about five.

Dorothea had redressed by the time Mike finished his call.

'I'm so sorry Dorothea. I have just been called to another Morton victim.'

'I know. I overheard Mike. I think next time, we will skip dinner,' said Dorothea.

'Well, I'm glad to hear that there will be a next time,' said Mike, 'and I will be happy to go straight to dessert and bypass the rest.'

After putting on his shirt and jacket, they embraced and kissed. Mike asked her if it was okay for her to go with Charlie back home.

'Charlie, this is Dorothea. Could you give her a lift to Llandaff and then come down to Barry?'

Mike kissed Dorothea once more, before helping her into Charlie's car. Charlie wound down the window. 'What about you, Mike, drink-wise, I mean,' he said.

'I'm fine Charlie. I'm under the limit. It's been four hours. I would have got rid of two of the units in my body and I've only had three, so I'm fine.'

Charlie drove off. Dorothea wanted to make conversation and the only thing she could think of to say was, 'Mike's a nice man. Have you known him long?'

'Mike's a brilliant man, a one-off and a fantastic detective to boot. They say he's the best we've got. Decent people love him, nasties hate him; everyone looks up to him. It's an honour to work with him. And by the way, he doesn't pay me to say all these things.'

Dorothea laughed. Even this little cockney chap she liked, Toby his solicitor friend too. You could tell a good man by his friends and colleagues. Mike was lucky.

Mike drove, siren blazing. He didn't do it to enable him to go faster, he did it because the noise kept him awake.

'So Evan, when did you arrive?' asked Mike.

'About ten minutes ago, I was just about to get into bed when Amber called,' said Evan.

'So was I, when Charlie called,' said Mike.

'Where is he, Mike?'

'Be here in about five minutes Evan.'

'Who's in charge, Evan?'

'We are, Mike. DI Dobson's gone to the hospital. His wife's expecting any minute. That over there is D.S. Morris; Doctor Read is the guy just over there, having a cigarette. We've got a few from the forensic department, four uniforms, a photographer just left and Jack Garner is in the lounge,' said Evan.

'Jack Garner, what role does he have in this?' asked Mike.

'The main one Mike, he's the victim,' Evan replied.

'What do we know?' said Mike.

'According to the Doc, time of death between nine and eleven last night. More likely between ten and eleven, found by his girlfriend at a quarter past eleven, sitting dead, watching TV,' said Evan. 'Three, four blows to the right side of the head. Blunt instrument, something round like a metal ball or stone.'

'Any signs of forced entry?' asked Mike.

'No,' said Evan.

Mike went and had a look at Jack. The TV was still on.

One of the boys in white space suits and gloves used a pair of tweezers and picked something from the matted wound on Jack's head. He put it into a small plastic pouch.

'What's that?' asked Mike.

'Don't know until we analyse it,' said the guy who was holding the plastic pouch.

'Can I have a look?' said Mike, taking it out of the guy's hand before he could answer.

Mike looked at it and passed it to Evan, who gave it to Charlie who had just appeared.

'Woollen strand,' said Evan.

'Homemade cosh,' said Charlie.

'A what?' said D.S. Morris.

'A sock filled with coins, marbles, stones, whatever and used as a cosh,' said Charlie.

'You finished here?' Evan asked the forensic boys.

'Just about,' said one.

'Fingerprints?' asked Mike.

'Yep, everywhere we could think of,' said one of them.

'Everywhere including the doorbell?' said Mike.

They looked at each other but didn't answer.

'There is no forced entry. The girlfriend who found him obviously has a key. I mean Jack didn't answer the door to her, did he? So the last person to use the doorbell was our perp,' Mike said.

'He was probably wearing gloves but even the best of us make mistakes,' Mike said.

'Our friend here was dragged in from the front. See those two scuff marks on the lino in the hall?' said Evan.

'Which means he didn't know his assailant,' said Charlie.

'Correct,' said Mike, 'which means that our perp had a good enough reason to get Jack to open the door and give him the time for the attack.'

By now the whole room had stopped doing whatever and were listening to the Four I's boys describe the scene.

'So we can eliminate the postman, milkman, insurance or double-glazing salesman. Who would you have a conversation with late at night, who was also a stranger?' said Mike.

'A delivery boy or person,' said Evan.

'And who delivers?' said Mike.

'Takeaway delivery,' said the Doctor.

'Evan, can we get the last number dialled on the landline and find his mobile. He's bound to have one, Charlie.'

'That's good, very good,' said D.S. Morris.

'Not really,' said Mike 'won't help at all.'

'Why?' asked the Doctor.

'Because I see no pizza or fast food boxes of any kind in this room,' said Mike.

'I see,' said the Doctor.

'It was just a ruse to get the time at the door for our killer,' said Evan.

'How many takeaways that deliver have you got in Barry, within a mile of the house?' Charlie asked D.S. Morris.

'I'd say six, seven or so,' said Morris.

'Okay, listen up,' Mike said walking to the front door and kneeling. He then went into the kitchen, opened the pedal bin, then the bread bin, and finally looked at the sink contents.

'Where's the girlfriend, this Helen Hartley?' asked Mike.

'In the car with one of the women police people,' said D.S. Morris.

'Could you ask her to come in please?' said Mike.

'She's pretty distraught and pissed off. She's been waiting God knows how long,' said Morris.

'Tell her you're sorry, D.S. Morris and get her in here. We're wasting valuable time,' said Mike.

A pretty young brunette, eyes swollen through crying, was led in by D.S. Morris.

'Hello, I'm sorry about the waiting. I'm Special Detective Inspector Karetzi and these two are my colleagues, S.D.I. Jones and

Mr C White, and we would like to ask you a few simple questions which will help us enormously,' said Mike.

The girl nodded, her eyes darting to the closed door of the lounge where her boyfriend still lay.

'Do you live with Jack in this house?' asked Mike.

She nodded.

'Do you have a key?' asked Mike.

'Of course I have a key,' said Helen.

'Did Jack ring you tonight?'

'Yes he did,' said Helen.

'At what time?' asked Mike.

'About half six, when he got home from work.'

'Did he ring again after that?' asked Mike.

'No, I rang him about eight-thirty,' Helen said.

'Why?' asked Mike.

'To tell him not to wait up for me. I usually finish at the Crown at ten, but tonight was very busy, what with the football on and Dave, that's the Boss, asked me to stay on.'

'What did he say about that Helen?'

'Told me he was tired and would grab an early night,' Helen said.

Evan handed Mike a piece of paper; a telephone number was written on it. Mike read it to Helen before asking her if that was her mobile number. She confirmed that it was.

'Does Jack have a mobile Helen?' Mike asked.

'Yes he does, but it's broken and being fixed. I took it in this morning for him. The shop said I could pick it up tomorrow. I mean today now,' said Helen.

'One last question, Helen. Do you know what all these keys are for? Although I can see that this one is a front door key and this one a car key,' said Mike.

Helen pointed with one of her scarlet painted fingernails. 'This is the back door key and the rest are something to do with the Agency. It was Jack's job to lock up at six every night and open up at nine every morning.'

Thank you Miss Hartley. Have you anywhere you can go tonight?' said Mike.

'Yes, my parents live nearby but I'll need to take some clothes and stuff,' Helen said.

'Go ahead, get what you need and one of the uniforms will drive you there,' said Mike.

'We've got an ambulance outside,' said the doctor. 'Do you need me for anything else?'

'No thanks Doc. I suggest we wait for the girlfriend to go and then move the body,' said Evan.'

'We've got the whole neighbourhood waiting behind twitching curtains to see what's going on,' said D.S. Morris.

'In that case, get the uniforms to go house to house. We're interested in strange men or cars seen yesterday evening between 18.00 and 23.00 hours,' said Evan.

'Get the four uniforms, do three houses each; three either side of this and the six directly across the street,' said Evan.

'At this time of night?' said D.S. Morris.

'Yes, at this time of night,' snapped Mike.

D.S. Morris walked away. He wasn't happy. Within a minute D.S. Morris was back, two paramedics in tow. They weren't happy either.

'Not yet,' said Evan. 'Hang on just a minute or two more.'

'We can't hang on whilst you people pass the time talking about things,' said the scruffy one.

'But you will,' said Mike, not even looking at him.

Scruffy was about to say something more when Helen came down the stairs, suitcase in hand. Charlie grabbed the case and walked her to the waiting police car. She had started crying again.

The ambulance boys did their job and suddenly there were only the three of them left. D.S. Morris was standing outside. Mike joined him and offered him a cigarette, which D.S. Morris accepted gratefully. They smoked in silence, both men with their own thoughts.

'Let's go back in and sit down,' said Mike.

Evan and Charlie joined them. Evan placed a saucer in the middle of the table. A window and the back door were open. Evan took out his pipe, packed it and lit up. Charlie pushed back his chair and tried to relax. Mike closed his eyes and wondered what Dorothea was doing at that very moment, asleep probably. His mind wandered to what she would be wearing, if anything. D.S. Morris was also taxing his mind. He was wondering what the crazy half asleep cop was thinking about.

'Something bothering you, Mike?' said Evan.

Mike opened his eyes. He'd nearly nodded off but now tried to focus on the subject in hand.

'Why knock off what amounts to a gopher, Evan? Tell me that. Why not at least the Manager, someone of importance.'

'That same question has crossed my mind a dozen times since I've been here Mike,' said Evan.

'Convenience,' said Charlie.

'You mean an easy target?' said Evan.

'Okay, but why go to the trouble, what is gained?' said Mike.

'The last agency the Mortons have will now surely close,' said D.S. Morris.

'Doesn't mean anything. They are still financially strong. The market's in the doldrums, they can dump the staff. It's probably a godsend to them,' said Evan.

'But does Yesterday's Man know that?' said Mike.

'Do we know what went down here last night?' said D.S. Morris. 'I mean exactly what happened?'

'I think so,' said Evan.

'Yes, we do,' said Mike.

'So how do you see it Mike?' asked Charlie.

'I see it like this: Jack closes up the shop in the High Street. He's last one out. It's just gone six. He walks home, takes about fifteen or so minutes. Comes in, puts on the lights and closes the curtains in the lounge for some privacy. He switches on the TV then phones his girlfriend. He then goes into the kitchen, makes some toast and opens a tin of beans. He also opens a tin of tomato soup, sits on this table and eats. He also has a glass of lager.'

'Excuse me, how do we know this?' said D.S. Morris.

'The guy's generally tidy, but there are breadcrumbs on top of the toaster which people usually forget to wipe down. There's a saucepan, plate, knife, fork, spoon and breadknife in the sink. The saucepan contains a red film on the side i.e. the tomato soup, in the bin; on the top is an empty can of soup and beans and an empty bottle of lager.

'The lager he drank without the use of a glass, the soup direct from the pan. He then returned to the TV room and watched TV. His girlfriend rang at half eight. He was alive and well.

'Sometime after that the doorbell rang. He answered and there was a guy with a pizza. Not an Indian or Chinese, I could not smell anything near the door. It had to be a pizza, or at least the box. Maybe the perp ate the pizza. Anyway, the vic and the killer had a discussion about the pizza coming to the wrong address etc. The killer saw an opportunity. He was armed. Bang, bang, bang and Jack's no longer with the living. The perp then drags him into the lounge and sits him on the sofa. That's about it,' said Mike, 'except to say that the killer followed Jack from the High Street, saw that he lived alone or was alone, then went and bought the pizza. The cosh he already had. I don't think he was after Jack in particular. He was after whoever was last out and easy to follow.'

By now the four uniforms had returned from their door-to-door. One had some news of interest: a man about five-nine, ten, wearing dark clothes and a cap of some sort was seen going past the house twice. He was walking very slowly and deliberately, or so it seemed. No further description of the man or his clothes was available. The time was approximately half-six, quarter to seven.

'Fits in with your theory that Jack was followed from work Mike,' said Charlie.

'My gut feeling is that this victim has nothing to do with the others,' said Evan.

'Why?' asked D.S. Morris.

'Because,' said Evan, 'because it seems unplanned. I mean let's get the facts straight: did our killer know where Jack lived? No. Did he know he had a girlfriend who worked at night? No. Did he know this Jack was a nobody? No. So I say what did he know? Nothing, anyone associated with Mortons would have done. Even the bloody cleaning lady,' said Evan.

'Beatrice had a lucky escape then,' said Mike.

'Beatrice?' queried Charlie.

'Yeah, Mrs Alibi the cleaning lady and mine too,' said Mike.

'One more thing, did he ring to tell us about it? No. Yet he assumed that the body wouldn't be found until 10.00 a.m. this morning at the earliest,' said Charlie.

'That's it,' said Mike. 'He isn't after the publicity as such. Maybe this guy's working independently or without the knowledge of his partners,' said Mike.

'But why?' said Charlie.

'That, Charlie, is the sixty-four thousand dollar question,' said Evan.

What time do these pizza take-aways open?' said Mike.

'Around four or five in the afternoon,' said D.S. Morris.

They all headed back to their respective homes.

# CHAPTER EIGHT

**AMBER** was having breakfast when Evan came in. As usual, he had come five minutes early. Charlie was on time and Mike turned up at quarter past, just fifteen minutes late. They all had coffee. Evan had changed his mind and had a second breakfast with Amber, a fried egg, two rashers of bacon and piece of toast. Amber didn't need to actually make any more, the food was ready, it was part of her breakfast, a small part of that.

'Any thoughts on yesterday, Mike?' Charlie asked.

Mike shook his head.

'What about you, Evan?' Charlie said.

'Nothing new,' replied Evan.

Amber carefully placed her knife and fork on her empty plate. She had finished eating for the time being. This was the signal that Mike could smoke, so Mike lit up one of his crumpled non-filters; his second of the day. The first he'd had with his breakfast coffee at eight. Half an hour later and Alex from the *Chronicle* turned up, surprised to find them all there instead of in Barry.

'I've some news for you,' Alex said. 'The Mortons have decided to remain here and not go away; they don't think it's right under the circumstances. They are all moving into the father's house in Llanbas village.'

'I suppose the Chief will arrange the necessary security,' said Evan.

'I guess so,' said Alex.

The phone rang. Amber answered it. 'It's Barry. They want to know if we want to sit in on the interviews with the staff.'

'Tell them no, just the copies when they've finished and the photos, lab reports on that strand and anything else they can conjure up,' said Mike.

'Off the record, can anyone tell me why this Garner bloke was killed? As far as I can make out, he's a glorified office boy,' said Alex.

Nobody answered.

'I guess you lot don't know either,' said Alex.

'You have any suggestion, Alex?' said Amber.

'The baddies aren't working together. They have either fallen out about something and one of them has gone out on his own for some reason, but my guess is it's not the old one, because he, that is, "Yesterday's Man", has not given us any tip-offs. Or has he?' said Alex.

'No, not to us,' said Evan.

'What would they argue about?  Money, their next victim? Who's in charge? What?' said Charlie.

'Well, if it's revenge, then it isn't money and logic tells us that the old man is in charge and decides who gets it next and when,' said Mike.

'Maybe the others or one of them at least, doesn't think the old man should be in charge.  Maybe he thinks that the old man is helping us too much,' said Charlie.

'And why is he helping us?' asked Amber.

'Because like everyone else in the world, he wants his fifteen minutes of fame,' said Alex.

'And how does helping us get him his fifteen minutes of fame? And before you say anything Charlie, "Fame" was a hit for David Bowie in, let's see, 1975.  Is that good or is that fantastic?' said Evan.

'He gets his quarter of an hour when he helps us catch him,' said Mike, coming back to the subject.

'That's when he will be in his element. TV channels, newspaper reporters, the lot will listen to his story,' replied Alex.

'But of course the other two, if we're correct in our assumptions, do not want to get caught and do life in jail,' said Evan. 'So why are the other two involved?' said Evan.

'Why does anyone get involved in crime? For the bloody money,' said Charlie, wishing he'd kept quiet and not spoken out.

Alex looked at Charlie. He knew that Charlie's past was a little unsavoury but wondered if the present was too. He would have to do some more digging into Charlie White aka Chalky.

Mike read Alex like he did the football scores. He needed to have a word or two with Alex a.s.a.p. Evan noticed Mike who was now sharpening some pencils with his father's knife. He could guess what Mike was worried about. Alex was after all a newspaper reporter and it would be difficult to divert him off the scent, Charlie's scent. He decided to have a word with Alex before Mike did.

The atmosphere had gone off in the 4, I's lounge cum office, cum laboratory, cum eating place, cum card playing area, so Amber decided that everyone needed to talk, get things off their chest. There was far too much not being said.

'Charlie, could you please get some fresh milk and bread, I'm running out,' said Amber.

'There's plenty of milk,' said Charlie.

'No, I want full-fat, not semi-skimmed. I intend making a nice rice pudding. Three pints will do. I've got the other ingredients: corn flour, vanilla essence, sugar, cinnamon and rice, just need the milk,' said Amber.

'I'll get it when everyone leaves for Barry, Amber, if that's okay with you.'

'I'd appreciate it now, Charlie. I want to make it soonest and then cool it off in the fridge.'

'Right, I'm on my way,' said Charlie.

'Me too,' said Alex.

'Could you just hold on a tick, Alex, I want to show you some photographs. I need your opinion on them,' said Amber.

'Sure, no problem,' said Alex, sitting back down and lighting up a small cigar.

Amber motioned for Evan, who was standing, to sit. Evan did.

'Do you wish to take notes Alex?' Amber said.

'Notes on photographs, what for?' said Alex.
'No, notes on Charles White, Alex,' said Amber.
'Why would I take notes on Charlie?' said Alex.
'It saves you trawling through his dirty washing,' said Amber.
'What makes you think that I'm interested in Charlie?' said Alex.
'Because you are, Alex, and if we are to remain friends and help each other out now and then, we suggest that you leave well alone,' said Mike.
'I have no intention of going into the laundry business, I've enough on my plate as it is,' said Alex.
'Good,' said Evan. 'Maybe some of Amber's rice pudding piled on your overfilled plate will be just reward, as will our continued friendship in keeping your nose out of Charlie's life.'
'What's past is past,' said Mike. 'Let's keep it that way, shall we?'
'Fine, we never had this conversation,' said a relieved Alex, who was now more determined than ever to delve into Mr White's murky past.
Alex left and the new car arrived. The red BMW 330. It was nearly two hours late but at least it was the new model, not their old re-sprayed one.
'Photos of the fire and cars of any use?' asked Amber.
'I don't think so. I think we've just wasted eighty pounds,' said Evan.
Mike flicked through them too and had to agree with Evan.

Forty-six year old Terry Medwin began his day by cashing in his winnings from Saturday's lottery. Eighty-seven pounds. His next stop was the nearest bookies where he invested £20 each way on a 40-1 outsider in the 2.10 at Newcastle. The horse, Medwan, came in second and Terry was two hundred pounds richer. His next stop was the first pub he came across after leaving the bookies. He ordered a pint of Brains Dark and a large whisky. He spotted the one-armed bandit and pushed a pound into the money slot; low and behold, he hit the jackpot, thirty pounds.

He guessed it was his lucky day. He bought drinks for the six hardy souls inside the place and tipped both the landlady and a barmaid. Within the hour, he had put away two and half pints and four large whiskies. He told anyone who would listen about his good fortune and bought them a drink for listening. One person in particular listened very carefully. Another was interested but too far gone to really make any sense of what Terry was saying. The careful listener left the pub and crossed the road where he patiently waited. After his third visit to the toilets, Terry realised that he was drunk and needed to get back home. He had come by bus; he had the foresight to leave his car at home. Unfortunately he'd also left his mobile. He now needed to find himself a taxi. For fifty or so yards, he zigzagged down the street, when suddenly he felt an arm around his shoulders. 'You need a taxi mate. Just come this way,' the careful pub drinker said as he manoeuvred the hapless Terry into a quiet alley, where he brandished a knife and told Terry to hand over his money.

Something told Terry that this was a bad situation and Terry made a pathetic lunge at the mugger only to run straight into five inches of Sheffield steel. The mugger panicked. He'd been caught by surprise and his initial reaction was to plunge his knife another three times into Terry's heart, before rifling through Terry's pockets and taking whatever monies he could find. He then legged it as fast as he could. From across the road another drunk from the pub had witnessed what had happened but wasn't exactly sure what he had seen. He crossed the road as best he could and saw Terry who by now was lying completely still in a pool of blood. The drunk also went through Terry's pockets and found about eight pounds in change and a crumpled five-pound note. He tried in vain to take off Terry's gold ring and watch, so he gave up and headed for the nearest off licence where he bought himself a half bottle of whisky, ten cigarettes and matches.

Somehow Bill Winters got himself back to his DHSS flat, locked the door and started drinking and smoking. By seven, he had drunk himself into oblivion. He reached out but just couldn't catch the many dragons breathing out flames of fire that were flying around the room. The fire was real enough. The Fire Brigade saved Bill and got him to hospital. He had only minor burns but had inhaled a lot of smoke.

In Barry, the four remaining staff at Mortons were being interviewed by Mike and Evan who had changed their minds about interviewing the staff. They learnt nothing of any use. Yes, Jack was a good chap, hard worker, no enemies, nice girlfriend etc. etc. etc. None of the take-aways had CCTV coverage and no, they couldn't remember all their customers between six and ten. Apart from trying out the new car, the journey to Barry had been a waste of time.

Alex on the other hand had learnt a lot about Charlie's past. He too had friends and informants everywhere. He needed them to make a living. Unfortunately, for Alex, one of his guys in the force was also a friend of big Mick Maloney who was godfather to Evan's daughter Jasmine. Mick phoned Evan who told Mike.

At half past five, Mike phoned Dorothea. They arranged for Mike to pick her up at eight. At five past six, Mike phoned Dorothea again and cancelled. They had another Mortons casualty to deal with: a Terry Medwin who'd been stabbed on the outskirts of Cardiff four times.

Patrick finished work at the local garage at one and immediately set off in his pick-up truck to Penarth. He parked, bought some soft drinks and a couple of sandwiches and headed for the promenade where he found himself a comfortable place to sit. He then spent the next five hours planning Louis Morton's death. That he owed to the only person apart from his mother and brother David who had given him the time of day. He would repay Walter once he'd made his plans.

After Patrick had finished eating, he wanted an ice cream of some sort so he crossed the road to one of the shops, brushing inadvertently against a newly painted pillar outside the shop. It was only a little red paint and however hard Patrick tried, he just couldn't get it off his jacket sleeve.

On arrival in their new BMW, Mike noticed that D.I. Foster was on the case and that he was speaking to Alex Symonds. Foster still had a big plaster covering his nose. For some reason it was Evan, not Mike who wanted to break it again.

'So what do we have?' said Evan to Foster.

'Simple,' said Foster. 'Our friend Terry Medwin, Manager of Mortons, the one that was burnt down but still on salary, had a few too many at the pub over there, the Red Lion, was followed here and stabbed fatally in the heart. No witnesses. Murder made to look like a robbery but as you can see Medwin still has his watch, ring and credit cards. Obviously part of this Mortons purge.'

'Fine,' said Evan, 'we will take over now. You can go home.'

'You're kidding me,' said Foster.

'We kid you not,' said Mike. 'Piss off.'

One of the SOCO boys came over and said to Evan, 'I understand you're in charge now. We're finished here. Anything you want to know?'

'Yes,' said Mike. 'Was he drunk when he died?'

'Very,' said another guy who had joined the conversation and introduced himself as a Doctor.

'How many stab wounds Doc?' said Evan.

'Four,' said the Doc, 'one there just above the heart was the first is my educated guess; the other three to the heart followed and anyone of them could have been the fatal one. It wasn't the first.'

'Weapon?' said Mike.

'Five or so inch blade, probably a flick knife, not a broader kitchen knife,' said the Doc.

'Any other marks or anything unusual?' said Evan

'None,' said the Doc, 'but I can tell you he didn't put up much of a fight.'

'Have we got a photo of him?' said Mike

A sarge left by Foster handed Mike a photo.

'I suggest that we get the body out of here. Anyone contact Terry Medwin's next of kin?' said Evan.

'Not yet, be doing so as soon as we move him. We can't bring his wife here, can we?' said the sarge.

'What's your take on this Evan?' asked Alex. 'Come over here Alex, we don't want the rest of the press boys onto what we think, which by the way is off the record, use the information carefully.'

Mike walked over to the other press lads. A young chap, twenty-two or thereabouts, probably weighing no more than the proverbial seven stone weakling who gets sand kicked in his face, was trying to get into the front row of the scrum. He had no hope. A grey-haired, bespectacled battle-axe of a woman and a balding fatso chewing on a cheap cigar kept blocking his way.

'Listen up,' said Mike, 'I'm only going to give it to you once.'

'Terrence Medwin, aged forty-six, married with one child, native and still living in Cardiff was murdered at around five o'clock today by person or persons unknown. He was a manager of the estate agents, Mortons, who have during the past month been targeted. Any questions?'

'Can we assume that there is a connection with the other deaths?' said Fatso.

'At this moment we cannot comment on an ongoing investigation. I've already told you that I won't or can't answer any questions.' That he thought should shut up the fat one. It did, but the grey-haired battle-axe wasn't satisfied.

'Why have you people taken so long to come up with a proper suspect? What are you hiding from us?' she said.

'Lady, I'm luckily not your husband, so I don't need to hide from you. Now please go and write something creative. It should be easy enough, you don't have to rely on us people for your lies,' Mike said angrily. Mike was about to turn when he remembered the young man who was still standing as if in a daze, all alone; the other press boys and battle-axe had dispersed.

'What's your name son?' said Mike.

'It's Joe,' said the lad nervously.

'And who do you work for then, Joe?'

'Freelance but mainly for the *Sun.*'

'Why are you still here? Shouldn't you be getting your story in before someone else beats you to it?' said Mike.

'I haven't got a story,' said Joe.

'Do you see that pub Joe, the Red Lion? Yes, well in about ten minutes I'll be there. Go and get yourself half a shandy or something.'

The lad moved off without a word and headed for the pub. Strange boy, thought Mike. Evan finished with Alex and came over to where Mike was.

'Everything okay, Ev?' Mike said.

'Yeah, told Alex, all off the record, that we expect more attempts in the near future on Morton's staff and that they should be extra vigilant.'

'Load of crap, Evan.'

'I know Mike. The thing that happened here started off as a mugging that went wrong. I'll bet my life on it. All the hallmarks of a drunk being rolled over by an opportunist.'

'That reminds me Evan, I've got us some help, a young reporter. He needs a break, he's waiting over at the pub.'

'Well, let's not keep our intrepid reporter waiting, Mike.'

They found Joe nursing a half of lager. He had a notebook and pencil in front of him; at least two pages were full of words.

'Right Joe, I'm D.I. Karetzi, this is my partner D.I. Jones, and you are Joe what?'

'Mellor,' said Joe.

'I'll get the drinks in,' said Evan, 'what's it to be?'

'Same as Joe,' said Mike.

Evan brought the drinks to the table.

'So you haven't got a story, Joe?' Mike said, and added, 'All the other boyos have.'

'I'm obviously not an expert,' said Joe, 'but who in their right mind follows a man from home, has an opportunity in the pub to drop him a Mickey Finn or even to finish him off in the toilets. There are no CCTVs in here, unusual these days. No, it was in my opinion a plain and simple mugging and I think with all due deference to your status in the police force, I know you agree with me.'

'I like this lad,' said Evan.

'Okay Joe, just sit tight and don't speak,' said Mike as he got up and moved towards the bar. Ten minutes later, he was back. He'd spoken to both the landlady and the barmaid.

'Medwin came in about two-thirty. They had about half a dozen customers of which three were regulars. One was still in the pub, a little worse for wear. Medwin bought drinks for everyone twice—he had a wad of money. He also hit the thirty-pound jackpot on one of those machines. One of the customers left at about four-thirty, a few minutes before Medwin and another man, Bill, who was completely plastered left at the same time. She has an address for him, as they usually have to call a taxi to get him home. The pub always paid for the cab and this Bill chap repays them when he has money.

'Today, though, he left early. Probably ran out of money, he lives about five, six hundred yards down the road. According to both the landlady and barmaid, Medwin had far too much to drink and was a little unsteady on his feet.'

'Do we have a description of the guy that left just before Medwin?' said Evan.

'Yes, dark hair, unshaven, five-eight, nine; broad shoulders; age: late twenties; dark leather jacket, black or navy blue jeans, trainers and a crooked nose,' said Mike, reading from his notes.

'I'll go and have a word with our other chap who was here at the time,' said Mike. Five minutes later and Mike returned. 'Forget him, he wanted to know if I was John, his uncle,' said Mike.

'Did "Uncle John" offer to buy his nephew a drink?' asked Evan.

'Uncle John wasn't in the mood for socializing today,' said Mike.

'This is what we know,' Evan said. 'Medwin lives over two miles away but comes into this part of town. Why? There are nearer places for him to have a drink.' said Evan.

'He came here because he had something that the shops local to him don't have,' said Mike.

'He had done no shopping of any kind unless he bought a piece of jewellery which was lifted together with his money,' said Evan.

'Not around here,' said Joe. 'There are only about six, maybe seven shops and there is no jeweller's.'

'So what shops are there?' said Mike.

Joe thought for a few seconds then said, 'There's a newsagent's, a small convenience store, a baker's, chemist, a bookies and a second-hand bookshop.'

Mike got up and walked back to the bar. 'Does your TV have Teletext?'

'Don't know,' said the barmaid.

'Where are the controls?' asked Mike. The barmaid handed them over. The TV did have Ceefax and Mike, after a while, got to the racing pages where he noted the first three horses in every race ran between 1.30 and 2.30 p.m. He returned to the table and pointed at a horse in the 2.10. 'My money's on Medwan. Is that bookies still open?'

'That's a big leap Mike,' said Evan.

'Medwin, Medwan, I'd back it and it was a 40-1 shot.'

The bookie was still open. He had half a dozen customers watching a live televised match. He showed Medwin's picture to the manager who confirmed that Medwin had placed a bet of twenty pounds each way on Medwan. He also confirmed that to the best of his knowledge Terry Medwin had never stepped through his door until that afternoon.

'Right then: Mr Terry Medwin wakes up this morning. He's in a good mood or he's bored or he just fancies a bet. So, he reads his morning paper, notices that there is a horse that sounds like his surname and decides to come into town, or the nearest place where there is a bookies. He gets public transport in; maybe he can't drive or his wife's taken the car. Whatever, he goes in and puts on his bet. He watches the race on TV at the bookies, collects his winnings and decides to celebrate at this dive that pretends to be a pub. He wins a bit more dosh on the slot machine, buys a few rounds because he's in a good mood and gets drunk.'

'So far so good Evan,' said Mike.
'Yes, it sounds reasonable but now we run into a few problems.'
'Like what?' said Joe.
'Like why he doesn't call a cab on his mobile or if he hasn't got it with him, why not ask the landlady or barmaid to get him one?' said Evan.
'Because Ev, in his drunken state, he thinks some fresh air will do him good and maybe he thinks he can pick up a passing taxi,' said Mike.
'Or he intends getting on a bus,' said Joe.
'Could be,' said Evan. 'He was going in the general direction of his home,' said Evan.
'But he only got a hundred yards from the pub,' said Joe.
'I think that the first guy, the one we have a description of, waited for him. Lured him into the alley and attempted to mug him,' said Evan.
'I agree, Evan, but the guy who left at the same time or within a minute or so, this Bill chap, would have been a witness, assuming that he was going the same way,' said Mike.
'Let's look him up,' said Evan.
'He lives down there, about a half of a mile,' said Mike.

As they passed the convenience store, Mike took the opportunity to pop in and buy some cigarettes. A seventy-five year old Asian with a fourteen year old girl, also Asian, were behind the counter. They had no customers. Mike bought his non-filters and decided to show them a picture of Medwin; both shook their heads but the old man requested to see the picture again just as Mike was about to leave. Medwin had indeed come in, about two p.m. He had won on the lottery.

The old man remembered him because he had four numbers, plus the fact that business was slow, people in the area were hurting. The last customer that paid over a five-pound note was a drunk who paid mostly in change and that was for a half bottle of the cheapest whisky and some cheap brand cigarettes. Mike thanked him and left.

How anyone drunk or sober, rich or poor could drink that much was beyond Mike's comprehension.

They arrived just as the Fire Brigade was leaving. A lone policeman stood outside the sealed-off area.

'What's going on?' said Evan.

'Small fire,' said one of the departing fire officers, after seeing Mike's badge.

'Anyone hurt?' asked Evan.

'Minor burns, taken to hospital. Most probably started with a cigarette whilst the man was asleep, drunk out of his mind,' said the officer.

'Can I have a fifteen second look inside?' said Mike.

'I can't allow that Sir,' said the fireman.

'Of course you can, it's important. I just need fifteen seconds or we can stand here until your boss, my boss, Rhodri Morgan or even Barak Obama comes down and I will still get my fifteen seconds inside. It's important,' said Mike.

'Okay Detective, follow me, you've got exactly one minute. Agreed?'

'Agreed and thanks.'

Once inside Mike's eyes darted everywhere. 'Is that where you found the guy, on that easy chair or what's left of it?'

'Yes, that's where we found him.'

'Anything moved?' said Mike.

'No, only what was moved unintentionally or to get at the fire,' said the fireman.

'Do we have a name?' said Mike.

'Yes, it's William Winterman,' said the fireman.

'Can you read me the name of that half bottle of whisky over there?' said Mike.

The fireman did.

'Thank you,' said Mike. 'That's it,' he said and walked out.

'Back to the car,' said Evan.

'Yes, but via the convenience store,' said Mike.

'It's our man, isn't it?' said Evan.

'Yeah, it's a Bill Winterman, I'm just going to buy him some lubrication,' said Mike.

'What type of lubrication?' asked Joe.

'Cheap whisky,' said Mike.

'I doubt that they will let us see him and more to the point is he in any state to say anything of use, even if they do?' said Evan.

With the half bottle of cheap whisky in his pocket they asked at reception for William Winterman. After ten minutes of waiting a young couple came up to them. The girl spoke: 'They won't allow you to see my father, even I'm not allowed in.'

'Is he in a critical condition?' asked Evan.

'No, the old bastard's pissed and sleeping it off,' said the man with the girl.

'Shut up, Dean, and stop talking about my father like that,' she said.

'Sorry Carol, but this is the third time he's ended up in here. He should be in some clinic where they can get him off the booze.'

'He's tried Dean. Every since Mum died. I said he should stay with us,' Carol said.

'No way. Especially now that we're going to have a baby,' said Dean.

'Anyway, who the hell are you lot?' said Carol.

Evan showed her his warrant card.

'What's he done?' asked Dean.

'He's a possible witness to a murder,' said Evan.

'A possible witness? What kind of a witness?' said Dean.

'The kind that might have seen a murder and could prevent further ones,' said Evan.

'That's rubbish,' said Dean.

'I will tell you what's rubbish,' said Mike. 'Rubbish is that man who has killed ten people in the space of a month, does not worry about hunting down a witness and killing him too. Now that's garbage, isn't it Dean?' said Mike.

'I didn't mean it that way,' said Dean.

'Let's get to see him. I'm sure he'd like to reach the status of grandfather,' said Mike.

'They won't let us, they keep on saying come back tomorrow at visiting time.'

'Do you know his room number?' said Evan.

'He's in a ward with three others,' said Dean.

'Let's go then,' said Mike.

At the top of the stairs, they were stopped by a nurse. Mike showed her his warrant card and barged past her. The others followed. By the time they reached Bill's ward they were confronted by the nurse, a doctor and a security man.

'We need to talk to Mr Winterman,' said Evan.

'And I need you all to leave with immediate effect,' said the doctor.

'We leave after we have spoken to Mr Winterman. Just a few minutes,' said Evan.

'Impossible, he's under sedation,' said the nurse.

'I see,' said Mike. 'A man who's brought in out of this world on cheap whisky is given pills or something to sedate him. Are you taking note of this malpractice, Joe? Sorry, I haven't introduced you to a reporter from the *Sun* or to his daughter, and we are the investigating detectives on a murder case which Winters witnessed and could possibly be his next target.'

'That doesn't cut any ice with me,' said the doctor. 'He's in my care now.'

'Call Mick and tell him to get a dozen uniforms down here now,' said Mike. 'I've a bad feeling about the treatment of patients down here and we need to get to the bottom of this.'

Evan got out his mobile phone and the security guard moved towards him.

'One more step from you, bonzo, and you'll be joining the patients in here.'

The security man stopped. This cop meant it. Evan started dialling. The doctor backed down, asked Evan to cut the line. Evan was relieved—he didn't know what he was going to say to his wife Edna.

'Look, I don't need any trouble. I know that in this situation I have absolute authority but we have fifty-odd patients on this floor and I can't have people disturbing them. The daughter can go in for two minutes with me and then one of you lot for another two minutes. The rest back to Reception please. Security will walk you down,' the doctor added.

'I'll see him,' said Mike 'and I'll meet you downstairs when I've finished.'

'It won't do you much good, Detective. I'm warning you now, Mr Winterman is in no position to make any sensible conversation if he can even talk, that is.'

Everyone left except Mike who waited outside whilst Carol and the doctor entered the ward. Three minutes of pacing up and down the hall outside the wards passed before Carol and the doctor came back out.

'He's sitting up but not making any sense as such,' said Carol.

'Did he recognise you?' asked Mike.

'Yes, he did, no problem,' said Carol.

'Does he know where he is and why?'

'He knows he's in hospital but not quite sure why,' she said.

'Okay Carol, I'll go in now,' said Mike.

'Hello Bill, I'm Detective Inspector Mike Karetzi and I've come to help you answer some very simple questions.'

'Who you?' said Bill.

'The Police, Bill. You saw a fight today, after you left the Red Lion. It was a fight between two people who were in the pub at the same time as you. After the fight you stole some change from the man that died in the fight and bought a half bottle of whisky from the convenience store on the corner.'

Bill closed his eyes and didn't speak. Mike turned to the doctor: 'You're going to have to leave the room now Doc. I cannot let you hear what I'm going to ask next, it's confidential.'

'I can't do that,' said the doctor.

'Two minutes Doctor, stand outside the door. This is really confidential police business.'

'Like I said, I can't,' said the doctor.

'You can and you will. Two minutes,' said Mike.

The doctor looked at his watch. 'Two minutes. Not a second more Detective,' and walked out.

'Bill, open your eyes and see what I'm holding in my hand. It's a present for you.'

Bill opened his eyes a squint then more and more until they were nearly popping out of his head. Mike unscrewed the top and put it to Bill's mouth. Bill took a swig and tried for more but Mike screwed the cap back on and returned it to his pocket.

'Now if you can't remember anything, that's fine, and I'm off,' said Mike

'I want drink,' said Bill.

'Did you see the fight, Bill?'

'I think I saw something,' said Bill.

'Thinking's no good Bill. Goodnight, I'll get one of the nurses to get you a cup of tea.'

'It was Mad Mitch! He got the other bloke, give me a drink.'

Mike unscrewed the cap and let Bill have another couple of swigs. He managed to put the cap on the bottle into his pocket just as the doctor walked back in, looking again at his watch.

'Does this Mitch have another name? Where can he be found? What's his job, something…'

'That's enough,' said the doctor, 'your time's up.'

'Doc, if you don't shut up, your time will be up. I'm investigating a murder. Ten murders actually. So please shut up.'

'At the boat,' said Bill.

'What boat?' asked Mike.

'The boat, the sailing boat. Lots of sails, they all go,' and with that Bill had closed his eyes and seemed out of it.

'That's it,' said the doctor. 'He's gone for the next three, four hours.'

'Okay doc, sorry about the hassle, just doing my job, saving lives, similar to what you do here,' said Mike.

'There is a marked difference though about how we go about it,' said the doctor.

'That's true,' said Mike, 'my way always works. Yours is hit and miss, Doctor. Goodnight.'

As Mike passed the bed next to Bill's an old man with a long, grey face pointed at Mike's pocket and said 'drink.' Mike stopped, picked up the medical clipboard hanging on the metal rung at the bottom of the bed and glanced quickly at it before saying, 'Sorry old boy, says here NIL BY MOUTH.'

As they left the room, Mike turned to the doctor: 'Tell me, do you know of any sailing boats around here?'

The doctor just walked away. Mike guessed he was tired and didn't want to play the find the boat with lots of sails game. Neither did Mike, but he had promised Joe a story.

The four were waiting downstairs. 'How was Dad?' asked Carol.

'He helped a lot. He also mumbled something about Dean being a good lad,' said Mike.

'He didn't,' said Dean.

'He did actually,' said Mike.

'I told you he likes you deep down, Dean. Now do you believe me?' said Carol.

'Yes love,' Dean said, not believing a word.

'So Mike, do you realise it's nearly ten-thirty?' said Evan.

'Have you called Edna and reported in?' said Mike.

'What did you find out then Mike?' said Evan, ignoring Mike's barb.

'So you did phone Edna,' said Mike 'otherwise you would be on the phone right now.'

'Very clever, Mike. Did you get anything out of him?' said Evan.

'He saw what happened then robbed Medwin, who was dead, of his small change with which he bought the whisky. He knows the killer as Mad Mitch. No other name and this Mad Mitch works or hangs out at some kind of sailing club or boatyard or owns a boat. Anyway, it's something to do with boats.'

'He's probably got previous. I'll ring it in to Amber, see if she can get anywhere with this Mad Mitch character.'

Evan rang in. Amber was having a drink with Charlie and Maggie. She had invited them around for a meal, which they had finished and were now on Rum and Black.

'Where to now, Mike? Not much more we can do,' said Evan.

'True,' said Mike, 'your story will have to wait a day or so Joe; where can we drop you off?'

'Can I tag along?' said Joe.

Just as Evan was about to answer, 'yes,' his mobile rang. 'That's Edna,' said Mike.

Evan answered. 'It's Charlie, he's with Amber. Mad Mitch can be found on certain days at the Cutty Sark. No one knows his real name. He mugs people, usually drunks, and steals their money, watches, rings, chains; he can get quite violent, short fuse, people are wary of him. Sells his ill-gotten gains at the Sark. Not a person to cross; doesn't drink much and always carries a knife, which he's not afraid to use. He lives on Bute Street, somewhere, with his mother, who's wheelchair bound. I'm waiting for someone to give me an address. It will cost twenty quid,' said Charlie.

'Thanks Charlie, we're going for a coffee and something to eat. Can Amber arrange through Mick Maloney a couple of uniforms to be on standby? This man sounds like a handful,' said Evan.

'Will do,' said Charlie, finishing the conversation and closing down the line.

After a coffee and stale sandwich left over from lunchtime, Mike and Evan, Joe in tow, headed for Bute Street. They parked halfway down and just sat. Evan in the driving seat, Mike next to him smoking and Joe in the back, writing frantically. Charlie phoned with a name: James Mitchell and an address. He also told them Big Mick with two uniforms would be there within a few minutes.

'Do we have a plan, Evan?' Mick asked.

'I'll go in the front with Mike and a constable; you, Mick, take the other uniform and cut off the back,' said Evan.

'Joe, you stay put in the car,' said Mike.

'And if he's not in?' said Mick.

'Then we will just wait for him, inside,' said Evan.

'Give us a minute or two to get around to the back,' said Mick.

'Fine,' said Evan, 'and Mick, watch the bastard, he's handy with a knife.'

'Don't worry Evan, he'll be no trouble. There's five of us for God's sake,' Mick said.

Evan rang on the door. A scruffy, thin, peroxide blonde opened the door, took one look and shouted 'Police!' before making a dash back down the narrow hall.

Mike was past Evan and first in, running down the hall only to run headlong into a wheelchair and being bowled over like a ten pin ball. Mad Mitch's mother then tried to hit him with a plate of fish and chips and attempted to gouge out an eye when she was restrained by Evan who managed to wrestle her to the ground. Still, the woman put up one hell of a fight, biting Evan on his arm and drawing blood.

Three up to Mad Mitch's woman, thought Mike as he managed to push a chair between himself and the maniac driving the wheelchair.

Outside it was bedlam. Mad Mitch wasn't a big bloke but he was fast. He sliced to the bone the uniform's hand and when Big Mick got the knife off him, he produced another from somewhere and nearly decapitated Mick who was only saved by the knife making contact with its dull side as mad Mitch had missed with his anti-clockwise attack and in his hurry to swing back in a clockwise arc, didn't have time to adjust the knife.

Big Mick lashed out, his fist connecting perfectly with Mad Mitch's chin and rendering him senseless for a while. Big Mick frogmarched a dazed and handcuffed Mad Mitch back into the house. The blonde was also handcuffed and the mother still trapped in a corner by a chair and a sofa.

'What happened here then?' said Mick, still a little shaken by his fortunate escape.

'Looks to me that I'm the last person standing,' said Mike. 'Let's get some back-up, we need a van for these two.'

'And her in the chair?' said Mick.

'Leave her,' said Mike. 'She hasn't finished eating her fish dinner yet.'

'It's back to the hospital for the two uniforms and Evan; you'll probably need a jab for rabies,' said Mick.

'Can we leave the rest up to you, Mick? You interview the madman and please give Joe our friendly reporter any updates soonest. We promised him a story and he's earned it,' said Evan.

'Where is this Joe?' said Mick.

'In the back of our car. I'll go and get him Mick, and thanks, we couldn't have taken on that bloody lot without you and the boys,' said Mike.

'Okay Joe, out you get. It's safe now. D.I. Mick Maloney will fill you in before he drops you off at the station. You've got the scoop of the year. Remember us when you make the big time,' Mike said, shaking Joe's sweating hands.

Joe thanked Mike profusely, then walked over to Evan and did the same. On the drive to the hospital, Mike driving, they caught the end of a very old Joe Brown song called 'A picture of you.' Nearly fifty years, thought Evan.

'I wish I had a bloody picture,' Mike said out loud, thinking of the strawberry blonde.

'What did you say Mike? I didn't quite catch it,' said Evan.

'Nothing Evan, just thinking about something,' said Mike.

Funnily enough, Evan was also thinking about his daughter Jasmine, Mike's strawberry blonde. He would miss her when she returned to Edinburgh the following day.

# CHAPTER NINE

**ON THE FRIDAY** morning, a fine bright day, Mike had his large espresso coffee and a cigarette. He felt good and decided he would walk to the office and still be early for a change. He'd grab a Chronicle on route and read it when he got to 4, I's.

Evan said his tearful goodbyes to Jasmine and left for Nelson Street. His wife Edna would take their daughter to the train station. A few minutes after Evan left in the BMW, his wife and daughter left in his Rover. Like her husband Edna was a cautious but good driver, eyes always on the road—viewing of her mirrors, mobile switched off and not much talking whilst she concentrated on her driving.

As the car approached Cardiff Central, Jasmine espied Mike. She shouted to her mother to stop the car but Edna couldn't. A car was right behind her and there was nowhere to turn off or park for about a hundred yards or so.

When Edna did stop, Jasmine told her to go and park at Cardiff Central whilst she went and found a long lost friend. It was too late for Edna to argue. Jasmine was already out of the car and running back the way they had come. Mike had not seen Jasmine otherwise he would also have run, in the opposite direction, and they would have met. Mike entered the newsagent's, picked up the *Sun*: Joe Mellor had made the front page. Mike felt pleased so he bought both the *Sun* and the *Cardiff Chronicle* which was running with the crap story like all the others.

Mike read a few back pages of the main dailies, bought himself twenty Players Medium and a small bottle of pure orange juice, which he drank before leaving the shop. As he was about to leave, his mobile rang. It was Tanya, an old girlfriend who'd left him for someone more accessible, or so she thought at the time. It seemed she was wrong and was now crying on the phone. She needed a friend to talk to desperately. Mike ascertained what type of friend she was looking for. He agreed to meet her for a coffee.

Mike had a new girl in Dorothea and a strawberry blonde he would love to get to know. At that very moment Jasmine was standing just ten yards away, tears streaming down her face.

Mike was happy with platonic. He could hardly refuse an ex a meet over a cup of coffee. He finished the call and immediately retrieved another. It was his mother Alice. She was sitting with her friends and they were reading the *Sun*. She was proud of her Mikhail.

Mike asked who had bought the *Sun*. 'Alfred, Mrs Alibi's husband of course,' said his mother. Obvious, Mike thought. Mrs Alibi's husband. Mike thought about ringing 4 'I's and letting them know that he would be late, but then that wasn't saying anything new, he was always late.

Jasmine just made the train but that was no consolation. She didn't even want to confide her feelings for someone she hardly knew to her mother and they were extremely close. It was a quarter past when Mike met Tanya at the designated coffee house. Everything was a little awkward. Did he hug her, kiss her on the cheek or just say 'Hello'? He opted for the latter but Tanya had other ideas and gave Mike both a hug and a kiss on the cheek. She was fifteen minutes late. Mike had only been five.

They ordered coffees. Mike listened to Tanya speak about Tony, the guy who turned out to be a real piece of work, or so Tanya said. She'd probably said the same things about him to Tony, he mused. It was twenty-five to when Tanya at last finished her vitriolic attack on the hapless Tony. Mike was about to say something soothing when she blurted out that she still loved Tony and then burst into tears.

All Mike could do was hand her a paper napkin and that didn't help at all. Mike wondered what he was doing there. He felt like a smoke but couldn't in the café. Everyone was looking at him with a 'you bastard type look.' Mike felt like a heel and he hadn't done anything.

Softly he asked Tanya how he could help and was told in no uncertain terms that he couldn't. He again wondered what he was doing there with Tanya. The crying stopped ten minutes later. She looked at Mike and said, 'All men are bastards!'—loud enough for everyone to hear.

Mike reached out and took her hand and she said, 'Sorry.' This was hardly audible and no one heard it apart from Mike. One guy sitting nearby with a toothbrush thick moustache seemed to be getting a little agitated. He was sitting alone, so Mike gave him a warning look that said 'don't get involved you asshole, it's none of your business.' The guy heeded Mike's advice and looked at the picture of a bunch of daisies on the wall.

A waitress came and asked Tanya if everything was all right. Tanya didn't answer so Mike did. He told her that everything was fine and dandy. The waitress walked away shaking her head. Out of the corner of his eye, Mike saw the waitress speaking to an older man who was obviously in charge. He wore a yellow tie. Mike slipped his warrant card out of his jacket and laid it open face up on the table. He was expecting a visitor. Mike was right; the man with the yellow tie marched through the café like one of Hitler's SS guards. He made sure that all the customers were aware of his movements. When he reached the table and before he had time to speak, Mike tapped the warrant card with his fingers. Yellow tie turned and crept back to his position behind the bar. Yellow was an apt colour for him; Mike and the other customers agreed on this.

Tanya meantime was oblivious to the drama unfolding around her. Her coffee lay untouched.

'Tanya, go find someone else. This Tony guy's not for you but there are plenty of decent people out there,' Mike said.

'You find anyone yet?' Tanya said.

'I've been lucky, Tanya,' said Mike.

'Does that mean you have or haven't?' said Tanya.

'I have,' said Mike.

'What's her name?' said Tanya.

'What difference does it make?' said Mike. Tanya shrugged her shoulders.

'I've got work to do,' said Mike.

'Yes, I read about you Mike. You're a big hero around these parts. It's a wonder you have time for any socialising.'

'I try to fit them in,' said Mike, trying make a joke of the whole thing.

'You bastard,' said Tanya, standing up and throwing her coffee over Mike's face before stomping out.

Mike just sat there wiping his face with a few napkins from an adjoining table; at least the coffee was cold. Mike's shirt would need dry cleaning. He took out some money, placed it on the table and left to the relief of all in the café. He'd only got ten yards when he heard Tanya's voice. He turned and she was standing there. 'I'm sorry,' she said. 'That was a stupid thing for me to do. It's not your fault I can't keep a man, but I do love him you know. I'll tell you what, why don't you have a word with Tony, tell him that I didn't mean to trash his suits, it was all a big mistake.'

'You trashed his suits—why, Tanya? said Mike.

'Because he lied to me! You know I can't stand lies,' Tanya said.

'Let me get this in perspective, Tanya. You left me. I guess that was a mutual decision. Anyway, you found someone new, this Tony guy, who lies to you and you trash his clothes. Tony gets mad and ditches you but you still love him and want me to talk to him after throwing a cup of coffee in my face in a public place where the people now think I'm some kind of monster.'

'It's nothing like you're making it out to be Mike, so stop saying things like that. I'm the one that's been hurt, you know.'

'I know nothing, Tanya. I'm not speaking to this Tony chap. You've made your own bed so go and lie on it with or without Tony, and please don't ring me again. I've had enough humiliation to last me a long time.' Mike walked away from a stunned Tanya.

Mike got to 4 'I's at eleven. Alex Symonds had beaten him by five minutes. 'Mr Symonds is very upset,' said Amber.

'Why is Mr Symonds upset?' said Mike.

'Because of this,' said Alex, slamming down a copy of the *Sun*.
'True story that,' said Mike.
'What happened to you scratch my back and I'll scratch yours?' said Alex.
'Ah that. We said that thinking you were going to use nails Alex, not a fucking garden rake,' said Mike.
'What are you on, some kind of drug?' said Alex.
'Alex, we said no looking into the past when it concerns one of our own. By that, I mean Charlie. The minute you began and broke your word, we knew about it and decided we would break ours,' said Evan.
'I didn't do anything,' said Alex.
'Don't deny it Alex, it's unbecoming of you,' said Amber.
'This is bullshit,' said Alex, 'I'm very disappointed in you all. You've made me look like a right prat by giving up a top story to some snotty-nosed freelance kid. You all know how useful I can be and have been,' said Alex.
'Give it a break man,' Charlie said, 'you made a mistake; we made a mistake. Maybe we understand each other better now.'
'I'm telling you that I've not broken our agreement,' said Alex.
'If you don't shut up Alex, I'm going to bounce you around the five corners of this room,' said Mike.
'Four corners,' said Amber.
'Five,' said Mike, 'I'm going to bounce him off one twice.'
'You're bloody mental,' said Alex.
'I know, that's why they call me "crazy Karetzi",' said Mike.
'Let's not get wound up about it all please Gentlemen,' said Amber. 'Let's have a cup of tea and a few biscuits. I'm sure Alex will welcome closure of this subject.'
But Alex was having none of it. He stormed out and back to his own office where he reflected on his own stupidity.
It was the Chief Constable who turned up next. She'd had a complaint from the hospital administration. Evan thought she would be gunning for Mike for being too aggressive. He was right on both counts, but there was a third. Mike had given a patient under heavy

sedation whisky, which according to the hospital had endangered the patient's life. The Chief wanted to know if this was correct.

'Partly correct Chief,' said Mike.

'Which part?' asked the Chief.

'We were not aggressive. More let's say persuasive than aggressive. Mr Winterman's daughter and son-in-law to be were witness to that and, as for the whisky, yes, Mike did take some in but only let Winterman smell it. And yes, he did indicate that he would leave the bottle if Winterman answered his questions.'

'Were you alone with Mr Winterman, Mike?'

'For a while yes,' said Mike.

'Why did you ask the doctor to leave?' asked the Chief.

'Because it was obvious that Mr Winterman was afraid of the man in the white coat. He had previous experiences in hospital,' said Mike.

'Did he tell you that?' said the Chief.

'He didn't need to. I could tell by his body language and I was proved right because most of what I garnered From Mr Winterman came when the doctor was not present.'

'But both the patient and doctor agree on one thing: that you gave the patient whisky. Why is that?'

'Because Chief, one thought that if he said I had given him whisky, then that might convince the doctor to give him more. After all Bill was in a state of delirium.'

'I see, and the doctor's reason?' said the Chief.

'He wanted to believe Winterman because it suited him and he could make trouble for me.'

'Why would a doctor who did not know you want to make trouble for you, Mike?'

'Because he had misdiagnosed Mr Winterman's condition,' Mike said. 'He said I wouldn't get a tweet out of the heavily sedated Winterman but he was wrong. Winterman sang like a canary.'

'I'd love to believe you Mike, but this is unfortunately an official complaint which I must look into,' said the Chief.

'Then we don't have a problem. Mike can prove it,' said Evan.

'How?' asked the Chief.

'Because Mike left the bottle we bought at the newsagent's in the BMW which is just outside. I'll go and bring it in,' said Evan.

'Good,' said the Chief, 'that's a start.'

Within a minute Evan returned, bottle in hand, and placed it in front of the Chief. 'Exhibit No 1,' said Evan.

'We have more?' said the Chief.

'We will when Charlie runs down to the nearest offi and buys a similar bottle,' said Evan.

Mike looked at the half bottle. It was full. Evan had added some still water that he always kept in the car. Good old Evan. What a clever little bastard, Mike thought.

The Chief tried the top. The seal had been broken. 'It's been opened,' said the Chief. 'Yes, I did that. You can't smell whisky through glass,' said Mike.

On Charlie's return with Exhibit No 2, it was obvious to even the one-eyed that the quantities were the same.

'Would you like a taste of each Chief, just to make sure?' said Evan.

'No thank you, but I'd love a cup of tea and some of those chocolate biscuits.'

'Tea it is then Chief,' said Amber.

'Whilst I'm here, I'd like to talk about your expenses,' said the Chief.

'Anytime you wish Chief,' said Evan.

'I wish now,' said the Chief.

'Chief, these can be sorted out when we return from Barry. We've a few loose ends to sort out regarding the Mortons business,' said Mike.

'Fine, so when will you be back?' said the Chief.

'A few minutes after you leave,' said Mike.

'A joke I presume,' said the Chief.

'Of course,' said Mike.

'Then don't disappear,' said the Chief.

'Chief, we're going to need at least a week of your time to sort them out,' said Evan, knowing that the Chief had barely a spare hour on any given day.

'I don't have the time, as you well know. That's why we have a Mr Drago to sort things out. He's a very patient man with lots of time on his hands. He will see you tomorrow morning. Nine sharp.'

'Yes Chief, a Mr Drago, nine sharp,' said Amber.

Mr Ken Drago arrived on time, nine sharp. Five foot five. Dapper with little black moustache; a neat dark three-piece suit and highly polished black shoes. A man who understood like Evan how to look after his shoes. He was about fifty, maybe older. Everything about him cried accountant from his hide leather briefcase to his black trilby hat.

He introduced himself to Amber, Evan and Charlie and requested an office. Evan pointed to the three desks. Drago picked one and sat down next to it. He noticed the clock was five minutes slow, that there were ashtrays on the desks, food, pencils only one inch long. Everything around the place screamed sloppiness.

He had been told that this unit was slightly unconventional but this was ridiculous. He was going to have a field day in Nelson Street. One of them, the one with the Russian name, hadn't even bothered to turn up yet. Another, the grossly overweight black woman, was eating some kind of pie whilst she was working one of the computers. One was playing patience and the other one was on the phone to someone in Edinburgh; it sounded like he was talking to his daughter.

Putting his hands behind his neck, he closed his eyes. Psyching himself up in readiness for the battle that lay ahead. He didn't care about how long it would take. His firm charged by the hour and that charge was heavy.

Mike surfaced at quarter past nine, 4 'I's time. Ken introduced himself; Mike did the same. 'I'm afraid you're twenty minutes late,' said Drago.

'Don't be afraid Mr Drago. You're in good hands. We are the Police,' said Mike, 'and anyway I'm only fifteen minutes late.' Mike looked at the big office clock.

'But that's five minutes slow,' said Drago.

'We know,' said Mike, 'but that's the clock we use, not your hand watch.'

So this is the guy they call 'crazy,' Drago thought. But from what he'd been reading in the papers, these guys were no fools. On the contrary, they were probably the best detectives in the UK.

'So time isn't a problem, Mr Drago,' said Mike.

'Every job has a certain amount of time allotted to it and we don't like to overrun. It's unfair on our clients,' said Drago who was concentrating on the number code to open his case.

'Are you Maltese?' Mr Drago asked Charlie.

'No, why?' said Drago.

'No reason, and I suppose you don't follow snooker,' said Charlie.

'That's correct Mr White. But why is it of interest to you, all these questions, why?' said Drago.

'He's just nosey Mr Drago, don't take any notice of Charlie,' said Amber, her mouth full of apple pie.

Drago opened his briefcase. Out came a fountain pen, two sharpened pencils, a rubber, a ruler, a calculator and three files, all coloured differently.

'I think we should start with last year's accounts, up to and including the 31$^{st}$ December. Then we will take them in monthly order: January, February and March.'

Evan having packed his pipe, lit up. Mike did the same with one of his cigarettes.

'May I point out to you that the laws in this country prohibit smoking in public places, which include offices,' said Drago.

'That's very interesting Mr Drago, but we are in our lounge and the law doesn't apply to lounges. There's a sign on the door Mr Drago, if you care to look.'

'This is preposterous,' said Drago.

'I agree,' said Evan, 'best you go upstairs to our designated office and we will call you down when we finish smoking.'

'Why can't we use the office upstairs then?' said Mr Drago.

'Because we can't smoke up there Mr Drago,' Mike said as innocently as he could muster.

Drago knew he was in a madhouse but he'd come to do a job and a job he would do. Nobody but nobody could beat him when it came to accounts. If there was a penny unaccounted for, he would find it. That's why he was the top man and that's why he was here: because he was the best.

'Can you tell me, Mrs Gilberts, what exactly is your role here?' asked Drago.

'Watching the detectives,' Amber replied.

'Elvis song. Good one I think,' said Charlie.

'Presley eh? Never heard that one,' said Evan.

'Costello, Elvis Costello,' said Charlie.

Amber cut the cake into six pieces; a walnut and almond cake with syrup of honey. She put a piece for all the men on individual plates, together with a small fork and napkin and kept two for herself. It was only fair; she had made it. It was a little too heavy for Mike but he took a couple of mouthfuls. Evan and Charlie were tucking in and poor old Ken Drago didn't know what to do.

'Eat up Mr Drago. It's got almonds and walnuts. Nuts that are very good for your BP,' said Amber.

'BP? I'm not familiar with ... oh, I see what you mean, blood pressure.'

'Yes, Mr Drago, and I only made it last night, it's not stale or anything.'

'It's great,' said Evan.

Drago took a forkful. DI Jones was right. It tasted good. No doubt, she'd be trying to get the ingredients on a future expense sheet, he thought. One more thing he wouldn't allow to go through.

It was gone eleven when Drago took control of himself and started the inquisition.

'Now then, let's start with this meal at Angelo's. When I say meal, I mean meals, drinks plural and a massive tip. Then we have various taxis. Look, it's all here in black and white. You can't claim this lot on expenses, your first day too!' said Drago.

Without thinking, Mike had taken one of Drago's two pencils and was whittling it down to nothing with his knife.

'What are you doing D.I. Karetzi?' said Drago.

'Looking at the figures and listening to you, Mr Drago,' Mike replied.

'I'm talking about my pencil,' Drago said.

'Oh, I'm sorry about that, Mr Drago.'

'So am I, Detective. I've had that pencil for over a year,' Drago said.

'Well it's time you had a new one Mr Drago. Amber's got some somewhere,' said Mike.

'Never mind the pencil. What about the meal and drinks?' Drago said tapping the offending document with his last usable pencil.

'It's been a while. I can't really remember what we ate or drank and as for the tip, well we must have had some excellent service,' Mike said.

Drago laughed. 'I'm fifty-five, Detective, not five. Stop fobbing me off and just agree that this cannot be classified as an out of pocket expense, which someone, in this case, the South Wales Police Force, has to cover.'

'Do you ever work from home, Mr Drago?' asked Charlie.

'Yes, on a few rare occasions,' said Drago.

'Are you paid extra for that?' said Charlie.

'No, I'm not. I'm salaried like your goodselves,' said Drago.

'Let's say you work all of Saturday on some audit, you're telling me that you don't get paid extra overtime, a bonus?' said Charlie.

'That's correct. Um, it's Mr White, isn't it?' said Drago.

'So, then, let's say six hours extra, is not passed on by your company to the clients. I mean, you don't charge Forbes & Forbes and they don't charge the six hours work you have done to the clients. Now, that's very fair and decent,' said Charlie.

'That is not a comparison with your case,' said Drago.

Mike passed a note to Amber. It read, 'Check out directors of Forbes & Forbes, or partners and managers, especially Drago, the non-snooker playing Malteser.'

Mike only wrote that last word because he liked the sound of it. It rolled off his tongue.

'I don't think we are progressing much, are we?' said Drago.

'If your boss or you yourself take out, say someone for lunch to discuss a problem at work or an account, do you expect to be reimbursed?' said Amber.

'Of course I do,' said Drago.

'We do the same,' said Evan.

'Let me make it clear to you. These expenses are not, I repeat not, going through. Look at this: hundreds of pounds for groceries, enough petrol to keep a ship going for an Atlantic crossing, Christmas trees, decorations—who do you think you are, Abramovich?' said Drago.

'Who's Abramovich?' said Charlie.

'Never mind,' said Drago.

'And what's all this business with a non-repaid loan for the purchase of forty-two DVD recorders, which I understand you gave away. One more thing, you can't just put down £300 as a charity donation without documentation proving which charity this money went to or the hundreds for informants without names. Everything must be accounted for,' said Drago.

'So how do we get around all this nonsense?' said Mike.

'By putting your hands in your pockets and making up the shortfall,' said Drago.

'Apart from Charlie, is anyone whiter than white?' asked Mike.

'Another joke, Detective?' said Drago.

'Not bad though,' said Evan.

'Look, this must be taken seriously, otherwise it could be classified as fraudulent,' said Drago.

'Can anyone help us sort out this misunderstanding?' said Mike.

'Yes, I could be passing these expenses as bona fide ones but I can't and won't,' Drago said popping another wine gum into his mouth.

'Time for lunch,' said Amber.

Drago looked at his watch. It was only ten to twelve.

'It's pointless delaying the inevitable,' said Drago.

'At last we agree on something,' said Mike.

'I'm glad you're seeing sense,' said Drago.

'We are, so just pass the expenses and we can all get on with our jobs,' said Mike.

'Have you understood what I've been saying all morning D.I. Karetzi?' said Drago.

'Yes, you're saying that our expenses are not refundable. We're saying they are,' said Mike.

'Well prove it,' said Drago.

'Let's eat first Mr Drago and then we will go on and prove it,' said Mike.

'Fine with me,' said Drago, 'I'll go for a walk, give you time to eat and talk. I'll be back in half an hour.'

'What do you have, Amber?' said Evan

'Looks like our friend Drago is squeaky clean, as is the company, Forbes & Forbes; but seven years ago there was a big to do with a rival company who accused them of poaching a big client and massaging that company's accounts to such an extent that the company in question could borrow twenty odd million pounds,' said Amber.

'So?' said Evan.

'The rival company says that they lost other clients who thought they were not as good as Forbes and it nearly bust them.'

'The rival company, Jacobson's and Jones say that bribes were involved and that Forbes not only acted unethically but illegally,' said Amber.

'The SFO were called in,' Amber said. 'One of Forbes' top people, a Mrs Sandra Elves, committed suicide just days before the SFO started looking into the case. Her husband, Edward, says that it wasn't suicide but something more sinister, but couldn't get anyone to listen.'

'Why would he think that?' said Charlie. 'And what did the serious fraud people find?'

'The SFO found nothing untoward and Sandra Elves died at her desk at work after taking a bottle of valium,' said Amber.

'Suicide note?' said Mike.

'No, no suicide note found,' said Amber.

'Did they have an autopsy?' said Evan.

'Yes, it was confirmed she had taken the pills, enough to kill her,' said Amber.

'How was she involved?' asked Charlie.

'She was the leader of the team that did the audit of the accounts for the client that they had poached,' said Amber.

'Her position in the company?' said Evan.

'Partner,' said Amber.

'Her husband, what's he do?' asked Mike.

'Don't know,' said Amber.

'Children?' said Evan.

'Don't know,' said Amber.

'Get me an address, work or home, preferably work,' said Mike. 'One more thing,' he added, 'who's the top dog at Forbes and Forbes?'

'Frederick Forbes,' said Amber.

'Isn't it strange,' said Charlie, 'this name business: Monroe Marilyn, Bunter Billy, Forbes Frederick—you see, people name their children with the same initials as their surname.'

'Most people don't, Charlie. Take yours, White and Charles; mine, Jones and Evan; Mike's... never mind, that's just coincidence,' said Evan.

'People with the same initial Christian and surnames usually are from the higher classes and they get on further in life,' said Charlie, 'that is a fact.'

'That's not fact Charlie, it's crap,' said Mike.

'What are we going to do about Drago?' Amber asked. 'He's like a dog with a bone. He's not letting go.'

'If we can get someone to request us to re-open the case, then I think we might be in with a chance to get Drago to help us sort our problem out,' said Mike.

'Why would he do that?' said Amber.

'To stop us re-opening the case, Amber,' said Evan who was now following Mike's line of thought.

When Ken Drago returned nearly forty minutes later, they were still finishing off the bacon butties. They were beginning to get on Ken Drago's nerves. All this stopping to eat, smoke, talk, he couldn't fathom them out. When did they find time to catch any criminals?

'Hello Mr Drago, had a nice walk through the park? I see you bought some wine gums,' said Mike.

'That's right. How did you know that I went through the park and I bought some wine gums?'

'You've got mud on your shoes and there's an empty packet of wine gums in the waste bin,' said Mike.

'Very good, but that's your job, isn't it?' said Drago.

'Yes, part of it, Mr Drago.'

'So are we now in a position to go through these expenses?' said Drago.

'Not quite yet, nearly there,' said Evan 'but we just have a few calls to make about an ongoing case and a possible cold case that needs looking into.'

'Would you like a cup of coffee or tea, Mr Drago?' asked Amber.

'Yes, thank you, tea would do nicely.'

'Do you want to contact Big Mick or shall I?' said Evan.

A perplexed Mike could only think of one answer to that. 'You,' he said.

Evan dialled. 'Hi Mick, how's Janet, the kids? Good, good, give them my best. Yes, I'm ringing you up about this cold case you want looked into. We really don't have the time Mick, what with the Mortons stuff and now we've got the bloody auditors in; a guy's actually telling us we can't eat, drink, drive cars. I'm not sure whether or not he's allowing toilet paper to be used as an expense.'

'What the fuck are you on Evan, speed?' said Big Mick, 'you know I'm not married and have no kids.'

'Mike agrees that it's probably not suicide but we don't have the time Mick.' Here Evan paused and pretended to be listening. Mick didn't say anything.

'Look, I said we agree Mick, this Elves chap could be right about his wife.' Again Evan paused. 'On the other hand Mick, it's a bit delicate for us to proceed. Yes, I do understand that some new documents have come to hand but it's seven years and if we start making waves those press boys will be down here like a pack of hounds.'

'For Christ's sake Evan, I've got work to do. I've got a pimp and six illegals down here. Translators, lawyers, so get to the punch line and let me get off the frigging phone,' said Mick.

'Okay Mick. We will have a talk about it tonight and see if we think it's worthwhile poking a stick into the hornet's nest, and Mick don't ring me, I'll ring you. Cheers for now, see you anon.'

'Charlie and I can do the preparatory work and pass it on to you and Mike,' said Amber.

'That seems fine. We can sort things out with Mr Drago,' said Mike.

'I'm maybe out of line,' Drago butted in, 'but I couldn't help overhearing your conversation about the late Sandra Elves. We worked together. It's very sad what happened. A nice young woman like that taking her own life.'

'It happens. The pressure of life gets to people sometimes, but in this case, we're not so sure. Put it this way, if we re-open the case it will be because foul play was involved,' said Evan.

'How will you know that? Everyone agreed it was a suicide,' said Drago.

'I can name you a few reasons: her husband said she wasn't suicidal, there was no note. A good detective, someone we trust says that documentation has surfaced that throws new light on the case and we are fortunate enough to have the Serious Fraud Squad's files on hand,' said Mike.

'And are you going to re-open?' said Drago.

'Probably, that's the way it's panning out,' said Amber.

'What about your other cases? Surely you should prioritise the estate agency murders?'

'We are on track, don't worry. Last night for instance we were called in at six for a fatal stabbing that happened at four. No clues, nothing. By midnight we had the killer in the Nick,' said Charlie.

'Stop boasting Charlie, Mr Drago is not interested in facts, just numbers,' said Mike.

'No, I'm interested. Let me tell you about Sandra. She was neurotic, scared of her own shadow. How she rose to the position of partner is a mystery. Her suicide came as no surprise to anyone who knew her well,' said Drago.

'Except her husband, who one must assume knew her best of all,' said Evan.

'Don't pursue a lost cause. Like you say, you've better things to do D.I. Jones.'

'We all have better things to do Mr Drago, but then we here at 4 'I's don't like doing the better things first, got it?' said Mike.

Mike took one of the pencil stubs and wrote a note for Charlie. It was a simple note that read: 'Contact Alex, make him apologise to you and tell him there is a potential story. Tell him we are reopening the Elves' suicide, get him around a.s.a.p. with any documentation he has on file.

Mike passed it to Charlie. Secretly Charlie read it, decoding Mike's writing as best he could. It's difficult writing with a one-inch pencil.

'I'm off,' Charlie said, 'unless I'm needed. I'll be about ten minutes, is that okay?'

Everyone looked at Drago who nodded.

Amber started typing first into one laptop then another before picking up the phone and dialling out.

'Let's get on with it,' said Evan.

'On with what, Evan?' said Mike.

'Getting Mr Drago to see the light with these expenses Mike.'

'Pity it's not the 5$^{th}$ of November, we could do with a massive bonfire,' said Mike.

'Angelo's, day one, let's begin with that,' said Drago who didn't seem to be in a rush anymore, his mind preoccupied and elsewhere.

'Excuse me!' shouted Amber. 'Before you start can I give you the police photos taken at Mrs Elves' office, the autopsy report and I want to let you know that we are fortunate that Mr Drago is here. He oversaw the work done by Mrs Elves' team. Oh, I thought you boys might be interested to know that Sandra Elves was made a partner just ten days before Forbes took the account in question,' said Amber.

'Can you get us the accounts filed? That caused all the controversy,' said Evan.

'They're on the way as we speak,' said Amber.

'Well done, Amber, keep at it. We need everything we can get,' said Evan.

'The usual, staff names, previous employment connections to anyone or anything, the S.F.O. should have the stuff. If they do and won't hand them over, phone Brian and tell him to arrange it. Also whilst you're on the phone to him I want to know of any undesirables who are in or out of jail that have been convicted for accountancy fraud. Tell them to check with Customs and Excise. We need an expert's advice and we will have to do with second best,' said Mike.

'Why second best Mike,' Evan asked.

'Because the best haven't been caught, Evan,' said Mike.

Drago was just about to speak when Charlie walked in followed by Alex.

'Has Alex made his peace with you Charlie?' Mike asked.

'Yes, he understands the situation and has brought a piece offering,' said Charlie.

'Glad to have you back on our side Alex. Amber kept some rice pudding for you,' said Evan.

'Like hell I did, but I can make some more,' said Amber.

Alex put down two files. No-one touched them.

'Alex, this is Mr Drago, auditor hired by our beloved Chief to sort out our expenses. It seems we're owed quite a bit, although Mr Drago doesn't see it that way, yet.'

'Mr Drago, this is Alex Symonds, the *Chronicles'* top man,' said Mike.

'Nice to meet you,' said Alex.

'Yes,' said Drago.

'Any biscuits, cake, I'm starving,' said Alex.

'In the usual place,' said Amber.

'Can you spare us just ten minutes, Mr Drago, whilst we have a quick peep at these files and photos?' said Evan.

'I don't see why not but I'm telling you, you are wasting your time,' Drago said.

'Oh Alex, I forgot to tell you, Mr Drago happens to work for Forbes and Forbes,' Mike said.

Mike read the autopsy report then handed it to Evan. He then read the doctor's report and handed it to Evan, then the newspaper clippings and notes that Alex had brought and handed them to Evan. He then spread out all the photographs that they had on one of the desks. Evan produced a magnifying glass and after Mike and Evan lit up their respective poisons they started to check out the photos.

After a good ten minutes Mike turned to his partner and said, 'You first, Evan.'

'Only one cigarette in the ashtray, glass full of water, no bottle in sight, pen and plenty of paper on her desk, one has something typed on it, body in sitting comfortably position, handbag at side of her desk, closed. No sign of any containers, that's about it from me for now Mike,' said Evan.

'Window closed on a hot summer's day, picture of what I presume is her husband in prominent position at the end of the desk facing more towards the wall than to her sitting position, picture of sailing boats behind her slightly askew, waste paper basket empty, no mobile phone in sight or cigarettes, lighter, no files on the desk, no coffee or tea mugs. I don't like it, not one bit,' said Mike.

'Charlie, any comments?' asked Evan.

'It's as if someone other than her tidied up her room. The handbag should be closer, the photograph nearer and facing her, and the window, why keep it closed mid-July, midday? The sun as you can see is streaming in and I don't see a fan or anything that looks like an air conditioning unit in the room,' said Charlie.

'How did she bring in the pills, loose in a paper bag, how, where did she get the pills from, when, how the hell did she wash them down, the glass is full to the brim and no note or files? What was she doing?' said Mike.

'Did she have financial worries, health problems, received some bad news?' said Amber.

'What happened that day Amber? I see you're holding a report from Central,' said Evan.

'Sandra came into work at about nine, spoke to the receptionist, made herself a coffee and went into her office. At ten she had a meeting with a Paul Baldwin about one of their clients. It lasted about twenty minutes. At about eleven she met with a Miss Jackson outside the ladies. It was just a quick hello, how are you type of conversation. That was the last time she was seen. She made three calls, two to clients, one to her husband, the last one being to her husband at about twenty past eleven. At twenty-five past she rang this Baldwin chap again on the internal system.

'She was found dead at 12:43 hours. Doc was brought in. He came about one o'clock.

'He couldn't find a suicide note. He felt uneasy and called in our boys who for one reason or another didn't appear until ten to two.

'That's it boys,' said Amber.

'Contents of handbag?' asked Charlie.

'Hang on, I'll find it for you. Ah here it is, lipstick, mirror, brush, mascara, tissues, purse containing credit cards, sixty-five pounds in notes, some loose change, bunch of keys, mobile phone, loose toothpicks, a gold, four-leaf clover type brooch, cigarettes, plastic lighter, cheap biro, notepad and a dry cleaning ticket,' said Amber.

'No empty pill box or bottle of water?' said Evan.

'Nor the kitchen sink,' said Mike.

'Look,' said Charlie, pointing at the photos. 'Amber said she came in, made herself a coffee, but there is no sign of a coffee cup on the desk or anywhere in the room.'

'You're right Charlie. Tell me, Mr Drago, do you use plastic containers for your coffees or china?' asked Evan.

'China for visitors, or in meetings, but plastic at any other time. Let me reiterate, this is a simple case of suicide, and you lot are trying to make it look like something sinister happened to Sandra.'

'Do I have a story or not?' said Alex, always the professional.

'The accounts are coming through on the fax. My God it's near on thirty pages,' said Amber.

'Is it clear? I mean is it legible?' said Evan.

'Good enough. The hard copy's coming by hand, will be with us in the morning,' said Amber.

'Tomorrow's Sunday,' Evan said.

'It's still coming tomorrow and anyway Brian's not come back with a name of a crooked accountant, so we can't really progress on that front,' said Amber.

'I can talk you through them,' said Drago.

'I don't think so, as from the moment we reopen the case, you, Mr Drago, will be on our list of suspects,' said Mike.

'You are crazy, Detective,' said Drago.

'A lot would agree with you, but you Mr Drago are stupid—who else would work on Saturday and not get paid, eh? Tell me that,' said Mike.

'We do Mike, *and* Sundays, *and* we don't get paid extra,' said Evan.

'But we will get our petrol and meals paid for whilst we are on duty,' said Mike, laughing.

'You won't get authorisation to reopen this case, Detectives. I can assure you.'

'You're wrong Mr Drago. We have insurance for such eventualities.'

'Insurance?' said Drago.

'Yes sir, insurance,' said Mike.

'What insurance? How can you have insurance?' said Drago.

'Mr Alex Symonds of the *Chronicle,* please stand up and explain to Mr Drago.'

'I think Mr Drago gets the picture. I print front page that suicide is murder, but somebody is keeping the lid on it and not allowing the Serious Crime Squad to investigate fully.'

'Okay, okay, but I'm sure a gagging order can be made to stop publication of such wild theories,' said Drago.

'We do have freedom of the press in this country Mr Drago.'

'We need George Lambis,' said Charlie.

'Who's he?' said Mike.

'George the Fraud, ex accountant, conman, document forger etc. etc. Sixty-five years old. If you want something found, George will find it; but I doubt if he'll work for the police. He's been inside three, four times for various scams and we are not his friends.'

'Where can this guy be found, Charlie?' said Evan.

'Usual office, between eight and ten every night,' said Charlie.

'He has an office?' said Evan.

'No Evan, Charlie means the Cutty Sark,' said Mike.

'How do we recognise him, Charlie?' asked Mike.

'Walks with a cane, ivory handle and always wears a white scarf around his neck,' said Charlie.

'Are we going to reopen or not?' said Charlie.

'Let's play the Q and A game,' said Amber, 'and then we can decide.'

'You take the chair, Mike,' said Evan.

'This is ridiculous. We're not getting anywhere. I'm off,' said Drago.

'I suggest you remain,' said Amber.

'Why? If you are going to start playing games?' said Drago.

'Because you might have some input. Just bear with us for a few minutes;' said Amber.

'Question: Why no pill container?' said Mike.

'Answer: She brought them in loose,' said Alex.

'Question: In her bag or jacket pocket?'

'Answer: Must be jacket pocket. She wouldn't have found them with all that crap in her bag,' said Alex.

'Question: Could someone else have brought them in?'

'Answer: Of course, if it's not suicide then she didn't bring them in,' said Amber.

'Question: If she did bring them in, how did she get them down her throat?'

'Answer: With her coffee first thing or when she went to the toilet. She could have used tap water in the washroom.'

'Question: What happened to her coffee?'

'Answer: Someone, either she herself or somebody else removed it,' said Alex.

'Question: Why?'

'Answer: It could be incriminating,' said Evan.

'Question: What would make somebody think that the coffee would be incriminating? After all, she poured that coffee herself.'

'Question: who brought the glass of water? Did she because all the containers at reception are plastic; the china and glass must be in the kitchen, isn't that so Mr Drago?'

'Answer: That is correct.'

'Question: Why wasn't she working on anything? It looked like she was ready to go out yet her jacket was hanging up.'

'Answer: She's just a tidy person,' said Evan.

'Question: So why not straighten the photograph or the picture hanging on the wall?'

'Answer: She couldn't see the picture on the wall. She had her back to it; as for the photo, I don't know,' said Charlie.

'Question: That last call to her husband, what was the conversation about?'

'Answer: According to her husband they talked about which film they were going to see that night,' said Amber.

'Question: What did Sandra talk about to Baldwin?'

'Answer: Sandra wanted to change the wording on some account that Baldwin was handling,' said Amber.

'Question: That typed piece of paper, do we know what that's about?'

'Answer: Yes we do. It's Baldwin's notes on the hours put in by him in respect of the job he was talking to Sandra about,' said Amber.

'Question: Why didn't she have an open file or something on her desk?'

'Answer: Whoever killed her either put it away or took it with him/her,' said Evan.

'Question: Why was the window shut?'

'Answer: Too much noise from outside,' said Alex.

'Question: Why worry about the noise when you're not doing any work. Like I keep on saying, there's no file on her desk.'

'Answer: Someone else shut it,' said Charlie.

'Question: Why?'

No answers.

'Question: Why bother taking something to the laundry if you intend to commit suicide?'

Again no answers.

'Is that it then? Are you telling me that your case revolves around a shut window, a glass of water and a missing coffee cup?' said Drago.

'Do you know what this reminds me of?' said Evan.

'Are you talking about King?' said Amber.

'It's not impossible, is it? Let's go through what may have happened,' said Mike.

'Forget everything until after her phone call to her husband. Everything is hunky dory. They have just arranged to go and catch a film. She then speaks to this Baldwin, time 11:25, and carried on doing some work. Between 11:25 and say 12:30 someone pops into her office with a cup of coffee which has been doctored.

'This person is somebody high up in the firm because first he closes the window because they can't hear themselves above the midday traffic and then stands behind her pointing out something in a file he has brought with him. Thus he dislodges the picture slightly. I say *he*, of course it could be a *she*. Anyway, this person goes around the desk and sits in the other chair but again, because they need room to both look at the file, the person moves the photo to the corner of the desk.

'Now let's go back to the coffee. He or she brings a coffee for Sandra and a glass of water for himself/herself. He/she hangs around talking until the drug starts taking effect. Why she doesn't shout out is a mystery. Either way he/she helps by restricting Sandra's movements and breathing. Not too difficult, she's only five one, two at the most and weighs nothing.

'When he is sure that she is dead, again I say *he* but it could be a *she*, he puts her in a sitting position, picks up the file and the two coffee cups, wipes down his glass which for some unknown reason he leaves and walks back to his/her office via the kitchen where he dumps the remaining coffee in the sink and washes it out before binning it,' said Evan.

'And motive. Why did this person take such a big risk? What's the motive?' said Drago.

'Firstly it was premeditated. He/she just waited for an opportunity which means that it has something to do with the past. Something to do with those accounts that she was involved in which caused all the controversy,' said Mike.

'I'm not sure,' said Alex. 'She could have taken the pills when she visited the ladies, dropped her coffee cup herself before going to the toilets, got herself a glass of water from the kitchen, in which case it leaves one question—why?'

'That also makes sense,' said Evan.

'It sure does. Maybe the husband's lying about everything being hunky dory. Maybe she'd done something wrong regarding the accounts and started panicking,' said Amber.

'Look, you're all mixed up. Sandra made her own coffee, so why would someone else bring her one, and if someone else brought another one how did he switch coffees without Sandra's knowledge? Your theories are all over the place Detectives,' said Drago.

'As is the coffee,' said Mike

'There is nothing wrong with these accounts; at least two partners would have scrutinised them apart from myself and when you get somebody in they will tell you the same thing. Forbes and Forbes are above reproach, unless of course this new evidence that's suddenly cropped up changes anything. You're just taking stabs in the dark—there is nothing to suggest anything other than suicide,' said Drago.

'May I have your phone number, Mr Drago?' said Mike.

Drago gave Mike a card.

Mike grabbed the phone, dialled the number on the card and asked for Mr Frederick Forbes, telling the girl who answered that it was extremely urgent and when asked who was calling, Mike told her that it was D. I. Karetzi of the Serious Crime Squad.

It took over two minutes for Forbes to come on the phone.

'I understand this is urgent, D.I. Karetzi? You are lucky to find me in the office on a Saturday. How can I help you?'

'I have actually one of your partners with me, a Mr Drago. It would probably be easier if he spoke to you and explained our predicament.'

'No detective, you rang *me*, you tell me!' said Forbes.

'Well, if you so wish Mr Forbes. In a nutshell we have reason to believe that Mrs Elves' death was not suicide; we are at this very moment contemplating whether or not to reopen the case,' said Mike.

'What is Ken Drago doing there, detective?' asked Forbes.

'He's here to sort out some accounts, not one of which we can agree with, Mr Forbes,' said Mike.

'Please pass me on to Ken, that is Mr Drago,' said Forbes

Mike passed the phone to Drago.

Mike nodded to Charlie, then pointed to the door.

The two men walked to the hall. Drago and Forbes were still talking.

'Apart from an unscrupulous doctor, where can someone get drugs like Valium? I mean someone like Mrs Elves who was not prescribed them,' said Mike.

'The obvious is the internet, but I guess you've checked hers,' said Charlie.

'Yes, at the time our boys checked both her husband's and hers at home and at work,' said Mike.

'Still easy, if you know where to go or who to ask,' said Charlie.

'Sandra Elves, she doesn't fit the type,' said Mike.

'Everyone's the type Mike,' said Charlie.

'Now get down to the Cutty Sark, find this Georgy Fraudy and tell him that unless you come up with something on those accounts, you will be chucked in the clink for something else, use your imagination, you're desperate, you will give him two hundred pounds, go to three hundred,' said Mike.

'Why would I have the accounts?' said Charlie.

'I don't know, you'll think of something Charlie,' said Mike.

'I'll see him tonight, but no promises Mike. This ain't going to be easy,' said Charlie.

Drago and Forbes were still talking; for what seemed an eternity they talked. Now Drago was giving Forbes a rundown of the Serious Crime Squad accounts.

Eventually, with a sigh of annoyance, Mr Drago handed the phone back to Mike.

'This is D.I. Karetzi.'

'Ah good, we do not think it is in the public's interest to reopen Sandra's case. It will cause unnecessary anguish to those who knew and worked with her; however, we understand you have a job to do and we will cooperate in any way we can, detective,' Mr Forbes said.

'Thank you Mr Forbes. We will keep your Mr Drago informed as to our intentions,' said Mike, closing the line.

Mike looked at Drago and sat down. 'Shall we proceed with the accounts, Mr Drago?'

'What about me?' said Alex.

'Let's talk later Alex,' said Evan.

Alex left. There was more going on, things he was not party to. These buggers had more faces than Big Ben but at least he'd cleared up the Charlie business, hopefully.

But one thing was certain, there would be no story, Alex was sure of that.

'Day one, Angelos, Mr Drago, that's where we're at,' said Evan.

Drago looked at Evan, then Charlie and finally his eyes lingered on Mike who was sharpening another pencil, his pencil, his last one.

'Do you realise detective that you are mutilating my last pencil?' Drago said.

'I'm sorry, I didn't realise. I do things automatically. I like to cut things down to size, Mr Drago, but fortunately we have lots of spares, don't we Amber?' Mike said.

'Oh yes we do Mike but they're all only an inch long,' said Amber.

'Shit,' said Mike.

'You can borrow my pen,' said Evan.

'It's okay,' said Drago reaching into his briefcase and bringing out a gold propelling type pencil.

'Angelo's, day one, who were you entertaining?' asked Drago.

'No one,' said Mike.

'Me,' said Charlie.

'You?' said Drago to Charlie.

'Yes, I wasn't employed here then. I was entertained a few times both outside and here,' said Charlie.

'Anyone else?' said Drago.

'Well, there were various informants. Alex, of course, all part of the job,' said Evan.

'Now we seem to be getting somewhere. The petrol!' said Drago.

'Five, six different cars, sometimes we are in different places when something happens so of course we use our own cars.'

'Furniture, Christmas decorations, can you help me with that lot?' said Drago.

'Mr Drago, you sort it out to everyone's satisfaction. Mr Forbes said you could,' said Mike.

'This television? I understand that this lady is repaying your goodselves monthly, say twenty pounds?' said Drago.

'That's correct. We're expecting a second payment any day soon,' said Evan.

'Then leave it to me. I'll send you a copy which you can all sign,' said Drago.

'Thank you Mr Drago. Is that it?' said Mike.

'Simple as that, detective; I think we all understand each other, don't we?' said Drago, getting up and closing his briefcase. 'Oh, one more thing, detective,' said Drago.

'Are you addressing me?' said Mike.

'Yes, D.I. Karetzi.'

'How did City go down at Plymouth?' Drago said.

'No idea Mr Drago, how do you know I follow the City?' said Mike.

'The glass bluebird on your desk,' said Drago.

'4-0,' shouted Amber.

'Great,' said Drago.

'Brilliant,' said Mike.

'To Plymouth,' said Amber.

'Shit,' said Drago. 'Shit,' said Mike.

After Ken Drago had departed, Amber brought out the chocolate biscuits.

'Now what Evan?' said Mike. 'Are you talking about Elves?'

'Yes,' said Evan.

'It was suicide, wasn't it?' said Amber.

'Looks that way,' said Mike.

'I agree,' said Evan. 'I think she had an argument with her husband the night previous, probably a week or two before, gave her time to get hold of the drugs, she came in, made a coffee, drank it, had a cigarette, did her phone calls, had her meeting with Baldwin, went to the ladies at eleven where she took the pills, dumped the remains of her coffee and refilled her glass which she took back to her room.

'Phoned her husband and told him, or threatened him with what she was about to do or what she had already done. She threw the empty pill bottle out of the window and then closed it. She then moved the photo of her husband to a position where she couldn't see it head on, tidied up her desk and sat down,' said Evan.

'Why ring this Baldwin chap at twenty five past?' said Charlie.

'That's the one thing that doesn't make sense,' said Evan.

'Maybe Baldwin's lying. If so, why? No-one can check the internal calls, can they?' said Charlie.

'Look Mike, we've got a result on the expenses. All this mumbo jumbo about the Elves' case swung it for us. I'm sure Forbes and Forbes don't want any upheaval in their offices,' said Amber.

'I think this Baldwin and the husband were involved somehow and I honestly don't think it's anything to do with those accounts, but I honestly believe that Sandra took her own life and we should let it rest. Charlie, forget George the Fraud. It would be a waste of three hundred of our money; you could hardly expect Drago to pass it off when the money is used against his own company,' said Mike.

'Back to Morton's again,' said Amber.

'Yeah, but all that can wait until Monday. It's Saturday night and I for one am dog-tired,' said Mike.

'And I for another am dog hungry,' said Amber.

'Now listen Patrick, it's finished. It doesn't make any difference to Walter any more. The house will be sold within a month or two and we will have enough money to open a petrol garage and workshop. Within a year or two we will have a chain of them.'

'You killed that man in Barry David. That was after Walter had died,' said Patrick.

'And the blood on your jacket, Patrick? Did you have anything to do with that business outside the Red Lion?'

'I don't know what you're saying. You know I wouldn't do anything without you David. I'm not stupid. I know that I'm not very bright. I don't know where the blood came from,' said Patrick.

'Christ Patrick, let's see your hands and roll up your sleeves,' said David.

Patrick did and David inspected them.

'You haven't cut yourself. Where were you when… oh, never mind Patrick, just sit down whilst I explain to you why it's finished. No more killing, we don't need to do anything stupid and going after the other Morton people would be just that—stupid.'

'David I was in Penarth, just sitting looking at the sea, I caught my jacket on some newly painted stanchion when I went to buy an ice cream.'

'Good,' said David. 'Never do anything without asking me first. That's the way we will become somebodies in the world.'

'I have a plan. I thought it out when I was in Penarth. Walter would expect us to get that Louis Morton. If you help me, I will kill him. I have a plan.'

'Have you listened to anything I've been saying for the past half an hour, Pat? Forget it. I know best.'

'I've told you David. Do not call me Pat, that's a girl's name and yes, I have been listening; but Walter was my friend, my only friend. He gave us money and a house. If he was alive now what would he say? I know—we must get Louis Morton.'

'Patrick, Walter was very ill. He'd had a very hard and sad life. Do you think he would want us to get caught and put in prison?'

'We're not going to prison. I have a plan. I told you. I thought it out all by myself.'

'A plan, you've got a plan, Patrick? Let me tell you about Louis Morton. He lives in a mansion, here next door to Walter's, protected by eight foot walls, a private security guard roams the grounds continuously. The gates are electronic with a guard who controls entry, CCTV's everywhere, a patrol car passing every fifteen minutes, servants, God know what internal protection; not even a fucking ant can get to Morton. Do you understand that brother, not even a cockroach can get through. And at night, floodlights, night cameras, alarms and so on.'

'David, I have a plan.'

'For Christ's sake Patrick, stop saying that. I've just explained there is no plan that will work and we do not need to take any more risks. Have you understood me?' said David.

'I'm doing it for Walter. He was my only friend.' And with that he told David his master plan. David was quite impressed.

With the football season done and dusted for Mike, his Sundays were free. He picked up his mother and took her to the cemetery.

'Every week Mikhail without fail, fresh flowers with the same card,' said Alice.

'Yes Mam, every week until either I die or they do, that's the price those bastards have to pay.'

Mike said a few words and then wandered off leaving his mother alone at his father's grave.

A lot of the graves were unkempt. The headstones dirty or broken; some were so old Mike couldn't read the names on the headstones. He felt sad. So this is what it all comes down to. At least some had made a mark in this world. He hoped he was one of them.

After a spot of lunch at a country pub he made do with just two halves of lager. He never got a pint; it got too warm before he could finish it. It was a carvery and Mike had the turkey. He finished five minutes before his mother and desperately needed a cigarette but he held on.

Turkey in April, Mike thought, pity they didn't have any Christmas pudding, he was partial to a bit of that.

He dropped off his mother, bought two Sunday papers, four/five papers when City won, and headed home.

After a good solid lunch of roast pork with all the trimmings, Evan and Edna sat down to watch a rented DVD.

That morning they had been to Chapel and during the sermon it had occurred to Evan that the reason they hadn't heard from Yesterday's Man was so obvious that no-one had caught on.

Yesterday's Man was either dead, seriously ill or compromised by his fellow criminals. He phoned and asked Amber to check out all the hospitals and the obituary columns for the last two weeks.

It was nearly two, Monday morning. Patrick had not spoken to David and vice versa for over six hours. Both went to bed with heavy hearts but neither was going to give in.

David sat up in bed. There was no way he could get to sleep. He was in a dilemma. Help Patrick and take a massive risk of getting caught or the alternative, cut ties with his brother, who wouldn't last a week on his own.

Patrick was also awake and restless. He needed his brother who was always there for him but he had made a promise to Walter. What was he to do?

It took two hours for Patrick to come to a decision. He could not survive without his brother and anyway he could not do the job alone. He would tell his brother first thing at breakfast.

It took David longer to reach a decision. He would agree to helping Patrick kill Louis Morton on the day of the first anniversary of Walter's death. By that time he had a reasonable chance of talking his brother out of it.

It was now half past six, David got up and walked to Patrick's bedroom. He knocked twice, hard. He heard Patrick switch his bedside light on. He opened the door; Patrick was halfway out of bed.

'I'm making a cup of tea, Patrick. We need to talk like brothers do; like we always have.'

'Okay David. I've something to say to you. I've been thinking about things.'

From the tone of his brother's voice David knew that everything was going to be alright; the killings had stopped.

Both felt good. David put an arm around Patrick's massive shoulders.

'Do you know bruv, your plan was good. I'm proud of you. All it needed was a little refining,' said David.

'So you liked my idea? I had no help with it,' said Patrick.

'It's great to a point Patrick. You've covered getting in but getting out is the problem.'

'I'll go through it again David.'

'No Patrick, I've got to get to work; so have you. Your plan was good but it's time to move on. It's time we had a holiday. We will go on Tuesday after the funeral on Monday and the reading of the Will. You decide where you would like to go; Disneyland, Barbados, anywhere. We will talk about it tonight. Decide what you want to do, where you want to go. Money is plentiful; we've earned it.'

# CHAPTER TEN

EVAN was the first to arrive as usual and found Amber sitting on his desk studying a road atlas, pencil in right hand and half a Danish pastry in the left.
'Morning Amber. You going somewhere?'
'I think I might have something here, Evan.'
'Something on what?' asked Evan.
'On the Morton business; it could be nothing but I have a gut feeling, a strong gut feeling; after all, its big enough, isn't it?'
'I've no comment. Anyway I guess I'm not in a position to pass judgement considering the size of mine,' said Evan.
'Grab yourself a coffee and a Danish before I finish the lot and then come and give me your insight on this.'
Evan duly grabbed a pastry and poured himself a coffee before pulling up a chair and sitting himself next to Amber.
Just as he was about to ask Amber what she had found Mike walked in with Charlie in tow.
After the greetings both Mike and Charlie headed straight to where the others were sitting and stood behind them.
'So, do we have something exciting going on here?' Mike asked.
'Could be; well maybe,' said Amber.
'Don't keep us in suspense Amber, give us what you got,' said Charlie.
'Well I have three Danish's left,' said Amber.
'You know we're not talking about them,' said Charlie.
'It's important to me and Evan,' replied Amber, picking up another pastry and taking a huge mouthful.
The three men waited, Amber swallowed what she had in her mouth and tapped a huge fat finger at the obituary column in the *Chronicle* and said, 'Walter Richard Cramp, who fits our profile for Yesterday's Man, with the added bonus that not only did this man

live in Llanbas but was Louis Morton's nearest neighbour; coincidence or what?'

'Okay, but is there any tangible connection to the Mortons other than they used to be neighbours?' said Mike.

'Let's phone the Mortons and have a word with the Land Registry boyos,' said Evan.

'Why the Land Registry?' asked Charlie.

'To see if there is any property connection, past or present,' said Amber.

'You can also include a call to the solicitor doing the probate,' said Mike.

'And any relations, they could know something,' said Evan.

'From what I understand there are no relations,' said Amber.

'Interesting,' said Mike.

'Why?' asked Charlie.

'Well, assuming he didn't have a mortgage, I mean he's quite old and the house, cottage whatever must be worth quite a bit. Then who did he leave it to, charity or someone close? It opens up another line into the investigation.'

'How did he die? That could also be important,' added Evan.

'That's if, and a big if, he's our man,' said Amber.

'You obviously think so,' said Mike.

'I do?' said Amber.

'Yes, your mind is preoccupied with this Amber, hence the two untouched Danish pastries,' said Mike, pouring himself a coffee.

'You stopped smoking?' enquired Charlie to Mike.

'Nearly,' said Mike.

'How nearly?' asked Evan.

'This will be my first today,' Mike said, tapping out a non-filter on his desk.

That was the cue for Evan to fire up his little pipe.

Charlie took the opportunity to grab a pastry and Amber grabbed the last one. It was looking a bit forlorn all on its own.

The detectives smoked, Amber and Charlie ate and for that brief moment of time all was well with the world.

And it got better as the morning ticked on.

It was gone eleven when they had finished their calls and sat around the desks ready to discuss their findings.

Amber spoke first.

'The land on which the Mortons built their house was originally owned by Cramp who sold the land and house to Carmo Ltd, one of Morton's subsidiary companies.

'That was how long ago Amber?' asked Mike.

'About fourteen years ago,' Amber said.

'Price?' asked Evan.

'Half of what it was worth, probably less than half actually,' said Amber.

'Why did Cramp sell then?' asked Charlie.

'There were problems with mineral rights and the Council who were about to make a compulsory purchase of part of the land for a new road to bypass the village,' said Amber.

'After the sale, the mineral rights problem went away and the Council changed their mind on the new road,' said Amber.

'Okay, so old Cramp lost a lot of money,' said Evan.

'Swindled out of a lot of money more likely,' said Mike.

The phone rang.

'That will be Alex for me,' said Amber picking up the phone and listening.

Five minutes later and Amber had concluded the call.

'Alex has delved into the papers, archives and found some interesting facts. Cramp's wife committed suicide three days before he sold up. It seems that she couldn't take the strain. Cramp was in serious financial difficulties because of the non-sale at the original price. He had ordered machinery and business had slowed dramatically. They lost workmen who Cramp could no longer afford to pay. Cramp took a mortgage on his cottage which he and his family were going to move into. To say things were bad is an understatement.

'The sister-in-law moved in to look after the daughter and Mabel his wife, who was continuously poorly. Then more bad luck. His little girl gets run over on her way to school.'

Evan butted in before Amber could carry on. 'Shouldn't somebody have accompanied her, she wasn't that old?'

'Alex didn't say but from what I gather she was young but Iris, the sister-in-law, was ill and Cramp himself was the worse for wear.'

'You mean pissed?' said Charlie butting in.

'Yes, he was drunk,' said Amber.

'Do you think he blamed himself?' said Evan.

'Who knows, it seems he was unlucky because I've not finished yet, six months later Iris gets taken by cancer and a few months later his beloved dog died naturally, of old age I think, just dropped dead leaving poor old Walter all alone in the world,' said Amber.

'No wife, no sister-in-law, no daughter, no dog—no wonder the bloke had a problem,' said Mike.

'I feel a song coming on,' said Charlie.

'A song?' asked Amber.

'Yes, one of those sad, wrist cutting country and western songs,' said Charlie.

'Don't be so bloody stupid,' said Evan. 'This is serious and it's our job to get to the bottom of it.'

'Sorry, but Christ, did all his lucky horse shoes land on his head?' said Charlie.

'What's that meant to mean Charlie?' asked Evan.

'Nothing, just that Cramp was about the unluckiest chap I've ever heard of.'

'Has anyone anything constructive to add?' said Amber.

'I have,' said Charlie.

'Spill it,' said Evan.

'It's not much,' said Charlie.

'Then drip it,' said Mike.

Amber and Evan shook their heads.

'The old man used to drink in the local pub, the Daffy,' Charlie said.

'The Daffy, what kind of name is that?' said Evan.
'The locals call it that but the real name is 'Dog and Affodill.' That's a double ff o d i and double l.'
'So who told you that?' asked Amber.
'A friend of a friend from The Cutty.'
'Sounds like a nice place, a cosy country type inn serving good food and good ales,' said Evan.
'You get anywhere Mike?' asked Amber.
'Not really. I spoke to a lady at the solicitors handling the Will and got nowhere. Funeral is on Saturday morning and the reading of the Will Monday morning in Bolt and Hopkins, solicitors offices in Penarth.'
'Evan?' said Mike. 'I contacted the locals who advised me that Cramp fell in his house and cracked open his skull. It seems that he was about to write a suicide note and had mixed various pills with whisky in preparation.'
'He must have got up for something, slipped and fell onto the fire grate,' said Evan.
'Why would he want to commit suicide Evan?' asked Mike.
'Because he was dying of cancer; the doctors gave him two, three months more and the pain was becoming unbearable,' said Evan.
'Couldn't chemotherapy or radiotherapy help the poor man?' asked Amber.
'From what I gather it was caught too late and Cramp wasn't interested anyway. It looks like he gave up on life.'
'But,' said Charlie, 'if he's our Yesterday's Man, he wanted his revenge before he departed this earth.'
'From what we know he was a physically weak man, hence his accomplices,' Evan said.
'Who found the body, Evan?' Mike asked.
Evan consulted his notes and read out aloud. 'P.C. Dodds, David and Patrick Barr.'
'What, all at the same time?' said Amber.
'Yes, this Patrick Barr, a local, was on his way to work but passing by Cramp's house with some teabags, couldn't raise the old

man so asked his brother David to phone Cramp as he didn't have his number. This David, the younger of the two, tried unsuccessfully to contact Cramp, got no answer, so, assuming something was wrong, got into his car and went around to Cramp's cottage. They gained access into the garden and saw Cramp through a window lying there. David Barr called the police. Dodds turned up and they go into the cottage through a window and that's about it, you now know as much as me,' Evan concluded.

'Why didn't the older brother have Cramp's number?' asked Charlie.

'No idea,' said Evan.

'How were they friends, two young people mates with a reclusive, bitter man?' said Charlie.

'Again no idea,' said Evan.

'So where do we go from here? What's our next step?' said Evan.

No-one spoke for a full two minutes. Mike lit up, inhaled deeply and said, 'One thing's for sure, we can't wait till Monday to know who gets what, so I suggest we need to get a look at the Will a.s.a.p. Don't you agree, Charlie?'

'Oh no, I've got a bad feeling coming on,' said Charlie.

'What are you saying Mike?' asked Evan, fidgeting uncomfortably with his pipe.

'I'm saying that we need to know who benefits from Cramp's death. He has no living relatives, few friends, maybe he's left it all to the RSPCA, somehow though I doubt it, and we need Charlie's special night time skills to obtain that information.'

'Not again Mike, it doesn't sit well with me,' said Evan.

'I'd tell you to stand up Evan, but then again that's just me being flippant,' said Mike.

'It's not the time for jokes,' said Evan. 'It's illegal and we could be in big trouble again. I stress the word "again" and Charlie's not happy, nor is Amber. We're the good guys, remember Mike.'

'Evan, I'm in two minds…'

'Mike might not be morally correct but then if it brings us nearer to closure, then I think that, assuming Charlie's up for it, we should go ahead,' said Amber.

'This Cramp might have nothing to do with the Morton's Murders,' said Evan.

'Do you really believe that?' said Mike.

'No, I don't but it's possible,' said Evan.

'Give me the address, tell me what we need and I'll deal with it,' said Charlie.

'Are you sure?' said Evan.

'Of course, I'm as sure as the Allisons in 1961,' said Charlie.

'Nice, very nice Charlie, but now is not the time for the music game,' said Evan.

'I agree,' said Mike, 'now is the time for a drink at the old Daffodil or whatever it's called.'

Evan's mobile started up, the Lone Ranger theme blaring out. It was D.I. Mick Maloney who not only was Evan's best and longest friend but also Godfather to his daughter Jasmine.

'Hi Mick, you okay?' asked Evan.

Whilst Evan was on the phone Mike had one cigarette and Amber two jam doughnuts. Charlie had left for home. He needed to do a recce on the solicitors. He liked to be prepared as they say down at his drinking hole the Cutty Sark—it's all about preparation.

'Everything okay?' Amber asked Evan when he came off the phone.

'Fine,' said Evan. 'Mick was just saying that the tea machine's broken down and everyone is dying for a cuppa.'

The new dark red beamer was a good runner; a twenty-minute drive still took double with Evan driving.

'That reminds me, Evan.'

'What does Mike?'

'The tea problem; you know Mick and co. dying for a cup of tea.'

'It's when you can't have one that you're more thirsty, especially tea which is a great thirst quencher,' said Evan.

'But what I'm saying is this, old man Cramp had no teabags, isn't that so? Well, he would be gagging for one; what did he do about it?' said Mike.

'Ring the Barr's I suppose, see if they could get him some, lend him some,' said Evan.

'Do we have the coroner's findings, the phone calls made? Something tells me all is not right about Cramp's death,' said Mike.

'It was just an accident Mike. He was ill, unstable and drinking, plus he was ready to write a suicide note,' said Evan.

'A piece of paper and a pen doesn't constitute readiness to write a suicide note Ev.'

'What are you saying exactly, Mike?'

'I'm not saying anything but let's keep an open mind about this. Anyway, we've arrived.'

'Christ this looks like a dump. Hardly your quintessential English country pub,' said Mike.

'Hardly surprising when we are in Wales,' said Evan.

'Yeah,' said Mike.

When they entered the pub, they doubled the customers. There was a man behind the bar cleaning glasses with a cloth, a woman reading a magazine and two other men sitting on separate tables.

The older of these wore a cloth cap and seemed asleep; the younger, probably in his late sixties, was reading a newspaper.

Mike's eye caught a picture which hung above the marble mantelpiece. Evan noticed that Brains was sold in the establishment.

'Right then gentlemen, what can I do for you?' said the man cleaning glasses.

'Half of that,' said Evan pointing to the Brains Bitter. 'And Mike, what do...'

'Half a lager,' Mike said.

'Any preference?' said the barman.

'Anything's fine,' said Mike who had no intention of staying long enough to worry about the taste.

'Anything else sirs?' said the barman.

'Just some information,' said Mike putting one of his 4 'I's police cards on the old oak bar.

The barman picked up the card and looked at it, carefully turning it over and over in his hands.

'Card hot?' said Mike.

'Sorry, I don't understand,' said the barman.

'Never mind,' said Mike.

'So what do you want?' asked the woman who was eyeing up Mike.

Not you, thought Mike.

'Does Mr Louis Morton frequent this pub?' asked Evan.

'Not in my time here,' said the barman, turning to the woman and saying, 'Louisa, have you ever set eyes on our reclusive Lord of the Manor in here?'

Louisa wasn't answering; she was still looking intently at Mike.

'So I guess you don't see Louis Morton in here? What about Walter Cramp?' said Evan.

'Yes, he was a regular,' said the barman.

'By regular, what do you mean?' said Evan.

'Three, four nights a week up until a couple of months ago, then maybe once a week,' said the barman.

Louisa was now in flirty mode. She'd run her fingers through her hair, applied another layer of lipstick and put a sexy smile on without taking her eyes off Mike.

'Never mind my wife, she will flirt with any man under sixty.'

'Shut up Barry,' said Louisa. 'You're talking crap again.'

Evan mentally checked his age and thanked God he looked older.

Mike lent on the bar, putting his face closer to Louisa's and said, 'Maybe you should do the talking Louisa.' Barry turned away and went through to the back room.

'He gets so jealous does Barry. Don't know why, it's part of the job flirting with customers,' said Louisa to Mike.

'Oh I understand him, you're a very good looking woman,' said Mike.

Louisa laughed and said, 'That's rubbish, but thank you, you've made my year.'

'Tell us about Walter Cramp,' said Mike.

Louisa told them everything she knew.

Mike supped his lager and still had most of it left when Evan ordered another half for himself when Barry re-entered the room.

'Any more questions Mike?' asked Louisa.

'Yes,' said Evan, 'did Cramp like spirits like whisky, rum, gin and so on.'

'Not to my knowledge,' said Barry.

'And the brothers, one you say is cleverer than the other brother, who is physically large and strong but not a full shilling,' said Evan.

'That's about it,' said Barry.

'The scrapbook, where do you think it is?' asked Mike.

'No idea,' said both Barry and Louisa.

'Funnily enough though, well not particularly funny, but all three of them were in here the night Walter died. That's when the younger, Dai as I call him, told us that Walter was terminally ill and contemplating taking his own life,' said Barry.

'Now that is interesting to say the least,' said Evan.

'Why is there an eye in each corner of your calling card?' Louisa asked. 'Is it something to do with private detectives; you know, "private eyes" as they say in America?'

'Near enough,' said Mike, leaning over and giving Louisa a kiss on the cheek.

Back in the car with Mike driving, Evan called Amber and asked her if she had sighted the coroner's report.

'Yes Evan, I have, it's in front of me.'

'Okay, two questions, when did they think he died?' said Evan.

'Between nine and ten the previous night.'

'So Amber, he was dead approximately ten hours, correct?'

'Yes Evan.'

'Phone records?' said Evan.

'I have them too,' said Amber, 'and before you ask, the last call that was made or received was at 16:33 a.m. on the previous day to the Council offices. It lasted a good fifteen minutes,' said Amber.

'Mobile?' Mike asked.

'No mobile Mike.'

'Thanks,' said Evan.

'Hang on Evan, get Charlie to come down to Cramp's house now with any tools he might need for entry,' said Mike.

'He's not in at the moment but I'll get him on his mobile,' said Amber.

'So we're going to Cramps, why?' asked Evan.

'Because we need that scrapbook,' said Mike. 'Before you say to me to ring and get a warrant or ask permission from Fowler or the Chief, I will tell you it's better at this very moment that nobody knows that we are looking for a scrapbook, Evan.'

'Why not, it's our case? We can look for whatever we want,' said Evan.

'Look, we're back at the pub. We will park here and walk,' said Mike.

'About asking permission, what's your reasoning on not getting help?' said Evan.

'No reason, I just know that we need to get inside and look around in peace.'

'Maybe we should ask Louisa to come and check out the bedrooms,' said Evan.

'I don't think Edna would be too happy about that, Evan. Anyway you're too old for her.'

Evan smiled; there was no point in doing otherwise.

Charlie had just finished his recce of the solicitors when he got the call. He didn't need any tools for breaking into a cottage so he was on his way. Fifteen minutes later and he was at the cottage where Mike and Evan were waiting outside.

'Round from the back Charlie,' Mike said.

Eleven minutes later and they were sitting in Cramp's front room, all three of them.

'Kitchen first,' Mike said. 'Look for the teabags and a scrapbook.'

Each took a cupboard; nothing.

'Drinks of any kind?' said Mike.

'Six bottles of beer and one cider, but no spirits.'

'Same with the other two rooms downstairs, nothing.'

'Bedroom one, two and bathroom, nothing except a few old photos.'

'This guy lived very frugally,' said Charlie.

Back in the dining room and Mike sat on one of the chairs before getting up and turning towards the fireplace.

'It's possible, no probable that he just fainted and fell, bam, bam, and out,' said Evan.

'Just one thing,' said Charlie.

'What?' said Evan.

Everything he needed was on the table, his booze, the drugs in the glass, paper, pen, why did he get up and head for the fireplace?'

'More importantly why, if he intended to take his life, didn't he have his Will on the table? Where did they find it anyway and who found it, and where is the scrapbook that, according to the people in the pub, he always had with him even when he made a visit to the toilet?' said Evan.

'Fuck, fuck, fuck,' said Mike.

'There's a lot of fucking going on in here,' said Charlie.

'I'm sure that he's our man,' said Mike.

'And the others are too,' said Evan.

'You mean the two brothers?' said Charlie.

'Too many coincidences; the teabag fiasco, telling Barry and Louisa that Cramp was thinking about taking his own life. I have this gut feeling that the brothers did for the old man.'

'Who's Barry and Louisa?' asked Charlie.

'Landlords of the Affodil,' said Evan.

'Also let's not forget Cramp didn't like spirits. Why did he buy the whisky or did somebody give it to him? Not a friend, they would know he didn't drink spirits; then again, why was the TV on and only his fingerprints were on the glass and the pill bottle?' said Mike.

'Two things we need to know, firstly did the Barr's know about the Will and if they did why kill Cramp who only had months to live, that is of course assuming they are the beneficiaries.'

'The other point?' asked Charlie, cutting into Evan's thoughts.

'Why did they kill Garner after Cramps' death? That was pointless and very risky,' said Evan.

'It doesn't make sense. A lot of things about this case don't add up. I can only surmise that they got wind of Cramp's messages to us. Cramp was about to change his Will or Cramp wanted the brothers to up the killings, possibly targeting Louis Morton,' said Mike.

'A lot will be sorted out tonight when I procure the contents of the Will,' said Charlie.

'I'm still not happy with that,' said Evan.

'You will be if we can tie the brothers Barr to all this mayhem,' said Mike.

'I might but that doesn't make what we're about to do right,' said Evan.

'What I'm about to do, not we,' said Charlie.

'We are one unit Charlie, so as far as we are concerned, it's we, that includes Amber,' said Evan.

'I'm relieved you said that,' said Charlie, 'it makes me feel better.'

'I'm glad of that,' said Evan, 'but…'

'You've made your point Evan and you're making Charlie nervous.'

'All I'm saying is that we could wait till Monday and know. Why take any risks?'

'We need to know now, that's why,' said Mike.

'You're impossible to fathom out when you're on your blinkered high horse where nothing seems to stop you going headlong into trouble,' said Evan.

'It's worked in the past. We have got to know it's important, time doesn't stand still for anyone,' said Mike.

'I've said my piece, and you all know that I'm with you all the way. It just doesn't sit well with me,' said Evan.

'So what's next?' said Charlie.

'You can drop me off at home and Ev, you take the BMW,' said Mike.

'Let's go out the same way we came in, said Evan, 'we don't need to get caught in here. It will be a little bit difficult to explain.'

In the car Mike called Amber and told her that Evan was probably on his way. Mike also told her of Evan's doubts. That was enough, Amber understood what was required of her.

'Why do you think Evan will go and speak with Amber?' said Charlie.

'He needs reassurance from Amber, then from Edna. He's a very Christian soul is Ev, a good man. Sometimes he finds he has a conflict of right and wrong. What I mean is, is it right to do the wrong things for the right reasons?'

'Have you ever met Evan's daughter?' Mike.

'No Charlie, why?'

'I don't know, it just came into my head, no reason, just making conversation.'

'Fine,' said Mike getting lost in thought.

Charlie was also thinking. Mike and Jasmine would make the perfect couple. Strange that they haven't met. He wondered if this was due to Evan's reluctance to let them meet, given Mike's womanising.

Evan walked in, umbrella in hand. It was chucking it down outside. Evan could smell food and felt hungry. He wondered what Edna was making for tea.

'I've just baked some scones. I've got cream and fresh strawberry jam,' said Amber.

'Were you expecting me?' said Evan, sitting down at his desk.

'Actually I was hoping Charlie was going to pop in, in all truth,' said Amber.

'Why Charlie?'

'Just to reassure him that what he was going to do tonight was the right thing and that I appreciated his willingness to take such high risks for the good of the S.C.S.

'I've had my doubts Amber, but I've come to the conclusion that what must be must be. It's the way forward and hopefully it will help us solve these crimes and put the criminals behind bars, that's what we're paid to do.'

'Eat up Evan,' and Evan did, demolishing three scones but losing out to Amber's four.

By the time Evan got home he was ready for his tea. Edna was preparing some lamb cutlets, chips and peas but hadn't started cooking yet so Evan opened a bottle of ale and went into the kitchen where his wife was peeling potatoes.

'I had some foolish negative thoughts today and I let myself down in front of Mike and Charlie.'

'What did you say, my love?'

Evan told her.

'I'm surprised at you, Evan. You owe both these men. There are times when you must see the end game, Evan. It's not all black or white; sometimes the grey needs to be diluted to suit a specific need to get a result that would benefit the good people.'

'I know Edna, it's my Chapel upbringing. I now feel ashamed about raising my petty concerns.'

'Well, ring and tell them,' said Edna.

'Amber promised me she would do it. I spoke to her before coming home.'

'That's not right, Evan, they would prefer it coming from you. Don't hide behind Amber's massive frame.'

'Good place to hide though,' grinned Evan.

Edna gave him her look of disapproval. It was not a nice look. Her face became ugly through distortion of her fine features.

'I'll go phone,' said Evan.

After speaking to both, a relieved Evan re-entered the kitchen and carried on drinking his beer.

After a while Edna said, 'I bet you feel better now Evan,' and Evan did.

On completion of Evan's phone call, Mike had gone to his mother's. He had intended to give Dorothea a call but this business with Evan had spooked him and he was worried about Charlie and decided he would stay in, have a takeaway from Angelos who obliged if Mike picked the food up.

He decided to have the three C's, calamari, chops and chips with a nice bottle of Pinot Grigio to go with the meal.

Mike looked in his fridge. He had a few tomatoes, red onions, a cucumber, a lettuce, some celery and some Clementines. Good old Mam, via Mrs Alibi his cleaner, because he personally had purchased none of the aforementioned items. Today he would have his five a day.

Mike took a stick of celery and cut it into small pieces of about quarter of an inch square. He de-skinned the onion and diced it into the same size pieces as the celery. Tomatoes went the same way and after peeling four inches of cucumber they met the same fate. He had no use for the lettuce. He threw all his ingredients into a soup bowl and drenched them with vinegar, virgin olive oil, salt and lots of black pepper. Mike then mixed the concoction and tasted with a spoon. He then added more olive oil and pepper, mixed again and put the contents, together with the dessert spoon, into the fridge.

By now it was time to pick up his food.

Mike took the car, picked up the food and returned home to eat.

Normally he'd add diced cold water prawns to the salad and that would constitute a meal, a main meal, but today what with the herby lamb chops, chips and calamari, he had an Evan-size meal. Another couple of dishes, plus bread and butter and a sweet, would be rated as an Amber-size meal.

It was as easy as getting into his own house; the alarm was a fake, the front door a simple Yale and a triple lever lock, nothing for someone of Charlie's experience.

The offices were situated on the first floor. The first space at the top of the stairs was obviously a reception area with two desks; to the left was a hall which had three doors leading off it. The hall to the right had four doors so Charlie turned right and walked down the hall to the last door and entered.

As an end of street property, all the rooms had windows and all the windows slatted blinds. The first room had windows on two walls; the blinds were open and the street lamp from outside gave adequate light, not that Charlie needed it. This was either a boardroom or meeting room, a large table surrounded by eight chairs. There were a few pictures on the walls and a large bookcase full of legal books, no files or papers. The next room had a desk, a lamp, two chairs and files piled everywhere. The blinds were closed and Charlie used his torch. The next two rooms were the same. It was hopeless; no wonder solicitors took so long doing anything. They probably spent most of the time looking for the correct files.

The two rooms on the other side of the reception were just as untidy. Either these people had a lot of work on, or very little work split up to make customers believe that they were hiring a top company. Charlie picked up a file at random; there were pages of just one line, twenty, thirty pages, and he read the name T. CLAY LTD No 1. Charlie picked up No. 3 and No. 4 but couldn't find No.2.

The last office housed a partner's desk, a big leather chair and two smaller leather chairs. It was bigger than the other rooms and in the corner was a large, old-fashioned steel safe. The blinds again were closed and Charlie swept his torch beam around the room.

Charlie sat behind the desk and opened all the drawers one by one, finding nothing of any interest. The same result on the other side of the desk.

This room was ultra-tidy, obviously the head honcho's domain. Now the safe could be opened but it would take time, a lot of time which Charlie couldn't afford bearing in mind that it was unconceivable that a crummy little Will would be held inside.

Charlie looked at his watch. He'd been there over an hour, far too long. He knew he was beaten; beaten by a bunch of untidy bastards.

Little did he know that Mr Arnold, one of the solicitors and the one handling W.R. Cramp's Last Will and Testament had inadvertently taken the file home with him.

On leaving he phoned Mike and gave him the bad news. Mike passed on the message to Evan who felt that somehow he'd put the mockers on the whole thing.

Mike slept fitfully that night; he surrendered to the sleep of the damned, those whose dreams become their demons.

It was the same story for Patrick and David who had gone to the Daffy for a drink and learnt that the S.C.S. were asking questions about them.

Friday, the last day of April, and Patrick was up early. The weather was foul, rain with a strong wind and it was still dark. The time was six in the morning.

David heard Patrick get up and got out of bed himself. His older brother was dressed for work.

'Do you realise the time, Patrick?'

'Yes, David, but I'm to be in earlier today to finish work on one of the trucks before nine when the council pick it up,' Patrick answered. 'They need it desperately.'

'Have something to eat before you go. It's nasty out there.'

'I will, don't worry about me.'

'But I do, Patrick. Anyway see you when you get back home. I'm not going in today so I'll prepare dinner for us.'

'Thanks David, see you later,' and David went back to bed and fell asleep.

His alarm was still set for 8 a.m.

By eight o'clock Amber was already down in the market, the taxi waiting nearby, the meter ticking over at the S.C.S. expense. Good food didn't come cheap, that was one thing Amber knew. A pineapple, a large oval yellow melon, white grapes, red grapes, plums, green apples, kiwi fruits, two pears, cherries and two mangoes, all the ingredients of a good fruit salad.

Five minutes later and Charlie received a call. It was from Mike.

'Do you know what the time is Mike?' Charlie asked.

'About eight.'

'It's Saturday,' said Charlie.

'God, you're quick,' said Mike.

'I usually have an hour or two lie-in on a Saturday and Sunday.'

'Well, have four hours tomorrow Charlie, I need you to get down here and help me find that scrapbook.'

'Can't it wait, Mike?'

'No Charlie, it can't.'

'Okay, I'll have a cup of tea and get down there.'

'Who was that?' said a sleepy Maggie.

'Just Mike, he needs me pronto,' said Charlie.

'See you later then Chas,' said Maggie.

Two espressos and four cigarettes later Charlie was at Mike's.

'Nearly forty minutes Charlie!' said Mike.

'You're lucky I came at all, Maggie gave me a bloody earful,' he lied.

'We'll go in your car Charlie, save some time,' said Mike.

Evan too was up at seven. He had a lousy sleep. He was desperate for a pipe smoke but had no tobacco as he had left his pouch in the office with a good four ounces left in it.

'I'll be back in an hour or so Edna my love,' he shouted through the bathroom door.

'What's that darling?' she replied but Evan had gone. He was looking forward to a good breakfast with Amber.

Edna was on some kind of diet and breakfasts were just bran flakes or yoghurt, not a decent meal to start the day, not for people like Evan that was for sure

If it wasn't for Amber's office extras he would be as thin as Charlie, just a few inches taller but as thin. Evan shuddered.

Amber was getting out of a taxi just as Evan parked behind the cab.

He helped Amber with the shopping and then helped her pile the fruit like a pyramid on a large tray which she placed on Charlie's desk.

'I'll deal with them later. No point in taking them upstairs until we've had ourselves a nice cup of tea and some lovely fresh cream cakes.'

'Great said Evan, Edna's on a diet.'

'And you're suffering, is that so?' said Amber.

'Not whilst I work here,' said Evan, sitting on his desk and opening up the first box of four cream cakes.

'Doing anything special today?' asked Evan.

'Picking up my daughter Jasmine; she's off till Tuesday. She'll then return to Edinburgh and work right through summer.'

'I've always wanted to go there,' said Amber.

'Yes, it's a great place, good breakfasts,' said Evan.

# CHAPTER ELEVEN

**PATRICK** finished his check-up. The big brute of a vehicle stood towering over him. He knew that the only problem still outstanding was the balance and tracking. The drivers had experienced steering problems at speeds over thirty but that wasn't going to be too much of a problem. It was just a four-mile journey, one-way only.

Now he knew what he needed to know; there was a guard at the big double steel gates, no problem for this twenty-six ton monster, the front of the swimming pool was mainly glass, Louis Morton took an hour's exercise swimming, from 8 a.m. to 9 a.m. and 6 p.m. to 7 p.m. every day without fail, that the in-house day security chap relieved the night man at eight every morning and after a walk around usually had a coffee with the cook-cum-cleaner at about twenty to nine. Sure everything was hunky dory. He knew that there were Morton's children and spouses living with him but he only needed enough time to deal with the guy who had ruined his best friend's life. He would get Louis and anyone who tried to stop him.

What he didn't know was how he was going to get away. His brother David always said that was the problem.

Time ticked away as Patrick contemplated. It was now twenty to nine and Patrick had to get a move on. He opened the large garage compound gates and eased the big garbage truck out.

He didn't bother reclosing the gates, the staff would all be in within the next ten minutes or so and Patrick was in a rush.

Charlie wasn't; his car was playing up.

'What's up with your car Charlie, it's shaking and do you hear that rattling noise coming from the engine compartment?'

'Strange, it was okay when we left your place Mike. We're nearly there so I'll slow down and have a look when we park.'

'Do you know anything about cars then Charlie?'

'No, but I'll look anyway.'

'Watch the ditch on our left Charlie.'

'Don't worry, I can see it.'

They were now in the village as was Patrick who had hit fifty-five. The truck was nearly uncontrollable, swaying and using the whole of the narrow road.

'What the fuck is that madman doing?' said Charlie looking through the side mirror.

Mike turned. 'Shit,' he said, 'the thing's all over the place and he's doing Christ knows what speedwise.'

Patrick tried to avoid the little Ford in front of him but caught it on the driver's right wing sending Charlie and Mike in a spinning roll into the ditch but landing upright.

Charlie was in shock. All he could mumble was Bill Haley over and over again.

'Are you okay, you hurt Charlie?' Mike said in a dazed state but still with the presence of mind to see the truck turn left just a further two hundred yards down the road.

Charlie said '1954.'

'You're delirious, don't move,' said Mike.

Two passing cars stopped. Mike got out. He was wobbling but as far as he could tell all in one piece.

One of the passers-by, a seventy plus year old man, had already opened Charlie's door and switched off the engine.

'You okay mate? I saw what happened. That truck's just turned into the Morton's side road. It's a dead end. He won't get far, that's if he doesn't kill himself first.'

'If he's still alive, I'll fucking kill him anyway,' Mike said.

No truer a word was said that day. Charlie got out, patted himself down and asked Mike if he had a cigarette.

'You don't smoke, Charlie.'

'Oh,' said Charlie.

'Bill Haley—what was all that about Charlie?' asked Mike.

'First record I ever bought,' said the old man. 'Rock around the Clock. They don't make them like that anymore.'

'That was 1955. I was thinking about Haley's first hit here, Shake, Rattle and Roll, which came out a couple of months earlier at the end of 1954,' said Charlie.

'My, my, you're a walking music encyclopaedia,' said the old man smiling.

'I'm not sure about the walking part, but I'm quite good in the first 25 years of the charts,' replied Charlie.

'The one after that was See you later Alligator—I'm right aren't I?' said the man.

'Mambo Rock,' said Charlie.

'Strange that, never heard of it,' said the man.

'You'd know it if you heard it again. It goes something like this, Mambo, Mambo, Mambo Rock....'

'Enough reminiscing, let's get after the bastard! Can we hitch a lift with you sir?' said Mike, showing the old man his warrant card.

'Police eh?' said the old man.

'That's us, the good guys,' said Mike.

As they got into the car Mike, who sat in the front with the driver, turned and said to Charlie, 'Shake, Rattle and Roll?'

'Yeah, my car started shaking, then rattling, then when we got hit by the rubbish truck we did a roll; get it?' Mike got it.

Patrick somehow managed to hit the gates just off centre, taking part of the large brick pillar with it on impact. The guard had no chance—he was crushed like a bunch of grapes under the wine maker's boots. The lawn, shrubs, small trees, flowers and ornaments fared no better in the dumper's track of destruction.

A security guard suffered the same fate as the gate guard. He was cut to pieces by flying glass from the swimming bath's frontage. He was just unfortunate he had finished his coffee early and was just passing the outside of the pool whilst doing his rounds.

Patrick was unhurt. If it hadn't been for the large R.S.G. the truck would have been in the pool with Louis Morton and the dead guard and now Patrick himself.

The crystal clear chlorinated water had turned red with the guard's blood.

A woman, hysterical with fright, was running up and down one side of the pool screaming.

Patrick was having a difficult time getting hold of Louis who was good in the water but Patrick had him trapped in one corner at the one end which was six foot, six inches deep.

The old man stopped near the entrance where the great steel gates once stood, as was one of the pillars.

Mike jumped out, Charlie followed. 'Call 999 and get them here fast and an ambulance quick,' said Mike to the driver as he ran up to the entrance, Charlie hot on his heels.

Both took in the devastation. It looked like something a tornado had passed through.

They could hear the screams. Charlie said, 'I'll check the guard.'

'Forget him, he's brown bread. Let's get to the garbage vehicle: there seems a lot of screaming going on,' said Mike.

Mike rushed ahead. Charlie followed slowly. He didn't like the sound of things. It wasn't his scene. This sort of police work wasn't for him and no amount of money could make him get involved in the rough part of the work which might involve broken limbs. That was D.I. Karetzi's department.

Mike got through. Morton and his assailant, who was twice as big and much younger, were at the bottom of the pool. The big chap had Morton in a neck lock. Mike took a great lungful of air and dived in fully clothed.

Mike tried to prise the giant's left arm from around Morton's neck only to be grabbed by a vice like a bear's paw by the guy's right hand.

Mike broke free. The assailant let Morton go and with both arms grabbed Mike's right arm above and below the elbow.

All three broke through to the surface, two gasping for air; the other, Louis Morton, had drowned but Patrick wasn't sure, so he let go of Mike and with both hands around Morton's throat together they descended to the bottom of the pool.

Charlie meanwhile had got the screaming woman out and led her into another room before returning.

The old man had by now contacted both the police and the press and was hanging around in the Morton's garden awaiting developments.

Patrick was now killing the dead man Morton for a second time. Mike was taking in air when suddenly just as he was about to unlock his knife, he was forcibly pulled down by his legs.

Patrick had given up killing Morton anymore and had now turned his attention to Mike who had broken free from Patrick's grasp and was now head to head with the big guy, both kneeling on the bottom.

Charlie, now more at ease without the screaming, grabbed a loose brick from the front glass debris.

Mike still doing his bit of training and his regular football games, was fit but he guessed that Patrick had the greater lung capacity but had been under a full minute more than himself.

His right hand still clasped the folded knife. Patrick had made his decision. He would last longer than the Curly haired fool—Mike was weakening. The giant had unlimited strength and looked like he could stay under indefinitely.

Charlie had expected reinforcements by now but nothing had come. He could sense that Mike was giving in. He had no choice; he launched himself in the direction of the big guy, brick in hand and somehow managed to hit him with the brick on the side of the head. He was not in the least surprised to see that his blow had no effect. It was like hitting a grown-up elephant with a pea shooter.

Mike couldn't take much more; he thought of his mother, his father, the strawberry blonde that he would never know. He closed his eyes but something inside him wouldn't let him submit to such a stupid death. He opened his eyes and with all his remaining strength rammed the folded knife straight into Patrick's closed mouth, breaking teeth and forcing a surprised Patrick to involuntarily open his mouth and take in the rush of water.

Charlie was now on Patrick's back. Patrick loosened his grip and Mike seized his moment ramming the knife once more into Patrick's now closed mouth.

Mike started counting. If he could only make it to thirty, he could still beat the brute.

Reinforcements arrived clambering over the rubble. Louis Morton was floating face down, halfway down the pool, the guard further down in the shallow end.

Mike had counted to thirty-six and thought that his time had come when he realised there was no strength left in the giant's grasp on his jacket shoulder and with one huge spring with both his feet broke the water's surface into open air. Mike gasped, went back under but now had the mental strength to resurface and hold onto the side spluttering and spitting out water between taking in the fresh air. Charlie was still clinging onto Patrick before he fathomed out that it was all over and paddled to the side to join his friend and colleague.

A dozen hands reached out to both and pulled them out. Charlie stood up, his legs wobbly, and someone gave him a helping hand. Mike was on all fours still breathing heavily.

Alex Symonds, another friend and Chief Reporter from the *Chronicle,* bent down and whispered in Mike's ear.

Mike just turned, still on all fours, and flopped into the water head first.

He picked up his knife, put it into a pocket and swam towards the shallow end not stopping until he reached the steps leading into and out of the pool.

Police had now retrieved the bodies of Louis Morton, Patrick Barr and the guard.

Mike went up to Charlie and hugged him. Charlie felt like a hero but he knew who the real hero was.

Mike thought the opposite. Without Charlie's intervention he would now be lying where the giant lay. Weedy, five foot six, little, non-violent Charlie had risked all. He was incredibly brave. Again Mike was in Charlie's debt. He thanked whoever had arranged their crossing of paths all those years ago. The little burglar was worth more than anything Mike could think of.

Oblivious to all this Amber and Evan sat eating and chatting. Evan would leave when the fishmonger, who was expected with a large fresh sea bass, had delivered.

'Shall I call Evan and Amber?' said Charlie.

'No, if they haven't yet heard, best not to alarm them,' said Mike who walked over to the corpses and looked carefully at Patrick Barr.

'Big guy,' said Alex. 'That's the older brother Barr, Patrick.'

Mike nodded, then said, 'I just helped kill a bloke I'd never seen before now.'

Mike felt sick, his right hand numb with no feelings.

Someone handed him a towel with which he rubbed his hair best he could with his left hand.

'Where the hell were the Morton children?' Mike asked.

'On a weekend break, Brighton, according to the cook,' said Charlie. Mike nodded.

The time was 09:37. Mike's Omega watch, a present from Evan, Edna and daughter, was still working.

Charlie's cheapo had stopped at 09:19.

Six minutes before at precisely 09:31, David Barr was finishing his breakfast whilst listening to the radio.

As he put the last spoonful of cornflakes with cold milk into his mouth, the programme that he was listening to was interrupted by some breaking news.

Four fatalities at the home of Louis Morton, Chairman of the Estate Agency Group in the village of Llanbas, near Cardiff, Wales. Two security guards, Mr Louis Morton himself and an unnamed intruder were the victims. More to follow on the story.

David knew instinctively the intruder was his brother Patrick, who was stupid enough to go through with a plan that had more holes in it that a fisherman's net.

First a feeling of sadness; he loved his backward brother to bits, then anger, then a thirst for some form of revenge.

Coolly, he went into the kitchen, took out the two largest knives and his car keys. He remembered the address on the policeman's card, the ones who had asked the questions at the Daffy, the ones with the card which bore an eye in each corner. He could visualise the address—111 Nelson Street in Cardiff.

In his car he reached into one of the side pockets and produced a Cardiff Street Atlas. He drove carefully into Cardiff; there would be more deaths that day. His brother had to be avenged and it was only fitting that the hunters were now to be the hunted.

Hunted to death, nothing else mattered, not his own life, not money, not glory, just retribution. Vengeance was his.

'What about the other brother?' asked Charlie.

We must move quickly, where does he work?' No-one answered Mike.

'Right, then where does he live?' Again no answer.

Mike turned to the D.I. in charge of the group of police reinforcements which consisted of a D.S. Anders and two uniformed constables. 'Can we find out where this David Barr lives and works pronto? He could be up to anything. We can't let him get away.'

Charlie moved into a corner and threw up. Mike asked if anyone possessed a cigarette. His were floating bits of paper and tobacco in his pocket. One of the ambulance crew obliged with one and a light.

With his left hand Mike broke off the filter and started smoking.

'This is a crime scene,' said the D.I., giving Mike a hostile look.

Mike brushed past him, stepped over some bricks and broken glass into the rain which had come during this bathing escapade.

He stood and smoked. He was soaked through anyway. A little rain made no difference.

Five minutes later and they had the addresses. A unit from Central was dispatched to David Barr's place of work.

Mike turned to Charlie and said, 'Go back to the office, Charlie, and I will take D.S. Anders and one of the uniforms and go to the house.'

'Who put you in charge? I understand that we've the same rank,' said the D.I. who introduced himself as Dan Cogling. 'It's my case, it's ongoing.'

'Chief Inspector Davidson didn't give me that impression.'

'Well I am. If you don't like it, call whoever, but don't get in my way or I'll get the Chief Constable to have a word with both you and your boss.'

'I've no car,' said Charlie.

'Hitch a ride with the ambulance or call a taxi,' said Mike.

'I'll tag along with you,' said Charlie.

'You'll both catch pneumonia,' said D.I. Cogling.

'Yes but we might also catch David Barr,' said Mike.

'Before someone else is killed,' added Charlie.

Just as they were leaving the call came through from D.I. Cogling's office. David Barr was not expected into work that day.

The D.I. passed on the information to Mike.

Tony from the fishmongers carried the polystyrene box which contained a large fresh sea bass covered in ice from his scooter the twenty yards to the 4 'I's office.

David Barr arrived at the same time and followed a few yards behind.

This, David thought, could be his lucky day and the occupants' of the building, unlucky day.

Charlie rang at exactly the time as that of the doorbell.

'Fishmonger,' Tony said into the speaker. Evan buzzed him in.

'My God, are you both alright? Where are you now? What about the other one?' Evan walked towards Amber.

'What's going on Amber? Anything wrong?'

Amber was about to tell him when a man's voice said: 'You murdering bastards! Time to pay—you killed my brother and now it's your turn!'

Before dropping the phone Amber said, 'He's here, he's got two knives, one with blood…'

'Shut up you fat, black bitch, shut up!' David Barr moved towards them slowly. Evan and Amber backed up until they hit the desks.

'I'm going to fillet you both just like I did the fish guy, appropriate eh? And when I've done you two I'm going to wait until anyone else arrives and do them.'

'You are mad, put the knives down,' said Evan. 'We have no idea what you're talking about.'

Barr circled them until he knew there was no escape. He advanced another step. He decided the man was first.

Mike commandeered the police car as soon as Charlie told him what the situation was at the office. They sped as fast as Charlie could drive. Mike still had no feeling in his right hand.

With difficulty he took off his jacket. He hadn't bothered with the seat belt. He unlocked his knife again with great difficulty and now he was ready. He just hoped he'd get there in time.

With his back to the desk, Evan felt around until he felt the honeydew melon. With one movement he threw the melon directly at Barr's head, stunning him and dropping him to his knees. Twenty years of playing rugby and he hadn't lost his touch.

Barr started rising only to be felled flat out by a pineapple thrown by Amber with the force of a lightning bolt.

Fifty years of food handling and prepping had honed Amber's throwing style.

Evan walked over, kicked the knives away and handcuffed Barr behind his back; then Evan used his tie, the one with the white sheep on it, to tie Barr's legs. He hated that tie. He preferred plain, red, blue, grey, whatever, but plain.

Mike burst through, stepped over Tony and charged into the office only to find David Barr trussed up like a turkey.

Charlie followed, saw the gruesome body and threw up again. Within seconds three police cars, sirens wailing, pulled up.

'How?' said Mike.

'We did him with fruit, a melon and a pineapple to be exact.'

The room was now full of people when Alex walked in holding a big sea bass by the tail.

'Is that evidence?' said one of the policemen.

'No, that's my supper,' said Amber.

Everyone laughed except Charlie who, on seeing the fish, was ready to throw up again.

'Statements are needed from all of you,' said Chief Constable Short, who had appeared from nowhere.

The Chief looked at her watch; it was 10:21.

'Five murders in less than one and a half hours. That must be a record even for you guys.'

'Four,' said Mike.

'Four what?' said the Chief.

'Four murders and a drowning,' said Mike.

'Sounds like a good film title,' said Alex.

'I'm going home,' said Charlie.

'Get yourself dried up, cleaned up and return here so that you can make your statement,' said the Chief.

'What about my car?' said Charlie.

'Amber can arrange for it to be picked up and taken to Curly's,' said Mike.

'Is the car evidence of some sort?' said the Chief.

'Yes Chief, car rage—we were run off the road by the brother who drowned.'

'Well, you need to take it to one of our compounds, not your local garage,' said the Chief.

'Curly works for us, the police I mean, you know the guy,' said Mike.

'Statements D.I. Karetzi, statements. It will be interesting to know how Mr Barr lost all his front teeth whilst drowning. This is serious. I don't think I'm going to like reading your particular statement and I would like to know why we retrieved a brick from the bottom of the pool.'

'They don't float, that's why,' said Mike.

Before the Chief could reprimand Mike, a dazed David Barr had come round and asked which bastard had killed Patrick.

'He drowned, simple as that,' said Mike.

'Patrick was a good swimmer, he couldn't drown in a swimming pool,' said David Barr.

'Get him out of here,' the Chief said.

'And use your own handcuffs and tie,' said Evan.

'Can we move the body in the hall?' asked a medic.

'SOCO finished?' asked the Chief.

'Yes,' said someone else who was in the dozen or so people in the room.

'Photographer finished?' asked the Chief.

'Yes,' said another bystander who was about to take a picture of the people assembled in the room.

'Don't even think about it,' said the Chief.

The guy lowered his camera.

'I'm off,' said Charlie. 'Can anyone give me a ride?'

'I will,' said Alex hoping that he'd get the inside info on what happened at the Morton's mansion.

The Chief was on her way out when suddenly she stopped and pointed to the melon and pineapple still on the floor.

'Why are they on the floor?' the Chief asked.

'Self-defence weapons,' said Evan.

'And they double up as a fruit salad,' said Amber.

'Very nice, good job all round, but the missing teeth—I'm dying to hear an explanation.'

'You fucking bastards,' said David Barr.

'Shut up!' said at least half a dozen voices in unison.

Evan drove Mike home. His mother Alice and his cleaner Mrs Beatrice Alibi were waiting, frantic with worry even though they knew Mike was okay.

'Best you come up with me Evan, just for a minute. Mrs Alibi's car is here which means she's brought my mother.'

As Mike opened the door he shouted, 'Hello Mam, hello Mrs Alibi.'

They came rushing out and his mother grabbed him. 'Are you okay Mikhaili, your clothes are all wet! What have you been doing?'

'Swimming,' said Mike sarcastically.

'We've been worried,' said Mrs Alibi.

'Sorry, I'm just tired,' said Mike.

'He's fine,' said Evan, 'and has promised me that next time he fancies a dip he'll take his bathing trunks.'

'What's wrong with your hand?' his mother asked.

'It's bruised, that's all, now can I get out of these clothes, take a shower, have a whisky, a cigarette and a lie down?' said Mike.

'See you anon Mike. I've got to pick up my daughter in an hour and I need to go home and pick up Edna and a new tie.'

'Bye,' said Alice.

'Bye,' said Beatrice and Evan was off.

# CHAPTER TWELVE

**SEVEN O'CLOCK** and Amber had just finished eating the sea bass. What was left would go into the big pot and join the shrimps and prawns which would later become a nice Bouillabaisse together with lovely French sticks with which to soak up the richness of the soup.

Hurry on Sunday, she thought. Meanwhile she had to make do with a few slices of Black Forest Gateau, which should keep her going until it was time to have a nice cup or two of tea with a few digestive biscuits.

Charlie was in the pub sitting with various other Cutty Sark regulars. For a change Charlie was holding court telling everyone how he had dived into the pool, brick in hand and brought down the madman Patrick Barr, a six foot nine mountain with the strength of a gorilla. In passing he mentioned the help of D.I. Karetzi but this was his moment. Charlie would be drinking free all night. Fortunately Maggie was on duty at the hospital otherwise he wouldn't have recounted the story in quite the same way.

After being told off by Edna for ripping his tie, something he had done himself in order not to wear it again, Evan also, over dinner with Edna and his daughter Jasmine, told them of his expert throw of the honeydew oval shaped melon. He did though mention that the pineapple thrown by Amber was the decisive blow that knocked out David Barr.

Evan didn't mention the fishmonger Tony, or that Barr was holding two kitchen knives with intent to kill him and Amber.

He didn't want Edna to worry unduly but realised that all the gruesome details would be in tomorrow's papers.

Evan had about thirteen hours to come up with why he didn't tell them the whole story.

Mike looked at the lasagne his mother had brought him. It looked good, homemade with good quality ingredients, but it was enough to feed four, even enough to keep Amber going. Now all he needed was some grated parmesan, a green leaf salad and a couple of bottles of good Pinot Grigio. That left someone to share it all with. First he rang Dorothea and thankfully she was more than happy to come to dinner; then he booked a taxi, went to the supermarket, bought the salad ingredients, parmesan, bacon, milk, eggs and a loaf of bread. Mike was thinking in advance, actually hoping in advance, was more to the point. If Dorothea stayed the night then she would probably like some breakfast, hence the milk which he didn't take in either tea or coffee.

Next stop, Angelo's where he picked up two bottles of his favourite white.

Back home Mike prepared the salad, but didn't dress it. The dressing, a simple oil and lemon with a small teaspoon of Dijon mustard, he made and put it into a small cup which he placed in the fridge. The wine and grated cheese also went into the fridge.

His mother and Mrs Alibi had given the place a good working over; everything was clean, neat and tidy.

Mike had a good look through all his cupboards to familiarise himself with what he had and where it was, or to be precise where Mrs Alibi and/or his mother decided where things should go.

He found a vase and left it out, then had another shower, shaved, cleaned his teeth and dressed.

Some English lavender brilliantine, helped to tame his unruly black hair and a few splashes of Grey Flannel aftershave completed the grooming.

Mike felt good because both products reminded him of his father who used them daily. He ran a comb through his hair twice with his left hand; his right now had movement but wasn't quite right. It seemed wooden and didn't respond as it should do but it was getting better.

Not well enough to drive, so another taxi was needed.

The taxi duly arrived. The driver was a young woman with lovely long red hair and a beautiful come-to-bed Welsh accent; any other time and...

Again Mike directed Eva, the taxi driver, to a supermarket where he bought thirteen red roses.

'That's so nice of you to buy me flowers on our first meeting,' Eva said.

'Here,' said Mike, giving her a rose.

'Thank you, that's the first time since I've been cabbying that someone has given me a flower, what a lovely gesture.'

'It's my pleasure,' said Mike. Sometimes thirteen could turn out to be lucky.

'That will be four pounds ten Sir and, if you ever need a ride, here's the number.' Eva handed over a card on which she had just written something.

'Thanks,' said Mike handing over a fiver. He liked her choice of words. Yes, who knows, he might just take up her offer of a RIDE.

'Keep the change,' Mike said as he stepped out of the taxi.

'My mobile number's on the back,' Eva told Mike as he closed the door.

As she drove away Eva thought, that's some lucky lady, a man like that and flowers. She sighed: how come she ended up with loser Brian, all mouth and beer gut. She would dump him and his boozy football mates.

Dorothea opened the door. Her beauty never failed to impress Mike. She was something else and yet she had the type of face and temperament his mother would approve of, not that they were ever going to meet.

Mike handed her the flowers before grabbing her and giving her a big fat wet kiss on her full red lips.

'So do you have a plan Mike for tonight?'

'I do. I have prepared a nice meal, chilled some nice wine. Is that of any interest?'

'Sounds perfect. I was hoping you would say that so I packed a small overnight bag—is that okay?'

'Are you doing anything tomorrow night Dorothea?'

'If you are asking me to stay Sunday too, then the answer is yes, and I have packed enough for two nights.'

'Great! You will have to drive; we could get a taxi, it's up to you.'

'Let's see your hand Mike.'

Mike stretched out his left hand.

'Your bad hand, you fool.'

Mike showed her his bruised hand.

'Umm, I think I will have to help you with the unwrapping of your Christmas present.'

'A bit early for that isn't it?' said Mike.

'It's never too early for presents,' she replied. 'I suppose you can lay your hands on a vase Mike?'

'I can,' said Mike.

'Well we can take the roses with us and watch them grow.'

'Sure,' said Mike. 'Nice idea,' he added.

When they got to Mike's flat, she had to laugh when she saw the vase standing there already, next to what looked like a lasagne.

'I like to be prepared and don't worry, I didn't make the lasagne, my mother did, but didn't leave me with any cooking instructions,' said Mike tongue in cheek.

'My cooking skills should just about cover that—and to opening a bottle of wine if you can't with your hand like that.'

'You go into the bedroom, unpack and the wine will be opened and poured ready for you in the lounge,' said Mike.

Dorothea had put the lasagne in the oven and they were just about to sit down and have their wine when the phone rang.

Agitated, Mike got up, picked up the phone and said, 'Unless it's a mass murder, I'm unavailable.'

'No Mikhail, it's your mother. I was just ringing to give you cooking instructions but I think you have made suitable arrangements.'

314

'Sorry Mam. Yes, I have got everything under control. I'm nearly forty for Christ's sake. I can bake a pie.'

'Mikhail, you are thirty-six and, and you don't need cooking instructions because you have a friend there with you who can cook.'

'How do you know that?' said Mike.

'I'm your mother Mikhail. I hope your young lady is someone who will appreciate what she has. Maybe you can introduce her to your mother—that would be nice.'

'It would be Mam but neither I nor my friend has reached that point,' said Mike.

'I see. Well, have a nice dinner,' said his mother.

'I will and I'll phone you on Monday,' said Mike.

Monday, thought Alice—what happened to Sunday?

'Your mother I assume,' said Dorothea.

'Yes, she's always worrying about me.'

'That's nice, a mother will always remain a mother however old you are.'

'I'm 36,' said Mike, unplugging the phone.

'What point haven't we reached, Mike?'

'Ah, she wants to meet you and, well, you know what I'm trying to say.'

'We need to get to know each other better; I think that's what you're trying to say.'

'That's right, and we can make a start after we've eaten,' said Mike laughing.

'It will be the perfect time for you to unwrap your Christmas present Mike, after we've eaten.'

'Great, how long is this lasagne going to take?' said Mike.

They ate, they drank and they talked.

Dorothea lit up a menthol, Mike his own non-filter. Mike got up, opened a bottle of the Hine brandy and poured one each.

Five minutes later Dorothea excused herself telling Mike she was going to get his present.

Mike waited five minutes, smoked another cigarette and started wondering what type of present took so long to wrap. It was obviously something small otherwise it wouldn't have fitted in her overnight case. Mike was about to go and see what was going on when she waltzed in wearing his multi-coloured dressing gown, something he wore once or twice a year and was like brand new even though it was probably five years old.

It was like a tent on Dorothea. Mike looked, Dorothea grinned.

'Well, come on unwrap your present! You just pull here, good or bad hand.' Mike pulled the dressing gown: it opened and parted. This literally was a gift from God—she was absolutely stunning! Just a little more unwrapping to go, although he could just sit and gaze at this beautiful woman for ever and a day.

A few minutes later and stockings, panties, suspender belt and basque lay on the floor together with all Mike's clothes.

The night passed, breakfast was forfeited for more worthy causes and eventually they surfaced at ten to one. Mike made coffee, one black, one white.

Mike turned on the TV and then put on the Ceefax, page 302.

'Looking up the news?' asked Dorothea.

'No,' said Mike, 'just checking how City did last night.'

'Football, is that right—Cardiff City?'

'It is Thea,' Mike had shortened her name, of course with her agreement. It was easier to say especially if required at the height of love making.

City had won. Everything seemed to be going Mike's way.

'I would have thought you would want to see the news, especially as it will be all about you and the others in your office.'

'No, I failed; we should have apprehended the brothers earlier and saved some lives.'

'I disagree, you risked your life trying to save that Morton chappie,' said Thea.

'But I failed,' said Mike.

'I can't understand why they had no pictures of you or your partners on last night's news.'

'The Chief Constable, thank God, has put a stop on the media; says it dangerous for people to know what we look like in case we are targeted. It's a new thing and we all agree.

'You hungry Thea?'

'Not really Mike.'

'Okay, I suggest we freshen up, shower is big enough for two, then go and have a rest. Later on when they open, we can order an Indian, Chinese, pizza, whatever takes your fancy.'

At midnight the games stopped and the two were exhausted—it was time for sleep.

Nearly seven hours later there was time for the final game of that particular series. They got up and got ready.

'Can you give me a lift to Nelson Street Thea? I think my hand needs a little more time?'

It was twenty to nine. This was going to be a very early start for Mike. He would be the first of the boys in.

As they hit the centre Mike spied Evan walking alone with his daughter. They were engrossed in conversation and didn't notice Mike because he wasn't in his own or the firm's car.

From what Mike could see was a very nice face and hair that reminded him of his strawberry blonde, obviously inherited from Edna, her mother, but the body unfortunately was Evan's shape, stubby and a little overweight. She was short too. Pity, thought Mike, pity.

'This is me, Mr Jones, give my best to Jazz, bye.'

'Will do Becky, have a nice day.'

'Same to you Mr Jones.'

Nice girl, Jazz's old school friend, Evan thought as he turned for the office.

All four were now there. Amber said 'Reports?' Mike, Evan and Charlie all nodded.

'I'll go first on the tape, tell my pack of believable lies, then Charlie can and then Amber can write it all up in a way that sounds

P.C.,' said Mike, opening up his knife and grabbing the pencil from Evan's desk.

'Anyway you want it,' said Amber, 'is fine with me.'

'Hold on,' said Charlie, 'I've got a corker here.' The three others looked at him.

' "Anyway you want it"—the Dave Clark Five, 1963, brilliant group. The lead singer, Dave Clark was also the drummer.'

'They did "Glad all Over" and "Bits and Pieces" too, didn't they?' said Mike.

'The same, both number ones if my memory serves me right,' said Charlie.

'Let's get back to the lies on tape,' said Amber. 'I'm hungry and need to get down the facts, so Mike, off you go.'

'Well, Charlie and I decided we would go for a ride. You see, Charlie was having a few problems with his car so we thought he should give it a run out to the countryside when suddenly…'

'Hold it there, Mike, no-one would believe that you got up early to go for a ride around the countryside testing Charlie's car on a Saturday morning,' said Amber.

'You're right as usual. The truth, let's see. I rang Charlie, told him we were going to break into old Cramp's house and find the scrapbook, that any better?'

'Much better; how about you rang Charlie to take you down to Llanbas early so that you could have a word with the Barr boys before they left for work; you didn't ring Evan because you knew he was going to pick up his daughter and you didn't take your car as it had a flat tyre which you hadn't time on the Friday to fix and, by the way Charlie, your car's now at Sandy's and they are awaiting the insurance people,' said Amber.

' "Anyway you want it" was 64, not 63,' said Charlie.

'I always get them mixed up with that Spencer Davis lot,' said Evan.

'They had a couple of big hits with "Keep on Running" and "Somebody Help Me", both 1966,' said Charlie.

'I'll make some nice bacon butties and we can resume our reports later,' said Amber, rewinding the tape before getting up.

Just as Amber left the room, the phone rang and Evan picked up; it was the Chief Constable.

'How are the reports progressing?' she asked.

'Fine, nearly there,' said Evan.

'Have you even started, D.I. Jones?'

'Of course we have Chief, at it since eight this morning,' said Evan.

'Karetzi doesn't get out of bed till nine, never mind the office,' said the Chief, slamming down the phone.

'Chief, was it?' said Mike.

'Yes, we must get these damn reports finalised,' said Evan.

'I can't see why I need to make one,' said Charlie.

'Because you work for the police and because you nearly brained a guy with a brick,' said Mike.

'Most people would say thanks for helping me out Mike,' said Charlie.

'Words wouldn't be enough Charlie, you saved my life again. I'm thankful for that and I owe you, again,' said Mike.

'I was only joking Mike,' said Charlie.

'I wish Amber would hurry up,' said Evan.

'So we can get on with the reports?' said Mike.

'No Mike, frig the reports, I'm bloody starving,' said Evan.

'By the way, nice new tie,' said Mike.

'I like the little men with different colour bowler hats, it's a great design.'

'Edna got it as a replacement for the one with the sheep on,' said Evan.

'The one you accidently ripped?' said Mike laughing.

'You're a cunning old fox,' said Charlie.

'Not that cunning, this tie is even more abhorrent then the sheep one,' said Evan.

'Foods up!' shouted Amber.

'Back to normal,' said Evan.

'Yes,' said Mike, and Charlie agreed.

'Funny how things work out,' said Mike as they sat around the desks eating.

'Like what?' said Evan.

'Well, David Barr will get Life whilst his brother Patrick got death.'

'Put it that way, I suppose you're right,' said Amber, stuffing her face with bacon.

'I'd call it weird, bloody weird,' said Charlie 'but we made the front page of every paper.'

'So we did, so we did,' said Mike, a look of satisfaction crossing the whole width of his face.

Now all he needed to make things perfect was a certain strawberry blonde, a big lottery win and promotion for City—in exactly that order.

Two months later and Mike was no nearer to finding his strawberry blonde, and there was no big lottery win, which was hardly surprising as Mike didn't play the lottery, but City were promoted.

One out of three wasn't a great result but it was better than nothing.